A REFLECTION *of the* SKY ON THE SEA

Book Four of the Adrift Series

TRINITY**DUNN**

Copyright

This is a work of fiction. Names, characters, organizations, places, events, and incidents are either products of the author's imagination or are used fictitiously.

I dedicate this book to you, my readers.

To those of you who took a chance on a new author,
who skipped over the occasional typo,
who shared, reviewed, and sent words of encouragement,
who stayed up all hours of the night to binge read these books,
or who simply loved the story I had to tell.

Thank you.

THE ADRIFT SERIES BOOKS
(IN ORDER):

Book 1: *More of Us to the West*

Book 2: *Feathers Floating Through Ember*

Book 3: *Remnants on the Tides of Time*

Book 4: *A Reflection of the Sky on the Sea*

Book 5 (Final): *The Stars that Call us Home*
(Coming Spring 2023)

PART I

Scattered Among the Stars

Chapter One

Alaina

Righteousness was going to get us killed. We'd made so many mistakes in preservation of what we believed to be the moral high ground only to find ourselves paying for it in the end.

To take a life—even if the life belonged to the most vile of individuals—was not the ethical thing to do; it was not what we'd all been raised to believe ourselves capable of, and so we imprisoned those that would harm us instead of ridding ourselves of the threat their continued existence posed.

It was a mistake; a mistake we were all reflecting upon as we stared at the gaping hole in the wall where Juan Josef, Phil, and Dario had escaped.

We'd had a plan. Bud and Chris brought enough evidence from the future to support the claim that all we needed to do to erase the actions of both Juan Josef and ourselves was go home. If my daughter, Cecelia, never lived in the 18th century to marry and have children, Juan Josef's wife, Gloria, could never be born.

If Gloria had never been born, Juan Josef would not have been exposed to the DEA officer, Richard Albrecht, and therefore, he would never run from him and into the storm.

All we had to do was get to the storm—get Cecelia through the storm. We had three months before the portal would open again and we planned to return close to the coordinates—ship and yacht loaded with supplies—to the island Maria and Chris had landed upon to wait for it. We would then go back to our time to gain memories where Juan Josef would've never kidnapped us, killed Anna, or caused us to poison the crew and therefore steal my sister's husband and child away from existence.

We *had* a plan.

And Juan Josef, with his hidden passageways throughout the ship, had heard us discussing every word of it in the dining room the day before.

'The knife is now at your throats,' he'd assured us in his letter, referencing the binder that was now in his possession.

That binder—chock-full of details pertaining to each of our ancestries—was now his weapon; one that could take us out, one by one, should we not bend to his will and appear at the battle of Great Bridge, Virginia to kill Richard Albrecht's ancestor, George Thomas Bennet.

"He can't be far," Lilly said as she stared out the small window of the cabin. "There's not enough fuel to get them to Virginia…" She spun around to face Chris where he was kneeling at the side of the hole in the wall Juan had escaped through. "How much fuel did you have when you got here?"

Chris raised a shoulder. "Not sure. It definitely wouldn't be enough to get to Virginia from here. Where would he go if not there?"

"The isthmus," Juan Jr. said softly, still sitting on the edge of the bed staring at his hands. "Panama… There's a trade route there he's familiar with. He could easily buy passage across land to board another ship in Portobelo. It would cut the journey to the colonies in half."

Beside me, I noticed Jack's fingers curl into fists at his side. "Did you know? Did you let them go?"

"No," Juan Jr. said, a breath of a word, shrouded in defeat.

"Bullshit," Jack seethed, jerking him off the bed by the lapels of his jacket and forcing him against the wall. "You've sailed with your father for how many years? And you expect us to believe you never knew he had secret passageways throughout the ship? Isn't that how you all spied on us? Wasn't this all *your* plan to get right with God? Why are you still here?"

Juan Jr. didn't so much as raise a hand in defense of his body and allowed Jack to shake him like a rag doll, his stance limp as his spine was pressed repeatedly against the wood paneling. "I do not know."

"Bullshit," Jack repeated, his fists tightening in the fabric of Juan's collar. "You're one hell of an actor, you know that? Playing the savior so we'd let our guard down… Did you send those men to attack us just so you could be the good guy? So you could let them get away then stay behind as the hero to secretly ensure we'd follow through on his mission instead of ours? Is that why you're still here?"

Juan Jr. shook his head. "I do not know of any other mission than the one to kill the Albrecht."

"No?" Jack slammed him against the wall again, an impressive feat since they were so close in stature. "Why would any of us believe that?"

Juan Jr. sighed. "There is nothing I can say in defense of my innocence in this matter you would believe at this moment."

"You're right." Jack's fingers unraveled from the fabric of Juan's collar to slide up the sides of his throat.

"Jack!" Cece shouted. "Stop! You can't kill him!"

"I can," Jack said, his grip tightening. "And I will. We've lost too much by not doing so sooner. We should've killed them all when we had the chance."

He was right. To put faith in Juan Jr. now—in anyone that wasn't one of our own—would surely add another mistake to the list. There was far too much at stake. Killing him wouldn't be permanent, not if we went through the storm. He would live again in another version of his life—just as Anna would.

"You'd kill a man that saved you?" Cece asked. "That saved your children? That has done nothing but try to help you in every instance you have needed the help?"

Jack shook his head, not taking his watering eyes off Juan Jr. as his skin turned shades of pink with the pressure Jack was applying. "It's too late. I'm done with *all* of this. No more threats. No more stupid mistakes. No more."

"Ay, Hoss," Jim said evenly, inching toward them. "We cain't sail this ship without him. *Those men* won't sail without him. If we're goin' back to the storm, we gonna' need him."

"We'll figure it out some other way," Jack hissed, his eyes unrecognizable as Juan Jr. began to choke and claw at the fingers encircling his throat.

"Let him go, buddy," Jim continued, eyeing Detective Haywood where he was moving closer with a hand hovering over the gun strapped to his hip. "You know we cain't kill him if we wanna' go home."

Jack shook his head, a tear sliding down his cheek as his muscles tensed further and Juan Jr.'s complexion turned dark purple. "They threatened my children—my *wife*. He pretended to be good and he let the bastards go. We'll never be rid of them until we kill them all."

"That's enough," Detective Haywood announced, drawing his pistol and pointing it at the back of Jack's head. "Nobody's killing anyone today. Take your hands off him and put them where I can see them."

Jack either didn't recognize the danger or could no longer hear us. He continued to squeeze, unable to take his eyes off Juan Jr. as he clawed and kicked to instinctively save the life that was being choked out of him.

"Hands up or I'll shoot," Detective Haywood warned again.

My feet were lead; glued to the floorboards as my voice caught in my throat. I should've moved closer; should've *done* something, but I couldn't. As much as I didn't want to see Juan Jr. killed, Jack was right. We'd let too much slip through our fingers. We couldn't afford to trust him with the death dates of both him and our son fast approaching. We couldn't risk any other setbacks on the way home.

Out of the corner of my eye, I saw Cece hand Cecelia off to Jim. She whirled past Detective Haywood and placed herself between the gun and Jack.

"Enough," she said softly, giving the detective a warning glare before she side-stepped into Jack's field of vision. "I can't let you kill him."

How tiny she looked beside them. She was barely over a hundred pounds and the top of her head hardly reached their shoulders. It was her instinct to speak up. She'd always had a sort of bleeding heart for any creature that was rendered defenseless. And Juan Jr. was certainly defenseless in Jack's grip, even with the sword at his hip. She reached up to wrap her fingers around Jack's, forcing him to meet her eyes. "He's not a threat to us. Let him go."

Jack frowned, regaining some bit of composure as he focused on her. "How can you say that? We don't even know him. You've barely met him."

She set her jaw, tugging at his hand where it was still applying pressure to Juan's throat. "You're wrong, Jack. *I—*"

Before she could say more, Bruce burst into the room.

"The yacht's gone," he panted, bending to catch his breath.

"We know—"

"Bud and Izzy are on it."

"What do you mean *they're on it*?" Lilly shouted, spinning back around to look out the window.

"They snuck out before dawn," Bruce said between heavy breaths. "Bud was going to lock the binder up in his safe and Izzy tagged along at the promise of ice cream."

The cabin erupted then. Lilly let out a shriek and collapsed into Jim's free arm, sobbing incoherent questions no one could understand. Bruce and Chris began to argue about how quickly we could catch up to them if we left immediately. Kyle appeared in the doorway, hair standing on end as Jim informed him of all that had happened that morning. And at the distraction, Jack released Juan Jr., allowing Cece the opportunity to wedge herself between them while Detective Haywood kept his gun in-hand, unsure where the threat might lie.

"We have to catch up to them," Lilly cried. "We can't let him hurt them."

"He won't hurt a child," Juan Jr. assured her through hoarse vocal cords, rubbing his still red throat.

"How can you guarantee that?" Jack snarled. "After what he did to Anna?"

"He was desperate with Anna," Juan choked out. "He thought we were poisoned and needed a way to ensure the mission would go on without him. He has no reason to harm either of them."

Lilly held the back of her hand against her nose as she turned to Juan Jr. "Did you see the two of them leave?"

Juan Jr. nodded. "He mentioned she wanted ice cream. I assumed you all knew. It hadn't occurred to me they'd not returned."

"How fast can this ship move?" Jack cut in.

My heart sank in my chest at the question. With it, an image flashed in my mind of that horrid piece of paper and the death date printed beneath Jack's name: 1775… Weeks away. If we pursued, he would *'die at sea'* as Bud had told me he'd seen on a handwritten chart as the evidence of it. And I could see in his face we would pursue… How could I possibly ask him not to when Izzy's life was in danger? We couldn't go to the storm without her.

"Eight knots in this weather," Juan said, considering, "fourteen if we catch a good wind and lose some of the extra weight."

"How fast can that yacht go?" Jack asked, turning toward Lilly.

She sniffled and her lower lip quivered. "At cruising speed, it can average eighteen knots… maybe more."

"It's what?" Chris asked, his brow furrowed. "Twenty-five-hundred miles between Hawaii and California? Add another two hundred or so for the trip here from the storm… How much fuel could they have left?"

"I… I don't know…" Lilly wept.

"Think," he insisted, "try to remember... Your grandpa said you used it more than anyone. We have to know how much fuel they have and if they can make it to Panama."

She straightened, closing her eyes. "It's got a... fifty-five hundred gallon fuel tank, and the holding tank's maybe another five-hundred gallons? But I don't know how many miles it can go on a gallon—I always had someone with me for that... I have no idea how far they might be able to go on what they have left."

Detective Haywood cleared his throat. "We can assume, on a yacht that big and modern, it can get at least two or three miles to the gallon... Let's say it's two... if we are where you say we are, they could make it to Panama from here... with fuel to spare."

"We cannot match their speed," Juan Jr. said, "even were we to toss every bit of furniture overboard. We will not catch up to them on the water, and with so much distance between us, we'll likely not catch them at the isthmus either. They'll be too far ahead."

"Your father has never been on a yacht like that one," Jack pointed out. "It will be Bud in the driver's seat, not him. And Bud is a smart man. He'll know that we'll be just hours behind them. He'd go slower and assume your father wouldn't know it could travel any faster... that's what I'd do."

"And if we cannot catch them?" Juan asked. "Will we follow to Virginia? You mentioned another plan?"

"We can't leave her," Lilly breathed, glancing at me. "We have to follow."

There was a long silence then as the entire room stared at Jack; all of us aware of his death date we'd intended on avoiding by idling near the storm coordinates for the next three months.

Jack's eyes met mine and I saw his answer. He wouldn't abandon Izzy. "We'll follow."

"Now hang on just a minute, Hoss," Jim said, frowning. "We got three months before that storm hits, and a few weeks still before that death date. There ain't no reason why we cain't drop yuns off near the storm to wait while the rest of us hunt him down. Ye' got babies to raise and there ain't no sense in you dyin' when the rest of us are just as capable of following him as you are."

Jack shook his head. "Juan Josef was listening to us yesterday. He knows that if we…" He stopped and glanced at Juan Jr. "He knows about our plan. I can't risk him harming either of them on my account if he intends to hold them hostage to ensure we don't go through with it. Nor can I risk him taking out our ancestors if the effects of our leaving aren't immediate. Cecelia won't marry for nearly twenty years still. It could be years before anything changes."

Bruce frowned at that, crossing his pudgy arms. "Then we should go to Virginia; go on with the plan to kill the Albrecht. We owe Anna her life, remember? I'm not willing to wait years to give it back to her. How long will it take to get to Panama from here?"

"If we do not stop," Juan said, eyeing Jack with suspicion, "and if we can manage good winds throughout, we might be able to get there in a month."

"A month?" Detective Haywood balked. "And then? How much longer will it take to reach Virginia?"

"Another month or so… if we can procure transportation for so many of us. We cannot take this ship. We'll have to go across the trade route on horseback to Portobelo, then find another ship with the same destination."

The detective pinched the bridge of his nose. "So… if we agree to go to Virginia, that's at least four months before we can return. We won't make the storm." He shook his head at Jack. "If that death date is real… you can't afford to miss it."

"So we go to Panama," I cut in. "And if we do not catch up, or if the yacht is not there, Jack and I will return on this ship with some of the crew while the rest of you go on to Virginia. We'll take these babies through time and pray the effects of our leaving will be immediate. If they're not, the rest of you will move forward with the plan to kill the Albrecht while we wait safely in the future." I looked up at Jack, hoping the compromise would be enough.

Juan Jr. nodded in agreement. "Gabriel is as good a captain as I. He could return you safely while I lead the others in search of my father."

"Why would you help us?" Cece asked sweetly, turning to face him. "Why *have* you helped us over and over again?

He reached into his jacket and produced a folded piece of paper. "He left this for me…"

Cece unfolded the paper after he offered it to her to reveal the ancestry chart with my and Jack's names at the top. A big black circle was drawn around baby Cecelia's name with the words, *'save your mother'* written beside it.

Juan Jr.'s shoulders slumped. "He knew, even before he got this, she was your descendent." He glanced at me. "That's why he wanted Jack killed. He ordered my brother and I to do it and insisted you and the child go unharmed. I put it together then—the likeness to my mother… the necklace—my mother descended from the two of you, from her…" He nodded toward Cecelia where Jim held her against his shoulder.

"And when he told me he planned to take control of the ship and steal your daughter, I knew he'd finally lost whatever was left of his morality. I may not be a good man, but I will not kidnap a child, nor will I murder an innocent man. I could not do it then. I will not do it now."

His gaze moved between me and Jack. "I can only assume, based on the year of death listed beneath your name, that your *alternate plan* is to return to the future… to remain there so my mother might never come to be; might never cause him to flee to that spot on the ocean… That's what he's referencing when he's asked me to save her, isn't it?"

None of us said a word.

Juan Jr. nodded, pursing his lips. "I do not look like like either of you. I have never resembled my mother in any way, and my name is not on this chart even though Dahlia's and Dario's are. Why?"

Again, we all fell silent, none of us sure if we could trust him with the truth.

"They were born after me," he said, looking at Cece for an answer once he realized we wouldn't offer one. "Why are their names listed and mine missing?"

"Because Gloria was not your birth mother," Cece said softly. "I'm sorry."

He looked past her then to Chris, his emotions unreadable. "Who is my birth mother?"

Chris swallowed. "A woman named Juliana Martinez. Do you recognize that name?"

Juan Jr. shook his head. "No."

He raised his brows as he inspected me, running a hand over the top of his head to smooth the hairs that had come loose from their ribbon. Clearing his throat, he dismissed the topic of his mother and shifted his attention back to Jack. "Do we sail to the isthmus then? If we're to stand any chance at catching them, we should not waste any more time."

"Yes," Jack said, his eyes meeting mine. "We'll try it your way, Red."

Juan Jr. bowed his head. "I can have my men pull the anchor and prepare the sails at once... assuming you still wish for me to sail it?"

Jack's shoulders sank in defeat and he nodded. "Go..."

Juan leaned in to whisper his gratitude to Cece before hurrying out of the cabin.

Jack watched him go and let out a long breath once the corridor was empty of his footsteps. "It's a mistake to trust him... This will be yet another mistake we will come to regret. You all know that, don't you?"

Cece touched Jack's shoulder. "We don't know that. What other choice do we have?"

"I don't know," Jack huffed, staring at the open door, "but I have a feeling, if we can't catch up to them, when it comes the time for us to go back to the storm, Juan Jr. will find some way to stop us. I can't let him out of my sight; can't leave him alone up there to potentially scheme with the other men. Let's go."

And then he was gone. Jim handed Cecelia back to my sister and followed, Lilly, Bruce, Chris, and Kyle hurrying out behind him, leaving only the two of us and the detective still standing in the cabin.

'Died at sea.'

That's all I could think of. What if we could never make it back? I held Zachary tighter. If we could never make it back, I would lose both Jack and Zachary. I couldn't bear it.

"He's going to die," I whispered, staring at the open door and the empty corridor beyond it. "Even with our knowledge of it… there's nothing we can do to prevent it. Is there?"

Terrence shook his head. "There's plenty we can do. Look around you. If all this is real, then we are holding history in our very hands; time is ours to command. There are at least twenty books in that room on 18th century history we brought with us—I know because I carried them down. Honey, we can prevent *anything* we want to."

With all the morning's commotion, I'd forgotten the "gifts" Bud had brought with him, including the vast collection of books on 18th century history. Maybe there was something in them— some reference to our journey or at least our destinations that would give us clues as to when and where we might save Jack's life. At the very least, scanning each page would keep my mind occupied.

"You're right," I said, turning toward the door. "We should start reading…"

Chapter Two

Alaina

While the others assisted Juan Jr. and the crew in pulling the anchor, turning the ship out of the bank, and hoisting the sails, Cece, Terrence, Maria, Magna, and I headed down to the cabin to begin rifling through the history books. Lilly would not be pulled away from the top deck, despite our insistence, and so we left her with Jim on the bow staring out in search of the yacht in the distance.

Fetia and her father joined us too, although they were much more interested in playing with Zachary and Cecelia than examining books they couldn't read. I was grateful for their help, anxious as I was to find answers. At four months old, the babies stayed awake longer and, with their improving attention spans, they required constant interaction.

Nearly six months pregnant herself, Fetia was a natural mother. I sank into the first book to the sounds of her gentle voice singing in Tahitian to both of them as they cooed back.

By the time we felt the ship's movement, we'd covered nearly every surface of our room with open books and papers darkened by our scribbled notes.

We were looking for any relevant historical event along our path, any mention of Juan Josef's ship in the Pacific, any text on the Panama region in 1775, and any ships or battles along the route from Portobelo to Virginia where Jack might be harmed.

The detective's words were a beacon of hope in the back of my mind. History was malleable. We'd proven that when our memories changed the first time. We literally had time in our hands if we could find the right passage.

"Anything on Panama in that one?" Maria asked, leaning over her own tome to peek at the open book in Magna's lap where the two of them sat crosslegged on the floor.

"Just this little bit," Magna said, marking the page she'd been reading and flipping back to another she'd marked with a piece of paper.

"It's talking mostly about the relocation of Panama City after a pirate attack, but then here, it mentions the Colonial Transisthmian Route of Panamá, which is the route I'm guessing we'll take to cross from the Pacific to the Atlantic as it stretches from Panama City to Portobelo... It reads here that it was a four-day stretch surrounded predominantly by jungle on both sides."

Her finger slid down the page. "And then here, it says... *'On route from Panamá to Portobelo flowed 60% of South American silver production on its way to Spain, as well as the tragedy of slave trade.'*"

"Slave trade?" the detective asked, lowering the book he'd been reading onto his leg.

Magna nodded. "It stood out to me as well." She marked the page once again with a slip of paper and returned to the one she'd been examining. "Here it speaks of it again, but there's not much. It says the slave trade in Panama began in the 1600s and flourished for more than 200 years... which would indicate it is still active today."

I saw the distorted look on the detective's face in response. Scanning the books laid out around him on the floor, I noticed every single one was opened to a page with an article referencing slavery in the 18th century. It occurred to me, for the first time, that the detective had made no small sacrifice in choosing to remain with us. He could've insisted on staying behind; on being dropped off at the island near the coordinates to return to his life in the 21st century… But he hadn't.

"Terrence, you don't have to do this," Cece said softly, evidently thinking the same. "We can take you to that island to wait for us. No one would think less of you. I certainly wouldn't. It'd be dangerous for you to step foot on that trail. They could mistake you for a slave."

He shook his head. "I promised you on that yacht I'd protect you, and I meant it. We'll go together. Jasmine would kill me if she knew I left you behind. Let some old white man attempt to take me as a slave… I *want* to see him try."

Cece rolled her eyes. "And Jasmine will kill *me* if I let you get yourself killed out here."

"You two know each other well, then?" I asked, glancing between them. I'd assumed they were only familiar through his assignment on the case, but their behavior was much more chummy—*particularly for Cece*—than that of mere acquaintances. She was far more timid with strangers than she was with him.

Cece nodded, keeping her pointer finger on whatever passage she'd been reading in the book resting across her legs. "You remember Jasmine from college? She was a Zeta too and my closest friend in school. When you went missing, I couldn't think of anyone better than her FBI-agent husband to help me find you. He was all too happy to look into it." She forced a smile at him. "Although, I do believe he's regretting that decision now."

The detective shook his head. "Honey, I regretted that decision on day one when you showed up with a mountain of spreadsheets, maps, and printed articles from the internet. Nearly lost my job over this case on several occasions. I'm too invested to turn back now."

Maria twisted her lips to one side in thought. "Do you think rumor might have reached Panama that the duchess of Parma had been spotted in the Pacific with James Cook? If it is under Spanish control, they will know the name…"

I shrugged, glancing down at the article on another Spanish captain I'd been scanning. "It's possible... why?"

She leaned forward, propping her cheek on her palm as she rested her elbow on her knee. "Look in your books for any mention of the duchess's travels. Maybe there is a clue there? If we must go across this trail, we will need identities. Her identity has worked for us before, would we not use it again to ensure safe passage? Particularly for *him*?" She winked at the detective. "No one would harm you if you are in the company of a duchess."

Terrence made a noise in his throat. "While you're at it, see if there's any reference to a duchess's escort murdering a whole mess of slave traders in Panama."

Magna chuckled and laid a hand on his knee where he sat in the wingback chair behind her. "We can't fix all of history's mistakes at once, honey... much as I would like to see every one of them burn." She turned back to the rest of us. "Maria does have a point though. If we must cross, we would use the duchess's identity and the gold we have in our possession to find safe passage. If we can find any mention of her in these books, we might be that much closer to a clue on Jack."

And the search for any text referencing Maria Amalia began.

We learned quickly that Maria Amalia was the sister of the infamous Marie Antoinette, and unfortunately, most references to her rule in Parma were but a short paragraph as it pertained to the history of the French queen. Very little was written exclusively about her, and the longer I searched, the more frustrated I became.

"Alaina," Maria said after about a half hour spent in silence, "your memories changed too, yes?"

"Uh huh," I mumbled, not looking up from the paragraph I was scanning on Marie Antoinette's letter from prison to Maria Amalia.

"But you still feel the same? You still choose Jack?"

I raised my eyes from the book then to find both Maria and Cece staring at me in anticipation of an answer. Clearing my throat, I frowned. "Jack is my husband and the father of my children. How I feel about him has not changed."

"But has how you feel about *Kreese* changed?" she pressed on, her expression telling me she would not allow me to skirt the conversation.

I massaged the back of my neck. Part of me had known this topic would come up when I got the new memories, but I hadn't been prepared to discuss it with Maria.

"I have always loved Chris," I assured her. "There was never a point, before or after the new memories, where that wasn't true."

She examined the ring on her finger where it was rested over her book. "We tried to get married twice, you know. Both times it fell through." She sighed, her big brown eyes meeting mine. "I think it was fate that stopped us. It would've been a mistake to marry him when he is still in love with you."

I clicked my tongue. "He loves *you*, Maria."

"Sí, I know that, but not like he loves you. I'm not sure he will ever love anyone like he does you. Can I ask you something?"

I nodded, not trusting myself to speak without coming across as heartless. I had chosen Jack the minute I'd kissed him on that beach and I understood what it might look like to the rest of the world. What wife lets go of a ten year marriage for a man she'd spent less than a year with? If I'd been on the outside, I might've thought I was heartless too.

"If Kreese had been more affectionate," Maria continued, "would he have been enough? And if the answer is yes, then do you only choose Jack because of a physical connection or is he really more than Kreese could ever be?"

"Wait," Cece said softly. "I can see your defenses going up, but she doesn't mean that as an attack. It's an important question. Honestly, I even thought about asking something similar when you first told me about Jack, but I know how defensive you are. You should think about it before answering impulsively."

My throat burned as I looked from my sister to Maria, my mouth falling open. It sure felt like an attack from where I was sitting with the eyes of the entire room upon me. "It's a question I have already answered, and it's never been impulsive. This was never about Chris not being enough or Jack being more. I love them both, and I chose Jack because I love who *I* am with him more than I love who I became with Chris."

"Even in the new memories?" Maria asked, drumming her fingers over the page in her lap.

"Those memories don't matter," I reminded her. "We're putting things back the way they were. I'm married to Jack and I'm happy. That wasn't a decision I made lightly, but it has always been the right one for me. I'm not going to change my mind and go running back to Chris if that's what you're asking. How many times do we have to have this conversation before you believe me?"

Maria narrowed her eyes at me. "The memories *do* matter. They mattered enough to him that he has barely touched me since he got them; hasn't been able to look at me the same knowing what you two could've been. Aside from one drunken night in Albuquerque, we have not been together at all. If there's any chance you could change your mind, he would drop everything for you—me included. He's lying to himself if he says otherwise. And if you are actively pushing those memories to the back of your mind to avoid them, that's not fair. They will still be there and some day you will have to acknowledge them; acknowledge who you became in those memories with him and if you still like who you are with Jack better. I'll have this conversation a thousand times if I must until I am certain I am not standing between two people who are meant to be together."

I groaned, but as I opened my mouth to speak, Cece laid her hand over mine. "You know what? We're all tired and cranky and there's time to figure out our relationships after we're done figuring out how to keep ourselves alive. No sense in arguing about love if we're all going to end up dead." She winked at me before she turned her attention to Maria. "Let's just focus on finding ourselves in these books for now, okay?"

After that, we all silently dived back into the research, everyone slightly more uncomfortable than they'd been prior to Maria's interrogation.

I read the words in my book over and over, but I couldn't comprehend them. Her question plagued my mind, and I found myself wondering if everyone saw us similarly.

At our own wedding, the stories people told had to do with catching Jack and I in some physical act—not how much love they saw between us. Did everyone assume I'd been so starved for affection that I mistook it for love?

It aggravated me that other people could make me doubt something I'd been so sure of prior to the question being asked.

I knew, with all my heart, Jack was the love of my life… but then again… I'd known that about Chris once, too…

If Chris *had* touched me the way Jack did, would I have made the same decisions? Would I have ever allowed myself to fall in love with Jack in the first place? And did that answer matter?

After several hours, Bruce called us all for supper, and having skipped both breakfast and lunch, we all paused the research long enough to join the others in the great cabin.

Jack escorted Juan Jr. inside, nudging him to take a seat at the far end of the table. As Jack took his beside me, I found my hand instinctively sliding over his. As he squeezed it softly, my anxiety melted away. What the rest of the world thought of us didn't matter. I knew the truth.

"Where are Lilly and Jim?" I asked.

"They're not coming," Jack said. "She won't move from that railing, and Jim won't leave her."

"I'll go up and check on her after dinner," I said, feeling horrible that I'd chosen to rush downstairs instead of remaining at her side as she would've done for me.

Maria groaned. "She's not going to help Izzy by just standing there wasting away!" She pushed back from the table and snatched up her dinner plate, already loaded with salt pork, potatoes, bread, and cheese. She snagged Chris's plate from him as well where he was just about to dig into the steaming slab of meat. "¡Mujer estúpida! Let me go feed this stubborn girl."

We all watched as Maria stormed out of the cabin with both plates, her Spanish complaints echoing down the hallway in her wake.

Without a plate in front of him, Chris set his utensils on the table and leaned back in his chair, his eyes meeting mine. There was a fondness in his gaze that told me the new memories had in fact changed things for him. It was only a matter of time before I'd have to turn him down... again. "Find anything?"

I shook my head and stared down at the potato I was pushing around my plate. "A bunch of promising leads that took us to a bunch more dead ends... There's a lot to look at, though. We've barely scratched the surface. Each of those books is at least a thousand pages... There *has* to be something. What I wouldn't give to have just ten minutes with a Google search right now. Speaking of..." I wiped a bead of drool from Zachary's chin. "Did you find out anything else on the storm? Any signs of other travelers or the back of the plane?"

Chris ran a hand over his face. "No trace of the rest of the plane, but the internet is loaded with time travel conspiracies. It's hard to know what might be a clue and what might have been made up by some guy who got bored one day and dreamed up a scandal. We had to look at everything, though. We pulled anything related to time travel we could find. Articles, photos, various time travel theories... Everything is in that binder."

"And Owen?" I shifted my focus to Cece who immediately stared down at her plate at the mention of his name. "Were you able to confirm we erased his existence?"

Chris followed my gaze and shook his head. "Owen's alive. He married after college and had children with someone else; still running his father's campground in Minnesota. I can only assume that whoever we erased when we poisoned those men had to have played a role in their initial meeting."

I remembered Jack speaking of his car accident where he'd scarred his sister... how fragile time had actually been. I recalled him regretting those few seconds he spent at a gas station scanning drink options, the signed autograph just outside… if he'd done neither of those things, they never would've crashed… I wondered what little moment was erased by our poison. Was it as simple as a man scanning drink options at a gas station and causing a delay in Owen's arrival at the party she'd met him at?

"Who's sailing the ship?" Cece cut in, dismissing the topic of Owen as she looked across the table at Juan Jr.

"Gabriel," Juan informed her. "I had intended to remain on deck, however, Mr. Volmer would not allow me to decline the *invitation* to join you."

He and Jack exchanged heated looks.

I blinked. "Wait, if Owen's alive—"

"As we are now on course to the isthmus…" Juan Jr. interrupted, his attention on Cece where her expression was begging anyone to change the subject. "We may very well encounter other ships along our route, and, as it is not uncustomary for Spanish captains to invite themselves on board other vessels, it may be time you all traded in your modern-day attire for clothing more… appropriate."

His gaze lingered on my sister. "I mean no offense, of course… Men in this century are not accustomed to seeing so much skin… Even the remaining crew have mentioned it on several occasions. With the heat, I was able to pass it off as a temporary reprieve in the lack of surrounding society, but now that we are at sea…"

I smiled. "We'll dress before we leave the room from now on."

Juan bowed his head in thanks and I couldn't help but notice that Cece hadn't touched her food, nor had she moved her gaze from Juan. She was having a silent conversation with only her eyes. She was thanking him… thanking him for silencing *me*.

How would I prepare her for the life she would be returned to if she wouldn't hear any of it? And why did she continue to dismiss any mention of that life? Didn't she want to know about her daughter? I couldn't understand her unwillingness to talk about any of it.

"About the *room*," Chris said, sitting forward as Bruce laid a new plate of food in front of him. "Now that there are more of us, and with Juan Josef gone, I was thinking we might spread out a bit… take the rooms on each side of the bigger cabin. A guard in the hall can watch three doors just as well as he can watch the one… I wouldn't mind sleeping in an actual bed tonight."

Kyle, beside him, nodded, focusing on his prosthetic arm as he attempted to tighten the fingers of it around the fork in his opposite hand. "Fetia could use the privacy of a room to ourselves as well. She's been getting more tired lately and I don't think she's sleeping with so many of us crammed together. Her father, too. He's too old to be sleeping on a mattress on the floor."

"Fine by me," Jack said, adjusting Zachary to prevent him from reaching for his food. "So long as we always have a lookout in the hall. I don't trust any of these men."

Bruce took a seat opposite me. "Neither do I. I'd like to sleep nearer to the kitchens with the rest of the waitstaff. After what happened with Georgie, it'd be good to have eyes and ears down there. I can take Jacob and Michael with me."

Memory of Georgie standing over Jack's unconscious body swept over me and I placed my fork and knife back down on my plate as I swallowed, squeezing Cecelia tighter in my lap.

"That's a good idea," Jack said, turning to Jacob. "You'd be alright sleeping down there?"

Jacob smiled and waved it off. "I worked the kitchens on a ship like this when I was a boy. I don't mind it, and it could do Michael good to help out. We're shorthanded as it is."

Jacob and Michael had spent so much time on the devil's island with Uati I wondered if there was anything that wouldn't be a vast improvement over their former living conditions.

"The men that remain are good, honorable men," Juan Jr. said. "I know that means little coming from me, particularly after all that has occurred under my father's command, but I assure you, they've no intention to harm any of you."

"Oye," Maria balked as she hurried back through the cabin doors to her seat beside Chris, "the one at the wheel has eyes that say otherwise."

Juan Jr. raised an eyebrow. "Gabriel is young and has spent most of his life at sea. He is unaccustomed to seeing women like yourselves dressed in such a way. He is pure of heart and means no harm."

"We're going back to the dresses," I said to her. "In case we're boarded by another ship and so we don't make the rest of the crew uncomfortable. We probably should've done that a while ago."

Maria rolled her eyes. "Do I have to wear those stupid stays again?"

"We all do… but only if we're venturing out of our rooms."

"¡Ay Coño!" she snarled, leaning in to Chris to whisper, not so quietly, "I am never leaving the room again."

After dinner, we all went our separate ways, Fetia and Kyle to their new room, Maria and Chris to theirs on the other side, leaving Magna, Cece, Terrence, and I to take the babies to the larger cabin.

Jack joined Juan Jr. on the deck, not ready to leave him to his own devices so early into the trip. I had a feeling I would be sleeping alone for the foreseeable future.

As I moved to take up my spot on the sofa and the book I'd been reading before dinner, Cece grabbed my hand to stop me. "Do you think… could you help me get dressed in one of those dresses you mentioned at dinner?"

I frowned. "Cece, you don't have to wear that now. We'll be in bed soon and you won't need to go back up until tomorrow."

"I…" She crossed her arms over her chest and set her jaw. "I *need* to get dressed."

"Why?" I asked, stifling the urge to laugh. She reminded me just then of her younger self… demanding to play with whatever toy was in my hand because she *'needed'* it. God knows, I could never say no to her.

"Because, A.J., I have never been able to sleep through the night and at some point, I might need to go get some air… I don't want to make Juan or the other men uncomfortable if I do."

Memory of the morning's events returning to me, I tilted my head to one side. "What's with you and Juan Jr.? This morning, you defended him, and then at dinner, you couldn't take your eyes off him. What's going on?"

I noticed the briefest exchange of looks between her and the detective before she brushed the hair back from her face. "Nothing… I just didn't want to see Jack hurt him is all. He seems like a nice man and you told me he saved you from an attack the night we arrived. Nobody else was doing anything to stop it and… well, you know me… I felt like I had to do something."

Unconvinced, I raised an eyebrow. "That's not all of it. What are you not saying?"

"Nothing. That's it," she lied.

I poked her rib. "You liar! What is it? Got the hots for him?"

She swatted my hand away. "No!"

I gasped. "You do!" I shook my head. "Cece, he may be handsome, but none of us knows who he really is. He could be tricking us. If he's anything like his father and brother, I wouldn't put it past him. Besides, we're going back, and you're going to have this wonderful life with a husband and child you adore. Trust me. It's not worth pursuing—especially if you return with two sets of memories like I did."

Again, there was an exchange of glances between her and Terrence; a secret conversation I was on the outside of. I knew it well. All our lives, we'd had the same ability to communicate with only a look. I felt suddenly estranged from her and I hated that.

Focusing my attention back on the detective, I huffed. "What is she not saying? What's going on?"

Terrence shrugged, plucking up the book he'd been reading from one of the wingback chairs. "I'm not getting in the middle of it. It's late and you'll need someone watching those doors. You two should get some rest."

I waited for him to leave the room before I closed the gap between me and my sister. "Cece, what's going on? We don't keep secrets from each other. What was with those looks between you and Terrence? You know you can talk to me… about anything."

She sighed. "It's nothing, A.J., I promise. I'm just… adjusting. All these new faces and stories and people and problems… We're in a whole different world with people who keep putting their arms around me like we're family and we're talking about changing history and there's this whole other life I don't know about that you keep insisting I will return to and…"

She took a deep breath, slowing her thoughts as she met my eyes. "It's just a lot to take in at once. You know? As for Juan, well, he's on the outside too. And it's not a crush, it's just my nature to be drawn to the person in the corner instead of the crowd at the center. You know that. I felt sorry for him this morning. That's all."

I knew that wasn't all there was to it, but we had all overwhelmed her, and Cece was someone who needed space and time to process, otherwise she was prone to panic attacks.

"I'm sorry." I squeezed her hand. "I hadn't realized just how much of an adjustment all this has been for you. Are you feeling alright?"

She ran a hand over her face. "I've been able to handle my anxiety so far, but with the lack of sleep, I want to be ready. That's why I want you to get me dressed. The air helps."

"Alright," I said softly. "I'll get you dressed." I pulled her to the changing screen and opened the trunk for her to pick something. "You don't have to stay, either. We could drop both you and Terrence off at that island to wait for us… leave a cutter and supplies just in case we don't make it in time… I know this is really hard—"

"I'm not going anywhere without you," she said, snagging a cream and blue flowered petticoat to hold against her waist. "I've spent too long searching for you to ever let you go again. I can deal with a panic attack just as well here as I can there."

Chapter Three

Cecelia

I laid in my small cot taking slow and steady breaths, cursing myself for insisting on getting dressed now that the stays inhibited any attempt to breathe deeply.

Having had panic attacks since college, I'd gotten good at identifying the early warning signs and was usually able to shut them down before they started. Here, however, I wasn't so sure I'd be able to stop them so easily, and the last thing anyone needed to deal with was my ridiculous levels of anxiety.

It was a strange thing for others to witness a person suddenly lose all control of themselves; a normal, functioning adult one minute, a crumbling invalid the next.

It was embarrassing, the wave of concern that always followed by anyone who'd witnessed it. They couldn't understand I didn't need to be worried over; didn't need to have people cooing and stroking my back as if I were an abandoned puppy left out in the cold. I just needed a second to put myself back together—to organize my thoughts—and I was always fine.

The people here already spoke and touched with a familiarity I didn't have yet. They knew more about me than I knew about them; already cared about me as if I were some part of their family.

If I had an attack here, I would undoubtedly be bombarded with sympathy; hugs and caresses and kind words which would make matters worse. I didn't want that—didn't need that kind of fragile image of me implanted in their minds when I was determined to be the one to get us out of here.

I needed to get ahead of my thoughts. However much I tried to evade it, the panic was gradually welling beyond my control. Where the euphoria of finding my sister had staved the anxiety off upon my arrival, my inevitable return to an alternate version of my life—one that looked nothing like the future I'd spent so many years working toward—was weighing heavily on my mind.

In this life, I had a mission; a vision for my future that gave me purpose in the world. One day, I would work with endangered animals to prevent their extinction. I'd spent years earning my Ph.D while running my clinic and had looked forward to little else before my sister's plane disappeared. I was proud of who I was and where I was going.

But in this alternate reality A.J. insisted on telling me about, I dropped out of college and moved far away from everyone I knew and loved to serve my husband and child.

It was eating away at me.

I didn't want to seem dismissive or cold; particularly when A.J. held so much affection for a daughter I couldn't envision. I tried to keep my mind open to it, but the more I considered who I might become; how utterly derailed my plans for the future would be and the lack of purpose to that existence, the stronger the sense of doom lingering in the outer crevices of my consciousness became.

A.J. had two sets of memories of her life. Would I wake up one day and remember both versions of mine? Would I recognize the two strangers that were supposed to be my family or would the pull of the life I knew now be stronger? Would memories of my accomplishments in this existence cause me to be unhappy in a reality I'd once been content with? Would this Owen person even recognize the woman he'd wake up beside when it all was over? How could I possibly be the mother that child was expecting if I woke up disappointed?

I could feel the little warning signals of an impending attack beginning to fire. I needed to get air before it took over.

A.J. was snoring softly, her mouth partially open, with both babies tucked into her chest. Smiling at the familiarness of her snore—one I'd never thought I'd hear again—I slowly sat up in my bed, careful not to let it creak and disturb the temporary reprieve her slumber would grant her.

She didn't need to be bothered with me and my reservations about the future. The poor thing had enough to worry about. Between the missing girl, Jack and Zachary's upcoming death dates, changing history to save Anna, and catering to general every day motherhood needs, it was a wonder to me she wasn't falling apart herself.

Wrapping my blanket around my shoulders, I tiptoed across the wooden floorboards and eased our cabin door open to slide out into the dark corridor beyond.

Just the darkness, the simplicity of being cloaked in shadow where no one might see me crumble, made my breath come a little easier.

"Where you going?" Terrence asked from his seat in those same shadows outside the door. His voice was kept low to prevent disturbing the others, but it still made me jump nearly out of my skin. I'd forgotten he was there.

"I need air," I whispered, anxiety welling in my stomach that I might collapse into an attack right there at his feet.

"I know it stinks down here, but I don't want you moving around this ship on your own, Cece. It's not safe."

I hugged the blanket tighter against my arms, hoping I could maintain my grip on myself with the weight of it. "I'm on the verge of having a panic attack. I'm sorry, but I have to get some air. I can't fall apart now."

He clutched my hand and began to rise from his chair. "I'll come with you."

"No, no." I squeezed his fingers in mine. "I know how to handle this myself, Tee. I'll be fine in no time. If there's danger here, I prefer you watch over them." I tilted my head in the direction of the door where my sister and her children slept. "She means the world to me. Besides, Jack and Jim never came down. I imagine they're both still up there to keep an eye on things."

"Did you tell her about Juan Jr.?" he asked, his grip tightening to prevent me from sprinting toward the stairwell.

"No." I sighed, not bothering to attempt an escape when I knew it was futile. Terrence was a relentless interrogator and would only release me once he got an answer that satisfied him. "There's no point in telling her when *I* don't even understand it yet. It could be nothing—some weird déjà vu or something. I could be wrong."

I said the words knowing full well Terrence wouldn't buy them. I didn't buy them either.

The truth was, from the moment I'd first seen Juan Jr., I knew, with all my heart, I *recognized* him. In the span of roughly thirty seconds, when his eyes first locked with mine, I knew every part of him—the midnight black hair and the way it slightly dipped into a widow's peak when pulled back, those sage green eyes and the way the tip of his nose flattened ever so faintly, the dimple in his cheek when his lips turned upward, and even the ruby ring on his pinky… I knew him. I could close my eyes and see every detail of him from memory, like he'd been a part of my life forever… and yet… I could not figure out how.

That, in and of itself, was contributing just as greatly to my growing sense of panic.

Terrence let out the breath of a laugh. "Cecelia McCreary, you are a terrible liar. We're in the past, honey. And you know damn well if their little plan works, that man could very possibly end up some place in your past if he returns to grow up through the 80s and 90s as he should have… You know it's *not* nothing. You have to figure out where you met him and if he gave you any kind of message or warning."

I groaned. "I know that, but you'd think I'd remember meeting him as clear as I remember the day I met you. As it stands, it's just an intuition; a familiarness to him, that's all. Maybe I saw someone who looked similar at some point."

"Similar to your Don Juan up there?" He chuckled. "I've never crossed paths with anyone who fits his description."

That was also true. His appearance was… unforgettable. When I'd laid eyes on him, I was instantly made a sixteen-year-old putz of a human-being, not quite knowing which direction to look or if I was smiling too much… or not enough… or if I was even smiling at all or just standing there baring my teeth like an idiot. I'd been completely unraveled in those seconds by not only the familiarity of him, but the familiarity of my desire for him.

I was awkward with men; had spent far too many years avoiding them because of that awkwardness, and the sudden pull to him had caught me off guard. I *wanted* to approach him; to know him in a deeper way. He was a stranger, but he wasn't, and my mind reeled simply at the thought of being near him.

I glanced toward the stairwell. "Maybe I could place him in a memory if I talk to him… I was planning to do that once I got my mind settled down."

Terrence clicked his tongue. "I really wish you'd wait until daytime to go up there."

I smirked. "I really wish I didn't have panic attacks at all so I wouldn't have to disappoint you. If you don't let me go, I might just collapse right here in this hallway for you to deal with. Trust me when I tell you it's not going to be pretty."

With a deep breath, he released my hand to reach into his pocket. "Then at least take this." I felt the weight of some kind of weapon pull down my palm. "If anyone so much as looks at you the wrong way, you pull this trigger here," he moved my finger down the surface to the trigger, "and tase the shit out of them. You've got two charges in there. Fire the first one and scream, loud enough I can hear you, and I'll be there in seconds."

"Thanks, Tee." I tucked the taser into the pocket tied beneath my skirts. "I'll be safe, and I promise, when we get home, I'm going to make this up to you."

"You better. Dragging my ass through time cause you can't let anyone else do their job!"

"And it's a good thing I did," I teased. "Otherwise you would still be chasing the hijack theory I told you from the start wasn't right."

"Yeah, yeah," he chortled. "Go on and figure out where you met your prince charming up there. I'll keep an eye on things down here."

I turned away from him, the lump once again expanding in my throat at the thought of speaking to Juan Jr., and padded up the stairs on my bare feet, anxious for the air on the top deck.

The moment I felt the cool night breeze on my cheeks, I took it deep into my lungs. With each breath, I began to feel my fingers, toes, and cheeks once more attached to my body… once more put together.

Salt and a hint of dampened canvas from the inflated sails filled my senses, washing away the fetid musk of the lower decks. My lungs rejoiced at being free from the odors of the ship's confines, and I wasn't entirely certain my feet would ever allow me to descend below deck again.

"Are you alright?" Jack asked, instantly there with a hand at the small of my back. "What are you doing up here? Are you having a panic attack?"

"I'm fine," I assured him, masterfully moving away from his too familiar touch in a way that might seem unintentional. "I just needed some air. It stinks below deck."

He laughed. "I thought the same the first time I got on Captain Cook's ship. You'll get used to the smells, eventually."

He scanned the deck, inspecting the shadows of men moving between lantern lights for any signs of a threat. "Given our history with this group and how little we really know the remaining crew, I'd feel a lot better if you weren't up here at night."

I forced a sweet smile. "I appreciate your concern, Jack, but I'm a big girl, and I don't need anyone to look after me. I can handle myself."

I presented my taser as evidence and winked. "Besides, if we'll be spending so much time with the remaining crew, now might be a good time to actually get to know them. Don't you think?"

I turned toward the quarterdeck and froze as my gaze locked with Juan Jr.'s.

Perhaps I *would* require a chaperone to escort me around the ship if the man insisted on looking at me like that. Did he recognize me too, or was the intensity in his stare that of a man who saw something he wanted?

I couldn't help the tiny ping of excitement at the idea that this man might reciprocate the desire that was nearly ripping through my skin. I felt his gaze warm parts of me I hadn't known were cold; felt a door open to awaken a romantic part of me that had lain dormant and dead for as long as I could remember.

My brain immediately forced that door back shut and locked.

'Now is not the time to open that door...'

Flirting with Juan, fun as it might be when he looked at me in such a way, was not an option. There were too many loose ends to tie up... too many answers we needed to find before we headed back to that storm... and too many mistakes made already when others had let their romantic parts rule over logic.

I returned his stare, ignoring my desire and attempting instead to find some background he fit into in my memory. I could almost see him with shorter hair... hands in his pockets... but where had I seen him? When? Had he come to warn me of something, or was I simply mistaking him for someone else?

"Careful there," Jack warned, nudging my elbow with his to pull me out of my stupor. "We don't know if we can trust him."

I cleared my throat, pulling the blanket back up over my shoulders where it had slipped. "Only one way to find out. If you'll excuse me..."

And then I was moving toward him.

And every step became heavier with the weight of his gaze, that part of me I'd locked away now pounding on the door and forcing my legs to quiver.

A muscle in his jaw ticked as I moved closer and I wondered if it was anticipation or frustration that caused it to do so. I hadn't spent much time with him since my arrival, but the déjà vu surrounding his image made me less hesitant to approach; made me assume he'd be welcoming of my company instead of dismissive.

I studied his expression where he kept whatever emotion was behind it shuttered. What was he feeling? Was that desire in his stare? Recognition? Hatred? Was he really disappointed about his father's escape or was he angry we'd thwarted his plans to rebel in some other way? Did he possess the kindness I'd sworn I recognized the moment I saw him or was it an act to get us all to trust him before he forced us toward his father's plans? Did it even matter which plans we moved toward? In the end, wouldn't it all end up with the same result?

We'd all go home with new memories one way or another…

I continued to stare, inspecting his dark features, the murky green of his eyes, and the sharp jawline. Where did I know him from? Who was he to me?

"Hello, Cecelia," he said when I reached him, and even that was familiar.

I cleared my throat, clutching the blanket tighter against my chest as my pulse beat even faster, my palms sweating while I tried to will my numb lips to form words, any words at all. Approaching him had seemed like a good idea, but standing this close, I second-guessed my own confidence in doing so.

Thankfully, this wasn't panic. It was timidness, which was just as familiar and just as infuriating in the way it debilitated me. My feet felt strange in their stance beneath me; my lips too tight. Even my own skin felt confining as I stood there, unable to look away from the sharp lines of his face, the breadth of his shoulders, and the one dark wisp of hair that'd escaped its ribbon to dance in the wind against his cheek.

He glanced at my feet and back. "Do you tremble because you are cold or because you are afraid of me?"

"I don't know," I admitted, curling my toes in against the wooden deck boards. "I… I have some things I need to ask you."

He scanned my features for a moment, and, as if he could see my struggle for composure beneath the surface, he let his guard melt away and offered an easy smile. "As I am in your debt, my dear, I shall be happy to offer any answers I can provide."

I might've gotten lost for days simply in that smile… It wasn't just the way the smile transformed an already perfect face into one almost God-like, but more the way it felt… As if *I'd* smiled and meant it for the first time in my life.

'Now is not the time to open that door…'

Shaking my head of its fog, I forced the words out in a tone a bit more demanding than I'd intended. "Do you know me?"

He raised his brows. "Know you? In what way?"

"You stare at me," I said, feeling slightly ridiculous for pointing out my awareness of it, "and I thought it might be recognition that caused you to do so… because I got this feeling like I'd met you before and have been unable to shake it."

I watched the change in him as he placed the icy guard he hid behind right back up between us. "You have mistaken me for another. I would have remembered meeting you, and you would not have been so quick to approach had you truly met me before. I am not a kind sort of man."

"No?" I asked, hating how stiff my own words sounded in my mouth. That silly romantic piece of my mind was desperate not to have him think of me as such a cold and demanding woman. "An unkind man wouldn't have saved my sister and her children in the dining room the other night."

He shook his head. "A *kind* man would've never taken them in the first place."

A bit of movement at his feet drew my attention away from his face, and I was delighted when a small cocker spaniel mix poked her head out of a pile of blankets. Happy for a distraction in conversation that might soften my stupid voice, I pointed at her. "Is she yours?"

"My brother's," he said, glancing down at the mutt with a smile. "Luna is her name. Your sister mentioned you were fond of animals. You're welcome to take her whenever it pleases you."

"Hello, Luna," I cooed, kneeling to let her sniff my hand. My heart was instantly settled at the feel of her gentle breath against my knuckles. Animals always had a way of setting me right.

I didn't look up at him, busying myself with the task of scratching her fluffy ears as I shifted conversation to a topic where my voice might be a little more recognizable as my own. "Do you have any pain in your throat after what happened this morning?"

There was a pause before he responded. "You are concerned for my well-being. Why?"

I chuckled as Luna flopped onto her back to present her belly to me. "I think we have some medicine that could help the muscles relax if they're swollen... We don't have any ice, but a wet cloth might help if you have pain."

"I've no pain, Cecelia," he assured me, my name on his lips awakening a familiar tickle in my sternum, like I'd heard it said with that same Spanish accent once before. "Why would you worry for me?"

Scratching the dog's pudgy pink belly, I kept my focus on my fingers for fear the burn on my cheeks might be visible. "Like I said, I feel like we've met before, and it doesn't feel right not to worry after what happened."

"We've not met before. I would have remembered your face even if I'd seen it only in passing."

I looked up at him in surprise at the hint of flirtation, but he straightened, adjusting the lapels of his dark jacket and staring ahead. "You should return to the others... where you belong."

"Where I belong?" I balked, standing and pulling the blanket back over my shoulders. "You're trying to change history and make it so you never end up going through the storm, right?"

"I am," he said, stiffening at my sudden nearness, his knuckles white where his fingers were coiled tightly around the tillers of the helm.

"You crossed through time in 1977, right?"

He nodded, avoiding eye contact as he pretended to check the compass. Was he just as awkward with women as I was with men or was my nearness so revolting to him?

Hoping he was just awkward, I softened my tone the way he had with me when I'd approached. "My sister said you were seven when you came through. So… if what you're planning to do here works and you never go through the storm, wouldn't it be possible you could end up growing up through the 80s and 90s? Wouldn't it be entirely likely you could wake up with memories of your time here somewhere around the year 2000 when I'm still young? Maybe with some sort of warning or message or… means to see that we all ended up here? It can't be a coincidence that the only other time travelers you've run into are related to your family."

Feeling a little more emboldened by his familiarness, I spoke freely; something I rarely ever did with a man who wasn't my family. "If I feel like I know you, do I not belong right here trying to determine where and when I met you and what you might or might not have said to me? Wouldn't that be more important than whatever self-preservation you're attempting to achieve by acting so dismissive? I'm not going to maul you, ya know. You can relax."

There was a twitch in his lip, so fleeting I might've missed it had I not been staring, and I could've sworn it was amusement; the faintest hint of a crack in his reserve. "Forgive me. I hadn't meant to be dismissive with you. I've spent too much time at sea and have forgotten my manners. This…feeling you met me… is this why you felt obligated to speak on my behalf this morning?"

"Partly," I admitted, leaning into the railing that separated the quarterdeck from the main one. "And partly because I didn't think Jack was being fair to jump to the conclusion you'd had a part in their escape, especially after what you did for them in the great cabin the other night."

His dark brow raised slightly. "You believe me innocent, then?"

I shrugged. "Are you?"

He nodded. "Aye. After what I did in the great cabin, my father did not trust me enough to share his escape plans with me. I suppose he did not trust me enough to share a great many things with me."

There were a million questions I wanted to ask him. I wanted to know who he was, what he planned, and if we could trust him, but right then, I saw the pain he was attempting to hide from me. Despite who he was or whether or not he could be trusted, he needed comfort, not questioning. There'd be time for more questions.

"You didn't know about your mother…" I said softly.

"No." His voice was little more than a whisper.

"I'm so sorry. I can't imagine how you must feel. Do you want to talk about it?"

"No." I watched the muscles in his throat move as he scanned the horizon behind me. I wondered how I might've felt if it were me reading someone else's name in place of my mother's on my own genealogy report.

My heart ached for him. I wouldn't pry—God knew, I always hated it when strangers pressed me to talk about things I wasn't ready to share—but I hoped I could come to know him in a way that would make him feel more comfortable to open up. He seemed like someone who'd been alone in his mind for far too long, and for whatever reason, I wanted to be someone he could talk to.

"You are the one who stares," he noted. "More so than I."

I quickly lowered my gaze. "I'm sorry. It's just that it's the strangest thing to look at you and recognize you without a clue as to where I know you from. I've had this weird pull to you for two days now, like I'd seen some old friend I'd been estranged from for years. It's so bizarre. I can't place you at all, but you're so damn familiar; your face, voice, even your mannerisms… it's like I remember all of it but can't figure out how. I'm not a person who just walks casually up to strange men and starts asking questions… but I couldn't stay away. I need to know why you're familiar. I don't mean to make you uncomfortable."

He loosened his death grip on the helm, his shoulders relaxing an inch. "You've not made me uncomfortable, Cecelia. As I said before, I've been at sea far too long and have forgotten how to interact with a woman."

I chuckled at that. "Is it so different from interacting with a man?"

"Aye," he said, those sage eyes meeting mine. "It is when the woman looks like you."

I cleared my throat, tugging the corners of the blanket back into place as a means to keep my hands occupied. The statement had me a bit unraveled. To have a man as stunning as he was admit to finding me attractive… It excited and terrified me at the same time.

As I tended to do whenever the discussion was pointing toward me, I steered the conversation right back to its original course. "Does this new detail about your mother change your plans?"

He blew out a breath and shook his head. "I've given a considerable amount of thought to where I might find myself when this is all over. Jack was right this morning. If your sister takes the child through the storm now, it's possible there would be a window of time where they could return. I cannot imagine the effects to history would be immediate as the child will not marry or produce my moth—*Gloria's* ancestor for several years still. My plan remains unchanged. God willing, I will continue on to Virginia to kill George Bennet after she's gone through the storm. It is my hope I might make memories I can hold onto during the years it would take for the changes to take place."

I frowned. "You really have no intention to stop it?"

"I considered it," he admitted, "but short of kidnapping the child to raise in this time, there's nothing to be done. I am not my father."

Perhaps it was the exhaustion setting in, or maybe it was just the honesty between us in that moment, but I felt encouraged just enough to pry. "My sister says you plan to kill him. Is that still true?"

He nodded, but there was pain in his expression.

"You plan to kill him," I continued, "but you don't want to? Did you love him?"

He let out the breath of a laugh. "Aye. In my way."

I could see the torment just beneath the stoic expression he was attempting to maintain. "If we catch up to them in Panama, you really plan to kill him?"

I watched his chest move with a deep breath as he stared ahead. "I can accept a few years of memories as a good enough compromise. He cannot. He will spend those years doing everything in his power to make sure your sister remains in this time. That is why he left that letter; possibly why he took the child and the old man. He may not have a plan in place now, but he will have one by the time we catch up to him. He is cruel when he is desperate, and if he overheard your plans, he will stop at nothing to impede them. I must put an end to this."

I chewed my lower lip. "I've never met the man, but it seems like it's hard for anyone to find a kind word to describe him. Is it strange to share your name with him? It doesn't seem like it suits you."

He smirked. "This matters to you?"

I smiled and nodded. "My family is one of those families that never used our real names when addressing each other… Everyone always had a nickname. That's just how it was. I have been Cece my whole life… and, between you and me, as an adult, I hate being called that name. It makes me cringe sometimes; like I'm still this little kid and no one takes me seriously. So, yes, the name I call you matters very much to me. I know you from somewhere, and as I plan to spend the next several months figuring out how, I'd like to call you by a name that doesn't make your shoulders tense."

He was silent for a long, awkward moment. I squeezed my palms against each other in the heavy quiet, cursing myself for getting too friendly as I debated what to say next.

"Gloria used to call me Joseph," he finally said, smiling at the memory. "She never called me Juan. Not once. Until I was seven, that was the only name I answered to."

"Would you prefer it if I called you Joseph instead of Juan?"

He studied me for a moment, only tenderness in his eyes then. "You, my dear, may call me whatever name you wish and I will be inclined to answer to all of them. I should be in far worse condition if it weren't for your intervention this morning."

"Did you want him to kill you?" I asked, observing the swirling silver handle of the sword at his hip. "You had your sword and Jack had no weapon. Why didn't you stop him?"

"I know the look of a man who intends to see you dead. He did not have it. I knew he was only overwhelmed with his anger—justifiably so—and would eventually release me. I had not expected it to be upon your insistence that he did so."

"Like I said," I yawned, "it didn't seem right not to speak up."

That glorious smile returned. "You should go back to your cabin lest you fall where you stand. We have time to figure out why I am familiar to you."

"I can't breathe down there," I confessed. "I haven't been able to get used to the smells… no offense."

"None taken," he said, resting his forearm on the helm as he grew more comfortable. "I've sailed this ship for over ten years and I've never been able to get used to the smell, either."

"Does no one ever sleep up here in the fresh air?"

"On occasion when the weather permits. I've a roll tucked away just there." He motioned to a pile of bedding behind him. "You're welcome to it if it pleases you, although I very much doubt it will please you long to sleep on such an unforgiving surface with so many moving around to disturb you."

"And when will you sleep?" I asked.

He let out a hint of a laugh, one deep in his throat. "You are too kind to be concerned about my well-being, Cecelia."

I straightened, my cheeks officially on fire. "I'm not. I just wouldn't want to take your bedding if you intend to use it soon is all."

His smile widened. "I'm not the least bit weary. I shall sleep when my body warrants it, whereupon I doubt you shall have any argument against being escorted to a more comfortable bed below deck. Take it if you wish."

Aware of his eyes on me as I did so, I gathered the bedding, unrolling it on the quarterdeck near where he stood at the helm.

"Are you certain you wish to sleep *there*?" he asked as I smoothed out the edges of the straw-stuffed fabric. "I doubt Mr. and Mrs. Jackson would mind if you joined them on the bow. I'm sure it would ease Mr. Volmer's mind to have you closer to himself. He is all but shaking at your nearness to me."

I laid down, inhaling the familiar cherry almond scent embedded in the fabrics and somehow knowing it was his. "I want to be here," I assured him, turning on my back to gaze up at the undisturbed starry sky overhead. "I don't sleep much at night anyway and, to be perfectly honest, I prefer your company to theirs just now."

He made a noise in his throat. "I noticed your spine stiffens and you attempt to move away every time any one of them finds cause to touch you. Why?"

I wrapped both arms around Luna as she curled into my side, her presence relaxing every part of my body. "I don't mean to stiffen. They all seem like very nice people. I just… I don't know them yet. You know? You think they noticed it too?"

"Only if they stare at you in the way, as you so kindly pointed out, I've a habit of doing."

I laughed as I closed my eyes.

"If it is your wish that I stopped, you need only say the word, Cecelia, and I shan't look upon you in such a way again."

I said nothing.

Chapter Four

Alaina

The sunlight on my closed eyelids was a welcome alarm in contrast to the usual sounds of crying babies that jerked me from my sleep. With both their bodies still pressed against my chest, I sighed as I blinked my eyes open to gaze down at them.

From birth, they'd always slept holding onto one another. Cecelia's face was buried in her brother's shoulder—much as it always was, her little arm draped over him and her fingers curled into a fist against his cheek. His legs were entwined with hers, and his fingers were tangled in the fabric of her sleeping gown. I wondered if they slept like that in the womb, and if it was strange for them to be separated when they woke.

I took a moment to just admire them. They were growing so quickly, and with all the chaos surrounding us, I'd hardly had the time to acknowledge the subtle developments I would otherwise be documenting daily. Zachary was becoming more vocal while Cecelia was becoming more observant. They both were developing personalities; laughing at each other and the world, reaching for things, rolling over, and they were beginning to recognize people. Zachary had taken a liking to Jim and Chris, always smiling when they entered the room, where Cecelia lit up with Fetia and Bruce.

No one, however, excited either of them more than Jack. They loved their father more than anyone, demanding to be in his arms if he was within sight.

I glanced across the bed to find his side undisturbed. He hadn't slept and would no doubt be exhausted. I wondered if, given his lack of trust in Juan Jr., this would become a nightly occurrence.

My mind returned to the chaotic reality we found ourselves in, and I looked further out to find Cece's cot empty as well.

My pulse quickened as I recalled her demeanor the night before. Had she had a panic attack in the night or had she simply woken early and snuck out?

I raised up on my elbows to peer across the room. Jim and Lilly's bed was empty too save for Izzy's new stuffed animals still lying where she'd left them on its surface.

Wherever Cece was, she was surrounded by people I could trust to take care of her.

I needed to go up and check on them all; needed to find some sign of us in those history books. I also needed to bathe and feed the babies, launder their diapers, and wash the bottles and pump Bud had brought through time with him.

Of course, all that would require me to get dressed at some point, a task in this century that took a considerable amount of effort when attempted alone.

I sat up, and the movement woke Zachary. I saw his little leg stretch in my peripheral. Pulling his warm body up against me, I offered him my breast before he had the chance to scream.

Anxious to start the day, I nudged Cecelia awake as well and fed them together, falling back into a half-sleep while I waited.

My thoughts drifted to Izzy. I wondered if she was aware of what was happening or if Bud had made up a tale to cover up the fact they'd been taken... *Had* they been taken? They could've merely been sitting down to a bowl of ice cream when the yacht was hijacked. Might they be hiding somewhere without Juan Josef's knowledge they were on board?

And what about Phil? He'd seemed sincere when he'd asked us to imprison him with Juan Josef. I knew he couldn't be trusted, but whose side was he on? If Bud made a move on Juan and Dario, would Phil join him in the attack or would he fight on Juan's side? Surely, he wouldn't have left Kyle behind of his own volition? Unstable as he was, I couldn't see him coming to the aid of the man who'd had his son flogged until the skin on his back broke open.

Between Phil and Bud, there was hope—there *had* to be. I had to hope they were hiding—pray Juan Josef was ignorant to their presence...

The doorknob turned and I hurried to pull a blanket up over the babies and my exposed skin.

Jim and Lilly, both of them with bloodshot eyes and paled skin, made their way into the room, their fingers interlaced at their sides. "Mornin,'" Jim managed, but there was no hint of his usual spunk in the tone.

"Morning," I said, scanning Lilly's devastated features. "Any signs of the yacht?"

Lilly shook her head as she sank down on her bed and pulled one of Izzy's teddy bears up against her chest. "Nothing."

"I was thinking," I started, pushing myself up so my back could rest against the headboard. "They might've been in the galley when Juan Josef and the others boarded the yacht. Juan might not even know they're on board. If anyone would know where to hide on that boat, it'd be your grandpa... And he'd be coming up with a plan right now if he hasn't already. Right?"

She shrugged, clutching the little fuzzy bear tighter. "Maybe... Maybe not. Either way, she's gone... She was right here between us in the bed... How didn't I hear her get up?"

"I didn't hear her either," I said, "neither did Jack or Jim or Magna or Kyle... It's not your fault."

Jim sat down beside her, draping an arm over her shoulders. "I done told her *all* that but she don't listen."

"It wasn't your jobs to hear her," she said, leaning into him. "It was mine. And if that man hurts her, I swear to God—"

"He ain't gonna hurt her," Jim said. "Ye' hear me? We gonna' kill him dead either way, I promise ye' that, but Bud ain't gonna' let *nobody* touch her. Juan Josef might be a conniving sack-of-shit, but your grand-daddy's smart as a whip and he'll be two steps ahead of him the whole time. And… much as I hate the ugly summbitch, Phil's with 'em too, and if he's still on our side, that means your grandpa ain't outnumbered. Bud'll fight if he has to, and I know that man well enough to know he won't start that fight 'till he knows he can win it."

She stared ahead at nothing, hugging the little bear. "They had to get on the yacht before Juan Josef and the others… You don't think he caught up to them on the top deck? Someone should've seen them leave, right?"

"Right," I said, juggling Zachary up to my shoulder to burp him. "I'm going up and I can ask the crew if anyone saw the two of them. Someone might've lowered Bud down to the yacht if they left on their own."

"Me and Junior done asked them questions last night to the crew," Jim assured me, guiding Lilly to lie down while he tugged off her shoes. "None of 'em saw Bud or Izzy or Juan Josef leavin.'"

"What about the service staff?" I asked. "Maybe one of them helped? Did you question the men on the lower decks?"

Jim shrugged. "Pretty damn sure we asked evra' man on board, but you're welcome to ask 'em again."

"I will," I promised. "If we know they left on their own and weren't forced, we can at least hope they're hiding and have a chance to fight back."

Jim yawned and toed off his boots. "Thank ye,' Freckles. We sure could use some hope 'round here."

At that, he laid down and pulled Lilly into his arms.

I stepped out onto the deck a half hour later, clad in an olive and white striped dress, the familiar sting of the stays once again tormenting my ribcage beneath the sling that held both babies.

Directly across from me, Maria stood on the quarterdeck in red fabrics, leaning back against the rail with Chris at her side. Cece knelt in front of them in the blue and cream she'd picked out the night before, a wide smile on her lips as she scratched Luna's belly.

Juan Jr. stood at the helm watching her.

"I believe your sister has taken a liking to Juan Jr.," Jack said as he appeared at my side. He laid a kiss on my temple and ran his palm over both babies' heads. "Did you sleep?"

"Yes. Did she?" I motioned to Cece.

Jack smirked. "Right there on a pallet beside him. Should we be worried?"

I shook my head, smiling in response to the laughter that came from her as the dog licked her face. "Not yet. She likely sought him out as a means to escape the rest of us; saw him on the outside of our group and found it more appealing. She's easily overwhelmed in groups."

He raked his knuckles over my shoulder. "She was having a panic attack last night when she came up; went straight to him. I don't know what he said to her, but it helped."

I let out a heavy breath of relief and laid my head against his bicep, inspecting Juan Jr. where he stood smiling sweetly at my little sister. "It's very hard to think he could kill those men in our defense and still be capable of deceiving us. Don't you think?"

"You really think he had no knowledge of those passageways?" Jack asked disbelievingly. "That he didn't hear that bed being pulled away from the wall? Thin as these walls are?"

"I didn't say that," I said. "I just… I don't think he's a bad man. That's all. Whatever secrets he may have… I don't think he'd hurt us."

"But he might try to stop us from taking these babies through time," Jack reminded me. "He said as much the other night in the dining room. He said he loved his mother more than anyone in the world and he was willing to do whatever it took to protect the ones he loved. *Whatever it took.* Why would he let us erase the woman he loves more than anyone in the world from history? The plan to kill the Albrecht was partly his… He could've helped them escape;

could've led Bud and Izzy to that boat in the hopes it'd be enough to deter us so he could see that plan brought to life."

He took my arms and turned me toward him. "I don't believe he intends to hurt us either, Red. I think he was sincere when he saved our lives. But if his father told him what we were planning, I *do* believe he'd choose to protect her; to do whatever it took to protect her."

"But he gave *us* the choice," I argued, frowning up at him. "He left it up to us to choose whether we followed or went to the other island to wait out the storm."

"Do you really think, if we'd have chosen the storm, he would've taken us there? I didn't choose to pursue them strictly for Izzy's sake. It was for all of us. Whether we want to or not, we're going to find ourselves in Virginia, face to face with the Albrecht ancestor, George Bennet. I'd bet money on that. And Juan Jr.'s giving us the illusion we're in control when he has *all* of it."

I swallowed, returning my gaze to my sister where she was still running both hands over Luna's exposed belly.

"So… what do we do?" I asked.

Jack shook his head and peered back toward the quarterdeck. "So far, our plans to fight them have done little else but cause us more trouble. We'll have to play along for now… but since he appears to have taken just as much of a liking to your sister as she has him, perhaps she can serve as an informant should he let some admission slip."

"No." I set my jaw. "Not Cece. She is too sweet and gentle for all these schemes and deceptions. I don't want any of this to touch her. We're going to get her home to Owen and Maddy where she belongs… not tangled up in this mess."

He shrugged, motioning with his head to where she'd risen to take the helm, Juan Jr. standing just behind her to offer instruction as she grinned. "Red, I believe she is already tangled up in it."

My stomach turned. I'd only ever seen her laugh like that with Owen. Seeing her act so casual with Juan Jr. wasn't right. There was more for her in this life than Juan Jr. "She's not getting caught up in this. I'll talk to her."

I spun back to him. "We need to figure out if anyone saw or helped Bud and Izzy get off this ship. If we can know for certain they left on their own and not as captives, we can hope they're hiding on the yacht without Juan's awareness. Can you ask around while I deal with my sister?"

"Of course. But Juan Jr. would've—"

I held up a hand. "You said it yourself. We don't know if we can trust him not to have a hand in this. We need to know if they were alone when they were lowered down to the yacht and if one of the crew worked the ropes for them. Ask everyone. Crew, service, kitchen… everyone."

"Alright, Red." He tucked a loose curl behind my ear. "I will. You go easy on your sister. She looked awful when she came up last night."

I huffed. "I know how to handle my sister, Jack."

"Yes, but do you know how to handle this version of her or the one that was married to Owen? Not once did you talk to me about who she became in your new memories—aside from how it played a part in your and Chris's altered relationship."

He had a point. I knew her as two very different people, but I'd been holding onto the memories of who she'd been with Owen. I knew the person she was now was far more independent than the more domesticated mother and wife, and I knew the *'older-sister lecture'* I was about to deliver her was not going to be well received.

"I can handle her," I said again, raising on my toes to kiss his cheek. "Go and talk to the crew, and then go take a nap. Chris won't let anything happen."

"Yes, boss."

"And make Terrence take a nap too. He's been up all night and needs to sleep. I left him by our door half-conscious."

He pressed a kiss to my brow, then spun on his heel to head for the stairwell and the crewmen on the lower decks. Taking a deep breath, I moved toward the quarterdeck.

"Is he gonna get some sleep?" Chris asked as I approached, glancing at the stairwell Jack had disappeared into.

"Yes. After he raids the kitchen a bit." I turned my attention to Juan Jr. "And what about you? We can't have a zombie captaining this ship. By the looks of things," I lifted an eyebrow at Cece who now had full control of the helm, "she's got us covered."

Juan Jr. bowed his head. "Aye. Gabriel will sail in the mornings while I sleep. Although your sister is more than capable of keeping us on course. Did you know she captained a ship of her own for a time?"

"I'd heard," I said, sounding a little too much like an overbearing parent dismissing an unwanted boyfriend as I crossed my arms over the babies.

Cece noticed and offered a wry smile.

"Oye," Maria said, leaning over the rail with her back to us. "This is where we found Jack before." She pointed at a plume of gray smoke against the morning sky. "The devil's islands. Yes?"

We all followed her gaze to the horizon the smoke sprang from and a small gray dot on the straight line separating the water from the sky.

"Indeed," Juan Jr. said, leaving my sister at the helm to move toward the rail. "Legend has it, only one other man has ever escaped those islands." He glanced at me. "Your husband is lucky to have made it out in one piece; luckier still the English captain turned toward it. No sailor with a head on his shoulders will go anywhere close to that smoke. Entire fleets have vanished by drawing too near."

"What's out there?" Cece asked in wonderment, standing on her toes to try to get a glimpse.

"Hell on earth," Juan Jr. assured her. "You just keep us straight ahead."

A chill ran over my spine at the sight of the smoke cloud. Jack still hadn't told me all that he'd gone through there, but the nightmares that plagued him almost nightly since he'd returned told me it was bad. I wondered if he'd ever talk about it or if he'd hold it inside forever.

"Juan," I said, turning toward Cece. "I wonder if you'd take the helm back now. I'd like to have breakfast with my sister. With everything that's happened since she returned, I haven't had much of a chance to catch up."

He bowed his head once and returned to the wheel.

"Are you hungry?" Cece asked him as she moved to join me. "I could bring something up for you…"

His smile returned as he studied her face too closely. "No, Cecelia. Thank you. You are too kind to offer."

"Indeed, she is," I blurted under my breath as I turned her back toward the bow and the stairwell.

Chapter Five

Alaina

Alone in the dining room with Cece, I watched her pour us each a cup of coffee while I laid the babies in the wooden cradle we kept there for them. I could see by the way she was avoiding my eyes she knew exactly what was coming; like a child mentally preparing for a scolding from a parent.

I sat down at the table and she moved around it to take the seat opposite mine, snagging a chunk of bread and spreading butter over its surface. "Well," she said, not looking up from her task, "go on and say it."

I turned my coffee cup on its saucer. "What exactly, Cece, do you think I'm about to say?"

Pulling her knee up into her chest on the chair, as she often tended to do, she took a small bite of bread before meeting my eyes. "Oh, come on, A.J., you think I don't know that look? You're going to go on and on about how dangerous it is to be spending time with Juan Jr. when we don't know if we can trust him and how I have this wonderful, perfect life waiting for me that I'll only be complicating. Isn't that right?"

I let out the breath of a laugh. "That's all true… and since you know it to be true, I wonder why you insist on spending your time with him? I saw the way you two were looking at each other. It's more than you just gravitating toward someone on the outside. Isn't it?"

"I like him—quite a bit, actually—and I'm curious about him." She inspected her piece of bread. "If he *is* dangerous, what better way to find out than to remain close to him? Keep your enemies closer and all that... How can he deceive us if I am always nearby?"

I leaned back in my chair and crossed my arms over my chest. "It looked like you were enjoying yourself a little too much to be playing the spy. That man had to have some part in this. There's no way he couldn't have known about those passageways. He wants to kill the Albrecht just as much as his father. I'm pretty sure, if we'd have chosen the storm, he'd have done whatever he could to talk us out of it."

"I'm not a little kid, A.J., I've come to those same conclusions, myself. I love you, but you don't have to do the whole protective older sister thing with me. I'm alright making decisions for myself. As a matter of fact, I'm not even your little sister anymore. Technically, I'm a year older than you now."

"That's—"

I hadn't considered the fact that, with time moving faster in the future, she'd suddenly become *my* older sister... it felt odd...

"That's irrelevant," I spouted, waving it off. "You'll always be my little sister and I will always feel the need to look out for you... I can't help it that I don't want to see you anywhere near him when I know what's waiting for you when we go back."

She dropped the piece of bread onto her saucer and hugged her knee to her chest, pursing her lips. "I don't want this to come off the wrong way, but has it ever crossed your mind that I might not want that life for myself?"

"You don't mean that. You don't know what I do."

"I know *myself*, A.J.," she said, her eyebrows raising high on her forehead. "And so do you. You have the memories now, right? So you should know how hard I worked to finish school, to open my own veterinary practice... to get my Ph.D... I am proud of myself for all that I have accomplished. Proud of who I became. You should be, too. But are you?"

I blinked. "Of course I'm proud of you, Cece! Are you kidding me? I've never been more proud of anyone."

"Then why are you insisting I give it all up?"

I tilted my head to one side, confused.

"In this other life," she continued, "I will marry Owen at twenty... and move to his campground before I am even twenty-one. Tell me I finished school?"

"Well, no... but—"

"And did I have a job at this campground other than helping him run it? Did I volunteer or help animals in any way? Did I do anything with my life to pursue my passion? To serve a purpose that wasn't his?"

"It's not the same, Cece. Your passion became—"

"It *is* the same," she said evenly. "Twenty is too young to decide your fate so instantly; to drop out of school and give up on your dreams to pursue another's. I spent all night thinking about it. That's not love, A.J. That's blindness. If that man loved me, he never would've allowed me to do that. He would've encouraged me to finish school; to pursue the career I dreamt of."

"He *wanted* you to finish school," I assured her. "But when his father needed him to run the campground, *you* chose to drop out and go with him rather than live separated. You loved him and he loved you... very much."

She set her jaw. "What if I have the choice again now? As an adult? I want to choose *me*, A.J."

"But your daughter," I argued. "If I could just give you some glimpse of how happy they both made you... If I could show you what I saw..."

"I choose me," she said again. "I want to be *Doctor* Cecelia McCreary more than I want to be someone's wife and mother. Can you understand what it feels like to be told you're happier as someone you don't recognize yourself in? Someone with no purpose or meaning? Someone who only exists to serve her husband and child? Living far far away from everyone she knows and loves? How often did you and mom and Bill come to see me in that life?"

"We all made the trip up at least once a year," I assured her. "And you came down to stay with us every November for Thanksgiving."

"Twice a year…" She shook her head, staring at the bits of buttered crust she was tearing into smaller pieces. "And somehow you know I was happier? How could you even know that with so much distance between us?"

"I just knew…"

When the bread had become nothing more than crumbs on her plate, she dropped it, wiping her hands on the napkin. "Let me choose for myself, A.J. If I don't want that life, I need you to support that choice."

"So you're just going to, what?" I asked. "Run off with Juan Jr. on a pirate ship in the 18th century? That's your better choice?"

She smirked, sipping her coffee with that slow, intentional attitude she always got when I tried to correct anything she did. "I don't intend to *run off* with anyone."

She placed the cup back on its saucer, folding her hands on the table in front of her. "You're making one night spent talking to a man into a marriage proposal. I like talking to him. So what? I'm here, aren't I? And I'm not exactly going to sit around with my thumb up my ass waiting for my life to start back up once we get to the storm. I can talk to whoever I want, A.J. I'm a grown woman. And at the moment, he's the only one who doesn't already know every little detail about me; who doesn't treat me like some long lost treasure to be coveted and cradled and locked away."

"Cece, nobody wants to lock you away. You have a husband that loves you and—"

"So did you," she blurted, her blond brow raising in defiance. "And you got to choose differently, didn't you?"

Jack had been right. I didn't know how to handle this version of my sister. While she'd always been smart, *Doctor* Cecelia McCreary was far more decided. She wasn't going to budge on this, but I didn't have the heart to tell her she didn't have the choice she thought she did. When I went through the storm—and I intended to—or when someone killed George Bennet, her other life would be returned, whether she wanted it or not.

She sat with both arms defensively crossed over her chest, waiting for my rebuttal, and I chuckled. "Look at us. You've been here less than two full days and we're already arguing."

The corner of her lip twitched. "Well… you started it."

I laughed out loud at the familiarity of that response. "God, I've missed you. I don't want us to fight. I just… I don't want to see you get hurt. This world is… hard."

She shrugged. "Life is hard, regardless of what time we're stuck in. I'm alright, A.J. And I'm not stupid, you know."

"I know. You're smarter than anyone I've ever met. And I am *very* proud of you."

"Good." She let out a long sigh and pushed back from the table. "We have a lot more research to do if we're going to figure out how to stop Jack from dying, and you're going to need my big ole' brain to figure it out." She smoothed her hands over the table. "This seems like a good enough spot as any to dig back in. Should I bring up some of the books?"

Doctor Cecelia McCreary was indeed a valuable asset when it came to research. She was nothing if she was not determined. For countless hours, the two of us sat with Magna and Fetia combing over the history books, page by page.

Where I often had to spend extended amounts of time re-reading the same passages over and over in search of any hint, Cece sped through page after page, jotting down notes and pulling over other marked tomes for reference. It was like watching DaVinci paint while I doodled stick figures. She was in her element.

I remembered then the way she'd been in the new memories. She devoted all of herself to her schoolwork, rarely ever deviating away for the occasional party or drink. She studied hard; harder still when she decided to continue on in pursuit of her Ph.D. in Veterinary Science, having absolutely no social life whatsoever during her early twenties.

Of course she found it hard to imagine a life where she'd given that up. She worked her ass off to become who she was, and I didn't want to take that accomplishment from her, nor did I want to take Maddy from her.

"Look for anything on the Las Cruces Trail," she said, moving her finger over the text on a page. "It says here Las Cruces Trail was the preferred route to travel across. Maybe there's some mention of a duchess there? This is a modern day image," she said, spinning her book to face me on the table.

I stared down at the photo of three hikers in bright blue and yellow windbreakers trekking uphill on a narrow dirt path, green jungle growing thick on each side of them. Everything looked damp and dark... and far too dangerous for a mother with two small babies.

I swallowed, wondering what kinds of creatures might be lying in wait beyond the brush in the photo... I didn't know much about Panama, but I knew, from one of the texts I'd read already, there were jaguars and vipers in those jungles...

I looked closer at the photo, imagining myself on that trail, damp, muddy, and trembling with Zachary and Cecelia pulled tight against my chest, every sound in the bushes a predator hunting us...

Would I have a choice to stay on the ship like we planned? Would Juan Jr. allow us to return to wait for the storm while the rest went ahead or were we headed into a trap?

Cece, clueless to the anxiety she'd implanted in me, spun the book back around, pulling her knee to her chest as she continued to read the page. "It was a treacherous trail. This is referencing an expedition in the earlier 1700s, but I imagine it still holds true."

She cleared her throat, moving her pointer finger as she read aloud in a tone that almost seemed excited to be heading toward danger, "*The road was just over sixty miles, passing through thick vegetation that grew so rapidly, it was in constant need of repair. In the rainy season it became impassable because of the many rivers flooding it. The high humidity would leave the clothes of any traveller completely saturated. Those who took the Royal Road had to contend with mosquitoes that carried malaria and yellow fever, and up in the mountains, where drops were precipitous, when a mule lost its footing it would be gone forever. There were other dangers too: the risk of ambush by Cimarrons - bands of runaway African slaves, and there was the very real threat of pirate attack—*

"Cece," I held up a hand. "We get it. It's dangerous."

She glanced at Fetia where she was rocking Zachary at my side. "Right. I'm sorry…"

"Afternoon," Jim said from the doorway, stretching his arms up over his frazzled head of hair. "Yuns find anything?"

"Aside from the constant threat of jaguars, vipers, floods, malaria, escaped slaves, and pirates in Panama?" I asked. "No. You want some coffee? I can run down and make you some."

"No need, Sugar." He yawned. "I caught Bruce on his way down. He's fixin' us up some now."

"How's Lill?"

"Still in bed," he said, pursing his lips. "She ain't gonna' be in the mood to climb out of it any time soon, neither. Poor thing's just eat up with guilt. I keep tellin' her it ain't her fault… Keep remindin' her Bud's with Izzy. Just goes in one ear and out the other. She ain't never gonna' smile till we catch up to 'em, you know. Did ye' find out anything about the night they left? Anyone see 'em?"

"No," I said, sighing. "Jack asked all the crew and service staff on board. No one saw any of them leave. But we know they left that room on their own. Either someone saw them and is lying about it or they're all that good at sneaking around in the shadows. We should poke around in Juan's secret passageway. See if there's some other way off the ship."

Magna growled, snapping her book shut and leaning back in her chair. "Everything I find on Panama stops at 1744 and starts again in 1820. There's nothing referencing this decade anywhere!"

I'd never seen Magna so flustered. She pushed back from the table and stood, running a hand hard over her face as she moved to the bay window.

"Same in these," Cece said softly. "But we know there's history there. Juan Jr. said his father was familiar with the Spaniards in the area… so we know there is still trade during this time… there has to be some mention of their activities somewhere… some clue— even in the 1740s that might carry us to 1775."

Magna huffed, staring out the window. "That may be, but even then, there's nothing on the duchess indicating she ever set foot in Panama or America… no mention of her encounter with Captain Cook… The only thing any of us have found is a paragraph on a Juan Perez that says he dies in November of 1775 on his return voyage. No mention of where or how or who was with him or even where in the Pacific he was heading. It's like this whole area just went silent for eighty years."

Jim closed one eye and scratched at the stubble on his jaw. "Well… what if we make some noise then? Burn somethin' down and create a bit of history? Wouldn't that be the surest way to locate ourselves in 'em books?"

I laughed at that. "Start a big fire and these history books will magically change?"

Jim shrugged. "Well, why the hell not? We *magically* traveled back in time through a dang thunderstorm. Anything's worth a shot, ain't it? Is they any old maps in 'em books?"

"Nothing with any landmarks, if that's what you're after," Cece said, pulling an open tome toward her. "There is, however, an entire section here on catholic churches that still stand in Panama City…"

She slid the book across the table, opened to a page with several photos of the giant temples.

Jim tapped the top most picture. "That one." He looked up at the ceiling as if God were within its wooden boards. "And don't you judge me. Ye' don't like the Catholics all that much anyway." He frowned and looked around the table. "None of yuns is Catholic, right?"

I shook my head.

"Then we'll burn it down," he said, returning to his divine conversation with the ceiling, "*at night* when no one's in there, and then I swear to ye,' I won't never set nothin' else on fire again… Amen."

He winked at me and slid the book back to Cece. "Now, yuns see if ye' can find any record of this church burnin' down while I go see what's takin' Bruce so long with the coffee."

Chapter Six

Cecelia

Long after the others had given up on their research and wandered off to either bed or the top deck, I remained in the dining room, reading page by page in the dim lantern light.

My mind was a tangled web of questions.

How did time work?

Did it move in a straight line or was it an endlessly looping spirograph pattern? Was every move we made here creating a new oval? And if so, what happened on the old one?

I stared down at the ancestry chart in front of me. At some point, inside some previous loop through time, Jack and Zachary had died in order for the chart to exist. If we found their cause of death and prevented it, what happened to the loop they'd died on?

Did it keep running? And if so, how many running realities were out there? Was there some timeline out there where I remained a wife and mother? And if we put things back, would the two looping lives mesh into one or would it set off the entire pattern?

I needed answers, and without the internet, I had little else than the old journals from Zachary William and old history books to form my hypotheses from.

But first, I needed to find noise.

What no one seemed to notice prior to my arrival was that Jack's death date was a threat to more than just him. Jack and Alaina had descendants. The rest of us didn't. Any one of us could die alongside him without a single word of it written in history. With no children to produce an ancestry chart, we all could've been easily forgotten.

There was also A.J.'s and the babies' death dates that had me concerned. The fact that there were actual years printed on that chart told me they'd died in some other loop through time as well. There was a very real possibility she might never make it back through the storm if we didn't find a way to alter our course.

With no technology and limited resources, I was fishing blindly for a clue.

While Jim's idea had seemed like a good one, I could find no mention of a specific fire at Saint Francis of Assisi other than that it had burnt down and been rebuilt several times. The same was true for many of the old churches in Panama, and I didn't think a simple church fire would be enough to earn us a spot in these history books. If we were going to make a noise, it needed to be louder.

That's what led me down a new wormhole, searching for anything that could be considered *louder* in the region.

I'd been investigating a ship that had mysteriously burst into flames just off the coast of Charleston when a male voice pulled me out of my mind. "You are still awake."

I didn't need to look up from my book to know it was Juan. I'd heard his voice so few times and yet, I could recognize it anywhere. The sweet dancing staccato of his Spanish accent made my heart quicken and the corners of my lips turn upward.

"I am." Marking the page I'd been reading, I stretched my arms and yawned, looking finally in his direction to find him leaning against the doorframe.

He'd removed his jacket with the day's heat and stood in his loose white shirt and black breeches, arms crossed over his chest. His hair was pulled back as it always was, held with a blue ribbon at the nape of his neck, the subtlest hint of a V forming at the center of his forehead. I did my best to conceal the excitement finding him there implanted in me.

"I think I might be onto something," I said, rubbing my eyes. "What time is it?"

He smiled. "Well past midnight. I only came down to see if I might find any bread or wine still left over. I didn't mean to disturb you."

"Oh," I frowned at the empty breadboard on the table. "I think I ate the last of it an hour ago… I could go down to the galley and see if there's more? If Bruce is still awake, maybe he could—"

"It's quite alright, Cecelia," he said, launching himself off the doorframe to saunter into the room. "I was hoping I might see you again tonight."

"You were?" I asked, blushing.

I'd hoped to see him, too. If I was being honest, the entire encounter with him both last night and through the early morning had left me unbalanced for the remainder of the day. Try as I might to read the words on a page, I'd often find my mind drifting away mid-research to remind me only of his name…

'Joseph…'

All day, he'd lingered right there in my head like a ping of hunger that would not relent until fed. As much as I tried to tell myself he remained there because of the odd feeling of recognition, I knew it was more.

Watching as he crossed the room, my mind and heart were finally satiated.

He raised the wine decanter, swirling it round to confirm there was still liquid inside. Plucking up someone else's wine glass from dinner, he poured the wine into it and took a sip. "I was indeed," he said when he'd swallowed, pulling out a chair on the opposite side of the table and taking a seat. "I enjoyed speaking with you last night."

Taking my own untouched wineglass into my hand, I pressed my shoulders against my chair to appear as relaxed as he was. "Oh yeah?"

He swirled the liquid in his glass and nodded. "Have you been able to determine where you might have met me?"

I shook my head, pushing the book to one side and massaging my temples. "No, and it's driving me crazy. I can almost see you with shorter hair, but—Wait... I thought you sailed the ship at night and Gabriel sailed through the morning?"

"I do and he does," he said, leaning back in his chair to rest one booted foot on the edge of the table. "But we lost the wind a few hours ago and it may be a while before we can catch it again."

Now that he'd mentioned it, I noticed the lack of forward momentum around me. I took a hefty sip of my wine, hoping it might calm my overly excited nerves. "You're not afraid someone might see us alone in here together and find it inappropriate? In addition to the research, I've been reading up on etiquette in this century. You all seem to put quite a bit of effort into avoiding being alone with us poor little females."

He raised his brows, sitting forward. "Would you prefer it if I left?"

"Oh, no, no. Stay. I was teasing... *poorly*. I have about a million questions I'd like to ask you."

"I shall give you an honest answer to anything you wish to know..." He raised an eyebrow. "...*if* you will allow me to ask a few questions of my own in return."

"Fine by me," I said, drinking until the wine in my glass was gone. I reached for the decanter, praying he didn't see it shaking as I poured myself another.

"What would you like to know, Cecelia?"

"Well," I said, "it's this whole Albrecht-Bennet thing... It doesn't quite add up to me... Your motives, that is."

He tilted his head to one side. "Is that your question?"

"No," I said, taking another sip. "I'm... organizing my thoughts in order to get to the question. They go all over the place most the time."

He grinned. "You've an interesting mind."

"Try living in it for a day and you'll think otherwise," I quipped. "Anyway, regardless of what we do, you still plan to kill

Richard Albrecht's ancestor, preventing everything you've done here from ever happening, and then you plan to kill your father once it is done. Right?"

"Correct," he said. "Is… that your question?"

"No… My question is… what then?"

He raised his brows. "You mean after I kill my father?"

"Yes. What will you do after you've erased everything you did here?"

"When it is done, my conscience will be clear," he said slowly. "I hadn't considered what might come after."

"No?" I asked, feeling a bit more confident as the wine warmed my cheeks. "You mean you didn't think you might return through time again with your new memories and run into your wife once more?"

He looked down at his wineglass then, frowning at the liquid inside.

"That's what you really want, isn't it?" I pried. "To start your life over with your wife? Live it differently so she and your sons would never get on that ship to get sick? It's what I'd be thinking if I were in your shoes."

He shook his head. "I only wished to see her once more. To see her alive and well and confirm my task was worth it. I would not condemn her to another life spent at the side of me."

"Why not?" I asked.

Lowering his leg from the table, he set his wineglass down and curled his fingers to each side of it. "Because I could not be the man she needed, Cecelia. She deserved better than me."

I tilted my head to one side. "Are you really so hard on yourself?"

He forced a smile that had no joy behind it. "My dear, you may know my father to be the monster among us, but it was I who did his bidding all these years. I required no command, either. I *wanted* to kill the Albrechts. I told myself it was to see Elizabeth's life restored and to see my mother's death undone, but there was a part of me that did awful things to silence my own guilt for the role I played in my family's deaths. So many innocent men died by my sword—even non-Albrecht men who got in my way. I went quite mad."

He flexed his fingers over the table, the candlelight catching the ruby in the ring he wore on his pinky, causing it to glow. "Other sailors refer to me as *El cazador*... The hunter... because of what I became for those years after she died; my own inadequacies as a husband vibrating on the edge of my sword. I *wanted* to do it. And I enjoyed it—God help me, I enjoyed the numbness of killing; it was a welcome relief from the guilt."

His eyes, which had ventured far off with the admission, returned. "This is likely more answer than you'd been expecting, but you wanted to know my motives. For me, it is more than simply restoring the lives of my wife and mother. Changing things will be the single kindness I will have ever done in this wretched life. To give those who have lost their lives by my hand the chance to live again... To give all that descended from those I have killed the chance to live... I must try. If not for them, then for my soul, for I am afraid it is eternally damned for the things I have done here. Would you not try if it were you and it were within your power to do so?"

"At the cost of yet *another* life?" I shook my head. "I honestly don't know. I understand why you'd want to do it, but... is it the right thing?"

"Is anything we do here right?" he asked. "Our very existence here is wrong. I must attempt to undo it. Your sister wants the same. She hopes to erase their deeds here; to restore all the lives lost as a result of the poison Anna and Bruce served us in their attempt to escape. That includes your husband and child. Were it not for my family, those men never would have died on the beach that day and your husband and child would live. My involvement in this time took them from you as much as hers did."

"*Life* took them from me," I said pointedly, "not you *or* her. We don't walk around the present day worrying about what lives will be affected by our involvement in it... We shape the future every day we live—all of us... Taking all the credit for the way my life turned out seems a little… self-important, don't you think? Maybe I like the way my life is going."

He sat quietly then, weighing my words for a long while as he studied the wine in his glass.

"I'm sorry," I said after the silence became unbearable and his evident guilt washed over me. "I didn't mean to discredit your cause. It *is* very honorable that you'd wish to save so many lives. I hadn't intended to upset you, only to understand the situation better." I took a deep breath. "Because I have another question."

He nodded, his shoulders slumping. "Which is?"

I squeezed my hands against each other, my leg bouncing nervously beneath the cover of the table. "I want to trust you—*need* to trust you for some strange reason. My sister and the others remain skeptical about you, so I have to ask… If your father and brother hadn't escaped and you'd learned of our plans before we'd told you, would you have let us take Cecelia through that storm?"

He closed his eyes. "No."

His answer stung, but I continued, hoping for a better response to the next. "And after we find Izzy and Bud, are you really going to let us go back then?"

"I do not yet know."

"Oh." My eyes watered at that. I wasn't sure why. I barely knew the man but it hurt. Some part of me—that silly romantic piece deep inside—wanted him to be more.

"I hadn't expected you," he said, still staring at his wineglass on the table as he curled and uncurled his fingers to each side of it.

"What does that mean?"

He ran a hand over his hair, loosening a few black strands to fall around his face. "Forgive my lack of reserve in saying so when we've only just met, but I have not looked upon a woman in such a way since Elizabeth, and I cannot answer your question because I do not yet know how to. Asking me to allow you to erase a woman I loved as my mother from history; to erase my brother and my sister… It is no small request. Were you not here, I would do everything in my power to prevent it… but now…" He shook his head. "Now, *you* sit in front of me with that look of disappointment on your face and I would agree to just about anything to see it erased."

That was certainly a much more silly and romantic response.

I hadn't considered what taking Cecelia back would've meant for him. It hadn't occurred to me that we'd be robbing him of Dario too; of the only family he had left... How could I ask that of him? Why wouldn't he fight that? I certainly would if it were Alaina's life on the line.

I traced a knot in the wood table with my thumb, unable to look at him. Flirting was one thing... this was something else. He'd just admitted he was considering giving up his whole family for me, a woman he barely knew. How could I let him do such a thing?

"I have embarrassed you?" he asked.

I shook my head. "No... you just... you surprised me. I hadn't been expecting that kind of answer."

"Hadn't you?" His lip twitched. "I would not have been so bold, my dear, if I was not already certain we both were well aware of our shared interest in each other."

I looked up at him then, raising a brow. "Shared interest?"

He nodded, leaning back once again in his chair with restored confidence. "Are you aware that our cabins are just beneath this one?"

"I suppose I knew that. Why?"

The corner of his lip turned upward, creating a dimple I knew would appear in his right cheek. "Because I can hear every word spoken in this room, and I heard your earlier conversation with your sister... I did not intend to intrude, but once I heard my name, I could not help myself listening... particularly to the part where you said you *liked me quite a bit*."

I was certain every inch of my body had turned bright red. Clearing my throat, I opened my mouth as if I might have any kind of response, then promptly closed it when I couldn't remember how to form words.

"And now that I *have* embarrassed you," he said, "might I ask my questions now? There are only two of them."

I nodded, hurrying to finish off my wine once more.

The dimple reappeared. "Do you really have no wish to be returned to a life where you would be reunited with your husband and child?"

"You mean, do I want to return to a life where I drop out of college, get married at twenty, and give up on every one of my dreams in order to pursue someone else's? No. I would much rather be alone than to lose myself so entirely to another person."

"But if your sister goes through time… or if one of us kills George Bennet?"

I raised my chin. "I will find a way to write my own destiny."

"You're sure?"

"I am positive."

"Well then," he leaned forward, "that will make me feel much less guilty about my second question."

I straightened in my seat, my heart beating faster as he'd leaned that much closer to me. My God, he was gorgeous. "Which is?"

"I would like to court you…" He held up a hand. "Which I know must sound absurd under these circumstances, but I'd still like to all the same—if only to understand your insistence that we've met previously… and perhaps to understand my own interest in you. Courting you would justify us spending extended amounts of time together so we could figure that out… You know… *Keep your enemies closer and all that.*" He grinned.

Blushing, I hid my smile. "You're asking me for a courtship? With you?"

"Yes."

I tapped my fingers on the table, considering it.

Part of me was screaming, jumping up on the table and dancing as she shouted *'yes yes yes!'* in response to his proposal. Who wouldn't say yes to courting a man that looked like him?

But there was too much at stake to want a fairytale. Within a few short months, it was very likely I'd never see him again. Getting romantically involved would do nothing but muddy things for both of us when we needed to think clearly.

A thought occurred to me, and I smiled to myself as both the logical and romantic halves of my heart fell into sync.

"I will agree on one condition," I finally answered.

He raised one dark brow. "Which is?"

I retraced the knot on the table. "If things *do* change… if you really wake up in that life with memories of this one, then I need you to promise me you will do whatever it takes to prevent my marriage to Owen."

At this, he tilted his head, brow furrowed while he searched my eyes. "How would I do that?"

"How old are you?"

He shyly dragged a hand through his hair. "Twenty-nine. Why?"

"So you were born in 1970?"

He nodded.

I perked up. "Alaina and Chris didn't go back to relive anything, right? Their memories changed, but they stayed the exact age they were before they'd changed them. If the same goes for you, and the change makes it so you never go back in time, you *should* show up in the year 1999. If you do, then only you would have the chance to prevent me from ever meeting Owen. I highly doubt I met him before 99 since I would only be thirteen years old. I can find out from A.J. where and how we met, and you could interfere."

He hadn't moved, nor had his attention faltered. "If it is within my power to do so, I shall prevent it… but only if you are certain."

"I am certain."

"A husband and a child are a considerable fate to give up so hastily," he said in a tone much older than his age. "I shall give you my word once *I* am certain you are sure."

"I am sure." I insisted, the frustration that'd been welling in me for days seeping out with the words. "I don't want to marry Owen. Not ever. To marry him would be the same as if I'd stepped off the side of this ship. There would be nothing left of me. Do you have any idea how devastating it is to work so hard your whole life and feel like you have no control over the way it's going to turn out? Save my life and I will let you court me; and I will let you court me for the sake of figuring out how we've met, nothing more. There's too much going on for anything more right now."

He pursed his lips for a moment then finished off his wine, pushing back from the table to stand. "Consider it done. Get some rest, *mi paloma*. I would like to begin our courtship in the morning."

'*Mi paloma*.'

My dove.

Dammit if I wasn't looking forward to the morning for more reasons than simply figuring out where I'd seen him.

Chapter Seven

Chris

Chris had been in a deep sleep when a crack of thunder seemed to shake the ship so fiercely he might've fallen out of bed.

It woke Maria too and the arm draped over his chest tightened. "Ay dios mío," she said sleepily. "What the hell was that?"

He turned his face into her hair, inhaling the rose water she'd washed with as he laid a kiss on the crown of her head. "It's alright. Just thunder. Go back to sleep."

She moved her body closer, curling one of her legs over his as she yawned. "Mmm, why are we not moving anymore?"

"Hmm?"

"The ship," she said softly, tucking her face into his chest. "It is not moving."

He frowned, realizing the constant forward motion he'd grown accustomed to over the past year spent sailing had indeed ceased. "That's strange…"

Another blast shook the ship and he recognized the sound, not as thunder, but as the firing of one of the ship's cannons.

He shot up from the bed, digging around in the dark until he found his shirt and pulled it on. Had they caught up to Juan Josef?

And if they had, why on earth would they be firing the cannons with Izzy and Bud in his custody?

"Go next door with Alaina," he said, sliding his bare feet into his boots. "Lock yourselves inside and don't come out until you hear one of us tell you it's safe. Understand?"

"What's going on?" she demanded while he strapped his sword to his hip and pulled a rifle over his shoulder. "Oye, is that gunfire?"

He listened closely and there was in fact gunfire erupting from the top deck.

"Go next-door. Take this." He pressed a pistol into her hand. "I don't know what's happening, but if anyone tries to come through that door that isn't one of us, you shoot them. It might be Juan Josef. You have your dagger?"

"Sí," she said, her voice trembling with concern. "And where are *you* going? What are you going to do?"

"If there's a fight," he said, pulling the door open and spinning round to take her hand, "they'll need help. Come on."

The hallway was lit by the lanterns' glow streaming out of the open door to Alaina's and Kyle's rooms. Kyle was ushering Fetia into the larger cabin with his prosthetic hand, a rifle strapped to his back and a pistol in his good hand.

"What's going on up there?" Chris asked as he nudged Maria toward the door.

"Don't know yet," Kyle said breathlessly, "but it sounds bad."

Alaina was there in a heartbeat, one of the babies cradled in her arm. "Jack's up there," she wept. "And Cece's not here either."

"They'll be fine," Chris assured her. "Lock this door the moment we're gone. Got it?"

Alaina nodded, clutching the baby tighter as another cannon blast fired. "The death date," she said, a tear sliding down her cheek. "It's so close… Don't let him die, Chris."

"I won't."

At that, he spun on his heel and sprinted for the stairwell.

The top deck was chaos. Juan Jr. stood at the rail with a rifle aimed out at the black night, shouting orders to the men around him. Jack and Jim stood at his side, each aiming their own rifles similarly.

"What's going on?" Chris shouted as he sprinted to them.

"The Nikora," Jack said as a cannon erupted beneath them. "We've been dead in the water for hours with no wind. They caught up to us."

"Summbitches must've been tailin' us all day," Jim spat, closing one eye as he aimed and fired at something Chris couldn't see in the dark water.

"What can we do?" Kyle asked from behind him as he caught up. "Where are they?"

"They're everywhere," Juan said, firing his rifle.

Chris squinted out into the darkness, at first seeing nothing, but then, he saw the whites of their eyes where the moonlight caught them. There were at least a hundred sets of eyes set in black shadows against the moon's reflection on the water…

"Jesus," he breathed. "What do they want?"

"Don't know," Juan said, not looking away from his target. "I've never heard of them pursuing this long. We need more men on the cannons while they're still far enough out. Kyle, gather as many service staff as you can—kitchen, waitstaff, anyone able, and get them to a cannon. Gabriel is down there. He will tell you what to do."

Another cannon fired and Juan Jr. shot another round at an approaching boat. "Then, I need you to go down to the armory and bring up as many modern rifles as you can carry."

"How can I help?" a soft female voice asked.

Chris spun around to find Cecelia standing on the deck in her flowered dress, raising on her toes to try to see over them.

Juan Jr. kept his gun steadied in front of him as he turned his head toward her, his expression softening. "Hide, Cecelia. When those men board, they'll want three things… Gold, blood, and women. Arm yourself, hide, and pray for a strong wind. We will not be able to hold them off while we are idle."

"Like hell we won't," Terrence said, jumping up to straddle the railing as he pulled out his pistol, aimed at one of the sets of eyes growing close, and fired. "Cece, go get us more guns and ammo. Kyle, go get men on those cannons. I'll be damned if I've come this far to go down like this. We might be sitting ducks, but we've got guns and they don't."

"Aye," Juan said, reloading his rifle with gunpowder, "but they've got poison tipped arrows and spears. If they get any closer, they'll be able to use them."

Cece and Kyle ran for the stairwell, another cannon firing below, shaking the deck and causing them both to hold onto each other to stay upright.

"What's the plan then?" Jim asked. "We gonna' just sit up here shootin' at 'em once they start firin' them arrows? Or we wanna' wait 'till they start climbing up? They cain't throw nothin' if they're climbing. They get up on the side of this ship, we could start knockin' 'em off with whatever we got up here to throw at 'em… save the bullets for the ones that get past."

Jack fired at another set of eyes. "There are too many of them and not enough of us. We have to pick off as many as we can now. Once they start climbing the ship, it'll be too late. It wouldn't be hard to break through the windows on the lower decks."

"Hell, I cain't see the summbitches to pick 'em off," Jim grumbled, moving his rifle slowly in search of a target.

Chris looked over his shoulder to the rest of the deck. Two men held rifles out at the stern, firing in turns. A single sailor manned the opposite railing, firing into the night as he paced along the length of the ship and back.

No one stood at the bow.

Shrugging the rifle off his shoulder, Chris moved toward the front of the ship.

As he approached, a face appeared over the railing, nearly black with the ink that covered it, the whites of his eyes and snarling teeth the only distinguishable characteristics against the darkness beyond him.

"They're on the bow!" Chris shouted, aiming and firing at the face without hesitation, hurrying his steps before another could appear.

He heard the distant splash as the man fell to his death, but pushed both the sound and the image to the back of his mind. His adrenaline was pumping too hard to make room for his conscience now.

"You know how to use that sword?" Terrence asked, suddenly keeping pace at his side.

"Yes," Chris assured him, reloading his rifle as they inched toward the rail.

"You better get ready to use it then," Terrence said as they both looked over the edge to find the shadows of at least ten men scaling the front of the ship.

Terrence wasted no time aiming his pistol at the topmost shadow and firing. As the body fell, the shadow behind him fell alongside him. "Two down, eight more to go," he said, firing again and missing. "Fuck."

"How many bullets you got in that gun?" Chris asked, glancing around the bow for something heavy to toss.

"I got nine rounds left in this clip. Three more clips on my belt. Can't afford to miss with this since the rest of you gotta' stop to reload between shots."

Tossing the rifle back over his shoulder, Chris hurried for the center of the deck, hoisting two canvas sandbags over his shoulders before returning.

Another cannon blast fired, then another, and another, forcing both Chris and Terrence to grip the railing to keep from falling over.

Kyle had gotten more men…

Three more cannons detonated, one after another after another.

The blasts caused one of the climbing Nikora to fall into the water, and Chris hurried to position one of the sandbags in the path of the one left in his wake.

"Bombs away," Terrence said, standing to one side as Chris launched it and took out two more. He wondered if the fall would kill them or only stun them momentarily so they'd have to fight the same ones off over and over again.

'*God,*' he prayed, feeling guilty that he only did so when he was in trouble, '*please send wind.*'

Terrence leaned over the rail again, aiming his Glock and firing two shots. This time, he didn't miss.

As he was doing so, Chris saw a dark line in his peripherals being launched from further out and overhead. He pulled Terrence off the railing and to one side just as a spear embedded its sharp edge in the wooden boards where they'd stood. They were indeed poisoned. A liquid oozed down the shimmering pointed edge, pooling on the deck boards beneath it.

"What kind of poison is this?" Chris shouted toward the others firing on the side rail. "Will it kill us?"

Juan Jr. turned toward him, and, seeing the spear embedded in the deck, pushed off the rail where he stood to join them on the bow. His steps did not falter as six more shots were fired from the cannons below. "How many on this side?"

"At least five left climbing," Chris informed him, slowly rising to stand with a watchful eye on the sky. "Can't see how many boats are in the water with the ship blocking the moonlight. They're close enough to use their spears and arrows, though."

Juan Jr. kneeled down at the side of the spear, lowering his face close enough to smell the liquid dripping from it. "Something sweet... maybe Angel's trumpet," he said, returning to his feet, "mixed with something much more foul. If it doesn't kill you, it'll paralyze you long enough so *they* can."

"That's reassuring," Terrence noted, crawling to the rail and squatting with his back against it as he checked his clip for remaining rounds. "How many you got on that side?"

Another round of cannon fire rang out.

"Too many to count," Juan said, plucking up the remaining sandbag and launching it over the side. There were two resounding splashes in the water below as he kneeled down to reload his gun. "My father has more modern weapons in the armory. He'd been saving them for such an occasion as this. I fear these rifles will not be enough."

Chris aimed his own rifle over the edge, praying Juan or Terrence would spot any flying arrows or spears overhead as he did so, and fired at a man within yards of reaching the top. The man had been close enough that he saw what the blast did to his face—the spray of blood colored black against the shadows as his nearly decapitated body fell lifeless from the ship.

Heart racing, Chris kneeled back down, watching the sky as Terrence rose and fired.

"How many now?" Chris asked.

"Ten," Terrence huffed. "They keep coming. What kind of modern weaponry are we talking? AR-15's? AK-47's?"

Juan Jr. stood and fired once, then returned to one knee to reload. "I do not know those names, but they fire many shots in a very short amount of time and there are enough of them to arm all on deck. My father dabbled in the arms business in addition to cocaine. His yacht was loaded with crates of them."

"There are AK-47's down there and lots of pistols," Chris said, waiting until the cannons stopped to continue. "We took an inventory after we poisoned the crew. Plenty of bullets too, which we made sure were kept separate. God, I hope Cecelia knows which ones to bring."

"I don't want her up here," Juan said, allowing Chris his turn to rise and fire before he followed suit. "You know where the guns are. Go down and take them from her. We can hold them in your absence. Make sure she's locked up somewhere safe in case they get past us."

"Are you sure?" Chris asked, peering across the deck to Jack and Jim as they each took turns firing.

"Go," Terrence said. "We got this. And you make sure Cece's got a gun of her own. I showed her how to use one and she can handle herself if one of these fuckers tries to get ahold of her."

As Chris turned toward the stairwell, one of the men on the stern shouted, "they've broken a window!" He then fired over the edge of the rail.

The cabins were on the stern side of the ship… The women were in the cabins… Alaina and the babies were in those cabins…

"GO!" Terrence repeated, and Chris bolted to the stairs.

Chapter Eight

Cecelia

"I'll go to the armory," I said, plucking a lit lantern from its hook as Kyle and I sped down the stairs. "You go get men for the cannons, then meet me down there to help me carry it all up."

Down two more flights, Kyle broke off. "Be safe. I'll be there soon," he said, and sprinted toward the crew's quarters.

Holding the lantern in front of me, I continued down one more flight into the bottommost floor of the ship. Luckily the armory was only a short walk off the stairs in the ship's store and I hurried past the cargo hold and through the door, placing the lantern on a long wooden counter in the center of the small space.

We'd taken water casks down when we'd planned to stock up and sail to the storm. Alaina had shown me the store and the armory then and I recalled thinking it was strange that they'd had so many modern-day assault rifles.

That's what I wanted.

I'd seen the shadows on the water, like a swarm of ants around decaying food; each one you might smash was easily replaced by another. No matter how many you killed, there were always a few ants that got past. We needed *a lot* of bullets…

I tugged an empty wooden crate across the floor and began unloading the shelf. I pulled every rifle and handgun available off the shelf and chucked it inside, saving a 9mm for myself when I recognized its shape and weight in my hand. I then moved to the next shelf: ammo.

I filled my arms with boxes, both wooden and cardboard, and let them fall into the crate.

My hands were shaking uncontrollably, and when the cannons fired above me, I dropped a box, cursing myself as I heard the brass spill out all over the floor.

I dropped to my knees, panting as I scooped up what I could.

'Hell on earth,' Juan had said when I'd asked what was on those islands… What kind of hell would be unleashed if they were able to get on board?

Over my head, I could hear their gunfire; could hear the rolling of cannonballs and the scraping of iron as they positioned more cannons for firing.

'Pray for wind,' was my order.

But what God would listen when I'd never prayed before? God had always been a sort of fairytale to me… something people used as a means to cope with life and death… Where Alaina would've taken that order literally and dropped to her knees, I had no one to pray to… I had only myself.

I had to think logically.

They were going to get on the ship. They outnumbered us ten to one—maybe more so—and it was inevitable that we'd come face to face with at least a few. I needed to be prepared for that; prepared to witness or even deliver death… Even if I locked myself in a room—which I wasn't planning to do—I'd need to be ready for a monster to burst into it.

I felt around for the bullets with trembling fingers, trying not to imagine the blood that would be spilled on the deck by the time this was over; trying not to imagine Juan Jr., Chris, Terrence, and A.J. lying dead in that blood…

No… Now was not the time to work myself up into a panic.

"You got the guns?" Kyle asked, breathless as he entered the store room.

"Yes, I just… I spilled some bullets…"

"Leave them," he insisted. "We have to go now."

The cannons blasted above, six shots in a row, forcing me to cover my ears.

"Cece," he said, kneeling down in front of me and waiting until the additional cannon fire ceased, "we have to go. Is that pistol loaded?"

"Not yet," I said, rising on quivering legs to place both palms on the counter. "None of them are." I plucked up the gun, swallowing the lump in my throat. "I need 9mm bullets. Do you see them?"

Kyle raised his lantern over the crate and rifled through the ammo I'd chucked inside. He handed me a small cardboard box. "You know how to shoot?"

"Yes," I assured him, releasing the clip to quickly slide the bullets inside. "Terrence used to take me and Jasmine to the range to practice."

"Good, cause I'm not good enough with this prosthetic to help carry this *and* point a gun. Best I can do is hold one side and hang the lantern from my fake arm."

Pushing the clip into the pistol, I removed the safety and chambered a round. "Alright. I'm ready."

"Put out your lantern. Don't wanna' leave that burning in a room full of gunpowder," he said.

I followed his order, then took one side of the crate as he took the other, the weight instantly feeling as if it was ripping the muscles in my forearms.

'*Let them rip,*' I thought, once again picturing the death that might be ensuing above.

We walked with the crate between us as fast as we could manage, out into the cargo hold with only his dim lantern to guide us.

I was focused on my feet and not tripping when I heard the strangest *'whoosh'* and Kyle let go of his side, pulling my arm down as the crate crashed onto the floor.

Everything moved in slow motion then. I looked at Kyle first. His eyes were like saucers as he stared down at the spear protruding from his thigh.

I then peered ahead and saw the massive shape of a man at the bottom of the stairwell. The lantern light danced across the swirling blank ink on his face, making him appear more like a demon than a man. He held another spear and reared it back just as Kyle blew out our lantern and the entire space went black.

I dropped to the floor and the spear clanked on the boards behind me.

Kyle's breathing became labored as he, too, fell to the ground.

I had no God to pray to…

Only myself… my mind… my experience…

No one was going to save me but me.

Forcing my shaking muscles still, I slowly and silently stood, pointing the gun in the direction of the stairs.

And I listened…

Just beyond Kyle's wheezing, I could hear the man who'd attacked us… I could smell his stench. Like rotting onions left in the sun. He was moving closer…

My finger was on the trigger, the barrel pointed at where the man's heart would be once he reached us…

And I waited…

My mouth filled with acid but I dared not swallow. My lungs burned, but I dared not breathe.

I listened and I heard the man inhale through his nose, getting closer… he might've been ten yards away.

He exhaled. Nine yards.

He inhaled again and the floorboards beneath his feet creaked at the weight.

He was close enough.

I exhaled the breath I was holding and pulled the trigger.

"Cece?" Chris shouted from the top of the stairs. "CECE?!"

I was frozen, both arms out as I held the gun steady. I watched the space where I knew the man had been as Chris's lantern light spilled down the stairwell. As he turned with it to move toward me, I saw the massive creature lying on his back, his face twisted in agony as he held both hands over a wound in his sternum.

"Cece!" Chris shouted, leaping off the final step. "Are you alright?"

Awareness returning to me, I turned back toward Kyle. He was alive, but his body was convulsing. "I'm fine, but he's not. We need to get him help… Those spears are poison."

"I'll send someone down for him," he said. "We need to get these guns up to the top deck before it gets worse. Kyle, can you hold on for someone to come fetch you?"

"Go," Kyle said through gritted teeth.

Swallowing the tears I so desperately wanted to cry, I took hold of one side of the crate as Chris stopped to drive his sword into the demon's throat to stop his writhing. He then sheathed it and took the other side. "You didn't kill that man, Cece. I did. Understand?"

I nodded, and we remained silent then as we clambered up the stairwell.

Halfway up, Chris shouted for Jacob, and we paused only long enough to inform him of Kyle's state. Jacob didn't hesitate in running past us down the stairs to collect him.

As we got to the top of the next flight, Chris stopped once more. "I can carry it the rest of the way. You go to the room with the others."

"No," I said. "The magazines are empty. I can load them while you shoot. Let me help. I'll go once they're all loaded, I promise."

I watched him struggle with it, but in too much of a hurry to argue as the cannons blasted again, he let me continue behind him up the stairs.

I didn't look up when we ascended. I knew from the way Chris dropped the crate and unsheathed his sword, from the sound of running footsteps all around me, the gunfire, and the crash of metal against wood, some of the Nikora had made it on to the deck.

I dropped to my knees before the crate, centering my mind on one single task: load the guns.

"You know what you're doing?" Terrence asked somewhere above my head.

"Yes," I said, not looking away from my hands as I pulled the first magazine out of an assault rifle and filled it. "Just make sure I don't get killed while I do it."

"That's my girl," he drawled proudly, firing two shots over my head. "Gettin' real tired of these motherfuckers."

I snapped the magazine back onto the gun and held it up. "Safety's still on," I said, reaching for another as Terrence took it.

"Jack!" He shouted. "Catch!"

Jack was still alive. That was good. I focused on my breathing as I loaded the second. I could have a panic attack later...

In through the nose... out through the mouth.

I held up the second gun when I was done, wobbling with the cannon blasts that fired as I did.

"Jim!" Terrence called. "This one's yours."

Jim was alive too... Good. What about Juan?

I heard the rapid fire of both rifles then and I imagined the sounds around me might've been comparable to that of a war zone. Somewhere to my left, two men were grappling, their grunts loud in my ears as shots and cannons fired in every direction.

Again, Terrence fired his pistol, and the sounds of their grapple were replaced by a choked, "thank you."

Over and over, I loaded the assault rifles in the crate, not daring to look up from my hands. When they'd all been handed out, I moved to pistols, additional magazines, and reloaded used ones as Terrence tossed them down once they'd been emptied.

"You're doing great," Terrence said as I handed him one of his own reloaded clips. "And Juan Jr.'s still standing... in case you're wondering."

Deep breath in through the nose... out through the mouth.

I had been wondering.

I slid a clip into a pistol and raised it over my head, but... something was wrong with my foot...

"Shit, shit shit!" Terrence swore above me.

Something… burned…

"Cece! Shit! Shit! Help!"

That burn ripped through me before I could even turn to see the arrow embedded in my foot, and every muscle in my body—from my fingers to my eyelids to the very tips of my toes—seized up in a clench as I collapsed onto my side.

I couldn't unclench. I had no control of my body as the fire of poison held me tight in its fist. My eyes were open, but everything was blurry. There were noises—cannon and gunfire and shouting —but it all faded into static.

Everything was a fist around my body.

Just before that fist squeezed the life out of me, I smelled cherries and almonds, and the little romantic part of me tried to reach for Juan.

"No, *mi paloma*," he said softly, "you cannot die yet."

Chapter Nine

Alaina

I stood in front of the cradle, my body paralyzed in the grips of fear, as Maria held a pistol steadily at the broken bay window on the opposite end of our room.

"You want to come in this room, pendejo?" she shouted with a ferocity that should've made any man quiver. "Come near this window again!"

She'd fired at the first Nikora when he'd broken the glass, catching him in the shoulder and causing him to lose his grip and fall back into the water, and now stood yelling at another we could hear fast approaching.

"I will kill any man who puts his ugly face near this glass," she warned, breathing heavily, her face wild with rage as she waited. "You hear me?! ¡Estúpidos hijos de puta! Come on then!"

The gunfire and cannons had set both babies into a screaming fit, and while every instinct in me told me to pull them out of the cradle and coddle them, I instead covered them in pillows and a mattress, placing my body between them and the window.

A knock on the door at my side of the room made me jump.

"It's Jacob!" the voice called, "I've got Kyle! He's hurt!"

Magna hurried to let him in as Maria fired another round out the window. I hadn't turned in time to see where she hit the man that had attempted to climb inside, but I saw the blur of his motion as he fell away.

She laughed deliriously. "You want to keep coming to this room? Eh?! You want to *die*?! Maybe you will find another window next time!"

We were going to need more bullets. Maria had a more modern pistol, but I wasn't entirely sure how many it could hold. I spun around to say so when I caught sight of Kyle's rigid body in Jacob's arms.

"It's poison," Jacob said, carefully laying Kyle on the bed. His arms were bent toward his face, the fingers of his hand curled into a partial fist, every part of him stiff, even his lips where they were pulled back to show a tightly clamped jaw. "Chris said they might be using angel's trumpet on the spears… I pulled one out of his thigh. I need to get back—"

"Wait, we need more bullets," I blurted, heart breaking as Fetia collapsed on the bed beside Kyle. "They're trying to get through the window. We don't have much left to fight them off with. Can you bring more weapons—more ammo? Do you have anything on you we can use?"

Jacob nodded, eyes wide as he took in the broken glass littering the floor near the window. "Take this," he pulled a rifle and powder horn off his shoulder. "I'll come back with more as soon as I can."

"This is not angel's trumpet," Magna said, leaning over Kyle and running a hand over his hair as I locked the door behind Jacob. "I don't think angel's trumpet would cause the muscles to do this… I don't know what this is. Kyle, baby, can you hear me?"

Kyle's eyes moved and he made a "Kkkkhhh" sound, but he was unable to control the muscles enough to speak.

"Alright baby," she cooed, placing her hand over his on the bed. "We'll get through this. You're gonna' be okay. Lilly, honey, come here and take this prosthetic off him… Take off anything that might be restricting. And let's get a tourniquet on his leg."

Maria fired again, striking a behemoth of a man in his chest. He grunted, but he grabbed onto the sill and attempted to pull himself inside.

"Did you not hear me before, you stupid motherfucker?" Maria asked, half-sobbing, half-mad. "I will kill every single one of you… Understand?" And then I watched the next bullet strike the center of his forehead before he, too, fell away.

How many shots was that? Four? Or was it five? And what would we do if we ran out of ammo before Jacob could return?

Both babies were sobbing from the cannon blasts and gunshots, but more than I needed to hold them, I needed to help fight. More and more men were coming. I couldn't stand there frozen any longer.

I took the rifle and, remembering Jim's lessons on how to use one, I placed it on its butt, poured in a bit of powder, and placed a lead bullet inside, pushing it down tight with the ramrod.

On shaking knees, I raised the heavy barrel, resting the butt against my shoulder to aim it at the window, and moved away from the cradle to stand at the side of Maria.

"Get back, Alaina," Maria reprimanded. "Your babies need you to stay alive."

"You're going to run out of bullets," I said. "And I can't let them get in here."

"You're going to fall over if you try to fire that thing," she spat, keeping her eyes on the window. "Let me handle this. The men have the big guns up there now. I can hear them. This won't take much longer."

"I can't just stand there and do nothing," I insisted.

"You're not doing nothing," Magna said, her hand suddenly on the small of my back. "Give me this and go back. If they fire an arrow or throw a spear, you could be killed, and those babies need you alive if they're going to survive. Go on."

I relinquished the rifle to her, laying the powder horn, lead balls, and ramrod at her feet as I inched back toward the cradle.

As if she'd done it a thousand times, Magna fired the instant a face appeared in the window, Maria taking out one that followed behind it with her pistol.

She knelt to reload the rifle, and I prayed… over and over.

I didn't know what the Nikora wanted, but I prayed they'd give up on it and retreat. I prayed Jack and Cece were unharmed. Prayed for Chris and Kyle and Jim and even Juan Jr… That was the only thing I could do.

A small eternity passed as Magna and Maria held their weapons toward the window, firing in turns. We all stood and listened to the rapid fire of modern weaponry above, the repeating blasts of cannons just beneath them, and the *'Kkkhhh'* sounds of Kyle behind us as he struggled for his life on the bed.

I counted the gunfire, attempting to make out how many different rifles were still up there… if I could count them… would that somehow assure me Jack was one of the ones firing?

'Died at sea,' my mind reminded me, referencing the cause of death Bud had informed me of. We were certainly at sea…

And then, my thoughts were interrupted. Suddenly, as if by some kind of divine intervention, the ship began to move… I could hear the wind skidding over the ocean; not a gentle breeze but a massive gust, and I gripped the back of one of the wingback chairs to keep myself from falling as the ship sped forward.

As the gunfire above died out and a sense of safety came over us with no additional Nikora coming to the window, Maria collapsed onto the floor and vomited, the shock of what she'd done settling in. I knelt beside her and held her, my own shock sitting in my throat and forcing me to cry alongside her.

"I can't take this no more," she sobbed. "I wanna go home."

I clung to her and rocked, one eye on the bed where Lilly, Magna, and Fetia were attempting to help Kyle.

"Bud brought medicine," Magna said softly, smoothing her palm back and forth over Kyle's trembling and stiff upper arm. "Maybe there are some muscle relaxers in there? I don't know if they'll help, but it's gotta be worth a shot."

Letting go of Maria, I went straight to the box of gifts Bud left us, fishing out the medicine bag to pilfer through it when the knock we'd been waiting for came on our door.

"It's Jim," he called from the other side, and Lilly fell over herself as she leapt off the bed to let him in, wrapping both arms tightly around his torso as she did.

His expression, however, did not reflect the relief in hers. "Ay Freckles," he said to me in a tone full of defeat, "you gonna' wanna' come with me now."

'Jack.'

We knew he would die if we pursued and how stupid we were to assume he'd be safe for the last few weeks of 1774… The dates weren't always accurate… and now…

In those few seconds, all I could see were Zachary and Cecelia's little bodies wrapped up in his arms, and my heart split in two as I realized I might never see that sight again.

Frozen in place on my haunches over the box, my words came out in a choke. "Is he dead?"

"Hoss is fine," he said. "It's your sister that ain't."

Clutching the bag to my chest, I stood and swallowed hard, my body going as rigid as Kyle's. "What's wrong with her?"

Jim tilted his head toward Kyle. "Same thing as him."

"The pills," Magna said, motioning to the bag in my arms. "I'll see what I can find for both of them. You go ahead."

Half dazedly, I handed her the bag and followed Jim out the door.

Down the corridor, I let him lead me to Juan Jr.'s cabin, and inside, in the lantern light, I saw her tiny body, curled and tensed at an awkward angle in the center of Juan's bed.

Juan, Jack, Terrence, and Chris all stood bloodied around her, all of their hands hovering over her body as if they wanted to help her but were afraid they might hurt her if they touched her.

Just as Kyle had, she made a struggled *'Kkkhhh'* sound, and thick white foam dribbled from her clenched teeth onto the blanket beneath her.

I climbed onto the bed and hurried around her to begin unlacing her stays. "I'm here, Cece," I whispered, scanning her rigid body. "Where did it go in?"

I wasn't sure why that mattered, but I needed to ask questions… needed to *do* anything.

"In her foot," Terrence said, his eyes watering as he watched me pull the laces of her bodice. "I cleaned it the best I could and wrapped it with one of her stockings. I couldn't stitch it with her body clenched like this, but I will if we can get her to relax."

"Jack," I said, not looking away from the lacework, "Magna's going through the medicine in the other room to try to find any kind of muscle relaxer. Go see if she's come up with anything while I get these clothes off her. Chris, finish unlacing these while I get her stockings and skirts off."

As both of them followed my orders, Juan Jr. moved the hair from her reddened face. "Is she breathing?"

"Yes," I said, watching her chest move, "but it's a struggle with her muscles taut like that. If we can't get them to relax, I don't know if she'll *keep* breathing."

"How can I help her?" he asked.

Try as I might to stay focused, the question broke me, and I felt warm tears stream down both cheeks. "I don't know."

"We should put somethin' in her mouth," Jim offered from the doorway, "keep her from bitin' her tongue." He unlatched the buckle on his belt and pulled it off, handing it to Juan. "Put it between her teeth."

"Good idea," I said, tossing Cece's remaining slipper and stocking to the floor as I moved to untie her petticoats. "Jim, go make sure they do the same for Kyle."

"Yes, ma'am," he said, hurrying off.

"The pills," Terrence said, helping Juan to open Cece's jaw long enough to place the belt between her teeth, "I don't think the poor girl can swallow on her own. How in the world are we gonna' get anything down her?"

"I haven't thought that far ahead," I admitted, pulling the first petticoat from beneath her and moving to the second. "We could try to give it orally first… try to help her swallow. If that doesn't work…. I suppose we could try it as a suppository. I remember reading somewhere that any pill can be a suppository in an emergency."

"Breathe, Cece," Chris said softly, finally finished with the laces. He tugged the stays from under her and tossed them to the foot of the bed, remaining behind her to smooth his palm over her arched back.

She was turning a darker shade of pink.

"I've got Valium," Lilly said, appearing breathless in the doorway and wincing at the sight of Cecelia. "Magna thinks it'll help with the clenching."

I took a deep breath as she handed me two small blue pills.

"All of you look away," I said, making the decision as her skin continued to darken that I was not willing to attempt an oral route. I waited until everyone's heads were turned, and then I became more familiar with my sister than I ever imagined I might. If she lived through this, she was not going to be pleased with what I had to do.

'God, let her live through this to be mad at me.'

Pills administered, I pulled down her shift and laid a blanket loosely over her legs. As her back arched even further and her fingers curled into her palms hard enough to leave indentations, my fear turned into anger.

"What the hell was she even doing up there?!" I shouted, attempting to uncurl her fingers. "Was no one paying attention? Did no one try to stop her?"

All I could see was her eight year old self smiling at me beneath a tangled head of bright blond hair; pure innocence and goodness as she clung to her little stuffed puppy… And now that innocence was slipping away; my sweet little angel of a sister, who I'd just gotten back, was dying in my arms.

"Why the hell did no one stop her?" I screamed.

There was a very heavy silence then that forced me to look up at the men standing around the bed.

It occurred to me that they were all still half-feral; all of them covered in blood and ready to attack any threat… And by the blood-thirsty looks on all three men's faces, I realized I had just become that threat.

"Because no one can stop her when she sets her mind on a thing," Terrence said in a low, steady voice. "And because whatever she has set her mind on doing is almost *always* the right thing to do."

He stared affectionately down at her as he continued. "That girl would jump into a burning building to save a complete stranger—hell, she'd jump into that building to save a complete stranger's cat—with no regard for the danger to herself. That's the kind of person she is. If one of us had stopped her from coming up there to load those guns, we'd all be dead—including you."

"I'm sorry," I said, thinking of my own feet frozen to the floorboards, paralyzed with fear, as my sister leapt into action two floors up. "I shouldn't have said that… I just…" I curled my fingers beneath hers and let her squeeze them. "I'm just scared."

"She's tough," Chris said, rubbing her back. "Tough enough to get through this. She shot one in the hull. Hit him right in the chest."

I stared down at her rigid body, trying to imagine the girl who wouldn't even kill a spider—insisting on carrying them out to set them free instead—shooting a man in the chest… or loading guns while the Nikora slung poison spears onto the deck and poured over its railing. When had she become so fearless? And how hadn't I ever noticed?

"Chris," Lilly said from the doorway, "you should probably come to the other room for a while… Maria's… well, the adrenaline has worn off and she's in shock."

I nodded, holding my sister in my lap. "You should all go. It's been a long night and you all need to rest. Wash off that blood.

There's nothing more we can do but wait to see if she comes out of it."

Chris and Terrence lingered for a moment before they followed Lilly back down the hall. Juan Jr., however, pulled a chair from near the window and sat down.

"You should go, too," I said. "I've got her."

He shook his head and leaned in to rest his elbows on his knees. "I cannot leave yet."

"Can't or won't?" I asked, aggravated that he was so evidently pursuing my sister with everything else that was going on.

"Both," he admitted.

Again she made that throaty *'Kkkhhh'* sound and my body tensed. There was nothing I could do to make it better.

Looking back at Juan, I attempted to shield her from his eyes, curling my arms around her and holding her against my chest. "What are you doing, Juan? What could you possibly hope to get out of this?"

He lowered his head, his bloodied hands falling limp over his knees. "What does any man hope to accomplish when he cannot pull himself away from a woman?"

"Are you really looking for *love*?" I balked. "With *her*? As we are on our way to rewrite history?" Holding her tighter, I rocked her gently, praying it was somehow soothing her. "You realize that, whether she likes it or not, the moment I step through that storm or someone kills George Bennet, she'll wake up with a whole different life. With a husband and daughter she adores. *If* she remembers you, what will you have given her but shame? Regret? Pain? Confusion? Say she falls madly in love with you here… what happens when she wakes up to her family beside her? Will you make her choose between them and you? Split up a once happy family over… what? An attraction you have for her?"

I sighed, smoothing back the bright blond hair from my sister's face, ignoring the veins protruding from her forehead as she continued to fight the poison in them. "Juan, I can see you are fond of her, and I know it's easy to love her, but I'm asking you not to… it can do nothing but hurt her in the end."

He sat silently for a moment, turning his palms up to inspect the blood coating them before he once again met my eyes. "Her future, Alaina, is hers to decide. Not yours or mine. She knows—*all too well*—of the life she's to be returned to, and still she has chosen to take an interest in me. Why, I do not know, but I'll not deny her if she finds in me something she wants."

"And if she does?" I asked. "What can you give her that her husband and child can't?"

He tilted his head to one side, frowning. "I should give her the only thing she has asked me to. Herself."

Chapter Ten

Chris

He laid in bed with Maria, images of the battle playing on repeat in his mind, keeping the adrenaline that had carried him through the worst of the fight still coursing in his veins. His heart was still racing… his hands were still shaking… he was still ready to kill.

As was Maria. He could feel her galloping pulse where his palm rested against her throat; could see something untamed in her eyes where she returned his stare.

When he'd found her, she was roaring with madness—crying and screaming—cursing the Nikora that had since been defeated for what they'd made her do.

He'd hauled her off to their room and held her tight against his chest until she'd quieted.

But while she'd silenced her tirade, neither of their minds had been able to fully quiet. They laid facing one another, both trembling with the effort of containing the ferocity of battle still lingering beneath the surface of their skin.

Her breathing was shallow, and even though she stared at him, he knew it wasn't him she saw, just as it wasn't her face he was truly seeing.

He saw twelve very different faces and nine climbing shadows, all dead by his rifle or sword. Over and over he saw himself fire or strike, and he knew every line in every face as it froze forever in its wince, every movement of the shadows that fell from the side of the ship, and heard every echo of his bullets as they struck and forced the shadows off.

He saw a nearly headless body falling from the bow of the ship…

He saw a tattooed face peering over the rail, one side of that face shattering with the blast of his rifle… a face that had been youthful before it became nothing…

Where Maria's fingers rested on his chest, he felt instead the grip of a Nikora man clamped onto him, attempting to stop his sword from slowly being pushed through his chest…

He'd never taken a life, and now he'd taken more than twenty… How could he ever be the same again?

It was only when someone knocked on their door that he was pulled partway back to present.

Maria's fingers tightened in the fabric of his shirt, both of them stiffening at the sound.

"Ay, Beanstalk," Jim called from the corridor. "Kyle and Cece's settled for a bit. Terrence is stitchin' 'em up. The rest of us are goin' down now."

He let out a long exhale, combing a strand of hair back from Maria's face. "Do you want to stay here or come with?"

Her brown eyes moved between each of his. "You would let me come with you?"

Tears threatening to spill over for the pain he saw coursing through her, he nodded. "It's your call. Once this is done, it's all over."

"You will kill him when you have your answers?" she asked, referring to the Nikora captive they'd tied up and hauled down to the hull for questioning.

"Yes." His spine stiffened at the thought of another death sitting heavy on his conscience.

"I think I have seen enough men die today," she said softly. "I will stay here."

Nodding, he unwound his arms from her and laid a kiss on her brow.

"Oye," she said, cupping his face in her hands to keep him in place over her. "When you come back to me, we will fix each other… however me must. Okay?"

"Okay," he managed, letting her pull his lips to hers.

"Go and get your answers," she breathed, pressing her nose against his. "I love you."

He closed his eyes and inhaled her rosy scent once more, letting his fingers commit the softness of her hair to memory—a memory he might be able to cling to while they did whatever was necessary to get answers from their captive about the poison.

What he was about to walk into would not be easy. They hadn't taken just any Nikora captive. They'd taken the one that had shot Cecelia with his arrow, and after all she'd done for them; after they'd all watched her cling to life in that bed, he knew the methods they'd use to get those answers would be brutal.

He prayed he could come back from it… prayed there would still be some bit of him left to fix when he returned to Maria.

He kissed her once more and climbed out of the bed, not bothering with a sword or a gun before he joined Jim in the hallway. They wouldn't use weapons… not on this one. It would be much more personal than that.

He shuddered at his own eagerness.

Jim held the lantern out in front of them as they made their way toward the stairwell. "Ye' ready for this?"

His fingers tightened on the stair's railing. "I'm ready to be done with it."

"Me too. Ay, when you was up on the deck," Jim leaned in as they made their way down, "did ye' get a peek at Junior? The way he fought with 'at sword of his?"

Chris shook his head. "I saw him fighting, but I wasn't overly focused on it. The only thing I was worried about was staying alive."

"Well," Jim continued, "I did, and I ain't never seen nothin' like it. When we was all worryin' about his daddy, we shoulda' been worryin' about him. That man coulda' killed evra' one of us at any point, whether we had the guns or not. I watched him kill four of them summbitches in seconds. If he decides he wants us dead, there ain't nothin' any of us could do to stop him."

"I don't think he wants us dead, Jim," Chris said as they started down the second set of stairs. "He saved my life at least twice up there."

"Mine, too. And Hoss's more than a few times. But we underestimated him… The man's a killer. Lordt knows what he might be capable of."

"The same could be said for all of us." Chris straightened his spine as they stepped off the stairs into the hull and peered down at the dead Nikora Cece had shot earlier. "I killed more than twenty men tonight."

Jim patted his back. "Monsters, Beanstalk. Ye' killed twenty *monsters*—not men. And ye' didn't get no joy out of doin' it… Junior, on the other hand… Well, I seen his face when he was swingin' 'at sword… looked like he was enjoyin' hisself."

Before Chris could respond, Jack hurried out of the shadows ahead, waving them toward him.

"Junior down here yet?" Jim asked.

"Not yet," Jack said, his words clipped. "Jacob and Michael are in there ready to translate now. We can't afford to wait. The Valium helped, but it'll only last so long. We have to know what kind of poison they used so we can figure out how to permanently treat them."

"Where are we holding him?" Chris asked, adrenaline resurfacing to quicken his heartbeat.

"This way." Jack turned to lead them to the far side of the hull where a sliver of lantern light shone beneath a closed wooden door.

He pushed it open to reveal a large, heavily tattooed man slumped over in a chair he'd been tied to. Jacob and Michael stood near the door as they entered, both looking more afraid than their captive.

"Michael doesn't need to be in here," Jack said, directing the statement at Jacob. "You know the language well enough."

Jacob nodded. "He wants to be here… For Kyle."

Jack laid a hand on Michael's shoulder. "If you change your mind, no one would judge you for leaving. Okay?"

Michael raised his chin. "I know this man. He name Malosi. I help make him talk."

At the sound of his name, the man raised his chin from his chest and sneered at them. His face was nearly completely black from the tattoos that covered it, and he bared his teeth as he recognized Michael, saying something in a low baritone.

"What's he saying?" Jack asked, his hands curling into fists.

Jacob crossed his arms over his midsection. "He's shaming Michael… He says they came for the ship so they could use it to rescue him… that he is Uati's son, not mine… that he should've fought with them, not us."

"There's no time for that," Jack spat. "Ask him what kind of poison they used."

Jacob translated, but Malosi did not look away from Michael, nor did he answer.

"Tell him we will beat the answer out of him," Jack said through his teeth. "The sooner he answers, the sooner this will be over for him."

Again Jacob translated, and Malosi only glared at Michael.

The door flew open and Juan Jr. rushed through it. Where the rest of them had washed and changed clothes after the battle, Juan remained in the same torn and blood-stained clothing. He looked savage with his hair hung loose and his eyes boring into their captive. He did not pause in step to take in the room or its occupants, but moved directly to Malosi and landed a hard hook to his jaw.

"What was in the poison?" he demanded, rolling up his sleeves as Jacob translated.

Malosi did not answer, but instead spit blood onto Juan Jr.'s face and laughed.

Juan Jr. grinned in return, not bothering to wipe off the blood spattered across his eyelids, brow, and nose as he struck him again. "There are worse things than death," he promised, allowing Jacob time to translate as he pulled a dagger from his thigh and placed it in his left hand. "I could keep you alive for years… cutting off a little piece of you every day… just enough to make those years agony. Do not think I would not enjoy doing that very thing if you take too long to answer. What was in the poison?"

Again, Malosi laughed once Jacob translated.

"He not tell you," Michael said, his spine stapled against the far wall. "He—he not afraid."

"He *will* tell me," Juan assured him, throwing and landing another punch to Malosi's mouth, hard enough to knock the chair and its occupant onto its side. "And if he is not afraid, he is a fool."

Chris watched as Juan Jr. placed a finger beneath Malosi's chin and tilted his face up toward him. His voice was as low and sinister as his father's. "What was in the poison?"

Malosi's bloodied smile returned as he responded in perfect English. "Death."

A muscle ticked in Juan's jaw as he moved the dagger from his left to his right hand. "What kind of poison?"

Malosi laughed deep in his throat. "Death," he said again, daring Juan Jr. with his eyes to strike again.

And he did. Turning the dagger, he struck him with the blunt end in the bridge of his nose, the break audible on impact. Malosi cried out then, struggling against his restraints to work one hand loose enough to prop himself up from the floorboards.

"Michael," Chris started, keeping his eyes on Juan Jr. where he lowered the heel of his boot onto Malosi's fingers, "you never saw them preparing the spears and arrows? Never saw the plant they used?"

Michael shook his head. "N—no. I not allowed near fighting."

"What did you use for the poison?" Juan Jr. asked again, keeping his voice even. "Answer or I shall break every finger."

When no answer came, Chris cringed as Juan slowly put his weight on the foot and a resounding *'pop pop pop'* followed as the fingers beneath his boot broke one by one.

Malosi didn't cry out, but smiled through his grimace up at Juan, a deep laugh rumbling through him as he once again said, "death."

"How does the poison work?" Juan asked, his composure slipping only enough to shake the words slightly. He cleared it from his throat and continued, folding his hands behind his back and removing his foot to reveal the twisted fingers beneath it. "How long does it take? Is it guaranteed death or can it be prevented?"

Malosi spoke then, his tone condescending even with the language barrier.

Jacob winced. "He asks if it was your woman he hit. He says…" He shook his head. "He says it is a shame he will not be able to bed her before she dies."

Whatever thread was holding Chris together unraveled then and he lunged for Malosi, coiling both hands around his throat as he rolled the chair and the large man onto his back.

He was sick of the charade; sick of this whole night. Cece and Kyle couldn't afford for this to take hours. They needed an answer now.

"He wants you to do that," Juan Jr. observed once he'd gotten the leverage he needed to tighten his grip on the man's throat and push down with all his weight. "Death is an easier way out of this interrogation than the exit I intend to give him."

"Fuck him," Chris growled, loosening his grip on his throat to bash his head against the floorboards. "How long do they have? How do we stop it?"

Once Jacob translated, Malosi spoke again in the same mocking tone.

Jacob blew out. "He says it cannot be stopped. She will die in hours… Days if she is strong."

Juan Jr. kneeled down beside them, unable to stop the quiver this time in his voice. "You will draw the plant you used for the poison." He met Chris's eyes. "You have medical books in the great cabin. I have seen the drawings and diagrams on their pages. If we can identify the plant, we might find a cure among your medicines, no?"

Jacob translated and Malosi shook his head, speaking again.

"He says he cannot draw death."

Juan tilted his head to one side, the seams of his composure cracking. "Death? Is this your only answer?"

Malosi nodded. "Death."

"That is not good enough," he said through his teeth, the fingers of his hand curling tightly around the handle of the dagger. "What is it made of?"

Malosi spoke and Jacob swallowed.

"He said it is made from the dead…"

"Wait a minute," Jim said under his breath. "I heard somethin' about this once… 'bout the bacteria from dead bodies being used as a poison in the old days… they weaponized tetanus."

Chris frowned. "It can't be. Doesn't tetanus take a week or so before you show any symptoms?"

"Yeah," Jim narrowed his eyes at Malosi, "but Junior mentioned there was a sweet smell on 'at spear. They musta' mixed it with somethin' else… Ask him if he means the liquid that comes off a rotting body."

Jacob translated and nodded when Malosi answered. "Yes."

"Can it be cured?" Juan asked. "Can you help her?"

Jim shook his head. "Don't know. We'll have to look in 'em books to see if they's anything can be done outside the vaccine. I know it's deadly. What we gonna' do with him now that we got our answer?"

Juan Jr. glared at his bloodied captive. "The rest of you can go start scouring those books for a cure… I'll finish this."

"Come on beanstalk," Jim said, grabbing Chris by the upper arm to pull him off Malosi. "You go on up now. Take Michael and Jacob. Hoss, you go too. 'At wife of yours is gonna' need ye."

Chris rose and let him shoo them all out the door.

"You're staying?" he asked as Jim began to turn back.

Jim nodded, leaning in to speak in a hushed voice. "He ain't lettin' that man die anytime soon. If we're gonna' be cozied up at the side of him for the next few months, I wanna' see exactly what kind of man he is."

At that, Chris watched as he reentered the room and pulled the door closed behind him.

"I'll go get the books from the dining room," Jack said, attempting to keep his voice even as they all headed for the stairwell. "Michael, you can help me. Jacob, you go check on Kyle. Chris, you do the same for Cece. Don't tell anyone about the tetanus yet…"

As he placed a foot on the first step, Chris cringed at the blood-curdling scream that sounded from the closed door behind them. Malosi deserved whatever torment Juan Jr. would inflict, but the sounds still made each step heavier, as did the weight of the word tetanus.

He could've stopped Cece from going up to the deck. He could've prevented this altogether. Did he not deserve to be tortured the same way Malosi was? Was it not just as much his fault she laid in that bed?

She was as much his little sister as she was Alaina's after ten years of marriage, and he knew, the moment Jim had said tetanus, the threat of her dying was very real.

Of all the people in the world to suffer in such a way, she was the least deserving of it. Always good and quick to put those in need above herself, she was the best person among them. He never should've let her up there for that arrow to land in her foot… He should've shoved her into a room and locked the door if that's what it took.

He followed behind Jacob into the corridor, all the things he could've done differently playing on repeat in his mind until he reached the door to Juan Jr.'s room.

It was there, standing at the threshold to the small cabin to look down at her sleeping body in bed, Alaina sitting in a chair at the side of it, that everything came to a head.

"Chris?" Alaina asked, sitting forward in her seat. "What's wrong? What happened?"

He shook his head, the weight of it all—the poison, the battle, time travel, surgery, Juan Josef, Maria and Alaina and Anna and Owen and Maddy and the memories—all of it forced his knees to buckle and he collapsed in front of her in tears.

"Jesus, Chris." She wound both arms around him, pulling him against her to bury his face in her shoulder. "What's going on? Talk to me, love. What happened down there? Is she going to be okay?"

How pathetic he felt. He shouldn't be here, clinging to a woman that didn't want him; a woman he'd driven away; didn't deserve to have her arms around him or to feel the immense amount of comfort her touch gave him.

But that didn't stop him from pulling her closer; from holding her as tight as he was able, inhaling the lavender in her hair and the distinct Alaina scent just beneath it; a mixture of citrus and maple.

God, he missed her...

And he hated himself for that, too.

"Chris," she whispered, gently scratching the back of his head, "honey, you have to tell me what's going on. You're scaring me."

Jack told him not to mention tetanus...

Fuck Jack. And fuck him too for letting the sonofabitch steal his whole life away from him. He should've fought harder to be right here in the only place that had ever really made sense, the only place he ever wanted to be: her arms. Fuck him for ever thinking she wasn't the only person that really mattered in his life.

She did matter, and he'd been lying to himself for far too long in telling himself she didn't. He hadn't let her go; wasn't sure he could ever truly let go. And that made him cry harder, clinging to her for as long as he could before she'd inevitably push him away; before he'd have to deal with the fact that he'd gotten comfort from her and not Maria; before he'd have to return to his room to look down at her ring on Maria's finger and try not to think it was out of place... before he'd have to watch Jack be the husband he should've been.

Could he be any more pathetic? What the hell was he even doing anymore? If anyone's ancestor should be hunted down to erase them from existence, it should have been his.

"Chris," she gently pulled him away to wipe the tears from his cheeks. "What happened down there?"

Feeling like a fool, he smashed his hands over his eyes, removing all traces of moisture from them as he took a deep breath and sat back on his ankles. "Tetanus," he said finally. "We think they found a way to weaponize tetanus. Jack and Michael are getting the medical books from the dining room now."

"It's not tetanus," she balked in a matter-of-fact tone. "It can't be."

He moved his sleeve over his nose and took another deep breath. "How do you know that?"

"Because Kyle's had a tetanus shot recently. Anna asked him about it on the raft when she treated his arm. He'd had a dirt bike accident, I believe, about six months before the plane crash. They gave him the tetanus shot then. Those last for what? Ten years?"

"But Malosi said the poison was made from the liquid that comes off rotting bodies. It was mixed with some kind of plant. Maybe the plant acts as an accelerant or something?"

She shook her head. "That's not how tetanus works, love. It's got to be something in the plant causing this. If it was tetanus, Kyle wouldn't be in the same condition Cece is. I don't think?"

"Could be strychnine," Jack said from the doorway, holding an open book in one hand. "Says here tetanus and strychnine have the same symptoms. The stiff muscles and arched back… What if they used the strychnine plant with the bacteria to accelerate the symptoms?"

"Can it be treated?" Alaina asked, her attention moving to the bed.

"They treat strychnine poisoning with muscle relaxers," Jack answered, scanning the page, "and a lack of stimuli… no loud noises or bright lights… round the clock monitoring for controlled seizures. It's pretty similar to the treatment for tetanus."

"So we'll keep them sedated," she said, a glimmer of hope appearing in her eyes, "and set them each in their own dark, quiet rooms with someone to watch over them, and we'll see if they pull through. How much Valium do we have?"

"I don't—"

Jack stopped short as he looked up from the book to find Chris still kneeling on the floor before Alaina, his hands gripping the arms of her chair. "I'll… ehm… go check."

Her eyes remained on the doorway even after Jack had sufficiently disappeared into the room down the hall. "You should probably go," she said softly. "Maria will be worried."

He nodded. "I can't marry her, you know."

"You don't mean that." She shook her head. "You just need more time."

He stood and turned toward the door. "With or without the new memories, you were the love of my life. It doesn't feel like there's any amount of time that can ever change that."

And he turned down the corridor before she could respond.

Staring at the door to his room, he felt his throat swell. He couldn't climb into bed with Maria after that… He couldn't keep dragging her along while he craved the attention of another…

How could he look her in the eyes after what he'd just admitted to himself? What kind of man would he be if he strolled into that room and pretended those admissions hadn't just happened?

He moved past the door toward the stairwell instead. There was work to do on the deck—cleaning up the dead bodies and bullets leftover from the fight. He'd immerse himself in that, and then… however difficult it might be, he'd need to find a way to let them *both* go.

Chapter Eleven

Cecelia

Between heavy blinks, I found myself in a room on the ship I hadn't been in before. The sunlight streamed in through a small window to one side, positioned just right so the light from it shined directly on my face and nothing more, the brightness forcing my eyes closed despite my desire to remain awake.

I turned my head away from the window, a bizarre sensation of euphoria sweeping over me at the amaretto scent embedded in the sheets beneath me. *'Joseph.'*

I had small fragments of memory returning to me, one specifically stood out in my mind as he'd asked Alaina, *'What does any man hope to accomplish when he cannot pull himself away from a woman?'* There was something exhilarating at the knowledge that *I* was that woman.

"Hello, Cecelia."

I smiled and opened my eyes again to land them upon Juan where he sat in a stool at the side of my bed. It was the first time I'd ever seen his hair hang loose, and he looked absolutely angelic in the light as the dark waves fell around his face.

"That is a wonderful sight to wake up to," I said, all too comfortably. "Am I dead?"

He grinned, enough so to awaken the dimple in his cheek, and shook his head. "Is this how you imagine heaven to look?"

I examined him closer as he leaned in to rest his arms on the bed. His white shirt was stained red and torn down his chest to expose the skin beneath. "If there's a heaven, I think you might be cleaner in it."

He laughed out loud, a deep rich sound that set my lips even further upward in their smile. "I should hope so," he said. "You are not dead, *mi paloma,* but I believe the medicine your sister gave you has yet to wear off."

"Mmm," I hummed, noticing a bit of black ink on the skin beneath his shirt as he leaned in closer… close enough to touch.

And without my normal hesitation, I did touch him, watching the ease with which I laid my fingers on the slit in his shirt. "What is this?"

His eyes closed for a moment as I ran my finger along the exposed skin, then he laid a hand over mine on his chest to still it. "A scratch. I avoided the poison."

The flesh on top of my hand tingled at the feel of his over it. It was the first time he'd ever touched me… and I liked it very much. I liked everything about him very much right then, uninhibited as I was with the effects of whatever medicine I'd been given. "You have a tattoo."

"I do," he said, "and I'd intended to tell you all about it… This is not exactly what I had in mind for our first day of courting."

I turned toward him, stealing my hand away to rest it beneath my cheek. "You mean, you hadn't planned for me to end up half naked in your bed?"

Again, he let out that throaty laugh as he scanned my face. "Planning and dreaming are two very different things, Cecelia."

I grinned. "I like that you use my full name and not Cece. Thank you for that."

He smoothed both hands over the edge of the bed and rested his chin on them, amusement dancing in his eyes as the sunlight made the ruby on his pinky glow blood red. How sweet and harmless he looked just then, like a child admiring a puppy through a window. "I am so very glad to see you awake."

I bit my lower lip to stop from smiling even wider. "I'm very sad to have missed our first date, Joseph. I had such high expectations for it."

"Did you?"

I nodded, sliding my hand out from beneath my cheek to rest it in a place he might be inclined to take it between us. "I even did a little late night reading after you left… to figure out what a *'courtship'* really entailed."

"And here I thought we agreed the courtship was for *the sake of figuring out how we met and nothing more,*" he teased, taking the bait and curling his fingers around mine.

Some little feather in my stomach began to float.

"Tell me, Cecelia, do you find courting very different from how it is done in your time?"

"I wouldn't know," I admitted. "I haven't been on a date in a very long time… Will you tell me what you had planned?"

"When you are well, I intend to *show* you what I had planned," he said, a hint of desperation in the tone as he squeezed my hand. "There are plenty of mornings left before we arrive at the isthmus."

I frowned, noticing the redness in his eyes from a lack of sleep, the medical book that sat on the bedside table, the second chair pulled up beside him where A.J. must've spent the night, and the still blood-stained clothes he hadn't bothered to change out of. "I'm not going to live, am I?"

"Of course you are," he said unconvincingly. "You're going to be just fine."

"Your face gives you away." I forced a smile. "While *I* am on heavy drugs to explain my lack of reserve, there is no excuse for *your* directness. You're being too sweet—too familiar with me. It should've taken at least a month for you to let your guard down the way you are right now and that tells me I'm going to die."

"You're not going to die, Cecelia." He moved his thumb over my palm. "The medicine is helping. There is plenty more of it…

We will keep giving it to you until the poison has passed. You'll see."

They'd given me some kind of muscle relaxer, I knew, but I could feel the lingering rigidity in my body. The poison was still attacking my nervous system and I knew, as the pill wore off, I would gradually clench back up the way I had the night before… I tried to think, in my foggy state, what kind of poison might do that… I'd seen rat poison do that in dogs… what was the primary toxin there?

Was there any point in diagnosing myself? If I was destined to die—and I was pretty sure I was given the way he was caressing my hand—I didn't want to go out working myself up into a panic attack… I wanted to die smiling, and the man sitting beside my bed could certainly make me smile.

'No, mi paloma, you cannot die yet,' he'd said before my memory got foggy. This man liked me with the same intensity I liked him. To hell with being cautious. I flung open that door inside and let the little romantic part of me dance for whatever amount of time she had left to do so.

"Will you tell me about our date?" I asked sweetly. "Describe it to me? How would you have started our morning?"

Keeping one hand over mine, he raised his chin from the other so he could brush the fingers of it over the bits of hair above my forehead. I kept my eyes on his as he watched his fingers move, the feather in my stomach returning to twirl against my abdomen.

"I'd hoped you might wake before the sun had risen," he began, the corners of his eyes crinkling as they met mine and he smiled. "I'd intended to go down to the galley and make the coffee you seem to like so much. It would've been disastrous, to be certain, as I've never attempted it, but… I thought it might please you to have coffee and watch the sun rise."

"That sounds lovely." I lifted my pointer finger to graze my knuckle along his calloused palm where it still laid over my hand. "I would've drank every last drop, you know—even if it was disastrous—and I would've told you it was delicious."

"Aye, but *your* face would have given you away," he assured me, closing his eyes briefly as the rest of my knuckles inspected the feel of his palm. "I knew you would try to appear pleased."

I pouted playfully. "Am I so predictable you could know so much about me already?"

He opened his eyes and shook his head. "Cecelia, you are anything *but* predictable. You are… so very surprising."

I chuckled, curling my heavy legs up and closer to him. "I like this unguarded side of you… Why do you hide it?"

He shrugged. "What was the term you used on deck the other night? Self-preservation?"

"But you don't want to preserve yourself from me now? Two days later?"

He shook his head.

'Because I'm dying…'

I kept that thought to myself.

I sighed, shifting the conversation back to its original track. "Well then, we are on the bow and I am drinking my awful coffee. Is it still dark?"

"It is," he said, his thumb tracing the edge of my hairline. "But the dawn is coming. There is the faintest hint of the approaching sun beneath the horizon. Not enough to drown out the stars, though, and the sky overhead is still painted with them, and below us is a perfect reflection of the sky on the sea."

I closed my eyes and could see it exactly the way he described; could almost feel the slightest breeze on my cheeks. "And what are we doing in the middle of this perfect sky?"

"Trying to figure out what makes us drawn to one another; seeking similarities and asking questions. That's what you do in a courtship. Didn't your book tell you as much?"

"So you *are* drawn to me." My cheeks were starting to burn from the smile that was glued to my lips. I supposed this wasn't the worst way to die. "Did you think up all the questions you would ask me, Joseph?"

"Perhaps a few."

"What would you ask me first?"

He raked his teeth over his lower lip. "My dear, I do not wish to impose on your mind when it is left so unguarded as a result of the medicine still in your body."

I laughed at that. "Please… ask your questions. I don't want to die pretending to be coy with each other."

"You're not afraid?" he asked. "Of death?"

"I suppose I would be if I thought there was any finality to it," I said, pursing my lips. "But, as it stands, death here wouldn't exactly be final, would it? Nothing is. It'd be no different than going to sleep. You all will go on with your plans to change things, and I'll inevitably wake up in some other life once you're done as if I'd never died at all."

He tilted his head to one side, inspecting my features. "So you *are* as fearless as I suspected."

"Far from it." I moved my fingers to interlace them with his. "Normally, I'm afraid of about a million other ridiculous things; things normal people aren't… stupid stuff like saying the wrong thing or being laughed at. I'm afraid of strangers and large spaces and small spaces and judgment; of failing or not being enough or being too much sometimes… I'm scared of the unknown, of change, of people. It's absurd and inconvenient and I have no control over it. That fear gets so strong sometimes I work myself up into a panic attack and can't breathe because of it."

He leaned in closer, smiling as he whispered, "I am afraid of many of those same things, *mi paloma*. And I still believe you are fearless."

Grinning like an idiot, I took a moment to inspect his room—it had to be his given his distinct amaretto scent embedded in the blankets beneath me. Stacks of journals, papers, books, and maps covered a desk to spill over into towering stacks at its side and even onto the nightstands. Shelves of them lined the far side of the room, each one overflowing. I wondered what I would find on the pages of those journals; wondered what made a man like him tick.

"Can I ask *you* a question now?" I asked.

His fingers tightened around mine. "Of course."

"If you hadn't traveled through time—say you were just born here like a normal person and you weren't trying to undo it all—what would you *want* to be doing? Do you enjoy sailing the ship?"

"Very much," he said, following my gaze around the room. "My affinity for it is why I could not be the husband Elizabeth needed. Being on land—the stillness of it—didn't feel natural. I couldn't wait to return to sea the moment I would disembark. I suppose, if none of this had happened, I'd be an explorer... Perhaps I'd have even found myself in the company of your Captain Cook, discovering new lands and plants and people... writing about the world I'd seen. I heard he traveled farther south than any man before and has seen the glaciers my father has only been able to describe from photos. I would have liked to see them myself."

He again ran his thumb over my hairline. "What about you? What do you want to be doing with this life you refuse to let anyone replace?"

I sank further into my pillow with his touch, utterly at ease with this man who should be a stranger. "I opened up my own veterinary practice a few years ago, but the end goal wasn't to just help pets—much as I love dogs and cats... I wanted to travel too, to heal and help preserve the lives of endangered species throughout the world... big cats and apes and elephants... I thought, if I could help prevent even just one species from going extinct, I'd have made my mark on the world."

"Why animals instead of people?" he asked. "Your sister mentioned last night you wanted to be a doctor when you were a child."

I tucked my legs up a little closer, feeling my calf muscles begin to cramp slightly but enjoying the moment too much to say so just yet. "Animals are pure. They don't cheat or deceive or judge. They live on instinct—*love* on instinct. You don't have to worry about saying the wrong thing or not being enough. Everything you need to know about that animal is right there in its eyes and body language."

'Kind of like him,' I mused.

"I knew at a young age I'd go into some kind of medical field," I continued, "and when the time came to make a choice, I'd seen enough human nature to know I'd prefer to save the life of an animal."

"Speaking of animals…" I turned our joined hands to inspect his ring, admiring the engraved eagles perched atop a shield in the gold band to each side of the ruby. "Do the eagles mean something?"

He nodded, shifting his gaze to our hands. "They're condors. The symbol is the coat of arms of Colombia. My father's father had it made for him when he was a boy and he gave it to me on my eighteenth birthday. If you look closely," he held the ring up between us, "you can see the isthmus dividing two ships in the bottom of the shield."

I squinted, pulling his hand closer to make out the tiny details on the shield. It was immaculately engraved by hand. Whoever made it had to have spent countless hours on perfecting each intricate detail. "What's this thing in the center of the shield?"

He smiled. "It's a Phrygian cap held on a lance. My father says it's meant to signify liberty and freedom—always seemed odd and out of place to me. And above that are two cornucopias, one spilling coins, the other fruit. It represents Colombia's agriculture and mineral wealth."

"It's beautiful," I beamed. "Do you remember Colombia at all from your childhood?"

"A little," he sighed, his face close enough to mine that the breath skated over my cheek to incite goosebumps along both arms. "Although most of my memories are of the interior of our home there. My father kept us locked away most of the time; afraid, given his business, someone might steal us away if we ventured too far. I wonder if that's why I am so restless when I'm on land… Perhaps I spent too many years being still."

"Same," I said, remembering we were searching for similarities. "My father left us when we were babies. Our mom raised us with the help of our uncle a few blocks away. Since she had to work, A.J. and I spent most of our childhood at home… We never really went on vacation aside from a few trips downstate to see our grandfather. I knew, as soon as I was able, I'd spend my life traveling. Not to say my childhood wasn't wonderful. A.J. and I made up our own adventures to make it fun… created stories and worlds in our bedrooms and in the backyard."

"Dario and I did the same."

I straightened one of my legs and winced as the bottom of my foot sent a lightning bolt all the way up to my inner thigh.

"You are in pain. I should retrieve your sister."

"Not yet," I argued, tightening my fingers around his. "The sun hasn't come up and I'm still working on this awful cup of coffee… remember? Besides, I'm not done asking questions."

He sat back a little, laughing as he brushed his hair away from his face. "Do you have another question, Cecelia?"

I nodded, scanning his torn, bloody shirt and scabbed over knuckles. "Why, my dear sweet Joseph, didn't you change out of those ripped clothes and wash all that blood off before taking me on our first date?"

At that, he tilted his head back and laughed heartily; the sound touching every part of my heavy body so I felt lighter for it. "I could not be pulled away from you for fear you might wake and I would miss it."

"Is that all your blood?" I asked.

He glanced down at what was left of his shirt and shook his head. "Some of it."

"I'm guessing, since we are both still alive—*for now, anyway*—we won? They're all gone?"

"Aye, we won," he said softly. "You're safe now."

Chewing my lower lip, I decided any remaining shreds of caution were pointless when my future hung in the balance. Whether I was destined to die right there in his bed or wake up a few months later in someone else's, caution in the present would not change either of those things. And with the cramping in my legs, I knew our little moment was coming to an end.

"You know," I said, "I thought my sister and her friends were out of their minds to spend so much time getting romantically involved with one another instead of focusing on how they got here in the first place."

"Oh?" He flashed his teeth in a wide smile. "And here I thought you far too virtuous for such prejudice."

I turned my face to shield my blush with the pillow. "I told myself I would be the voice of reason while they all lived out their little fairytales. Swore I'd focus solely on finding some mention of Jack's death in history, be the one to figure out how the portal works, and make sure our path home would be the least disruptive to the history we knew… and yet…" I turned my face back toward him. "I like you… so much, in fact, I think I might cry the moment you remove your hand from mine."

I moved my legs again, attempting to rid myself of the growing cramps climbing up both. "And I know how pointless that is to say or feel when literally everything we're setting out to do will make anything more between the two of us impossible, but… I wanted to at least say that out loud; wanted to feel that out loud… just this once."

He raised his brows as he scanned my face. "I am unworthy of your affections."

"I disagree."

He hid a smile. "Then I shall not argue for I am far too greedy to let them go." His cheeks reddened ever so slightly. "Because I like you, too. Very much, I'm afraid. There is little else that occupies my thoughts outside of you."

"So can I call this a *real* courtship then? Even if it's just for as long as I can remain alive?"

He tightened his fingers once again over mine. "I never considered it anything less."

"Then I shall die a happy woman." I pulled our joined hands closer, squeezing him through a spasm of pain in my legs. "Much as I want to stay here in this spot with you forever, if I'm going to die soon, I should probably say goodbye to my sister and check on Kyle. Will you take me to them while you rest?" I touched the purpling skin beneath his eye. "You look so very tired."

"Of course I will," he said, frowning as if he felt guilty for keeping me to himself for so long.

"Before we go…" I said, forcing him to freeze halfway out of his seat. "Isn't it customary for the male to offer the female a gift at the start of their courtship? You cannot expect me to be satisfied with only a cup of terrible imaginary coffee."

"It is indeed," he chuckled, removing his hand from mine to slide the ruby ring from his finger and press it into my palm.

Before I could object to taking something so much more personal than what I'd been expecting, he scooped me up into his arms. The feather in my stomach exploded, and its fragments formed a million smaller ones, all of them dancing along the edges of my skin, rendering me hypnotized by the feel of his body against mine.

Chapter Twelve

Alaina

"Helloooo!" Cece sang from where she dangled in Juan Jr.'s arms as he carried her into the room.

I did not fail to notice the way her arms were wound affectionately around his neck, nor did I overlook the light shining upon his ring now rested loosely upon her pointer finger.

"Helloooo!" Kyle echoed back in the same giddy tone, both of them evidently experiencing the more pleasing side effects of their second doses of Valium.

Adjusting the blanket I'd hung over Zachary as he fed, I stood from the wingback chair. "You're awake," I said stupidly. "How are you feeling?"

"My teeth hurt," she said, scrunching her nose. "And my legs are starting to cramp."

"Where would you like me to put you?" Juan Jr. asked, smiling down at her.

She pointed at the bed where we'd propped Kyle up against the pillows. "I think I want to sit with Kyle if that's alright?"

Kyle gave her a glossed over grin and nodded.

"How's your leg?" she asked as Juan pushed a few pillows against the headboard before carefully lowering her down on her bottom. He hovered there until she'd found a comfortable position.

Kyle rubbed the bandage on his leg. "Well, it's still there, so that's good. I'd have been pissed if I woke up missing another limb. How's your foot?"

She frowned down at her foot where Terrence had stitched and bandaged it. "Also still there." She giggled and looked at me. "What kind of drugs did you give us?"

"Valium," I said, unable to prevent myself from laughing at both their overly happy faces as I moved to the foot of the bed. They looked like children sitting side by side grinning at nothing. I hoped this wouldn't be my last memory of them.

"I *really like* Valium," Kyle confessed.

"Me too," she whispered, nudging his shoulder with hers. "And I think I need another one."

Juan Jr. straightened then and cleared his throat. "If there's nothing else you need from me, Cecelia, I must beg your leave so I might change clothes and relieve Gabriel at the helm for a bit. I can stop in the galley and have some food brought up if you'd like?"

She pursed her lips as she gazed up at him. "But you haven't slept…"

He bowed his head. "I shall before the day is through, you've my word."

"Will you meet me for coffee in the morning and a real sunrise?" she asked sweetly. "If I'm still around?"

He smiled, looking at her with so much affection I hated myself for disapproving. "You will be, and I shall look forward to only that."

"I'll teach you how to make it," she added, turning in the bed to watch him bow to me before he left the room.

Spinning back to face me, she covered his ring protectively with her other hand. "Don't."

"Don't what?" I asked, sitting on the edge of the bed and pulling Zachary up to my shoulder to burp him.

"Don't try to take this from me."

And just like that, she was fourteen years old again, pouting because I'd told our mom she was talking to an older boy I knew only wanted one thing from her.

"I can see the look on your face, A.J. Just leave it, okay?"

Kyle's attention danced confusedly between the two of us.

"Cece, I don't want to take anything from you—least of all something that makes you happy."

"But...?" she asked, rolling her eyes and looking at Kyle as she waited for me to say more.

"But nothing," I said. "You're an adult and you can make your own decisions. I won't interfere... but—"

"Ah ha!" She pointed at me and then Kyle. "And there it is... the infamous *'but.'*"

Kyle hid a smile by pulling his lips inward, attempting *poorly* to keep the rest of his expression neutral.

"But," I said, trying to keep my voice even and not sound like our mother, "there is an amazing little girl that I have to try to save in all this. You can do whatever you'd like with him, but you will let me tell you about her—for *her* sake."

If it was only a contest between Owen and Juan, I wouldn't interfere. I didn't even really like Owen all that much. He was always a bit of a boob in my opinion. But I loved Maddy and I knew Cece did too, and I was mortified that, if she lived through this, she might one day wake with a memory of her daughter and resent me for not doing more to save her life.

She sighed. "Fine."

"Fine," I echoed.

"Anything else?" She raised a defiant blond brow.

"Yes, you little jerk-face." I pinched the big toe of her uninjured foot. "I love you and I am so proud of what you did up there... Thank you... for being you and saving all our lives."

Chin still up in the air in defense, I saw her lip twitch. "You're welcome, butthead... I love you, too." She scanned the room. "Where is everyone?"

"Jack, Terrence, and Jim are all off in various cabins sleeping. Lilly, Magna, Bruce, and Fetia are helping the crew clean up the deck. And Chris is… somewhere. He said you shot one of them. Is it bothering you?"

"Are you asking if I'm regretting what I did?" She tilted her head to one side. "Not at all. I saw what that man had intended for me if I wouldn't have fired. I'll never regret taking that shot." She smiled at Kyle. "Besides, it was both of us that took him down. I couldn't have stopped him if you hadn't blown out that lantern."

He flashed his teeth happily back at her. "You made the most badass shot I've ever seen in my life. I'm glad it was you with the gun and not me."

"We both kicked ass," she said, pinching his cheek and glancing back to me. "Remember how bad we used to want a little brother?"

I chuckled, patting Kyle's ankle. "Well, we have one now."

Pupils still dilated, he looked from me to Cece. "Does that mean I get to call you guys names like jerk-face and butthead?"

Cece nodded earnestly. "Oh, yes. Insults are a requirement in this family. If you're gonna' do it though, you gotta' start strong. A.J. is ruthless with name-calling." She adjusted her back against the pillows, attempting to get comfortable. "Jesus, my back is killing me… I think it's going to start back up soon."

Kyle's jubilant expression faded. "Chris told me what the captive said… Do you feel like you're dying?"

"Captive?" she asked, frowning at me. "They took one captive?"

"Yes," I said, a little hesitantly. "They took one to try to find out what kind of poison was used and if there was anything we could do to fight it."

She crossed her arms over her chest. "Well, what'd he say?"

"Tetanus," I sighed, "mixed with something else—we think strychnine. The muscle relaxers should help if we can ration them."

"That's reassuring," she grumbled, running a hand through her hair. "Is he still alive? The captive?"

I shook my head. "No… Juan… well… he beat him until there was nothing left to beat."

"Oh," she glanced down at the ring. Straightening her shoulders to dismiss the image I'd surely implanted of him in her mind, she turned back to Kyle. "I can feel my muscles tensing back up already. Can you?"

He nodded. "You think it'll be as bad as it was last night?"

She shrugged. "Not if we take another Valium before it can... And maybe antibiotics... They can't hurt and I know we have plenty. We'll need to eat first... If we're going to stand any chance at fighting this, we'll need the nourishment."

"I'll go get you something," I said, standing quickly.

"Wait," she said, taking my hand in hers. "Is anyone else hurt? Did we lose anyone? Are you okay? Are the babies okay?"

I laughed at the way her mind always spit out a million thoughts at once. "Everyone is fine, Cece. We didn't lose anyone... *thanks to you*. And a few tried to come through the window but Maria and Magna took care of them. As far as injuries go, you two are the only ones that got the poison. There are a few minor cuts and burns on the ones firing the cannons. Most of the men down there had never even been near the cannons before last night. Everyone will heal."

Kyle coughed. "Most of us, anyway."

She patted Kyle's hand. "We're not dead yet. Have you had a tetanus shot recently?"

He nodded. "Have you?"

"No. I'm way overdue for the booster"

It was early evening when Jack appeared at the cabin door. Both babies as well as Cece and Kyle had passed out, and in the silence, I'd dug back into one of the history books, unsure what I was even looking for, but looking all the same. The few seconds I'd thought he was dead when Jim had come in the room after the battle were the worst few seconds of my life. I wasn't willing to feel that again any time soon.

He eased the door closed and crept silently across the room to the wingback chair I was seated in.

"Did you sleep?" I whispered as he lowered to his knees in front of me and slid his arms to each side of my thighs.

"A little," he breathed, resting his head in my lap. "Did you?"

"Not yet," I yawned, closing my book to embed my fingers in his hair. "Are you alright?"

He nodded against my legs and sighed. "Just tired... So ungodly tired of *all* this."

"Me too," I admitted, folding forward to lay a kiss on the back of his head.

"How are Cece and Kyle holding up?" he asked, pushing his arms further back to curl them around me and pull me closer.

"Sore," I said, glancing at the bed. "But alive. We'll need to ration the Valium; cut it in half maybe... but if we can keep their muscles relaxed, they might make it."

"And how are *you* holding up?"

I took a deep breath. "I'd feel guilty to say I'm anything but perfect given the way I reacted last night. Everyone stepped up while I froze in fear... So I suppose I'm holding up just fine... aside from feeling like an asshole for lecturing our goddamn heroine on her life choices when it's mine that need evaluated."

He let out a chuckle that was muffled by my skirts. "You're not an asshole, Red. Cece may be our heroine, but, as her sister, you've got every right to lecture her when she's very clearly making a bad life choice."

"Is she, though?" My fingers froze against his scalp. "She doesn't know the life I've seen her in. Trying to sell her on it is like trying to sell someone a book they have no interest in reading. And Juan Jr.'s sweet to her. Why wouldn't she fight me? I couldn't imagine someone telling me to avoid *you* back on that island because I had a life I knew nothing about waiting for me."

He laid a kiss on my stomach and tilted his head up to face me. "I wouldn't have let you avoid me even if you tried."

I nodded. "I don't think he'll let her, either."

He smiled. "When she went down last night, he went mad getting to her… He took out six Nikora before she even hit the deck. *Six*. And he's only known her for, what? Four days?"

"Right," I said, glancing up at the bed to make sure she was still sleeping. "And assuming she lives through this, in three months, there's a very real possibility she's going to wake up in a life with Owen and Maddy. What happens to her marriage if she remembers what happened here?"

He shrugged. "You've warned them both of all this, right?"

"Yes."

Laying his head back against my lap, he yawned. "Well then, you've done your part. If they both know the risks and still choose to play out this little fling they've got going, that's on them. They're adults and you're not their mother."

"But… It's been four days… Four days, and he took out six Nikora to get to her… Four days and her eyes might as well turn into cartoon-beating-hearts every time he smiles at her. They're both going to get hurt."

"And they know that," he assured me. "Let them get hurt, Red, if they're willing to take it. You're not her mother. We have our own children to worry about in all this… and each other."

"Speaking of…" He pulled away to sit back on his haunches, moving his thumbs over my knees. "What was all that with Chris last night? Should I be worried?"

"No," I said. "He's just having a hard time adjusting to the new memories… He'll be alright."

"And you?" He raised his brows. "They're not bothering you at all?"

"I chose you, Jack." I smoothed my palm along the side of his jaw. "Even after the memories changed, I still chose you. No, they're not bothering me."

But Maria's words were. I was acutely aware of the fact that we were both touching one another, and I hated the tiny bit of insecurity she'd implanted in me.

That awareness became amplified as Jack's fingers crept beneath my skirts to skate over the skin of my calves.

"Jack…" I shook my head and covered his hands beneath the fabric where they'd ventured up to grip my thighs. "We've never talked about what happened on that island, and I can see you now burying what happened on the deck. It's not an easy thing to kill someone. What kind of wife would I be if I let you shoulder that burden by yourself? I need you to talk to me."

He shook his head. "I've already told you, my burdens fade away the moment I'm with you. I don't need to share that ugliness with you. They're gone the moment I put my hands on you."

"No, they're not." I pressed my palms firmly over his fingers where he'd attempted to move them farther. "You dream about that island almost every night. I can't bear watching you fight in your sleep any longer. And now… what happened last night… I'm terrified it'll only add to your nightmares. I want to know the ugliness as much as I know the good in you. Our relationship can't just be the good stuff."

He glanced toward the bed where Cece and Kyle were fast asleep before frowning at me. "What do you want me to say, Red? You want me to tell you that I strangled the life out of an innocent man with the same arms I hold you and our children with? What for? You gonna say some magical words to make it go away? You want me to tell you how much I enjoyed killing those men on the deck last night? How it was the first thing I felt I have gotten right after I have failed you over and over and over? How every second we move farther away from that storm, I feel like I am failing you again? Is that what you want me to say?"

"Yes," I said softly.

"Why?" He squeezed my thighs. "What good will it do to have both of us feeling inadequate when we have two children that need us to be whole? When we have a whole goddamn group of people looking to us for all the answers?"

"Jack, honey, you don't need to have the answers." I let go of his hands to move my palms over his cheeks. "And I want you to tell me these things so I can step up when you need to step down. I can't have you fall apart, and you will if you don't share this with me."

"I do share it with you," he said, "when I put my hands on you; when I feel your skin beneath my fingers, or mine beneath yours… When I move inside you or hold you in my arms… It is the only thing that pulls me back together."

"It can't only be that," I whispered. "I want to know what you know, feel what you feel so that when I'm putting you back together, I don't leave anything out. I love you, and I don't ever want either of us to keep things like this inside."

Letting my thumb skate over his cheek, I smiled. "You're not failing us, love. There is no right answer, and we are all doing the best we can with what we've got. There are other people here that can make decisions too. It doesn't always have to be you. Let us in; let us help. And if we fail, we shoulder that burden together. Okay?"

He nodded, laying his head in my lap and letting me comb my fingers through his hair. "You really want to know about my nightmares?"

"Yes." My heart swelled at the vulnerability in his tone.

"They're not about what happened, you know." He turned his head in my lap to rest his cheek on my thigh. "They're about what I *made* happen in order to do it. Killing that man was a choice I'd make over and over in order to get back to you. I knew I would either kill that man or be killed by him, and with you pregnant and at risk of dying during the delivery, I couldn't afford to be killed just then. So I had to make myself do it."

He took a deep breath. "I had this image of what our child would look like. He was this little red-headed boy with your freckles and my blue eyes… Maybe two or three in my mind, and… I could see you standing with him on the beach, his little hand wrapped around your finger."

He moved his fingertips lazily up and down my calves. "And I used that image to make the man in front of me into the monster I needed him to be… I saw him—clear as day—ripping your clothing from your body, tearing you away from our little boy… Watched as he violently had his way with you over and over while our son screamed… Then I stood there helplessly as he clawed you both to shreds and left the beach covered in blood... I forced that scene to play on repeat in my mind as I fought him... Forced myself to hear your cries when I wrapped my arms around his throat and held until his breath ran out... And those nightmares I have? They're not of me killing him... They're of what I made him do to you in my mind. Over and over I'm on that beach watching helplessly as he tears you both to pieces and I can't erase it."

He looked at me then. "I am so afraid it could come true. I'm terrified I'll make the wrong decision and you and our children will be the ones to pay for it. When I saw Cece go down, I was so sure I'd find you the same way. It felt like my nightmare was playing out before my very eyes. And seeing you come barging in that room was the most relief I've ever felt in my life. I never thought I could love anyone the way I love you and those babies, and my nightmares won't stop until I get you all home where I know you'll be safe; where I know no one can hurt you."

I shook my head. "No one's going to hurt us. You made sure of that when you taught me to defend us, remember? You showed me how to fight; how to get away. The next time you find yourself in that nightmare, you watch as I claw *him* to shreds. Okay?"

He smiled, his hands exploring farther upward, the warm metal of his wedding band dancing along my skin. "I love you so much."

Wrapping my arms around him, I laid my head against his shoulder, letting myself finally feel the relief that came with knowing he hadn't died on the deck. "I love you, too. And for the record, you can't afford to be killed just now either. And we're going to have to do whatever it takes to make sure that doesn't happen."

Chapter Thirteen

Alaina

Someone squeezed my nose… hard.

Waking suddenly surrounded by darkness, I swatted the hand away from my face and sat up abruptly. "What the—"

"Shhh… It's Cece," she whispered. "I need your help."

"Help with what?" I asked, still frazzled by being awoken in such a way. "Are you okay? Do you need more Valium?"

"I want to get washed and dressed," she said. "I can't stand my own stench any longer, but I can barely move my legs, they hurt so bad. I tried and failed several times to walk on my own before waking you. Fetia and Kyle slept in here with her father, so I was wondering if you'd just help me get to their room so I can clean myself up?"

"You need to be resting." I took a deep breath and massaged the bridge of my nose. "This wouldn't have anything to do with a certain Colombian who's promised to have coffee with you this morning?"

"It might," she admitted. "Will you help me or are you gonna' force me to crawl? I promise, you can go back to bed as soon as you get me in there."

I yawned and stretched my arms over my head. "What time is it?"

"I don't know," she whispered. "It could be midnight or noon for all I can tell with that window boarded up."

"You're a pain in the ass, you know that?" I said, sliding my legs over the edge of the bed, careful not to disturb Jack. "And how many times have I told you not to wake me up like that?"

She giggled. "A.J., I've waited three very long years to wake you up like that. Grab my purse. It's under the bed."

"You brought a purse?" I laughed. Of course, Cecelia McCreary would grab her name-brand purse before she was hoisted up the side of an 18th century pirate ship.

"And thank God I did," she huffed, "it's got my toothbrush, toothpaste, and perfume in it. Plus my contacts case and glasses are in there and I've had these contacts in for way too long."

Yawning and half asleep, I felt around beneath the bed until my fingers landed upon a strap. Placing it on her cot, I crept to the trunk to dig out a stack of clothing—unsure what I'd fished out in the dark, but certain I had the essentials—then returned to loop her arm around my shoulders and assist her out into the corridor.

Easing the door to our room closed, I frowned down at her where she was barely holding herself upright, even with my help. "You should be in bed. You need another pill."

She shook her head. "I'll take a half of one. I can't stay in bed any longer. I want to be on deck in the fresh air, and I need to get back to the research today. Before the attack, I was reading about a ship fire close to where we're headed… and it might be the *'noise'* Jim was referring to. Besides, you said some of the crew had injuries, and I'd like to help treat them while I'm able. I *am* a doctor, ya know… and I imagine cuts and burns are treated the same way on a human as they are any other animal."

I grinned at her inherent need to help others as we hobbled into Kyle's cabin and I dropped her on the bed to light one of the lanterns at its side. Holding it up, I turned toward the grandfather clock and groaned. It was 3:30 in the morning.

Following my gaze, she dipped her chin abashedly. "Sorry."

"Pain in my ass," I teased, carrying the lantern with me as I lit the candles around the vanity.

"Will you tell me how it worked?" she asked, limping the two steps to the vanity stool to sit down. "When you changed things before… did you go back to relive it all or just… wake up knowing it was different?"

I could see the gears in her brain spinning as I collected the basin and pitcher and joined her at the vanity. "I just woke up knowing," I said. "Tilt your head back."

She did so, her hazel eyes staring sweetly up at me, waiting for further explanation while I poured water over her hair.

"Nothing here changed," I continued, working the moisture down to wet her ends. "I didn't have any new memories after the crash. Everything that was different had to do with you and Chris before our plane went down."

"Like what?" she asked.

"Well," I sighed as I scrunched her wet hair, "he and I were on the brink of divorce in the original timeline. I didn't have you living down the street after I lost Evelyn to talk me off a ledge and things got bad. I left him for a very long time alone to deal with her death…"

I lathered rose soap into my palms and began massaging it into her hair. "The memories didn't come right away… It was about ten days after we killed those men on the beach when the new memories started trickling in. Right about the time Chris left. At first, I thought they were dreams… but then I knew I'd lived them… Started recognizing myself in them—knowing what happened the same way I knew the originals. Saw you there with us to help us get over her death… remembered him planning the trip to Bora Bora as a surprise instead of me trying to save our marriage… it took a while before I realized it was Owen that was missing."

Catching myself going off the topic she likely was looking for, I redirected it back to her. "Why do you ask?"

She stared at me in the mirror as I scratched the soap into the back of her head. "Just want to know what's waiting for me," she said, pursing her lips. "I might die here and wake up there, ya know? I won't go back and relive anything?"

"You're not going to die… and no, you won't relive anything. Well, I don't think so anyway. We're still not entirely sure how any of this works."

"And Juan," she said, frowning at her bobbing head in the mirror as I massaged the sweet-smelling suds into her hair. "If it works for him the same way it worked for you… he'd wake up with changed memories sometime in the late nineties or early 2000s since he never would've crossed through time, right? Twenty years before we wake up with our own changed memories?"

"Theoretically," I said, tilting her head back to rinse.

I waited until I'd finished to continue. "Why?"

"Just curious." She inspected the giant ring on her tiny finger.

Reading her concentrated expression, I pried into her ever-racing mind as I ran a towel over her hair. "Are you worried that he'll be nearly fifty when you wake up and remember him?"

"No," she whispered, spinning his ring on her finger. "I'm thinking about Gloria and his brother and sister… If he got to the Albrecht ancestor… would it be possible he could have those twenty years with them—twenty years worth of new memories, plus the ones he'd make when we change things—before we erase them?"

I placed my hands on my hips, looking entirely too much like our mother when I caught sight of my reflection. "We can't afford to miss the next storm, Cece. I'm not going to risk Jack dying so Juan can have a few extra memories."

"I'm not suggesting that." She matched my serious expression in the mirror. "There's no way the changes could be immediate when you take Cecelia through time. There would be a possibility for you to come back for years. He'd have time to kill the Albrecht after you go through the storm—might even have time to kill the Albrecht before you go through if we can find him."

"The genealogists could only locate George Bennet at the battle of Great Bridge in December. We don't know where he'd be before then."

"We have three months, right?" Again, she spun the ring on her finger. "If it takes two to get to Virginia… we could have a whole month to ask around about him. Surely, someone in the British army would know of the regiment? And he'd have to be close by if he fought in Great Bridge in December. It's worth a shot, right?"

I twisted my lips to one side. "You keep saying *'we'* as if you're planning to get off the ship in Panama."

She raised one blond brow in the mirror. "A.J., I am years overdue for my tetanus booster. If they mixed tetanus into that poison, there's a very real possibility I won't make it to Panama… I'm feeling better now, but tetanus takes time. In a few days—possibly a few hours—I'm going to get *much* worse. If, by some miracle, I live through this, I want to go with him. I want to see this century with my own eyes and have my own adventure… make as many memories as possible before I potentially wake up as someone else's wife."

"Cece, you've known him for five days," I said, plucking up a brush to begin working the knots out of her head. "Those jungles are dangerous. You'd really take that kind of risk for someone you just met?"

She shook her head. "I haven't just met him… I met him before. In our time."

"You what?" My mouth might've dropped open, and I froze in place with the brush midway through a section of hair.

She nodded. "I don't know where or when, but I recognized him as someone I'd met before. That's why I want to spend as much time with him as possible. A.J., everything about him is familiar—the look, the smell, the accent, even the way I feel about him is familiar… And I can't figure out how. That's got to be something big, right? Something bigger than logic? Something bigger than time? Something bigger than all the reasons I can come up with to stay away from him?"

I didn't have an answer. I was… dumbfounded. If Juan Jr. could've made it to her years prior to her arrival here… he should've had some kind of message for us… And… his existence there was proof in itself that whatever we were about to do would work. Anna could live again. And if Anna could live… so could Jack if we were unable to figure out the cause of his death before it happened.

"You don't remember any kind of warning as to what was going to happen or a clue we might be able to use in any way?"

She shook her head. "No… not yet… but I'm trying as hard as I can to remember where I met him and what he might've said."

"You should've told me you recognized him." I began to brush again.

She laughed at that. "And what would that have done but make you just as confused as I was? Besides, I was much more interested in your stories about Jack and the babies at the time. I planned on telling you once I figured out how I knew him."

"And you haven't come up with any clues?" I asked.

She twisted her lips to one side, watching herself in the mirror as she spun the ring on her finger once more. "I can see him with shorter hair, but I can't hear what he's saying to me or make out the backdrop… it's driving me crazy."

"And you're sure it's him?"

She nodded. "With all my heart. And every moment I spend with him, I feel a little closer to remembering."

Sighing, I placed the brush back on the vanity, pointing at the ring on her finger. "You're gonna' need a chain for that. You'll lose it otherwise."

As I moved for the clasp on my necklace, she stopped me.

"No, no, no!" She held up her hand. "Don't you ever take off *that* necklace. I don't need it, anyway. I'm giving this back to him today."

I watched the way she pressed it to her heart and I frowned. "Why?"

"It's too much too soon," she said. "I was teasing him about a courting gift. I expected an origami swan or something cute like that… not his ring." She winced as she reached down to grab the edges of her shift. "Turn around so I can wash off."

I laughed at that. "Cece, I've seen you naked plenty of times before. Let me help you."

"Not since we were kids, you haven't," she countered. "Turn around. I can do this myself."

Groaning, I turned to face the bed. "So he's courting you then?"

She grunted. "Yes, and that's all we're going to say about it right now. I'm not in the mood for a lecture. Okay?"

I rolled my eyes. "Fine. And for the record, I've seen more of your naked *adult* body than I'd like to have."

Behind me, I heard her suck in air through her teeth as she pulled the shift over her head. "When?"

"Last night," I admitted.

"What? How?"

I cleared my throat. "I, uh, had to get that pill in you one way or another… swallowing wasn't an option."

She gasped. "Tell me you didn't have your finger in my…"

"I did," I assured her, chuckling. "We are much closer than you think we are, Cece."

"Gross."

I smiled. "I'd do it over a thousand times to keep you alive, jerk-face."

I heard the sound of dripping water as she wet the washcloth. "Thanks, pervert."

"Ass-hat."

Again, she winced audibly as she washed, but still bantered through clenched teeth with: "Turd-burglar."

"Seriously, let me help you. I'm not going to look at anything"

"No," she said decidedly, half-panting. "I'm fine. Grab me a clean shift from that pile if there's one in there… skittle-tits."

I burst out laughing at that one. I hadn't heard her use it in close to twenty years. "We weren't very nice to each other, were we?"

"The names were your fault," she noted. "You came home from kindergarten and started calling me fart-face."

"How can you possibly remember that?" I asked, giggling as I fished out a fresh shift from the pile of clothes on the bed. "You were barely four years old."

"You'd be surprised what you remember about a person when you think they're dead." The amusement faded from her voice. "I remembered every single thing you ever said or did… every laugh we shared… every tear you ever cried… The hardest day of my life was the day your plane went missing."

I backed up and held the shift out for her to take. "I'm so sorry, Cece."

"It's alright," she said between grunts. "I'd feel it a thousand times over just to climb onto that ship and find you alive on it."

I smiled. "That was easily one of the greatest moments of my life. I never thought I'd see you again."

"Well, you can turn around and see me now *butt-sniffer*," she teased. "And bring the rest of the clothes and that pill to cut in half. I have a hot date to get to."

Chapter Fourteen

Cecelia

Every inch of my body felt as though a steak knife were embedded in it—*multiple* steak knives. The simple act of holding myself against the bed post long enough to be dressed was torture. My legs, back, shoulders, and arms felt as if I'd spent the night trying to hold up an eighteen-wheeler, and my jaw was in almost a permanent state of lock.

The wound, though cleaned, stitched and bandaged, continued to burn, and I could put no weight on it without screaming.

It was absurd to be going on a date in my condition, I knew, but I didn't want to lay in bed and wait for death. If I was going to die soon, I wanted to make as many memories as I could before I was revived in some other life.

I pulled Juan's ring up against my mouth as A.J. finished lacing my stays. The thick gold band was warm from where I'd been holding it tightly in my palm, and I smoothed it over my lips, imagining what it'd be like to have him do the same with his thumb... with his lips...

Just the thought of his touch made my heartbeat quicken; made my lungs light and ticklish on every inhale so I forgot to notice the muscles aching around them... so I forgot I might die at any moment.

"You really like him, huh?" A.J. asked, pulling the corset strings so the bones pressed into my ribs. "That too tight?"

"It's fine," I panted. "And yes, I like him *very* much. I hadn't intended to... Told myself over and over that it was ridiculous to like anyone given our circumstances... but here we are... and I like him so much I can barely stand the waiting."

"I know you don't want to, but I really wish you'd rest a little longer," she said, stepping back after she'd finished tying the laces to inspect my appearance. "You're not going to be able to walk around the ship on your own when you can barely hold yourself up. Do you expect him to carry you everywhere?"

"I don't mind," a muffled voice called out from the other side of the cabin door. Suddenly my heart was racing so fast I had to hold the bed post with both hands to keep each beat from knocking me over.

He was there...

And the tremors coursing through my muscles from the pain were replaced by new ones—ones brought on by sheer anticipation.

I hadn't seen him since the morning prior when we'd both been entirely too familiar with each other, and without the same amount of Valium in my system, I wasn't sure what I'd say or do when I saw his face. Would I be embarrassed? *Was* I embarrassed? Was he? God, I hoped not.

I'd been enchanted by his contribution to our conversation. His words replayed in my mind over and over... awakening a flurry of feathers every time I thought of them.

"Spying on us, Juan?" A.J. asked, moving across the room to the door. I quivered as she pulled it open and added, "It's not polite to listen to other people's conversations, you know."

His gaze never paused to take notice of her on its way to me.

And every inch of my face grew warm—even my eyelids—as the corners of his lips curled upward to form that dimple in his cheek. "Hello, Cecelia. Are you feeling well?"

His still-wet hair was pulled back in its usual ribbon, and he wore a navy and gold jacket over his white shirt and black breeches, sword ever-present at his hip. He was stunning. So stunning, in fact, I forgot to respond… forgot to even breathe.

"It's four in the morning," A.J. said, crossing her arms over her chest. "Exactly how long did you plan to stand out there waiting for her? And who's sailing the ship?"

He didn't move his eyes from mine, but his smile widened. "I woke Gabriel early so I could wait as long as it took."

A.J. might've left the room for all the two of us would've noticed right then. My eyes were as glued to him as his were to me, and as he moved closer, my lungs felt like they might float right out of my chest.

"Oh, you two have got it bad," she observed. "I'll go ahead and see myself out… Have fun with your coffee. And be careful with her. She's got another half pill in her pocket if the pain gets bad."

And then we were alone.

And he was moving toward me.

And I still hadn't exhaled.

"I like the glasses," he said softly. "Are you still in pain?"

I shook my head.

"The agony on your face says otherwise, *mi paloma*." He frowned at my hands where they were gripping the bedpost tight enough for the knuckles to turn white. "Perhaps you should rest."

I slowly let out a breath. "I can't go back to bed. Please don't try to make me."

"I will never try to *make* you do anything, Cecelia," he assured me, leaving no room for amusement in his tone. "But I do not wish to make matters worse. Shall I escort you to the deck where you might find a more comfortable place to prop up your legs?"

"The galley," I managed. "I promised to show you how to make coffee and I just took another half a pill. I'll be fine. I could hardly sleep waiting to go on this date with you. There's a certain way I envision this morning going, and it won't be the same without the coffee I've been dreaming you'll make me."

"Oh, aye?" He moved closer and the world stopped spinning. Slowly, he pulled one of my arms from the bedpost to wrap it round his neck while his own glided round my waist. "I've got you," he breathed against my temple, his lips close enough to brush against the skin. "You can let go now."

So I did. And he didn't give me the chance to stumble before he swept my legs up into his cradled arms as if I weighed nothing at all. Resting my head against his shoulder, I inhaled his familiar almond scent, and for a moment, my muscles were too delighted to hurt.

"I meant to ask yesterday, what happened to your hand?" I winced at the gashes and bruises lining the knuckles against my knees as he carried me out of the room.

"Nothing you should be concerned about," he said, his breath exciting even the pores on my forehead where it danced across them.

In the darkness of the stairwell, I laughed. "Are you planning to be this cryptic with your answers all morning?"

He chuckled. "No. If you must know, I hit the man who drove the arrow into your foot… a few more times than I should've. My hand will be fine."

I remembered Alaina's words the day before as she'd informed me that he'd *beat him until there was nothing left to beat,'* and, not willing to speak any more on the Nikora during our date, I laid my head back against his shoulder. "Good. Will you tell me about your tattoo?"

"In a moment." His voice had shifted to a whisper as he navigated us through the darkness we'd descended the stairs into. "We wouldn't wish to wake the staff so early."

I heard the sounds of gentle snoring around us and remembered the hammocks and bedding I'd seen near the galley on a trip down previously.

As we moved into the ship's kitchen and the half Valium began to kick in, I couldn't help my palm roaming beneath the lapels of his jacket where I could feel his heart beating rapidly.

"You'll give me away," he whispered, removing my hand as he lowered me onto a wooden stool in the darkness.

I laughed, admiring the sight of him as he closed the galley door and lit the lanterns around the room. "I think we both gave *ourselves* away yesterday."

"So you remember," he said with his back to me, cupping the flame on the edge of his match as he moved it to the brick stove. "And do you regret the things you said?"

"Not as much as I should," I admitted. "Do you?"

"No." He blew out the match and moved to the counter I was seated before, reaching over our heads to open a cabinet.

"You meant all those things?" I asked. "You weren't just being sweet because I'm dying?"

He rifled through the cabinet with a smile in my direction. "You are not dying, *mi paloma*, and I am never *sweet*. If I am awake, I am thinking of you. If I am asleep, I am dreaming of you. It is not a nicety that I am entirely captivated by you. It is just a fact. You've bewitched me."

"I've bewitched *you*?" I tittered. "I'm a chronic pragmatist. I don't dart off in the early morning hours looking for romance with a practical stranger. You're the charmer between the two of us."

Placing a burlap sack and an odd looking box with a handle in front of me on the wooden counter, he scratched the side of his jaw. "The kettle's there," he said, pointing to a cast-iron looking contraption. "What else do we need?"

I frowned at the items littering the counter and shook my head, unable to stop the laughter from escaping me. "I think I have gravely underestimated the complexity of 18th century cookware!"

He leaned back against the counter, crossing his arms casually over his midsection. "This is not how you do it in your time?"

"Not even close," I chuckled, inspecting the little bowl that sat around the handle on the box. "But I like a good challenge. I'm guessing this is a coffee grinder… and the beans go—"

"Oh!" Bruce exclaimed, holding a heavily bandaged hand over his heart where he'd come through the door, equally startled to find us there as we were him. "Cece! What… eh…" he glanced at Juan, "what are you two doing down here so early?"

I smiled at him, sliding Juan's ring into the pocket of my dress. "I thought *I'd* make the coffee this morning, and since I can't exactly walk just yet, Juan agreed to escort me. What are you doing up so early?"

He narrowed his eyes at Juan before turning to beam at me. "It takes a few hours to make bread properly. I'm always up this early."

"What happened there?" I asked, pointing at his bandaged hand as he limped into the room and placed himself between us at the counter.

"Just a little burn, sweetheart. Got a bit too confident on the cannon last night. It's nothing that won't heal."

I frowned. "Well, you can't make bread with one hand. We'll help. You can tell us what to do."

"Oh, no honey," he blushed, "I can handle it—"

"Don't be silly, I insist," I said, patting his arm and enjoying how outgoing I was as a result of the Valium. "I've always wanted to learn how to make bread, anyway. I'm sure Juan would love to learn, too…"

I dared to glance at him over Bruce's head and was surprised to find amusement in his features instead of agitation.

"I'd be happy to," he said with a mischievous grin before removing his jacket to roll up his sleeves.

"And when we're done," I added, "I'll take a look at that burn for you."

Bruce's cheeks reddened around his wide smile. "Well this sure is a surprise, Cece, but you really should be in bed resting. Your sister mentioned you might have tetanus. I don't want to get in the way of you healing."

"Not at all," I assured him. "If I'm dying, I'd much rather spend my final moments drinking coffee and making bread with new friends than laying in bed waiting for something to happen. That said…" I waved my hand over the coffee supplies in front of me. "I have absolutely no clue how to even make coffee in this century. You'll have to give me *very* close instructions… on everything."

He chuckled, his expression shifting from sweet to sour when he looked up at Juan. "There are some aprons in the pantry through there." He pointed at a narrow wooden door on the opposite end of the room. "Collect us a few along with the Kolea eggs and a bag of flour."

He waited until Juan disappeared beyond the door to lean in. "Are you in trouble?"

"Not even a little," I said. "He's not our enemy, you know. If he was, he could've saved himself the trouble and let the Nikora kill us all."

Bruce nodded and glanced at the door. "I still don't trust him. You shouldn't either. He had to know about that passageway."

He straightened as Juan reappeared, arms full of supplies with an expression indicating the walls separating us from the pantry were extremely thin.

I winked up at him as I unloaded the eggs and aprons from his arms. "Bruce, maybe you can show Juan how to make a proper cup of coffee while I get set up here?"

Over the course of the next hour, and with the assistance of strong coffee, Bruce walked us through the steps of 18th century bread making. Juan and I mixed and kneaded and folded while Bruce reminisced about his early days as a chef in Los Angeles. He boasted proudly about the restaurant he'd worked so hard to open and all the celebrities that occasioned to pass through it.

The more I learned about him, the more I adored him. He had a natural warmth that made me immediately at ease in his company; something that was rare for me to find outside my family and close friends.

As much as I enjoyed his stories, I was fascinated by the things he knew about food. For him, cooking was art—each ingredient a color on a canvas to be tweaked and blended until he'd formed a masterpiece. I could've stayed down there all day learning from him… were it not for the approaching sunrise.

Juan had remained silent as he worked, but we stole every possible opportunity Bruce was occupied to exchange playful glances or touches. It became harder and harder to look away once he'd managed to get bits of flour sprinkled over his eyebrows, the bridge of his nose, and streaked across his black hair. He was positively disheveled by the time we set the dough to rise, and I liked the look of him so unkempt.

"Alright, let me see that hand," I ordered Bruce, patting the counter in front of me.

"It's not that bad," he said, though he obediently laid his arm out for me to unwrap.

"You've got this bandage too tight," I said. "Did you do anything to treat it before you wrapped it?"

He shook his head. "I stuck it in water for a while."

I frowned at his palm once I'd removed the wrapping. It was red and several blisters had appeared over the skin, some oozing puss. "Not that bad, eh?" I looked around the galley, thinking. "Do we have any honey?"

"Honey?" Bruce tittered. "There's some in the pantry. What do you want it for?"

"It'll soothe the pain," I assured him, "and fight off infection. Plus, it'll help it heal faster and take down the swelling."

I grinned at Juan who stared at me like I'd just invented electricity. "Indigenous people have used honey to treat burns for ages. Do we have enough to treat the other burn victims?"

Bruce smiled. "Whoever was in charge of stocking this ship must've had one hell of a sweet tooth. There's a whole case of it in there."

Juan didn't wait to be instructed, but moved past me toward the pantry, grazing the back of my arm slowly with a finger as he did so. That touch seemed to linger on the skin there, a permanent imprint of the feel of him sinking down into the muscle beneath.

"I can see you're in a lot of pain, Cece," Bruce said between us, "you should be in bed, not down here taking care of me."

"I'm fine," I promised, leaning over the wound to make sure there was no smell of an infection. "I want to live while I'm able."

"You show me how to treat it," he continued, shaking his head, "and you leave the others for *me* to take care of. I'd intended to do that anyway. I brought fresh bandages with me." He dug into his apron to present a rolled strip of fabric. "I boiled it last night to make sure it was sanitary."

"Very good," I said, surprised.

"Anna taught me…"

I nodded. "A.J. told me you cared about her a lot. Do you think we'll get her back when all this is over?"

"God, I hope so," he said, straightening as the main door to the galley opened.

"Ay, Tiny!" Jim shouted, stopping in his tracks as Juan returned simultaneously from the pantry and they nearly collided. "Junior…" He said in greeting, turning to find me at the counter and jumping. "What the hell you doin' down here, lightnin' bug? You should be in bed!"

"Lightning bug?" I asked as he propped himself up against the opposing wall to observe me work.

He winked. "Fierce as lightning, cute as a bug."

Bruce chuckled. "He's got a nickname for all of us. Pretty sure he doesn't know any of our actual names."

I smiled, taking the honey from Juan and exchanging it for the bandages. "Can you cut off a small bit of that and pour some clean water over it? The one we use for drinking, *not* bathing."

He took it, his gaze lingering long enough that Jim cleared his throat in a manner that told me he'd noticed.

"What are *you* doing down here so early, Jim?" I asked, returning my attention to the opposite wall where he was flashing an all-too-knowing grin.

He pushed off the wall to help himself to the carafe. "Me 'n Tiny's got us a bit of a ritual. We drink coffee and sneak cigarettes and talk shit about the rest of yuns 'till the sun comes up." He sniffed the liquid in the pitcher before pouring himself a cup. "Seriously though, you orta' be in bed."

"Waiting to die?" I countered, taking the cloth Juan offered and scrubbing the blisters on Bruce's hand. "No, thank you. There's plenty more things I'd rather spend my time doing."

Bruce sucked in air through his teeth and I lightened my touch. "I'm sorry."

"It's okay," he lied, holding his breath while I continued to clean the wound.

"Oh quit carryin' on," Jim teased, smacking a hand on Bruce's shoulder. "Look at ye, shaking like a dog tryin to shit out a sack of prunes. It ain't nothin' but a couple blisters. You shoulda' seen what ole' Juan here did to that behemoth last night… and he didn't carry on half as what you are right now." He sipped his coffee and spun back toward the pantry. "Ye' got anything to eat down here? I'm 'bout starved to death."

I noticed Juan had stiffened when Jim mentioned the Nikora and I wondered if he was hoping I was ignorant to the fact they'd tortured and killed the captive.

I applied a spoonful of honey to Bruce's wound and began to loosely rewrap his hand, smiling up at Juan. "So you played the hunter—"

"Ow ow ow!" Bruce jerked his hand free, and I realized the fingers on both my hands had curled into fists.

Jim frowned, holding a biscuit halfway to his lips. "Umm, sugar, your mouth's doin' somethin' weird… Ye' got them pills with ye'?"

I nodded, motioning to my pocket. "In here," I said through my clamped together teeth. "It's okay. Don't freak out."

"Don't freak out?" he balked as Juan immediately moved to my side and began fishing around the pocket at my hip. "What ye' mean *don't freak out*?! Woman, ye' supposed to be in a dark room with no stimuli, resting… not traipsin' around makin' googly eyes with the likes of him! Of course I'm freakin' out! None of us is ready to watch ye' die today."

Ignoring Jim, Juan held the half pill in front of me. "Can you swallow?"

"Yes," I said through tightening teeth, "but you'll have to help me open my mouth. I… I don't think I can."

He didn't hesitate, and while it was an odd thing to have his fingers in my mouth, I was grateful when I felt the pill on my tongue, and I swallowed while I still had the ability.

I glanced at the clock on the wall. 5:30. The first half a pill had lasted less than two hours. There was no way the Valium was going to last… And without my muscles relaxed, I would asphyxiate and die… so would Kyle.

I huffed, bracing both fists on the counter. "This won't work."

"What won't work?" Juan asked, his hands hovering to each side of me in case I fell over.

"The pills won't last," I managed with a locked jaw. "I can't keep taking them like this when Kyle needs them too."

"We got booze," Jim noted. "And plenty of it… Couldn't that act as a muscle relaxer between doses?"

I considered it. "It might… but I'd have to drink a lot of it and do it round the clock…" I attempted a smile at Bruce that I imagined, with my tightened jaw, resembled more of a growl. "And I'm a *terrible* drunk. You'd all hate me before it was over."

Bruce chuckled, laying his hand over mine on the counter. "I don't believe that for a second. I bet you're a blast."

I shook my head, wincing as my teeth clamped down harder, the muscles around them tightening to pull my lips back. "I puke mostly… and black out. I've only been drunk a few times; enough to know I'm terrible."

Jim leaned over the counter and winked. "Oh, ye' just ain't learned how to drink properly is all. I'll teach ye' everything ye' need to know about gettin' pissed. I used to be somethin' of an expert at it myself."

"Should I take you back to your bed?" Juan asked, his entire face distorted with concern.

"No." I motioned to the loaves of bread where we'd set them to rise. "Bread. Oven." I spun back to face Jim as Juan moved to follow my order. "I want to try the alcohol and leave the pills for Kyle."

"Sugar," he breathed out a laugh, "just quit talkin' till' ye' can open ye' mouth again. I cain't understand a word you're sayin."

"Jim," Bruce chuckled, "not a one of us can understand half the crap that comes out of your mouth, and it's never stopped *you* from yammering on."

The two of them stared at each other for a long moment before they both burst into laughter.

That laughter was contagious, and I couldn't stop myself from joining, mortified with the spit that bubbled past my teeth and down my chin as a result.

Before I could get enough control over my arm to cover it, Juan reappeared and ran his thumb over my chin, silencing the laughter around us with the entirely too-sweet and too-familiar gesture.

"Christ almighty." Jim shook his head, turning to pour himself another cup of coffee. "I knew yuns two was gettin' doe-eyed, but shyit. What the hell kind of way ye' think this is gonna' work out for either of yuns when we're fixin' to send her happy ass through time?"

I rolled my eyes, attempting to uncurl my fingers and failing. "That's none of your business."

"Oh it ain't?" he huffed. "This big ole' summbitch is s'posed to lead us through Panama to find Izzy and Bud. How's he gonna' do that with his head stuck up his ass after you've sailed off?"

"I'm coming with," I said simply.

"No you're not," all three men said in almost perfect unison.

For as much as I wanted to argue, I couldn't right then. Even if my jaw wasn't clamped shut, the muscles in my entire body began to seize, forcing me to squeeze my eyes closed and focus solely on maintaining my breathing.

"They's a bath tub up in one of them cabins up there," Jim said. "We should put on some water and fill it. That orta' help some."

Before I could insist they didn't need to bother themselves with a bath and that the pill would kick in any moment, the three of them were moving around me, the clang of cookware and the sound of water being poured filling the galley.

By the time I was able to unclench, three large pots of water were steaming on the stove and all three men were staring worriedly and silent back at me.

"Still alive," I assured them, smiling despite every muscle in my jaw protesting the motion. I ran both hands over the moisture at my chin, utterly embarrassed.

"This will be ready in a few minutes," Bruce said. "I'll have some of the kitchen staff carry it up."

"Thank you." I stood on shaking legs, shooing all three men where they attempted to catch me. "If it's alright with you," I said to Bruce, wincing as I untied my apron, "and if I live, I'd like to come down more often. I've never been much of a cook and I would love to learn more."

He smiled. "Let's get you better first. Once you're up for it, I'd be happy to teach you anything you want to know. It's been a pleasure talking to you this morning."

"You too, Bruce."

My arms were on fire as I pulled the apron off and turned toward Jim. "You know, I think I'd enjoy being a part of your morning smack talk. I like it down here."

Jim chuckled. "Oh, I knew you was a gossip the minute you stepped off that boat. We gonna' have us a good time once you get better." He affectionately brushed a hair away from my face. "I'm serious now. You take your time gettin' well. Dark room, no stimuli."

He narrowed his eyes at Juan. "And yes, by stimuli, I mean you. I don't wanna' see her nowheres but a bed for the next several days. You might be big, but I'm scrappy and I could still whoop ye' if I had to. Got it?"

Laughing, Juan nodded, and the moment he scooped me up into his arms, I melted into them, my aching body going limp against his as he carried me out of the galley.

"You promised me an explanation about this mysterious tattoo of yours," I said, snuggling into his chest to savor the closeness before he would inevitably put me down. "I have one too, you know."

"I know. I saw it," he confessed, starting up the stairwell.

"You saw my ankle?" I teased. "How very scandalous for a gentleman."

He pressed his cheek against my temple to whisper, "I am no gentleman, *mi paloma*."

My temple was officially my favorite part of my body, particularly when he replaced his cheek with his lips for a fleeting second. The softness of them lingered and goosebumps erupted over my arms and along the back of my neck.

"You don't call me Joseph around the others," he whispered.

I smiled up at him. "It didn't feel right... Feels... I don't know, like something just between us... something I don't want to share with anyone else just yet."

"I like that." He held me closer and inhaled my hair. "Christ, how do you manage to smell like this?"

"Smell like what?" I asked, yawning as my eyelids grew heavy with the medicine. "Bread and coffee?"

"Like..." he inhaled again, resting his brow against the side of my head so his exhale skated over my ear. "Daisies..."

I grinned. "Very expensive perfume. How do you always smell like almonds?"

"I smell like almonds?" he asked, chuckling.

"In a good way," I assured him as he came out of the stairwell and into the corridor. "You smell like... the taste of amaretto. Almonds and cherries and a hint of wood..."

He adjusted my weight in his arms. "My father bought a case of soap from a Frenchman before we shipped out. I hadn't realized it smelled like almonds."

"I like it," I said, taking in the corridor and frowning. "Where are you taking me? *You* can't bathe me, you know."

"I can't?" He laughed. "I'm taking you to your sister. I assume you have no qualms with her assisting you in the bath?"

"So, no sunrise then?"

"Not today, Cecelia." Again he pressed his lips against my temple. "There are plenty more sunrises between here and Panama, and I mean to share a great deal of them with you once you are well."

Chapter Fifteen

Alaina

Kyle's condition was worsening again. He'd woken up in a tremendous amount of pain, his fist curled tightly into the blankets on the bed as he buried his face against the mattress to muffle his cries.

We'd tried to give him more Valium but he'd refused it, choosing instead to writhe in agony rather than take the risk of developing a dependency to Valium resemblant of his father's alcoholism.

Lilly, Fetia, and I surrounded him, massaging what we could in an attempt to relieve his pain. Magna had her nose buried in a book on Pacific Island plant history, searching for a poison similar to strychnine that might've been used that could explain his ongoing symptoms. Where Cece could potentially develop tetanus, he couldn't because of his recent vaccination, so we had to assume whatever was mixed with the bacteria was setting off their early symptoms.

Nothing we did would help him, and I couldn't help but worry Cece might be experiencing the same—or worse—wherever she and Juan Jr. had ended up.

It had been hours since I left them and the sun had sufficiently risen. I was torn between comforting Kyle and seeking out my sister.

Luckily, the door opened and she appeared before I was forced to make the decision, wrapped in the arms of Juan Jr. with a smile plastered across her face. That smile faded when she took in Kyle's twisted form on the bed.

"What's wrong?" she asked.

"Muscle cramps and more spasms," Magna said, frowning over her book. "Do you have them, too?"

"She does," Juan answered for her, his fingers curling into a fist against her legs.

Cece shook her head. "Not like that, I don't." She focused on Kyle. "The crew is pouring us a hot bath. He should get in first."

Juan frowned down at her. "But it will cool before you've had a chance—"

"Jack," she continued, ignoring his would-be protest, "the tub is down the hall and should be just about ready. Can you carry him?"

"I can walk," Kyle growled against the mattress, awkwardly sliding his knees beneath him.

"No you can't," she argued. "Not if your legs feel anything like mine. Now's not the time to be proud. Did you take another pill?"

Jack was already at the side of the bed, preparing to lift Kyle with an arm beneath his torso.

"No, and if *your* legs are this bad," Kyle winced, allowing Jack to hoist him up, "you should get in first."

"Take a pill, Kyle," she insisted. "It's the only thing keeping you alive."

"I don't want it."

She rolled her eyes. "I don't care. You're taking it and then you're getting in that tub first."

I'd been in the single tub the ship had, and I knew both of them were small enough to fit inside it—if only to be a little cramped. "You *both* are getting in," I said, standing. "You can wear your breeches and you can wear your shift." I handed a half pill to Jack before spinning back around. "Juan, I'm sure you have plenty of work to do on deck. Terrence and I can take it from here."

Terrence had already gotten the same idea and was out of his seat moving toward them.

"Wouldn't want you to catch a glimpse of my scandalous ankles again," Cece remarked, bouncing her brows at him. "Thank you for today. I'll see you soon?"

He smiled and nodded, reluctantly transferring her tiny body into Terrence's outstretched arms.

He bowed to me. "If you should need anything…" He stole a worried glance at my sister. "Anything at all… Please do not hesitate to send for me."

"We will," I assured him, turning him toward the door. "Thank you for taking care of her this morning."

When I turned back, my heart lightened at the sight of Kyle and Cece in Terrence and Jack's arms.

"He take the pill?" I asked, feeling again like an overbearing parent with two rebelling children.

Jack nodded.

"Good." My shoulders relaxed a little. "I'll grab some fresh bandages for when you both get out."

"Race ya there," Cece said, forcing a smile though I could see her jaw muscles were clamped tight around it.

She'd just medicated and she was still in pain… and I was terrified.

Both of them submerged to their necks and looking like a couple of toddlers in the steaming tub, I shooed Terrence and Jack out of the small cabin so only Fetia and I remained kneeling at each end of the basin.

Cece's eyes were closed and she tilted her head back against the tub's edge to let out a long breath. "Do you remember when we used to take baths together like this, A.J.?"

I laid a wet washcloth over her forehead and chuckled. "I do… you used to kick your little legs to keep me from stretching mine out. You were so tiny but you somehow managed to hog the whole damn tub."

"She still hogs the whole tub," Kyle teased, his eyes closed and head rested similarly at the opposite end.

"Still would kick my legs to get more room if I could move them," she bantered, flashing her teeth in a genuine smile. "Are you uncomfortable?"

"No," he said with a sigh, "I don't think I've ever been more comfortable in my life."

"I am going to find Bruce and Jim and Juan and kiss them right on the lips for this when we get out." She pulled one hand out of the water to expose Juan's ring still loosely fitted around her pointer finger.

"You're both getting another half a Valium and going straight to bed in a dark room when you get out," I informed her. "You can kiss them tomorrow. I thought you were going to give that back?"

The flattened white sleeves on her shoulders peeked over the water's surface as she shrugged and held the ring against her lips. "I changed my mind."

"I told you I don't want any more Valium," Kyle said, opening his eyes. "I'll take it if it's life or death, but if it's manageable, I'd prefer not to take anything. We don't have enough for both of us."

I groaned. "Kyle, honey, you need it."

Cece smiled, moving her leg beneath the water. "We won't be addicts. We'll just be fun for a few days."

"Said every addict in history," Kyle retorted. "Is that Juan Jr.'s ring?"

She smoothed it over her bottom lip and grinned. "Yes."

"It looks good on you." He put his hand over Fetia's where she was caressing his cheek and met my eyes. "Even if it doesn't quite fit."

I sighed as I caught his meaning. He'd been much more observant than I'd given him credit for in his Valium induced state the day before when Cece and I were speaking of Juan Jr.

I didn't want to be the bad guy. I just wanted to look out for Maddy. Neither of them could understand that… They didn't know her.

"I'm going to have to put it on a chain or a string," Cece said, oblivious to Kyle's undertone as she lowered her hand just beneath the water to hug the ring to her chest. "I don't want to lose it."

"Juan Josef sent a whole trove of jewelry to that room we're staying in," he informed her. "I'm sure there's something in there you could use."

He frowned down at the water. "Is it terrible that I'm kinda' glad Izzy wasn't on the ship to experience the attack? I mean…" He pursed his lips. "Juan Josef is an asshole, but… she would've been scarred for life if she'd been here to see what we saw. And, brutal as he might be, I don't think he'll do anything to scar her. You know?"

"He scarred you," I noted, remembering the whip slashing into the skin on his back and shuddering.

"Yes, but he only did that because we were plotting to escape when he needed us. He was desperate. And he was only ever evil when we threatened to disrupt his mission. I wonder, if we'd just been compliant, would he have done any of it?"

Maria burst suddenly through the door, cutting conversation short as she wildly scanned the room. I might've seen steam pouring from her nostrils had her temper been any more evident. "Kreese is not in here?"

"No." I frowned. "I haven't seen him since the night of the attack."

…when I had to turn him away in tears and it had nearly ripped the heart out of my chest. I left that little detail out, of course.

"That makes two of us," she growled, closing the door to lean back against it. "¡Ese hijo de puta! He's avoiding me."

Realization washing over her features as she took in the tub and its occupants, she shook her head and straightened. "I'm sorry. How are you two feeling?"

"Good, all things considered," Cece assured her, eyes closed as she rested her head once more against the back of the tub. "*Why* is Chris avoiding you?"

With her spine pressed against the door, Maria slid down it to curl her knees into her chest. "I imagine for the same reason he's been avoiding me for months now. These stupid new memories."

Dunking the washcloth back in the warm water, I repositioned it over Cece's forehead. "He just needs some time," I attempted to reason. "He'll bounce back."

"I don't think so," she grumbled. "Not every love story has a happy ending. I think mine is over and he is avoiding me because he doesn't have the balls to tell me it is over."

"You love him?" Fetia asked in perfect English, her fingertips lazily caressing Kyle's arm where it was draped over the side of the tub.

"Sí. Of course I love him."

"Then not over," Fetia said simply.

Maria frowned at her. "Oh yeah? And what would *you* do if one day Kyle just stopped looking at you?"

Fetia's face lit up in a wide grin. "I make him look. Show him love he can see."

"Is that right?" Kyle laughed, tilting his head toward hers to press their temples together. "What exactly would you show me, my Fetia?"

"I show you food I cook just for you. I show you why you look first time; tell you of first night we spend together… I show you laughing and dancing and happy together." She laid a kiss on his brow. "I show you baby we make in my belly. I show you…" She bit her lower lip and leaned in to whisper in his ear, prompting a scandalous giggle to escape him. "I make you look. Yes?"

Grinning, he nodded. "Yes, I would look."

"Jesus, how are you so goddamn insightful for so young a person?" Maria snarled. "What are you, seventeen? Eighteen?"

Fetia blushed. "No matter. Show him love he can see. Not argue. Not angry. Not worry. If he not look, then it over."

Cece removed the washcloth from her head and sat forward, extending it to Kyle. "I don't think I've ever heard you speak, Fetia. If I didn't already think you were perfect, I certainly do now. Where on Earth did you find her, Kyle?"

"Tahiti," he said proudly. "And she's mine, you can't have her." He tilted his head back and placed the washcloth over his eyes. "She has a point, Maria. We've all been under a lot of stress, but it's still important to laugh or smile here and there to remind us of what we're doing all this for. It can't all be doom and gloom, you know? When was the last time you two laughed? Reminded yourselves of what brought you together in the first place?"

Maria let out a long, heavy breath. "I don't even know… When we went back, it was all research and the surgery and recovery… and then we had to worry about the FBI and Dahlia and Liam and getting home… and then we came here and there was the escape and the Nikora… we haven't had fun in a very long time."

"So make some time for fun," Cece said, adjusting her leg and forcing Kyle to groan as he was forced to move as well. "Life's too short. You could turn up with an arrow in your foot trying to make the most of whatever minutes, hours, or days you have left."

"You're not going to die of *tetanus*," Maria informed her, "so long as you continue to take antibiotics and sedatives. It'll be a rough few weeks for you, not so bad for him since he's had the shot," she motioned to Kyle, "but you *can* survive it."

"How do you know?" Cece asked.

Maria flipped her hair over her shoulder and stood. "My father grew up in a very remote and poor part of Cuba. He got tetanus from a cut on his arm when he was a boy. He had the scar all his life. His parents used opium and alcohol to keep his muscles relaxed and they cleaned the wound twice a day. He said it was the most pain he ever felt in his life, but he lived. So will you."

Cece sat forward with a splash, a lightbulb going off in her brain. "Laudanum… Laudanum was made from opium and alcohol and they prescribed it for just about everything in this century. I bet there's some on this ship. These pills won't last more than a few days at the rate we're taking them but enough Laudanum might be just as effective… I could ask Juan—"

"*I'll* ask him if we have any once you're tucked in somewhere," I assured her, placing a hand on her shoulder to ease her back down. "You relax. No more excitement for either of you for a few days… that *includes* Juan Jr."

Chapter Sixteen

Alaina

Once I'd gotten Cece and Kyle each into a dark, quiet room, I was able to procure three bottles of Laudanum from the infirmary.

Juan Jr. informed me they kept a case of it there, and I'd been surprised to find out we even had an infirmary on the ship. Aside from a few medical tools covered in dust and the case of Laudanum that had already been rifled through by some of the crew, it could've easily been mistaken for any other sleeping cabin… which is probably why none of us knew it existed.

I was on my way to deliver the Laudanum and attempt to figure out how much of a dose Kyle and Cece might need when I ran into Chris coming down the stairwell.

"Maria's looking for you," I said, instantly regretting the harshness in my tone in my attempt to make our encounter brief and painless.

He tucked his hands into his pockets and stared down at his feet as he blocked the path back up. "Al…"

"Chris, please…" I shook my head. "I don't want to turn you away again."

"Then don't," he all but begged as his eyes met mine. "Our marriage—our goddamn life—is worth fighting for and if I'd been thinking clearly the first time around—if I'd been able to see what I was giving up on, I would've fought harder for it."

I hugged the Laudanum bottles against my chest to keep myself from hugging him at the sight of his watering eyes. "We grew apart, love. We've been over this. We weren't happy together, and we both grew into better people—happier people—once we were separated. You told me as much before you left."

"And I meant it," he assured me, "until the new memories showed up and I saw what we became... saw what it was to be happy with you past Evelyn... It's not the same. Nothing will ever be the same as us."

"Chris, you have a woman that loves you more than life itself wandering this ship in search of you. Please, don't give her up because of these new memories, especially when we're planning to change it all back. For her sake, you have to let this go."

"You think I haven't tried?" He ran a hand over his face. "Of course I've tried. I've told myself we're changing it back over and over and over to no avail. I told myself she meant more to me... tried with everything I have to love her the way I do you. The last thing in the world I want is to be standing here begging you while I knowingly string along a woman who deserves the world. I don't want to be this guy, Al... but I can't help it. Maybe the new memories hit me harder because I went back through... or maybe you just haven't acknowledged them because of everything that's happened here with the babies and Juan Josef... but standing here looking at you—even as you prepare to turn me away—is more home to me than anywhere else in the whole goddamn world. I can't love her the way she deserves when you are still my home. And I can't deny that any longer."

"The new memories aren't real, though," I attempted to convince him. "Much as I would love to be the girl in them, that's not how things happened."

"It *is* how it happened and the memories are real. You can deny it all you want, Al, but you *are* that girl. You're my Ally, the same one who cooked a lasagna at 3am when we'd stayed up all night talking in bed one night and got hungry; who forced me to dance with her whenever a Billie Holiday song came on—even if that meant dancing in the cereal aisle at the grocery store; the one that would make me hide dishes in the oven when surprise company showed up because we'd been too preoccupied with each other to bother with them after dinner. You're my wife—my beautiful, neurotic, playful, funny, and talented wife, and I want you back. You might not look at me with the same desire you do him, but you loved me and I loved you and I can still feel that."

He shook his head, inhaling deeply through his nose. "Jesus, I feel that all the way in my bones and have ever since I bumped into you in that bathroom all those years ago. Tell me you weren't happy; tell me we'd grown apart when we stayed up all night making love to one another before we got on that airplane… Tell me what I felt when we laid in each other's arms on the living room floor afterward wasn't real…"

"It didn't really happen like that," I insisted, despite the memory of it flooding the forefront of my mind to make me feel the way he'd touched me in the new memories on every inch of my skin.

He blinked the welling tears from his eyes. "If you want to deny who we became once we were actually capable of letting go of Evelyn's death, then I can't stop you. But those memories will find you at some point. When they do, I need you to know there is nothing—not the time you spent with Jack or the babies or the fact that you choose him still—that would ever make me love you any less; that would ever make me turn away. I'm sorry if it's inconvenient, and I'm sorry if it makes me look desperate, but I'm not sorry for what I feel. I want *you,* Al. And maybe I'll never have you again because of the way I fucked everything up the first time around, but that won't stop me from waiting for you to change your mind."

I wanted to cry; for him and for all those new memories I couldn't bring myself to acknowledge as real. I knew I'd been happy in them, but it was pointless to accept any of it as reality. I *remembered* reality, and for me, there was no way we could ever mend what we broke the first time.

For as much as I still loved him, I couldn't give him what he wanted. Jack was my husband now and I could never go back to the person I'd been with Chris.

"I won't change my mind," I said with finality, hating myself for having to be cold, but not willing to offer him any shred of hope for a future we'd never have together. "And before you make such a rash decision to spend your life waiting for something I'll never do, perhaps you should open your eyes to what's in front of you. Figure out what it was that drove you to Maria in the first place—I know it wasn't just attraction; you wouldn't do that to her —and see if you can get it back. You don't have to get married; hell, you don't even have to sleep in the same room… But don't cut her out when she would literally make the same argument as to why she'd wait forever for you. Maybe the new memories were stronger in the future, and maybe you just need time here to remember the original version and what made you fall in love with her so quickly. I won't change my mind."

I moved around him and began climbing the stairs when he added over his shoulder, "And if he dies here?"

I froze on the step, a sliver of ice sliding down my spine. "He's not going to die, Chris… We're not going to let him."

He kept his back to me, but I could see the rigidity in his muscles as he flexed his fingers at his sides. "But if he did… How could I move on if there was even the tiniest chance you might come back?"

"If he died," I said, the ice in my spine slipping out into the words as they were made defensive by his almost hopefulness that Jack might be killed, "my heart would die with him. I will never come back to you, Chris. That decision is final. Move on."

And at that, I hurried up the stairs before my anger forced me to say things I would regret.

Laudanum delivered and small doses administered to both our patients, it was determined that, since the babies still tended to wake on occasion at night, Terrence would spend the night watching over Cece in Juan Jr.'s room so she wouldn't be disturbed. Fetia and her father had done the same for Kyle, keeping him sedated in a dark, quiet room next door.

With Jim, Jack, Magna and Lilly still on the deck assisting with the clean up efforts and ship repairs, and both babies asleep in their cradle, I sat down with one of the history books, anxious to distract myself from my own thoughts.

'Make a list of places and ships Jack should avoid,' Cece's voice echoed in my mind, and I began the hunt.

I must've read an entire 700 page book cover to cover by the time Jack crawled in bed beside me.

"What's this?" he asked, plucking up the list of locations I'd jotted down.

"Places you could die," I said, curling both arms around his chest and clinging to him.

"I'm not going to die," he chuckled, smoothing a hand down my hair. "How are Cece and Kyle?"

"Sedated," I managed, face plastered against the warmth of his chest as I inhaled him. "Did you get the deck cleaned up?"

"Yes," he said, moving my books and papers to one side as he slid down onto his back on the bed with me still clamped to his torso. "Red, I'm not going anywhere. What's going on?"

"I just miss you," I mumbled against his shirt, squeezing him as if I could somehow get closer to him by doing so. "Things are hard enough as it is, but they're made that much harder when you're not with me."

He kissed the top of my head, tugging gently on one of my curls. "Much as I love it when you speak vaguely and squeeze the life out of me, I feel like I should ask you to elaborate. Did something happen?"

I sighed, loosening my grip to roll into his side. "Everything, Jack. Everything is just... slipping. Izzy going missing, Cece and Kyle getting sick... Chris... I just... it's all too much."

He swept his fingers up and down my spine. "Chris?"

I nodded, closing my eyes. "He can't let the new memories go. He's talking about leaving Maria… As if we didn't have enough to worry about…"

He made a noise in his throat. "I could go talk to him if you want me to?"

"And what would you say?" I groaned. "That he shouldn't be in love with me anymore because I love you? He knows that. There's literally nothing I can say to him or Maria or even Cece to give them the slightest clue as to what you and I have that makes it worth defending."

"Cece?" The muscles beneath me tensed. "She's made you defend our relationship as well?"

Rolling my eyes, I laid my cheek on his chest. "Well, no… but Maria did—accused me of mistaking affection for love—and Cece didn't exactly disagree."

"I don't know why you let that woman get under your skin." He chuckled, but then his chest froze mid-breath. "Unless she's made you question it, yourself? Are you regretting your decision? Is that what all that was about last night asking me to talk to you?"

"No," I assured him, laying a kiss against his collar. "Well… kind of, but we needed to talk about that. I just… I don't want to have to defend us anymore. And I absolutely hate hurting Chris. I was so glad when he found happiness with Maria. I felt like we could finally move past it… but now… Jesus, we're right back where we started and I'll have to hurt him all over again."

"No, you won't," he said, combing his fingers through my hair. "You don't have to do anything you don't want to. I'm here for the hard stuff too, you know. All you have to do is ask, and I can step up when you need to step down. As your husband and as the father of two babies who are beginning to pick up on our moves and actions, I have every right… particularly if he's professing his love for you and attempting to steal you away."

I nodded, glancing over at the cradle. "They really are growing too fast. Did I tell you Cecelia rolled onto her back earlier? And Zachary peed on me this morning when I was changing him. Pretty sure he was aiming because he laughed like a hyena as he was doing it."

He snorted. "Little shithead did that to me yesterday, too. I told you he was gonna' be bad."

I sighed, closing my eyes. "They shouldn't be growing up in all this chaos. They're beginning to understand us, and I want better for them."

"We'll give them better," he promised, resting his chin against the top of my head. "Your sister and Kyle are gonna' pull through, we're going to get Izzy and Bud back, and we'll take them home to live out a normal life. Let me handle Chris."

"The last time you *handled* Chris, you both came out bloodied and bruised. I don't want that."

I felt him grin against the back of my head. "I promise not to punch him this time."

Chapter Seventeen

Chris

In the hull with only the livestock for company, Chris fought an invisible opponent with his sword, practicing his advances, lunges, and fades.

Much as he'd been disappointed in John Edgecumb, he missed the man's company; missed being *Der Mutige* among the other men and sparring with them in the mornings.

After his encounter with Alaina, he'd spent the week alone in the hopes he might return to the others resembling something more like the man he'd once been. With no brain injury now to blame his muddled thinking on, he hated the person he'd become.

He hated himself for what he'd said to Alaina; hated himself more for being pathetic enough to wish for Jack's death, and even more for stringing along Maria. There was a constant ache inside him; a longing to go home, but the word itself had no meaning.

For so long, home had been Alaina, and almost immediately after, he'd found it in Maria... But now, home was nowhere. And foolish as it was at his age, he felt the loneliness of an orphan, lost in the world with no place to turn.

Bleh. He even hated the way he felt sorry for himself.

Dropping the sword, he collapsed against a bale of straw to swig from a bottle of whiskey that had been his only companion that week.

"Ay beanstalk!" Jim called, pushing the squeaky wooden cart he used to clean the pigpen. "Where ye' been? Kyle's up and movin' round the last few days; good as new from the looks of him. Been askin' for ye.' I tell ye, that kid impresses me a little more every time I see him." He frowned as he took in Chris's sunken shoulders. "What's got your panties in a bunch?"

He blew out a breath. "Nothing. Just feeling sorry for myself, I suppose."

"Welp," Jim parked the cart and pulled on a pair of gloves. "We all got to do it some time, don't we? Ye' beatin' yourself up cause that girl's gettin' worse up there or cause ye' wished it was somebody else laid up in that bed… somebody sharin' a different bed with a certain someone ye' used to be married to?"

"Both," he hiccuped, plucking his sword up off the ground to rest it across his knees.

Cece had gotten considerably worse after her trip to the galley. They'd been dosing her with Laudanum to keep her body relaxed, but every time they attempted to wean her off, she clenched right back up. He couldn't watch it and not relive the moment on the stairwell where he should've insisted she go back to the room.

"Yeah, I figured." Jim grabbed a shovel from the wall and leaned his forearm against its handle. "Look, I'm gonna' shovel some shit here, and I can do it quietly or I can tell ye' what I think while I do it. It's up to you."

"By all means," Chris said, waving the bottle out defeatedly before bringing it back to his lips. "Fire away."

"Alright then." Jim hopped over the fence of the pen and dug the shovel in. "First of all, ye' ain't gonna' find no answers at the bottom of that bottle, that's for damn sure. I know cause I spent a whole lotta' years lookin' myself. What ye'll find there is a surefire way to make matters worse."

He lobbed a shovelful of waste into the cart. "I think ye' lost your way is all. Women got a way of makin' us think there ain't nothin' else out in the world for us *but* them women. They's a whole hell of a lot more to it though, and a man without a place in this world ain't worth a good Got damn to none of them women he's chasin after. You gotta' find your *own* way, buddy; a way that don't necessarily land ye' between a purdy set of legs right away, if ye' catch my drift. Figure out what ye' want for yourself that ain't a woman and go get it. Then, once ye' got a life of your own to be proud of, ye' can find ye' some legs to wrap around ye'."

Chris laughed. "A life of my own. Everything I have done with my life has been for her."

"You ain't got to tell me that, bud. I could see it from a mile away. And now look at ye. She done run off and ye' cain't see up from down cause ye' head's been stuck up her ass for so long."

He grunted as he unloaded another shovelful. "What'd ye' want with your life *before* her?"

Chris shook his head. "I don't even remember. It's been so long."

"Well," Jim drawled. "Ye' gonna' have to figure out somethin' big man, 'for ye' drown in your own tears. And ye' ain't gonna fix your problems sittin' there grumblin' *'I don't know'* and drinkin' yourself stupid. What ye' *like* doin?"

"I don't know… Building things…" He drummed his fingers over the helm of his sword. "Swinging this thing around."

Jim grinned, leaning over the fence post. "Well, there's a start. Figure out what ye' life's got to look like for you to be proud of it. Where ye' gonna swing your little sword around and build stuff, then ye' can figure out who ye' want beside ye' when you do it."

Chris nodded. "Thanks Jim."

"That said," Jim sucked on his teeth. "Ye' need to sort out ye' business with the other one. I know you know it, but ye' ain't makin' it no easier for yourself or nobody else puttin' it off. She's up there fixin' ye' supper right now, thinkin' that's gonna' make things better."

Chris ran his hand down his face, guilt welling in his gut. "I hate doing this to her. I was hoping, if I stayed down here long enough, I'd fix myself somehow; go back to her looking a little more like the man I was before I got these memories."

"She ain't goin' nowheres." He pursed his lips. "She might give ye' the hairy eyeball and call ye' evra name in the book, but she ain't goin' nowhere. They's nothin' wrong with askin' her to give ye' space to work out your self." He chuckled. "Just… ask her when I ain't nowhere close by. That woman'd scare the dark out of the devil."

Chris sighed. "I should've waited before starting anything with her. Given it time."

"You ain't the type." Jim shooed a few pigs from the corner. "From the looks of ye', I'd guess you was one of them boys growin' up that always had ye' a girl. Jumped from one to the other without comin' up for air. I'd bet money you ain't been single longer than a few months in your whole life."

Chris chuckled. "I got my first girlfriend in 7th grade and haven't been single since."

"Well, no wonder you ain't got no sense." Jim lobbed another shovelful over the fence, then hoisted himself up to sit on the post and pull a cigarette from behind his ear. "Your brain ain't never been the one doin' the thinkin' for ye'."

Lighting the cigarette and letting it hang loosely from his lips, he hopped off the fence and motioned to the sword in Chris's lap. "You're pretty good with that thing. Wonder if ye' might show me a thing or two once ye' get your head on straight. Might come in handy when we get off the ship and don't have no modern guns."

Chris smiled, taking the familiar weight of it in his hands. "I'm out of practice, but I'd be happy to show you what I know."

"Go on and deal with your business first. I'll be around."

Rehearsing the right words to say to Maria, Chris was halfway up the steps when he ran into Jack on the stairwell.

"I've been looking for you," Jack informed him, blocking the path up. "I'm assuming you'll know why."

With a sigh, Chris leaned his hip against the railing and crossed his arms. "She sent you?"

"No. I came on my own," Jack said pointedly. "She's got enough on her plate and we've already been through this once. I don't dislike you, Chris, but I won't let you do this again. It was hard enough on her the first time."

Chris laughed out loud, the whiskey obviously still heating his blood. "Oh, was it hard on *her*, Jack? To turn away the husband that spent a year looking for her so she could snuggle up beside *you*? Forgive me for being so very insensitive to the difficulties you two must've gone through when I finally found my goddamn wife."

Jack took a deep breath. "She's *my* wife now. You gave her your consent to marry me, remember? And as her husband, it is my obligation to tell you to back off. She's got a sick sister and two babies to worry about, not to mention everything else we're about to face. I won't watch her cry because she's had to turn you away again on top of it."

"Oh fuck off, Jack," Chris spat hatefully. "I'm not going to beg for something she doesn't want to give and you don't need to come down here with your pompous ego puffed out like you're some goddamn hero. I said my piece to her and I'm done."

"You're done?" he echoed.

"Yes, Jack, you win." He ran his hand hard over his hair. "I had to at least try, and now that I have sufficiently failed, I'm done. So you can turn your little high horse around and fuck right off now."

Jack laughed, filling the step with his body as Chris moved to continue past him. "We're not done."

"The hell we're not," Chris growled. "Move."

Jack grinned and crossed his arms. "And who's got their ego puffed out now? You and I have done this, too. Don't let your wounded pride make us enemies again."

"*Again?*" Chris balked. "When were we ever not enemies? You stole my wife, asshole."

"And *you* busted my lip," Jack reminded him. "We're friends now and—"

"Oh ho no," Chris snorted. "You and I were never friends."

Jack held a hand over his heart in mock outrage. "And this after I carried you in my arms?" He clicked his tongue. "You reek of whiskey and loneliness, dickhead. Now's not the time for you to start ostracizing the people that care about you. Let me help."

Chris tilted his head back and groaned. "Don't you dare stand there and act like you care so you can feel better about yourself. I don't need a self-important friend to make me feel better about losing my self-important wife. I'd rather reek."

"Oh, we're the self important ones?" Jack sneered. "Funny. Neither of us is keeping a second option waiting."

At this, Chris's fingers curled tightly into his palms. "Move."

Jack set his feet. "No."

Growling, Chris smeared a hand down his face. "I've given you my wife. What the hell else do you want from me?"

Jack lowered his shoulders and shook his head. "Alaina cares about you—*I* care about you, and I can't stand to see you bury yourself in misery like this. Maybe it is for self-important reasons, but the last thing either of us want is the anguish we would suffer if you did something stupid."

"Rest easy," Chris snarled. "I'm not going to kill myself."

"No?" Jack asked. "You're drunk at four o'clock in the afternoon and have spent the last several days avoiding everyone. What the hell else are we supposed to think?"

"I'm wallowing," Chris assured him, "not preparing to hang myself. Jim already did the pep-talk, and as you can see, I am now making my way up to deal with my life. For the final time, Jack, fuck off and move. If I want your help, I'll ask for it."

Bowing his head once, Jack turned to his side, allowing Chris the room to move past him. "I'll be here anytime you need it."

Climbing the steps two at a time, Chris grumbled to himself, his spine stiffening when Jack yelled up the stairwell, "because we *are* friends, dickhead!"

One down… one more awful conversation to go… He might've considered remaining in the stairwell a little longer. The awkward pissing contest with Jack would be a hell of a lot easier than confronting Maria.

His shoulders tensed as he made his way down the corridor to his cabin and he winced as he pushed the door open to find a table with two place settings of food set out.

Maria jumped from where she'd been lighting a candle between the plates. "Mi amor! I was just about to come look for you. Sit down. Bruce and I made you smoked tuna."

"Maria," he sighed. "We have to—"

"Ay, you look terrible, Superman." She clicked her tongue and pulled out a chair, motioning for him to sit in it. "Sit down and eat. You've drank yourself ugly."

He sat down, but made no move to touch the food. "Maria, really, I need to—"

"You need to eat," she cut in, taking the seat opposite him, "and *we* need to laugh. The world has gotten too serious for us both. Look at that scowl on your face! You are too handsome, mi amor, to be looking so ugly."

"Maria—"

She smiled playfully. "Do you remember that night in Albuquerque, when—"

He pounded his fist on the table, rattling the plates. "Dammit, I'm trying to tell you something important!"

She sat back in her chair and crossed both arms over her chest, one eyebrow arched high on her forehead. "Okay, Kreese. You want to do this now? Go ahead. Punch your little fist down on the table and tell me all the things I already know."

He blew out a shaky breath, splaying his fingers wide on the table. "I'm sorry. I just… I can't do this to you any longer."

She plucked up her wineglass and narrowed her eyes over the rim. "What is it, exactly, you think you are doing to me? Eh? You think I didn't know when you were all *'Oh Maria, there is only you… Oh Maria, you are everything,'* that you didn't still love her? Eh? That you weren't using me as a fallback to her? I told you as much. Over and over, I told you this would happen, but *'no Maria, I love only you. My heart belongs to you! Oh, Maria, let me prove you're wrong and I love you and I want to marry you more than I've ever wanted anything.'* ¡Hijo de puta, comemierda! Go ahead and pound your fist on the table and tell me I was right all along."

"I should've waited," he said softly. "But I—"

"Ay, but you couldn't wait, could you?" she taunted. "Not when John Edgecumb was holding my hand and threatening to love me. Eh? You couldn't have enough of me when I was someone else's!" She smirked. "Maybe I will go find another man and you will love me again. That's how it really works with you. Isn't it? You didn't touch that wife of yours at all; *couldn't look at her as someone you needed to touch.* That's what you told me. But now that someone else is touching her, it's all you can think about. And *oh, poor Maria... I can't do this to you no more!*"

"You done?" he asked, instantly regretting it.

"*Am I done?*" she scoffed, sitting forward. "You come in here to tell me we are finished after you have dragged me behind you like some dog on a leash and you have the balls to ask me if *I'm* done?" She flung the wine from her glass to splash it across his face. "Yes, I am done. Take your stupid little ring," she pulled it off her finger and spiked it on the table, "and your big man attitude and get the hell out of my life."

Calmly, he took the napkin from the table and wiped the liquid from his face, holding in a laugh as he watched her seethe across from him. "Now that you've had this entire conversation for us both, can I say what I came in here to say to you?"

Her eyes watered but her lips remained in a straight line. "I swear to God, Kreese, if you spout off some bullshit about how you still love me, I will tear out my eardrums."

"I do, though," he said softly. "Very much. The thought of losing you absolutely kills me, but—"

"But." She snarled.

"*But,*" he continued firmly. "I have not taken the time I needed to put myself back together after I lost my wife. I rushed into things because I was terrified you'd marry John Edgecumb and I'd never get the chance to be with you otherwise. That wasn't fair to you, and I can never express how sorry I am for it. I came in here to tell you that I won't ask you to wait—you deserve better and no one would blame you if you went out looking for it—but if you did wait... If you gave me the chance to put myself back together... To figure out who I am without her and what I want... Give me a chance to get over her... I think what we could have would be amazing."

She shook her head, hurriedly swatting a tear from her cheek. "That is the very definition of asking me to wait, estúpido. Get out of my room. I don't want to look at your face right now."

"Maria—"

"Get out," she said with finality. "I am done."

Chapter Eighteen

Alaina

I sat at the side of Juan Jr.'s bed, my throat heavy as I watched Terrence, once again, administer another dose of Laudanum to my sister. We'd let it begin to wear off to feed her broth, but her entire body had seized and we'd only been able to give her a half bowl before we'd been forced to stop and sedate her again.

This was becoming a nightly occurrence.

Where Kyle had gotten better after forty-eight hours and had been able to be weaned off the Laudanum, Cece had worsened over the past ten days. It had to be tetanus causing her symptoms to last so far past his, and as I watched her skin pale and her muscles deteriorate, I was horrified she might not make it through.

Juan Jr. had joined us to look over her, as he did every evening after dinner, his face distorted as Terrence poured the liquid past her lips and held her there until she'd swallowed.

"She is withering away," he observed, shaking his head. "How is she to fight without nourishment? I can nearly make out her bones beneath her skin."

"We'll have to keep trying," I said. "Keep bringing her to the edge of consciousness, enough to get a bit of food down her...

until she's able to stay awake without her muscles clenching. She's fought it this long… She has to make it."

"She'll make it." Terrence agreed, gently laying Cece back down as the Laudanum instantly relaxed her muscles. "How much longer before we reach Panama?"

Juan Jr. sat back in his chair, opening the journal he often wrote in during his visits across his lap. "Two more weeks if we continue to encounter good winds."

Terrence nodded, stretching his arms over his head. "I've had enough of this century… No offense."

"None taken," Juan Jr. said with an uncustomary smile. "I've had enough of it myself."

"You're really going to let Gabriel take us back to the storm?" I asked. "You won't try to stop us?"

He shook his head, his eyes returning to the bed as he mindlessly dipped his quill in ink at the table beside him. "Would that I could adjust course and take you there now, but I've already moved too far south in order to catch the eastern winds. I've no wish to see her suffer any longer than she must. You have my word I'll not interfere in your journey home."

I smiled, following his gaze to Cece's face where she'd relaxed against the pillows. "She wanted to see Panama; was determined to get off the ship with you and help you find George Bennet before we could go back… She wanted to make it so no one would lose anyone…"

"That's Cece," Terrence noted, climbing out of the bed. "Always trying to save the world." He stretched his back with a grunt. "I'm gonna go wash up and snag what's left of the wine from dinner. You two want me to bring anything back with me?"

"No thank you," I said, hurrying to the babies' baskets as Zachary began to squawk.

"I'll be back in a bit," he said.

Pulling Zachary up against my shoulder, I watched as he disappeared down the corridor, grateful he was with us.

We'd assumed, since she needed to be constantly supervised and undisturbed, Cece wouldn't be opposed to Terrence sleeping beside her at night. The babies couldn't be trusted to sleep in the same room without disturbing her, and I certainly didn't trust Juan Jr. to share the bed with her given the way he looked at her.

The babies and I spent most of the days and evenings alongside her, only leaving if Zachary and Cecelia got fussy or if I needed to eat, and always making sure someone was there to keep an eye on her in my place.

There was no shortage of volunteers.

Even outside our immediate group and Juan Jr., Cece was well-loved throughout the ship. Many of the shipmen made their way to the room on multiple occasions to check on her well-being and offer any assistance should she need it.

I couldn't help the pride that welled in my heart at the impression she'd made. She had been there for such a short amount of time and it seemed like the entire ship had fallen in love with her. Who wouldn't? She lit up every room she entered with that smile that was almost permanently affixed to her lips. I was anxious to see it again; to hear her voice… She *had to* recover.

"What was she like in her other life?" Juan Jr. asked, his gaze fixed upon her face. "Was she happier?"

I shrugged, balancing Zachary's legs on my knees to build his strength in them. He liked standing and insisted on being lifted into the position almost constantly. "It's hard to know which life made her happier. It's a very rare thing to see Cecelia McCreary with a frown on her face. She's a naturally happy person."

Juan scribbled something in his journal, grinning. "I noticed. Did she enjoy being a mother?"

I nodded, kissing Zachary on the forehead as he cooed at me. "Oh yeah. Cece was everything you could ever want in a mother; attentive, playful, loving while not being too overbearing… It's like she was born to be a mom and didn't even know it. She was just… natural. And Maddy developed faster because of her. She was so smart; far more advanced than other kids her age. She could carry on a conversation with an adult and hold their attention. And Cece beamed with pride. Maddy was her whole world."

"And the husband?" he asked. "He was a good father?"

"Owen?" I smiled. "He adored Maddy and would've spoiled her rotten were it not for Cece. Whatever she wanted, he gave her, but Cece always made sure Maddy was grateful for it. Together, they made good parents… balanced each other out."

His eyes remained on Cece's face, the quill in his hand dripping on the page beneath it. "And was he kind to her? Did she love him?"

"It seemed like it," I said, covering myself with the nursing blanket before I positioned Zachary at my breast. "They lived too far away for me to have any insight into their daily lives, but we spoke on the phone almost every day. Cece would never complain, even if things weren't perfect, but the bits and pieces I saw and heard, he seemed like he was good to her. And I know she loved him fiercely."

He pursed his lips. "How did they meet?"

I smiled at that, relaxing as Zachary latched on. "At the end of her senior year in high school, Cece went on this college tour—she *had* to go alone, mind you, none of us were allowed to influence her decision. She was valedictorian of her class and had no small selection of schools and scholarships to choose from. And the thing about Cece is she doesn't want anyone making decisions for her. I've never met anyone more independent. She'd been working at this pet store and saved up for a car just to be able to go on the trip herself. Made a calendar and spreadsheet of where she was headed and what she wanted to see at each. It seemed like every weekend in April and May she was off visiting a different school. My mother was a mess worrying about her."

I sat back in my seat and sighed. "Anyway, one of those schools was Ohio State University. They had this great veterinary science program she was interested in. And while she was out there, she met this girl who was also studying to be a veterinarian. They hit it off and the girl invited her to some party her sorority was throwing that night. It always struck me as odd that Cecelia agreed to go. She was never comfortable in a crowd."

I waved my hand to dismiss it. "Regardless, she went anyway; maybe she wanted to face her fears before college—she's like that, doesn't like being hindered in any way. Now, I don't know all the details because she refused to tell me, but I do know she met Owen at that party, and I know my adorable little sister—who had never had a drink in her life—got drunk for the first time while she was there."

"Yes, but do you know *how* she got drunk?" Chris asked from the doorway, causing my spine to stiffen. We'd been avoiding each other since our encounter on the stairwell more than a week ago.

"No…" I frowned at his all-too-comfortable demeanor, feeling slightly guilty for immediately checking to make sure the nursing blanket covered me. "I take it you do?"

He leaned against the doorframe, looking over her body in the bed with a hint of disgust on his features. "Owen told me at the wedding… It was him that was feeding her shots of tequila. Got her so drunk she could barely stand up. He had a bet with his fraternity brothers he'd take the *fresh bait* home that night… and he was all too proud to inform me he won that bet. That's why I didn't like him at first. Knowing she was just barely eighteen when he did that… it didn't sit right."

I stared up at him in disbelief. "You never told me that."

He shrugged. "What was the point? They'd already said their vows by the time he told me and you all seemed to like him. I wasn't going to spoil the wedding for you when it was only our second date."

"Why didn't you mention it afterwards?" I asked, feeling suddenly defensive that my little sister was the subject of such a nasty bet at such a young age. "Even once you and I were married?"

He shrugged. "Seemed irrelevant. Yes, it was disgusting of him, but he still went on to date and marry her. And eventually, after they'd had Maddy, he started to grow on me. She seemed happy. What would've been the point of bringing it up if it would only cause tension in an otherwise happy family?"

I stared at the bed, my fingers curling into fists. "She was a virgin when she left for Ohio…"

Chris ran a hand over his hair and blew out. "I didn't know that detail. Now, I *really* don't like him."

"Me neither," Juan Jr. chimed in.

"Oh," Chris blinked, wobbling a little as he focused on Juan. "Gabriel asked me to retrieve you. Says there's a storm coming."

Closing the journal, Juan gazed at my sister for a moment more. "This event… did she also attend it in the new memories?"

I chewed my lower lip as I considered it. "I'm not sure. If she did, she never mentioned it. She was very secretive with the colleges and she only told me about the party the first time because she'd spent the rest of the weekend with Owen…"

He nodded, rising to tuck the journal into his jacket and bow to each of us. "Very well. Good night, Alaina. Mr. Grace."

Chris placed a hand on Juan's shoulder before he could move past him into the hallway. "Juan, I was wondering if you might spar with me in the mornings? I've never seen anyone use a sword the way you do, and I could use the practice before we get off in Panama."

Juan promptly removed Chris's hand. "I am no teacher, Mr. Grace, but if you wish to join me before sunrise, I will attempt to show you a few things. Good evening to you." He bowed his head once more and hurried off.

And then we were alone together.

And the room felt smaller as Chris took Juan Jr.'s seat on the opposite side of the bed, his gaze heavy as it landed upon me.

I cleared my throat, adjusting Zachary beneath the blanket. "You look like you've had a few drinks yourself. Are you doing alright?"

Cupping his hands behind his head, he leaned back and propped one booted foot on the bed. "Does it matter?"

I groaned. "Does it matter to me that you're doing alright? Yes, as a matter of fact, it does. We've already done this whole hurt-feelings-tough-guy act once before, Chris. Please, don't make me do it again. Not now."

He raised an eyebrow. "I've simply come to check on my sister-in-law, Al. I'm not here to play the tough-guy with you.

Besides, you're the one sitting there all rigid and anxious… what is it you think I'm going to do?"

I frowned. "I don't know… Where's Maria?"

He shrugged. "If I had to guess, I'd say she's off flirting with random crewmen in an attempt to make me jealous."

I rolled my eyes as I pulled Zachary up to my shoulder to burp him. "Why do you do that?"

He raised his other foot onto the bed, crossing his ankles as he sank comfortably into the chair. "Do what?"

"Demonize the women you care about… Does it make you feel better about yourself?"

He laughed but there was no amusement in it. "I tell you I cannot help myself from loving you—despite my multiple attempts to stop it, give up a woman I care about because it is the right thing to do, willingly step aside at the request of the man who has replaced me as your husband, and still you accuse me of demonizing either of you to feel better about myself? Jesus, Al, who's demonizing who? And what did I do to become such a fucking monster to you?"

I covered Zachary's ears. "Keep your voice down."

He tilted his head back and let out a long breath. "Relax Alaina. I'm not going to beg you or pin you down and force you to be my wife like your body language indicates I might. I am stuck here alongside you until we get to Panama, whether you like it or not, and we can't very well avoid each other the whole time. I'll be out of your hair soon enough." He tilted his head toward Cece. "How's she doing?"

"Same," I said, rocking Zachary more to ease my own nerves than his stomach. "She tenses back up the minute we try to bring her out of it… and I don't know what else to do."

"You do know she can't die, right?" He lowered his hands onto his lap. "Whether you take Cecelia through time or Juan Josef kills George Bennet, all of this will cease to have existed… she'll be fine… might even wake up with no memory it ever happened. You don't need to worry so much. None of this is real. You know that, right? That nothing since Tahiti has been real? We're all going to wake up soon with completely different lives."

I hugged Zachary tighter. "You don't think she'll have two sets of memories like we do?"

"Not if she never gets on that yacht to come back with us." He removed his feet from the bed to sit forward in the chair, resting his elbows on his knees. "The original plan was to send Anna—not Bud. Maybe, without his involvement, we end up on a boat she can't hide in… or maybe my memories don't change to prevent me from thinking clearly, and I never leave that ring behind to cause her to become so suspicious in the first place. She doesn't remember the original… I can only assume it's because she wasn't here when we changed it. If we prevent her from coming through, maybe she won't remember this either."

I nodded, inspecting her tiny body beneath the blanket. "I kinda' feel guilty handing her back over to Owen after what you told me about the night they met. I never saw that side of him; never saw anything but a doting husband in him. You talked to him more than I did… Do you think he was a pig or was he just putting on a show in front of his fraternity?"

"I don't know, Al," he uttered. "He acted one way with the family and another when it was just the guys… hard to know which one was authentic, you know?"

I frowned. "What was he like when it was *just the guys*?"

He shrugged. "Oh, you know… he told perverted jokes, made backhanded comments about certain women… things like that. A lot of guys do, though. Doesn't mean they're pigs. Might just be some need to feel more masculine, particularly when he spent so much time secluded with two females at that campground."

Zachary let out a loud liquid belch and I quickly moved him to my lap to wipe the spit up from his mouth and chin.

I cursed myself for not spending more time with my sister to know exactly what kind of life she was living. "Did you ever get the impression he was mean to her?"

"No," he said softly, smiling at Zachary when I spun him around to stand wobbly on my thighs. "He might've been a dick around the guys, but never to her."

Zachary extended his slobber soaked hands toward him and babbled happily, kicking both legs as he inhaled and exhaled with excitement.

Chris chuckled. "His eyesight is getting better. You want me to take him so you can feed her?"

I pursed my lips, attempting to keep my grip on him as he squirmed. "Are you sober enough not to drop him?"

He laughed. "I didn't drink that much, Al. I promise, I wouldn't offer if I thought I'd drop him."

Cautiously, I stood and extended him across the bed, stifling a smile as Zachary giggled happily and a trail of spit bubbles immediately landed upon Chris's forearm.

I turned back to the baskets to collect Cecelia, surprised to find her eyes open. "You think you'll go back to feeling the way you did about Maria without the changed memories?"

He balanced Zachary on his legs the same way I had, smiling as he then attempted to jump against his grip. "God, I hope so. Contrary to what you might believe about me, I absolutely hate feeling this way. Hate the way you both look at me now… I don't want to be this person, you know."

"Me neither," I admitted, snuggling Cecelia against my cheek before I positioned her beneath the nursing blanket. "I wish I could give you what you want… be that woman again. But I can't."

"I know," he said, smiling as Zachary explored his vowel sounds rather loudly. "The heart wants what it wants, and I can't change yours any more than I can change mine. Much as I try to convince myself I might. What I said the other day… about Jack dying… I shouldn't have said it like that. It's not like I'm hoping for it to happen."

I felt my shoulders relax. "I knew what you meant by it and probably shouldn't have reacted the way I did. According to that chart, there's a very real chance he could die out here… and it's only natural to wonder what I'd do afterward, having been married to you once before. You and I have never been good at talking to each other."

"That's not true," he said, his green eyes focused on the wiggling baby in his hands. "We talked just fine… it was the arguing part we were never good at. One of us was always storming off to deal with our anger elsewhere." He swallowed and met my gaze. "Do you argue with him?"

I nodded. "There weren't many places to storm off to on that island, and Jack's not one to back down from an argument, so I had to learn how to bicker. So did you," I noted. "These walls are thin and I've heard you and Maria at each other's throats on more than one occasion."

Bouncing Zachary against his thighs, he laughed. "I tried to storm off a few times… she'd just follow me and get louder."

I glanced at Cece. "You think she and Owen argued very much? I never saw it if they did. Even during the time I spent up there, she never seemed to get angry with him."

"Oh, they argued," he assured me. "She kicked him out once. Made him sleep in one of the smaller cabins for a whole week. He called me to see if she'd spoken to you about it."

I laughed at that. "Really? When?"

Placing Zachary on his butt in his lap, he closed one eye as he thought about it. "It wasn't long after they came out of the hospital… maybe a few weeks after Maddy's pneumonia cleared up."

"What'd he do that made her kick him out?"

He shook his head. "He didn't say but it seemed like it had something to do with that day she fell through the ice. Whatever it was, it was bad enough he was terrified she was going to leave him for good."

Again, I couldn't help but feel guilty I didn't know more about their relationship and what kind of man Owen was. I wondered if she'd been unhappy and some part of her subconscious mind avoided the subject of Owen because of it. Had she been planning to leave him? Had he done something horrible that day on the ice?

"Don't feel guilty, Al," he said, holding in a laugh as Zachary shoved half his little fist into his mouth and growled. "Cece wouldn't have stayed if she was unhappy. You're doing the right thing by changing things back."

"Am I?" I asked. "Juan Jr.'s sweet to her. He barely knows her and he's already willing to give up so much just to make sure she gets home... Owen sacrificed nothing for her. He could've told his father no when he asked him to run the campground. He could've insisted they stayed until Cece finished school... What if I go back and steal away a life that's better for her?"

"Ally, she's laying in bed dying from a poison arrow. This life isn't better for anyone."

"I'm not dying," she mumbled, forcing both of us to jump up from our seats.

"Cece?" I called, hurrying to the head of the bed. "You're awake? Are you hurting?"

She didn't respond or open her eyes, but there was a slight upward curve in her lips, and some part of me recognized it as a sign she would live.

Chapter Nineteen

Cecelia

It was so dark I wasn't sure if my eyes were open or closed, but I knew I hadn't died by the weight of an arm draped across my abdomen and a large, warm body pressed against my spine.

I remembered taking a bath… and then there were bits and pieces of time spent in this room—in *his* room… but it was all fuzzy.

I rolled onto my back, my muscles aching at the movement, and slid my fingers along the arm to a shoulder, then a jaw, then a wide set mouth.

I smiled. "Jasmine's not going to like this at all."

The lips beneath my fingers formed a smile. "You're awake."

"You say that as if it's a bad thing. Did you want me to sleep a little longer so you can continue to snuggle with me, *adulterer*?"

Terrence chuckled deep in his throat. "You needed to be locked up in a dark room undisturbed. Your sister's got two babies to take care of, and I wasn't about to let anyone else crawl in bed with you. I'll figure out a way to tell Jasmine… sometime in the next forty years or so. How are you feeling?"

I bent my knees to test them and found no stabbing pains in either, just an ache from a lack of use. "I feel fine, I think… how long have I been in here?"

"Close to two weeks," he said. "It got worse… so we kept you sedated. I normally give you another dose in the morning… must've slept in."

"Two weeks?" I sighed. "How's Kyle?"

"Much better," he assured me. "We put him in a dark room too and after about two days, he started recovering. He hasn't had a sedative in ten days and has shown no signs of another spasm."

I stretched my arms above me, grateful they'd returned to their normal weight, if only a bit sore. "I wanna see him… and Bruce. I need to check on his hand. It looked really bad when I treated it."

"You will. Later." He moved away from me and I felt the mattress lighten as he got out of the bed. "First, we need to make sure you're not gonna' do that weird thing with your face again."

I rolled onto my side in the direction he'd headed. "If it looks half as creepy as it felt, I'm sorry you had to witness it."

"Not as sorry as I am. That was some real exorcist shit you had going on. I don't think I'll ever be able to sleep right again. You think it's over?"

I closed my eyes to get a read on my body. "Close to it. My muscles are a little tight, but nothing like they were before."

"You think it's safe for me to open these shutters then?"

Taking a deep breath, I gripped the blanket and prepared for the worst. "Only one way to find out. Open 'em up."

A few clanking noises later, the warm glow of the morning sun poured through the window, tiny dust particles dancing in its beam where it traveled across the room to shine upon my face.

I squinted until my eyes adjusted to the light, but was grateful nothing inside me decided to curl, arch, or tighten. I hummed happily and laid on my back. "Thank God," I said through my exhale.

"Thought you didn't believe in God?" he asked, moving to lean against the bedpost and look down at me with one raised brow.

"I don't," I admitted, sliding my body up to sit. "But it can't hurt to say thanks anyway. I never want to feel that way again." I glanced down at my hands where I balanced them on my knees, noticing Juan's ring was gone. Sucking in a breath, I spun round to search the sheets, squinting without my glasses to see in the dim light.

"I got it," Terrence said calmly, digging into the pocket of his black jeans. "I put it on a chain for you." He tossed the ring toward me then leaned his shoulder against the bedpost. "You know he's been down here every night to check on you… and your sister barely leaves this room."

I squeezed the ring and the chain in my palm. "Did you find any noise in those history books? Any more clues about Jack's death date?"

He nodded. "They've got at least three pages full of locations he should avoid along our route. You hungry? I can go grab you something after I wake up your sister to tell her the good news."

I grinned. "I'm starving, but I can't stay in this bed for another minute. What time is it?"

He glanced at his watch. "Quarter to seven."

I smiled even wider. "Then there's still time for me to get cleaned up and join you all for breakfast, isn't there?"

He snorted. "Looking to make a dramatic entrance, Cece?"

I slid my legs over the edge of the bed and tested my weight on them, amused when Terrence rushed to my side in case I fell on my face. "A dramatic entrance seems like a hell of a lot more fun than laying in this bed stinking like death while I wait for them to come to me."

Able to stand on my own, I swatted his hovering arms away. "You don't need to fuss over me, Tee. I'm not as feeble as I look. Do we have soap and a pitcher in here?"

"I'd call you a lot of things, Celia," he chuckled, "but never feeble. There's a pitcher and basin there." He motioned to a small table with a mirror that I assumed was as close to a vanity as Juan would make room for among the books and maps that covered nearly every inch of the room. "You should let me get your sister to help you."

"Pshh," I scoffed, limping on numb feet to the mirror to inspect my appearance. "I can bathe myself and you can turn your head just as well as she can. Jesus," I pulled the shift tight and squinted at my reflection. "I can see my ribs... at least... I think I can. Where are my glasses? And what have I missed? Did anyone die while I was asleep?"

His teeth flashed white against his dark skin as he moved to the desk to retrieve my glasses from a stack of papers. "No one died and you've missed a whole lot of theatrics between your sister's two husbands. I don't think Chris is as accepting of the new beau as we thought."

He offered me the glasses and I took them, hurrying to reinspect my condition once they were affixed to my face. "Who could blame him?" I grumbled, turning to one side to poke my ribs. "He was crazy about her... and she just... replaced him like it was nothing." I dared to sniff my armpit and winced. "Oh my God. How can you sleep next to me when I stink this bad? Go over there and turn around so I can get rid of this stench."

He did as instructed, chuckling as he turned to look out the window. "I love the shit out of you. You know that?"

"You must," I snickered, pouring a bit of water over my hair, "to sleep next to me for two weeks smelling like a wet dog."

"I'm serious, Cece." He propped an arm over his head on the windowsill and took a deep breath. "It hasn't been easy watching you suffer... not knowing if you'd come out of it. I can't tell you what it means to see you up and being a little smart ass again."

Lathering soap into my hair, I smiled at the uncharacteristic admission of feelings. Terrence wasn't a sentimental guy. "I love you, too, Tee. And it means a lot to know you're here looking out for me. I'd be lost if you hadn't jumped on that boat after me."

"So what's your plan after this dramatic breakfast entrance?" he asked. "Back to the history books?"

"I've had some time to think about that," I said, moving the soap down my arms. "I think we've been going about this research all wrong."

"What do you mean?"

"Well…" I kept my gaze on the reflection of his back as I worked the soap beneath my shift… a little too worried he might accidentally get a glimpse of my naked body if I removed it entirely. "We've been looking for noise in the history books, right? But… I remember Juan from somewhere in my history. And it occurred to me, I have the ability to tell him exactly where and when he needs to show up so I can remember. We don't need the books, Tee. He *is* the noise we're searching for."

"Oh, it's that easy, is it?" he snorted. "It might work, but you left out one very important obstacle in that method. *You*."

Positioning the basin on the floor beneath me, I flipped my hair over to rinse it. "What's that supposed to mean?"

"It means a man that looks like him can't just walk up to you and give you a message from the future… or past… or whatever. You'd find an excuse to run away before he even got past his greeting."

Squeezing my eyes closed, I felt around for lingering soap suds in my hair before moving on to rinse my body. "I'm not so unapproachable, am I?"

"Cece," he laughed, "there are wild bears more approachable than you are when it comes to the opposite sex. Do you remember that time I tried to hook you up with a guy from the department? You didn't even make it past the appetizer before rushing out because your *mother needed you*."

I groaned. "Tee, he ran his middle finger up my palm when he shook my hand. He was gross."

"Okay, fine, what about that guy in college? The one Jasmine said drooled over you for four years before working up the courage to ask you on a date?"

I snorted. "Jerry?! He came out of the closet shortly after graduation."

"Give me one example then, Cece, where a guy you'd never met came up to you and you actually talked to him."

Wrapping my hair in the towel, I searched the room for my purse. "I talked to lots of strange men at the shelter and at my clinic. Have you forgotten about Greg? Is my purse in here? I need my toothbrush and toothpaste."

Without turning around, he motioned to the foot of the bed where a pile of folded clothing sat on a bench alongside my purse. "Greg was a piece of shit and doesn't count. Give me another example, outside work, Cece. One instance where a man approached you in any other setting."

I fished my toothbrush out as I considered it, squeezing a large glob of toothpaste onto it before shoving it in my mouth. The mint was heavenly, awakening my near dead tastebuds. I brushed harder than I ever had, trying as I did so, to find a social setting in my mind where I hadn't found a way to escape the attention of an unfamiliar male.

Spitting into the basin, I grinned as I moved the toothbrush to one side of my mouth. "2004. Ohio State. There was this guy—"

I froze as I remembered sitting in the passenger seat of a black sedan, attempting not to throw up the tequila I'd consumed as I stared up at the driver… Juan Jr.

I'd never been to a party before that night. Jasmine had been so sweet to invite me after I'd met her during the campus tour. I'd wanted to attend Ohio State more than all the other schools I'd seen, and I remembered thinking it wouldn't hurt to make a few friends before I moved so far away from everyone I knew.

I must've stood on the sidewalk staring up the stairs to the front door of the sorority house for fifteen minutes in an attempt to calm my nerves. Beyond it, loud music and the sounds of far too many people made me contemplate running back to where I'd parked my car to drive away as fast as possible. I'd nearly decided to do that very thing when a tall, light-haired boy nudged my elbow.

"You Cecelia?" he'd asked, crossing his arms the same way I was to look up at the house in a similar fashion. "Jazz mentioned she had a new potential pledge coming. Scared to go in?"

I nodded. "She made it sound like a small get together, not a full-blown party."

He chuckled. "Wouldn't want to scare you off, would we? It's alright to be nervous. I was the same way before my first frat party. I almost left before going in. Would've been the biggest mistake of my life. My brothers mean the world out here." He slung an arm around my shoulders and led me toward the door. "You know what got me through it? Tequila. If you plan on going to school here, you *definitely* want to go in."

And so I did…

And the light haired boy gave me several shots of tequila…

And I danced and laughed and let go of my anxiety…

Until *he* approached.

Hands in his pockets, those murky green eyes locked with mine and I didn't run away… Couldn't run away if I'd wanted to. I was frozen in place.

"Cecelia," he'd said with a deep Spanish accent that caused my heart to skip at least three beats. "I think you should let me take you back to your hotel now."

"I should?" I hiccuped, wobbling as I tried to focus on his face. "Are you a professor here?"

He gave me the hint of a smile. "No. You've had too much to drink and I wouldn't want you to be embarrassed for it later."

Unable to stop myself from staring at him, I shook my head. "You're too old to be a student… what are you doing at this party?"

He raked his teeth over his lower lip. "Looking for my wife."

"Oh," I frowned, squinting around at the blurry figures dancing around me. "Did you find her?"

"I did," he said, offering me his arm. "Let me drive you home."

"Why should I?" I asked, staring at his offered arm and debating whether or not I should take it. "I don't know you."

"You don't know anyone here. Besides, if you stay, that boy there," he pointed to the light haired boy who'd escorted me in and had been dancing with me all night, "is going to take advantage of you."

I glared at the boy. "How do you know?"

He kept his arm extended, waiting for me to take it. "Because I heard him make a bet with his friends that he'd take you to his bed before the night was over. Is that where you wish to be?"

My cheeks flushed at the thought of being a prize in some little douchebag's bet. "No." Without a second thought, I looped my arm through his. "You're not going to kill me, are you?"

"I'll not harm you, Cecelia," he said, turning me toward the door. "I only wish to see you safely returned to your room."

In my inebriated state, I believed him, and I leaned into his side as he escorted me to his car down the street.

"Your wife won't be mad you're driving some stupid drunk girl home?" I glanced behind us toward the house for signs of an enraged woman hurrying to catch up to us.

He opened the passenger door of a shiny black BMW to reveal an immaculately clean leather interior. "I assure you, she will not mind one bit. Please, get in."

Unconvinced, I did so, painfully aware of the world spinning around me the instant I sat down. "I might throw up... I don't want to throw up in your car. Maybe I should walk..."

He smiled down at me. "It is only a car, *mi alma*. I would rather you were sick inside it than walking alone in such a state."

At that, he closed the door, and I sat there wondering what *mi alma* meant... I'd taken a few Spanish classes during my junior and senior years of high school, but not enough to have a full conversation.

After he got in the driver's seat, the memory got hazy... I remembered pressing my forehead against the glass of the passenger side window, its coolness the only thing preventing me from vomiting during the drive. I remembered glancing over at him on occasion where he drove with one hand atop the wheel, praying I hadn't drunkenly agreed to get in a car with a murderer. And I remembered wondering what in the world his wife was doing at a college party but not trusting my queasy self to ask any questions lest I vomit in his lovely almond-smelling car.

I didn't remember arriving at the hotel or the walk from the parking lot to the elevator… nor did I recall the elevator ride up… but there was one flicker of a memory at the door…

I was attempting to figure out how my key card worked when he took it from me and inserted it, opening the door to my dimly lit room as he remained in the fluorescent hall.

"There are two things I need to tell you before I go," he said softly. "And you won't understand them now, nor will you remember them for a very long time… but you *will* remember and that's why I'm here."

I blinked, trying only to stay upright with a hand against the doorframe.

"The first is that… what your sister is afraid of? It won't happen if everyone gets off the ship in Panama."

I hiccuped into a laugh. "You're right. I definitely don't understand. You know my sister?"

He nodded but didn't elaborate. "Panama. You'll *all* get off the ship. Say it back so I know you heard me."

Feeling ridiculous, I rolled my eyes. "Panama. We'll *all* get off the ship."

"Good." He gently slid his knuckle beneath my chin as if he might tilt my face up to kiss him… I wasn't sure why I didn't move away when I knew he was a married man, but I didn't. Instead, I leaned into it. "The second," he breathed, "is that I'll not be an old man when my wife comes back to me. I shall go back to wait."

It was the briefest of moments, so brief, I might've blinked and missed it, but he pressed his lips to mine and then stepped back. "Goodnight, Cecelia."

And before I'd even watched the elevator doors close all the way, I threw up on my shoes, passing out right there against the door to black out the memory for nearly sixteen years.

Chapter Twenty

Alaina

I yawned, struggling to get Zachary to sit still in my lap long enough for me to have a single sip of the coffee I so desperately needed. He wiggled and fussed because he wanted me to stand him up, and I was determined to teach him that fussing wouldn't always get him what he wanted.

As I took a sip and nearly spilled it on his head when he threw a punch into the side of the cup, I gave up on that lesson, raising him onto his feet to lean against my chest.

"There, happy?"

Beside me, his sister was content to sit obediently in her father's lap, and I glared at both of them as Zachary reached for my coffee again.

He growled in response to my moving it away from him, then loudly shouted "bah" sounds in the direction of Jim and Lilly with his little fists raised in the air.

"Look at ye' standin' there bein' ugly," Jim teased, gnawing on a piece of bacon. "You're too damn cute to be so mean."

As if he understood him, Zachary raised his volume, shouting various vowel sounds back across the table at an ear piercing decibel.

Kyle pinched the bridge of his nose. "Are all babies this loud?"

"No," Jim said, sticking his tongue out at Zachary and going cross eyed, "this one's just practicin' to be a politician. Ain't ye?"

Zachary blew spit bubbles in response and I hurried to wipe them with my sleeve, groaning as it only seemed to encourage him to blow more.

"Oooh boy," Jim howled over his coffee cup. "He's fixin' to be meaner than a two-headed snake. Lordt help us all when he gets his legs to moving. He's gonna' run all over hell's half acre with us chasin' after him, and he ain't gonna' quit till he's…"

His words trailed off as his attention moved to the doorway where Cece strolled into the room, clad in navy and white skirts with her hair pinned up neatly. If I'd have been standing, I might've fallen over at the sight of her.

"Good morning," she beamed, as if her appearance was no big deal, sauntering to the head of the table to pull out a chair.

Terrence followed behind her, grinning from ear to ear as all our mouths fell open. "She wouldn't let me come get you," he said as he plucked up a plate and began filling it with an assortment of bread, fruit, and meat on her behalf. "She wanted it to be a surprise."

"And I have an even better surprise," she informed us, her teeth showing in a wide smile as she met my eyes. "I *remember*."

"Remember what?" Lilly asked, leaning forward in her chair.

"Juan." She grinned, helping herself to a piece of bread to smear jam over it.

I sat there gawking at her, unable to move my lips in even a lame greeting. None of us were sure she'd be able to function before we got back through the storm to a doctor, and even then, I thought it'd take a considerable amount of time before she'd be able to move normally. Her muscles had been so rigid for so long… I didn't think she'd ever recover entirely.

I'd been intent to keep her sedated and in bed until we could return through time. While the idea of it had me worried sick she might develop a long-term reliance on the Laudanum, it was a risk

I was willing to take to keep her alive. To see her moving and speaking as if none of it had happened… I was frozen in shock.

"Whatever we do here works," she continued. "Juan never goes through time with his father and because of that, he was able to show up in my past to give me a message about Jack."

She took a bite of the bread and closed her eyes to chew it for what felt like a small eternity. When she swallowed, the smile reappeared. "He said, *'what your sister is afraid of won't happen if you all get off the ship in Panama.'* He emphasized the word *'all.'* So," she snagged a piece of bacon to hold it near her lips, "we get off the ship in Panama and find another way to go back to the storm. Jack won't die if he gets off this ship. That message was clear."

"And how are you only remembering this now?" Lilly probed.

Cece shrugged. "It was the first time I'd ever been drunk… I blacked it out and… I don't know… when I woke up, I suddenly remembered it."

Chris and I exchanged knowing glances. It couldn't be a coincidence that three days after we'd given Juan Jr. the date and location where she'd met Owen, she suddenly remembered him. "This happened at Ohio State?" I asked. "At the sorority party?"

She frowned, moving the food in her mouth to one side. "I never told you about that party… How could you know that?"

"That party," I said shakily, still in awe that she was sitting at the table without a hint of tetanus, "is where you met Owen…"

She tilted her head to one side, the happiness dwindling away from her features. "Light hair, blue eyes? Likes to make nasty little bets with his friends?"

Cheeks suddenly on fire at her knowledge of the bet, I nodded.

She bit into another piece of bacon. "Sounds like Juan did me a favor. That guy was a real prick."

Speechless, I watched as she shifted her attention to Bruce's hand, pulling it to sit palm up on the table and run her finger over the small bits of scar tissue where he'd recovered from his burns.

If her sudden appearance hadn't rendered me awestricken, her revelation certainly did. As it was, I couldn't believe my eyes or my ears. The poison we'd served those men hadn't prevented Owen from running into Cece... Juan had. It was Cece's traveling back through time that changed our memories... not their deaths. The moment we sent Bud, we made it possible for her to come through, and because she'd come through, Juan went on to prevent her marriage. That's why our memories hadn't changed the instant those men died...

I glanced back down the table at Chris who was just as wide-eyed as I was, evidently putting the same pieces together in his own mind.

Lost in my astonishment, it was only a hard tug on my hair when Zachary managed to wind it into his death grip that dragged me back to the conversation.

"He didn't say anything about Izzy?" Lilly asked.

Cece twisted her lips to one side as she pushed her fork into a piece of guava. "No. I'm sorry. But maybe that's a good thing. Maybe that means we find her soon and she's unharmed? If she was in any kind of danger, he'd have mentioned her too. Don't you think?"

A glimmer of hope appeared in Lilly's eyes for the first time in nearly three weeks and her lips turned up in a smile. "You're right. They have to be safe and we must be getting close." She scanned Cece's face in bewilderment. "Are you sure you're feeling alright? No lingering signs of tetanus?"

Cece beamed sweetly back at her. "No, just a little sore and starving. I think the worst of it's over though."

"Good." Lilly reached across the table to lay her hand over Cece's and the interaction between the two of them warmed my still racing heart. "You look absolutely fabulous. And I love those glasses on you. They really bring out your eyes."

Cece touched the frame as if she'd only just realized she was wearing them. "Thank you."

"You think it's a trap?" Jack finally spoke next to me, his eyes narrowed in thought. "I mean... wouldn't Juan Jr. benefit a great deal if we got off the ship and followed to Virginia? It'd give him time to form a plan before we could make it through the storm to eliminate his mother and brother. He'd have a chance to change our minds... There'd be no way for us to ever know it was a lie... and he'd have years from when he arrived on his original timeline to manipulate our histories and get us to come back to this time for good."

Cece frowned across the table at him. "You couldn't really want to take the risk of staying on board?"

He brushed his palm over the top of Cecelia's head where she cooed quietly in his lap. "You think it's wiser to risk the lives of my children by taking them through the Panama jungle? With malaria and floods, pirates and wild animals, thieves, gypsies, and escaped slaves? All at the word of *Juan Jr.*?"

I saw her flinch at the disdain in his voice when he'd said the name. "What reason has he given you not to trust him?"

"What reason has he given me *to* trust him?" he countered. "He's the son of the man that took us captive, Cece... This was all his idea too... to make peace with God or whatever bullshit he spouted. He was right there when his father took us captive and he didn't do anything to stop it. I don't trust this or him. I'm sorry."

"Jack," I laid a hand on his shoulder. "Honey, this is the only real clue we have. We can't very well ignore it."

He shook his head. "What if he's planning something bigger? Planning to adjust course so we can never learn of the way back? I'm not taking these babies through Panama, Red. Not on his word."

Cece crossed her arms over her chest and leaned back in her seat. "And if this ship sinks? He didn't say *how* you would die, only that you'd live if you got off it. You'd risk taking them all down with you?"

Jack took a deep breath. "If the ship were to sink, it'd be more than just my name with the death date of 1775 printed below it. Someone on board intends to see me dead... so I'll remain armed and alert until we get to that storm."

"And if it's the storm that kills you?" she asked, one blond brow raised skeptically.

"I'll take that risk," he assured her, "before I willingly put my children in any more danger than I already have. The dates listed beneath their names come years and decades beyond mine—giving them time to make it back to the storm if I don't. If I must die to ensure they live, so be it."

"Your argument doesn't make any sense," Cece grumbled, not willing to let it go. "If you die and she *is* able to make it to the storm with both babies, none of their names would have death dates listed below them at all. As it stands, whatever happens on this ship after Panama may very well force her to stay as a result."

"We got that report with us," Jim cut in, his eyes darting between the two of them. "Ye'd think 'em dates might change if we do somethin' different… Wouldn't they?"

Jack shook his head. "I'm not taking my children into Panama or into a war zone afterward. They're going to the storm. That's final."

Back in the larger cabin below deck with the women, Cece groaned as she eased herself down into one of the wingback chairs. "You really fall for all that macho muscle man crap he spews?"

I sighed, laying Zachary on the bed to change his diaper. I was too relieved to see her awake to want to argue with her, and she and Jack had already done enough arguing over breakfast for the lot of us. "He's not wrong, Cece. It'd be dangerous to take these babies into Panama."

Maria leaned against the door with her arms crossed over her chest, looking more exhausted than I'd ever seen her. "So would ignoring his warning, Alaina. You can't seriously be considering staying on this ship? Your sister is right. If you could make it to the storm after his death, you wouldn't have your own death dates on that report. You *need* to take Cecelia home. You can't risk getting stuck here."

I focused on unpinning the linen at Zachary's waist as he kicked both legs wildly, attempting to keep my emotions out of the conversation that was unfolding. "I don't know what I'm considering. It's a lot to think about."

Cece huffed. "You mean it's a lot for *Jack* to think about. Are you really going to let him make this decision for you? I don't want to attack you, A.J., but we've spent weeks searching for a clue as to where, when, and how he might die… now we know and you're just going to let him ignore it? What the hell were we looking for all this time? And when have you ever been the type of woman to surrender your opinion to a man? You at least had your own mind when you were married to Chris."

I swallowed the hurt from my throat and positioned a new diaper beneath Zachary's bottom, my response coming out through my teeth. "Whether we get off the ship or not doesn't matter. It's all going to change the minute we undo things. And we're *going* to undo things. Juan Jr. showing up in your past is evidence of that." I met her eyes then. "I have my own mind, Cecelia, and I share it with my husband before the *two of us* make any decision regarding our children."

She clicked her tongue. "Juan Jr. showed up in my past with a warning. What if the only way to undo things is to heed that warning? What if none of us can ever make it back because you're letting him ignore it? It *does* matter, A.J., and I won't see us all pay for a decision your husband has taken it upon himself to make on our behalf."

I took a deep breath, fastening the pins to the edges of the new diaper. "Nothing has been decided yet. I love you, Cece, very much, and I'm so very glad you're awake, but I won't spend another second defending him. To anyone."

"Alright, alright," Lilly said calmly, stepping between us to smooth her hand over my back. "This is getting a little heated for a day that should be spent celebrating. We've got what? Two weeks before we arrive in Panama? Let's not fight over it today. Not after we've waited so long for Cece to wake up. You and Jack have time to talk about it and make a decision… We don't need to be turning on each other. Not now. Okay?"

I nodded, stealing a glance at my sister as Lilly shifted the conversation away from Jack. "Did Juan Jr. say anything else to you in the memory?"

Cece pursed her lips, pulling his ring from her breast where it hung from a gold chain around her neck. "He did… I'm pretty sure I'm going to end up married to him before all this is over…"

"What makes you say that?" Lilly asked, sitting down beside Zachary on the bed and staring at Cece with disbelief.

Cece smiled. "Because when I asked him what he was doing at that party, he said he was looking for his wife… and he kissed me before he left."

"He kissed you?" Lilly and I both asked in unison.

She nodded, her eyes staring forward at nothing in particular. "It was a peck really… but… it was so effortless, like he'd kissed me a thousand times before that. And as the memory played out in my mind, I was almost looking forward to living out whatever led him to that moment."

She slid his ring back and forth along its chain. "Before the Laudanum, we had a couple super sweet moments together… I was pretty sure he was being sweet to me *because* I was going to die and I figured there was no harm in letting it excite me when I wouldn't live much longer anyway. But now, I'm relatively certain I'm going to survive. And I keep looking at that clock wondering how much longer it might be before he wakes up; how much longer I'll have to wait before I can start living out whatever life we're supposed to have together here; how much longer before he might kiss me like that again… Does that make me naïve?"

"Not at all," Lilly said sweetly. "I think it's romantic."

"Lilly!" I hissed.

"What?" she snarled. "It is!"

"Ay," Maria agreed, swooning as she slid into the wingback chair beside Cece's and went limp against its cushions. "Very romantic."

I shook my head. Jack had a point at breakfast. Juan could very well be manipulating my sister so he could tamper with our pasts once he got to George Bennet. "Cece, do you remember Mark

Mitchell from junior high? What if he's Mark Mitchelling you and you're falling for it all over again?"

"Who's Mark Mitchell?" Lilly asked, frowning.

"Cece's first kiss," I answered, watching my sister for a reaction. "He'd hold her hand after we got off the bus and he'd kiss her behind this big oak tree by our house. He told her he was scared he would fail math and his parents wouldn't let him see her anymore if he did, so she let him copy her homework and look over her shoulder during tests... *And* she took the fall for it when they got caught; stood by it even after he stopped talking to her when he realized he couldn't get away with it anymore. She cried for months over that."

Lilly shook her head. "What makes you think Juan is anything like a stupid kid?"

I sighed. "Cece's always had this giant heart. She trusts too easily. Mark Mitchell took advantage of it. Why wouldn't Juan?" I spun to face her. "Honey, what if Jack's right? What if Juan's only being sweet to get you to convince us all to do whatever he wants done? What if he only showed up there and kissed you to give you the illusion you both meant more to each other?"

Lilly clicked her tongue. "If it's an illusion, he's one hell of an actor. Come on, Lainey. He's spent the past two weeks obsessing over nothing but her. You saw it. If he wasn't asking about her, he was sitting in that room beside you staring at her. I don't think I've ever seen a man more preoccupied."

Cece let the ring fall against her chest. "You don't think it's a trick? A really *really* well thought out one?"

Maria snorted. "Go wake his ass up and find out."

Chewing her lower lip, Cece frowned over at her. "You don't think that'd be inappropriate?"

"Oye, who cares about appropriate?" She folded her hands over her stomach. "He obviously doesn't if he showed up and kissed you in your past when you didn't even know him. I'd wake his ass up and glue myself to him for however long you can to figure out why."

She looked at me then, her eyebrows high on her forehead. "I know you don't approve, but I have to know what this is." She turned back to Maria. "Where is he?"

Chapter Twenty-One

Cecelia

On the pads of my bare feet, careful not to lower my wrapped heel, I crept down the stairs to the hall and past two doors to the one I knew I'd find Juan behind. I didn't knock, but turned the handle and slipped inside, easing the door closed behind me.

Heart beating in my throat, I turned to find him lying across the bed on his stomach.

He wore only his breeches, and his arms were splayed out and wrapped around the pillows, his face turned away from me.

His tattoo took up more than just a space on his chest. In the dim morning light, I could just make out a pattern that started at his shoulder blade, crawling wide across his upper bicep and disappearing on his chest where it was rested against the blankets he laid on.

Luna's tail began to wag a steady beat where she'd blended with the blankets at his ankles, and his arm moved an inch at the disturbance.

I should've knocked...

I'd been presumptuous to sneak into his room without thinking it would be considered inappropriate... Seeing him there, so vulnerable in his sleep, I realized I'd overstepped. We weren't familiar enough not to knock on each other's doors. Not yet.

Holding my breath, I placed my hand back on the doorknob and turned to make a stealthy escape.

"Cecelia?" he called groggily, forcing me to freeze where I stood.

I turned slowly around, cheeks on fire as I pressed my spine against the door. He was lying just as he'd been, but his face was turned toward me, and those dark sage eyes were fixed on mine.

"I'm sorry. I didn't mean to wake you."

"Cecelia!" He pushed himself up suddenly to sit on the edge of the bed, the front part of his tattoo becoming clear as he did so. "You're awake," he said sweetly, rubbing his eyes as if he wasn't sure what he was seeing was real. "Are… are you feeling well?"

"Yes," was the only word my lips could form as I stood there gawking at him, the swirling ink sitting on his sun-kissed skin like he'd been born with it… as beautiful a part of his body as the rest of him. The black lines created a tribal looking face set in a winding circle of patterned blocks on his chest. The blocks spiraled round and formed the shape of a serpent slithering over his upper arm and onto his back.

"You're not in pain?" He stood, and if I hadn't already been mesmerized by the sight of his exposed upper body and sleep swept hair, I certainly was once it was put on full display and heading toward me. I'd never seen anyone built so perfectly.

"No."

Luna, not to be ignored, stretched her front paws with a yawn and hopped off the bed, hurrying to my shins ahead of him to wiggle in demand of my affection.

I knelt down to scratch behind her ears, grateful once again for her perfectly timed distractions to allow myself time to settle my racing heart.

He lowered down to crouch across from me, sliding his fingers over her fur until they reached mine. "You are awake," he said again, moving his thumb over the side of my wrist. "And you are here instead of with your family. Why?"

I cursed my stupid nerves. Unable to explain what I remembered for fear I might somehow prevent any part of it from happening, I instead pointed at the tattoo. "Is that a face?"

"Aye. It is the face of an Aztec God." The dimple appeared in his cheek. "Have you come to ask about my tattoo then?"

I bit my lower lip and reminded myself that, if this was real, this man would be my husband very soon. I didn't need to be nervous with my own husband...

And despite that little voice in the back of my mind questioning it all, I couldn't help the excitement that welled in my stomach simply thinking of this beautiful creature as *'my husband'*. How strange it was to have my entire life plan unraveling before my eyes and feel so utterly unscathed; so strong was the desire to be called this man's wife. I wanted to know everything about him; wanted to stay in this room and soak up every second we had left together.

Blinking my daze away, I cleared my throat. "Why do you have the face of an Aztec god on your chest?"

"My wife's grandfather was a Paiute native."

When I said nothing, he continued. "The Paiute are relatives of the Aztec and his father passed many of their beliefs and practices down to him. He gave me the markings."

"What eh..." My words stumbled over themselves as he took my fingers in his and raised them to his lips. I was thrumming with the touch, like an electric current had been shot from his lips to set a pulse coursing through my body. "What does the snake mean?"

Keeping my hand in his, he lowered my fingertips to the sleep-warmed skin on his chest, tracing them over the ink that crept over his upper bicep. "This was the first one he gave me. The serpent is meant, in their culture, as a symbol for good fortune and fertility. He gave it to me on our wedding day."

My heart sank. Had I known the tattoo was for his wife, I'd have asked *any* other question. Touching something meant for her felt like an invasion... Like I was imposing on her memory—on something sacred reserved only for the two of them.

Before I could pull my hand away, he moved my fingers to the circle the serpent stemmed from and the face inside it. "This, he gave me after our first son, Philip, was born. It is Tezcatlipoca, the warrior… meant to give me strength and balance as a father and protector."

"And these," he moved my palm over the boxes surrounding it and I could see the symbols in each now that he was so close. "These he gave to me after they died. Three eagles separated by three suns… Meant to remind me that my family soars around me as I walk in darkness, guiding me with their light."

"It's very beautiful," I breathed as Luna scurried back toward the bed.

He shook his head, flattening my palm against his chest so I could feel his heart beating just as rapidly as mine. "I was so afraid I might never see your eyes open again… Why are you here… with me?"

I dared to place my other hand on him, letting my fingers trace the three lines of a scar running up his ribcage. "Because I remembered," I said, my voice unable to produce anything beyond a whisper at the memory of his lips on mine; at the hope they might return to mine in the coming seconds. "You did what you promised. You stopped me from marrying him… I came to tell you that… and to thank you for it."

"I gave you my word that I would." He reached out to move his palm along my jaw, his thumb dancing softly over my cheek. "I knew the moment your sister told me where you'd met him, I would go and stop it. I heard enough to know he did not deserve you. Did I give you the answers you were hoping for?"

I traced the eagles on his chest with my finger. "You said Jack won't die if we all get off the ship in Panama."

"All of you?" His thumb froze its movement against my jaw. "I cannot have asked that of you. The isthmus is not safe for you or those babies… and to procure transportation for so many… it would be no small feat."

I tilted my head into his palm where it still rested against my cheek. "You made me repeat it back to you so you were sure I'd heard. You said, *'Panama. You'll all get off the ship.'* You emphasized *all.*"

He frowned. "You are not afraid I might have deceived you?"

I shook my head. "No. I don't think you would."

He took a deep breath. "Before you got sick, you called me the hunter. I have not been able to silence that name on your lips in my mind… They told you what I did to the captive?"

"They did."

He winced at that. "And you are not afraid of me for it?"

I slid both my hands over his chest. "I did not call you the hunter because I think it's a part of you I should cower from. I'm glad for what you did. Whatever torture you inflicted on him in those few hours was far easier than the torment he served me these past few weeks. I feel safer because of it."

"You do?"

"Yes, *mi alma*," I hid a smile as I used the term he'd called me and felt his heartbeat quicken beneath my palm as a result. "I like you… very much. Perhaps even to my own detriment. Whether you are the hunter or the man who looks at me like you're looking at me now, it's all a part of the person I want."

He took my hands in his, pulling me onto my feet to stand before him. "*Mi alma.*" He smiled, tucking a stray wisp of my hair behind my ear. "Do you know what that means?"

"No," I lied. "But it's what you called me that night… in the memory."

Again, the dimple appeared in his cheek. "It's not a term to be used lightly, Cecelia. It means a great deal to call someone that name. When we use it, it is like saying in English: my soul, my heart, my spirit, my everything… All of it wrapped up in that one word."

"Oh," I blushed, not realizing it meant quite so much. "I suppose I must end up being a pretty big deal to you then, huh?"

"I suppose you must," he said softly, closing the gap between us to awaken the feather that had been lying dormant in my stomach. "Tell me, *mi alma,* have I kissed you before?"

"If I said that you did," I whispered, trembling with anticipation as I felt his breath on my lips, "would it stop you from doing so now?"

His eyes danced between each of mine. "Is that why you've come? Is this what you want?"

I nodded. "Maybe more than I've ever wanted anything."

And then his fingertips were sliding beneath my chin, tilting my face toward him.

And my heart leapt up into my throat…

And as his lips closed over mine I felt all the versions of all the lives we'd each lived or would ever live explode into a thousand pieces, drifting up high over our heads to scatter somewhere among the stars.

I was going to fall in love with this man. I knew it all the way down to my bones, whether it was foolish or not… And melted against him, I wasn't afraid of whatever would come next. He'd given me the life I chose for myself when he'd stepped in front of Owen, and I would forever be grateful.

Releasing my mouth entirely too soon, he pressed his forehead against mine, both hands roaming over my shoulders. "We cannot remain in this room alone together."

I could see the restraint in him moving his chest a little heavier and causing his jaw to tighten. I knew all I had to do was raise my lips an inch to meet his once more and that restraint would crumble. It wouldn't be the gentle, sweet, and too-brief kiss he'd just given me.

One single inch and I'd feel the very same level of passion that drove him to beat a man to death on my behalf with only his hands. I would taste him, feel every inch of him pressed up against every inch of me, and I would know exactly what it was to be his wife.

"I don't want to be anywhere else," I admitted. "There's so much I want to know about you and so little time left before the storm. I've already lost so much being sick… We don't have to be alone… Come with me?"

"Where?"

I laughed. "Anywhere… The deck, the dining room, the galley, the hallway… I don't care so long as I'm with you."

He pressed his lips against my brow. "Have you had any coffee yet? I'm afraid I've grown quite accustomed to drinking it since our last meeting."

I trembled with my own struggle for restraint. "Not enough of it," I said, no longer speaking of coffee, "not nearly enough of it."

I'd remained against his door as he slid on a loose shirt, not bothering to pull back his hair or add a jacket before escorting me out into the hallway.

The moment we were out of the room, he offered his arm, and when I wrapped both arms around it, he let out an audible sigh.

As we made our way down to the galley in silence, my thoughts returned to Mark Mitchell. I'd been so cautious since then… I'd spent twenty years building a wall around myself as protection from another Mark, and within seconds of seeing Juan for the first time, that wall had shattered to pieces. I had never reacted to any man the way I had so instantly reacted to him. No man had ever looked at me the way Juan did. Nor had they ever touched or kissed me with the same level of tenderness he had. Was I falling for another Mark? And now that I'd felt his lips over mine, would I be able to pull myself away long enough to figure that out? Did I even care if he ripped my heart to shreds? Would the time spent together leading up to my heartbreak be worth it?

Stepping into the galley to have my senses overwhelmed by the heavenly smells of onion, garlic, and basil, I smiled at Bruce's back where he and a young sailor were leaning over a book on the counter.

Juan cleared his throat and both men spun around.

"Captain!" The young sailor bowed nervously. "Mistress McCreary! You are awake."

I grinned. "You can call me Cece. And you are?"

"Tomás," he said, lowering his head to stare at his feet. "My apologies, Captain. I do not wish you to think I am neglecting my duties while you rest. I only come down for an hour in the morning after my work is done."

Bruce beamed at him. "If Tomás is in trouble for being down here, it is my fault. He's been teaching me Spanish. And I'm teaching him to read in exchange."

"Why on earth would he be in any trouble?" I snorted. "I think that's a wonderful use of your time, Tomás."

His dusty brown eyes glanced up at me for only a second. "Thank you mistress."

"Cece," I corrected as he lowered his gaze back to the floor.

"I should return to the deck." He bowed his head even farther. "Good day to you both."

He hurried out before any of us could offer a farewell, like a child who'd been caught stealing.

Bruce chuckled, closing the book on the counter and sliding it up onto a shelf over his head. "Back so soon, Juan? You couldn't have slept more than… what? Four hours?"

My arms still wound around Juan's, I looked up at him in fake outrage. "You were down here already today? Without me?"

"Oh, he's not half the brute he pretends to be, Cece." Bruce grinned. "He's come down every morning since your last visit to help with the bread and check on my hand. I think your Juan is a bit of a softie."

I smiled proudly up at the man at my side. Mark Mitchell wouldn't have been so thoughtful.

"What brings you down again so soon?" Bruce continued, moving to a massive pot on the stove to pull off the lid and inhale the plume of garlicky steam that rolled off it. "Are you hungry?"

"I thought I'd make Cecelia some coffee," Juan said. "And steal a bit of bread and cheese if you've any left."

"Plenty leftover in the pantry. Help yourself. I'll get the coffee." Bruce returned the lid and limped to the opposite counter to pull down the coffee supplies from a cabinet.

"That limp," I started as Juan untangled our arms and moved to the counter alongside him to get started. "Is that from the plane crash?"

Blowing out a breath as he turned back toward me, Bruce nodded. "Couldn't move my lower half when we came out of the plane on the raft. I thought for sure I'd be paralyzed for life. Anna didn't believe that for a second, and she got me walking again. She thought, in the end, I might've had a fracture and as the bone fused back improperly, it created a herniated disc to then cause sciatica."

I pursed my lips. "If it's sciatica, regular stretches and massages will help with the pain. I can see it's hurting you quite a bit to move around. Can I take a look?"

"That's very sweet of you, honey, but you're skin and bones after being in bed for so long. The only person who needs taking care of down here today is you. Sit down and let us handle things. You can worry about my limp another time."

Unable to argue with him as he pulled out a stool, I sat down in it, feeling the instant relief on my still sore muscles. I tilted my head toward the stove. "What are you cooking that smells so heavenly?"

"Salt pork stew," he said with a laugh. "Which is basically salt pork, peas, beans, broth and all the spices I could throw in to make it taste like it's not another salt pork dinner."

"I can't wait to try it," I assured him, smiling as Juan turned around with concentrated focus to place his coffee kettle on the stove beside it.

Bruce glanced between the two of us as he untied his apron and tossed it on the opposite counter. "Will you keep an eye on the stew for me? I promised Jim I'd go down and help him with the pigs before lunch, plus I need a bit of Wanda's milk."

"Of course," I said. "A.J. said you had a pig die a few weeks back. Maybe I could come with you tomorrow to see if there's anything to worry about. I'm a vet, you know."

Bruce winked. "I know. And I'm sure you'd put a lot of minds at ease if you looked them over... *When you're well.*"

"It's a date then," I promised, resting my forearms on the counter.

"We'll see how you're feeling." He patted my shoulder on his way to the door. "Try not to burn the ship down."

"I'll do my best," I beamed as he closed the door behind him.

I leaned over my arms to get a whiff of the warming coffee while Juan disappeared into the pantry to retrieve a loaf of bread and a chunk of questionable looking cheese.

"What was your youngest son's name?" I asked when he placed the items in front of me.

"Hmm?" He didn't look up from his hands as he shaved the layer of mold off the wedge of cheddar.

"You said your oldest was Philip. What was the younger one's name?"

"Nicolás," he said with the softness of true fatherly affection, slicing off a few pieces of bread before his eyes met mine.

"Is it alright if I ask you about them?"

He nodded. "Of course. What would you like to know?"

"Everything…" Sliding my arms over the counter between us, I moved my palm over the top of his hand. "I want to know how you met Elizabeth… what she was like… what you were like with her… What your sons were like… I want to know… well, everything."

He bent down to rest his arms on the counter as well, lacing the fingers of both our hands together between us as he took a very deep breath. "I have not spoken of them since their deaths. I was so certain my heart died with them, I couldn't bring myself to even say their names out loud."

He squeezed my hands in his. "Having spent so long mourning them, I thought it a betrayal to their memory when you came down those stairs the first time and I felt my heart beating once more."

"Do you feel that way still?" I asked, chewing my lower lip. "That it's a betrayal?"

He shook his head. "I don't know why, but I found myself hoping I might have the chance to tell you about them someday.

Odd as it may sound, I believe, in some miraculous way, it is them that is pushing me toward you."

"You think so?" I wasn't sure why that mattered, but it did.

His teeth shone bright white in a smile. "I know it. Much as every man, woman, and child on this ship loved you within hours of your coming on board, they would have too."

I blushed. "Will you tell me how you met her?"

"Aye. We grew up together," he said fondly. "When my father arrived in California to find it vastly different from the one he'd been expecting to land upon, it was her family that took us in and helped us settle."

"They were natives, right?" I asked, glancing toward the spot on his chest where the tattoo was covered by his shirt.

"Her mother was," he corrected. "Her father was a Spaniard. Their relationship was a great scandal among the other Spanish settlers in the region and they'd been cast out to live on a very remote piece of land... which also happened to be where we came ashore."

He smiled, running a thumb over my knuckles. "I liked it there —after the initial shock of time travel wore off, of course. Our fathers would leave for weeks at a time, and her grandfather would take Dario, Elizabeth and I out into the wild to teach us how to hunt and fish... We'd stay out in the woods for days, sleeping by a fire while he told us old Aztec stories. We spent two years practically living in the wilderness."

"Sounds like a dream."

Where his focus had been glazed over in memory, it returned to my face. "It was."

"Where would they go?" I pried. "Your father and hers?"

He smirked. "My father was a bit of an amateur historian before all this happened, and the moment he accepted that we'd indeed landed ourselves in the 18th century, he began traveling east to the mountains." His eyes lit up with mischief. "The two of them were searching for the untouched gold that would one day lead to the California gold rush."

My eyes widened at that. "That's where your money came from! Why he was able to afford such a large ship and all these lush furnishings?"

He nodded. "I'll never forget the day they came back with it. My father said it was more gold than anyone would have ever seen in one place… We all drank wine together and the adults laughed and sang and, for Dario and I, it felt like we were part of a family for the first time since our mother and sister were lost to us."

He unlaced our fingers as the kettle began to hiss, removing it from the stove to turn his back to me and pour the liquid through a filter on the opposite counter. "He buried some of that gold in the event we should ever return to the future… And the rest he used to take us all south to a new settlement off the coast where no one knew of Elizabeth or her family. There were about thirty Spanish families spread out through the area, and my father built a home there that could house all of us plus servants and no small amount of guests."

He turned back with two steaming cups, placing one on the counter before me. "He kept her mother and grandfather well hidden when visitors came through, and because Elizabeth was lighter skinned, he was able to pass her and her father off as his niece and brother from Spain."

"She was light skinned?" I asked.

He smiled. "Aye. With thick black hair and light blue eyes. Even as a young girl, she was striking to look at. No man could stop his head turning when she entered a room."

He leaned back against the opposite counter and sipped his coffee. "She and I lived as siblings for those early years, though we both knew we weren't blood… She'd tag along wherever Dario and I went… Lizzie is what we called her as children. She was unlike any other girl we'd ever met. She wanted to be able to hunt and fish the way we did, and we'd pretend to be annoyed when she'd tag along, but she made everything more fun. She'd get just as muddy as we would; play just as rough; was always laughing or turning our hikes into some wild adventure. As we got older and she began to develop into a woman, she didn't want *me* to call her

Lizzie anymore. And it was during the seven years war, when both our fathers were off fighting, that we became… more."

"More?" I raised a dubious eyebrow.

He grinned. "We'd gone out fishing early one morning and left Dario asleep. I think we both knew what it was we were about. We'd been looking at each other differently for weeks. As soon as we got to the creek, she kissed me… and after that, I didn't want to do much else *but* kiss her."

He chuckled at the memory. "We found every possible excuse to sneak off together. My father hadn't really been there to teach me about propriety and, living so remotely, I didn't realize I was doing anything wrong when kissing turned into touching…"

He let out a long breath. "She became pregnant with our Philip about a year after our first kiss. And with both our fathers still at war, her grandfather wed us in a traditional Paiute ceremony."

"How old were you?" I asked, fascinated.

"Sixteen. She was fifteen."

"So young!" I gasped.

He shrugged. "As soon as Philip was born, I was forced to grow up quickly. He cried so much those first few weeks, I thought I'd never sleep again. And Elizabeth cried almost just as much."

I leaned in. "What'd her father say when he came back a grandfather?"

He shook his head. "He didn't come back. He died in the war. Mine *did* come back a year after Philip was born and he was none too pleased with either of us, particularly after he'd just acquired this ship and was intent to set sail in search of the way back."

I propped my chin up on my fist. "What'd he do?"

Placing his cup down on the counter behind him, he leaned over the one I was seated at. "He had us wed by a Catholic priest, forced him to forge a date on our marriage certificate before we could've conceived Philip… He'd built something of a name for himself among the Spanish during the war and didn't want society knowing he had a bastard savage for a grandson. He gifted us the house and set sail for three months with Dario."

His facial expression changed then, a shadow seeming to pass over his eyes as he mindlessly toyed with the fabric at my elbow. "I grew restless in their absence. With the gold, my father procured servants and maids and staff to do most of the work for us. All I needed to do was manage the finances and father my child. But I wasn't made to sit still… Every day, that house felt more and more like a prison. I couldn't breathe. I started spending nights out in the woods with her grandfather again, hunting and fishing… Needing some kind of excitement lest I go mad. And when my father and Dario returned, I begged to go out with them on the following voyage."

He pursed his lips, smoothing his hands over the wood countertop. "I loved being at sea… loved the freedom of it. And every time we went out, we stayed out longer… I *wanted* to stay out longer, especially when each time we came back, Elizabeth would beg me not to leave again."

He sighed. "I was too young to know what to do with her. As far as I understood, being a husband was a physical act more than it was anything else. And once that physical act had been done, I didn't know how to just exist beside another person… particularly when that person had her own ideas of what my *existence* should look like."

He ran a hand over his hair. "When Philip was six, Nicolás was born. And my father and I were preparing to sail to the Atlantic… It was a long trip, and Elizabeth refused to let me go without her… She hated being apart… After hours and hours of her pleading, I agreed to bring them along… Nicolás was no more than a few days old when we set sail. And, well, it was on that trip they all got sick."

I clicked my tongue. "I'm so sorry."

He nodded, raising off his forearms to slice off a small piece of cheese. "Her mother and grandfather went back to the Paiute after we delivered news of their passing… I haven't been home since. That was more than five years ago."

I took a piece of bread and fumbled with the crust as a means to have something to do with my hands. "What do you think will happen to Elizabeth and her family without your father and his gold?"

He raised his shoulders, biting into his piece of cheese. "I have always hoped she would meet someone who wanted her heart instead of her body. Someone older that could understand the difference. I'd intended to return to make sure she had."

"And if she hasn't?" I pulled apart the bread in my hands, swallowing as I dared to pry further. "You're older now and know the difference."

"I have only *just* learned the difference, *mi paloma*," he said, scanning my face with an intensity that left no room for questions around his meaning.

My toes curled beneath me. Less than a month ago I'd been sitting in my jeep spying on Chris, convinced my whole life would be spent attempting to prove he'd murdered my sister. Now I was staring up at a man who wanted my heart, contemplating what a life spent beside him might look like. I hardly recognized myself.

"Philip used to do that." He pointed to the flakes of bread on the counter where I'd been mindlessly pulling it apart. "He'd pick pieces off his bread until there was nothing left of it. It used to drive my father mad."

I laughed, looking down at the pile of crumbs. "I didn't even realize I was doing it."

"He didn't either." He refilled my coffee and brushed the flakes away. "I have told you about my family. Tell me something about you."

"Oh," I folded my fingers around my coffee cup. "I don't have a story nearly as romantic as yours. A.J. was the boy-crazy one as a teenager, where I never developed the same desire she had to be someone's girlfriend. While she was off kissing boys at the mall, my life revolved around becoming the best in my class and spending time with my family."

"Your family matters a great deal to you then?"

I nodded. "My mother, uncle, and A.J. gave me all the love I ever needed. When her airplane disappeared, we *all* went mad searching for her. We bought a boat after they called off the official search to look for signs of her ourselves."

He smiled, breaking off a piece of bread and stacking a piece of cheese on it. "You mentioned you'd captained your own ship once. Did you sail these same waters?"

"I did," I answered proudly. "I mapped out every possible island she could've landed on within a five-hundred mile radius of their last known coordinates. We hired a few hands to help us and teach us how to captain it and we went to every single one of those coordinates."

"Fearless," he breathed, taking a bite and moving it to one side of his mouth. "Is that when you got her name tattooed on your ankle?"

"*Somebody* was looking very closely!" I teased, glancing down at my wrapped ankle where her name was concealed. "My mother and I got matching tattoos of the name last year on Alaina's birthday. Mom never said so, but I think she was giving up. For her, I think the tattoo was a sort-of surrender that A.J. was gone. For me, it was a permanent reminder that my sister was out there somewhere and needed me to find her. I went out on the boat again a month later, just me and a few crewmen, more determined than ever."

"Did you enjoy being at sea?"

"Very much," I confessed. "Particularly at night… when there's nothing to block out the stars and you can't tell which is sky and which is ocean because the water is so still. There was something about it that made me feel like I was a part of something much bigger than myself. I don't necessarily believe in God, but I do believe there's more to this life than we comprehend…"

I stole a piece of cheese and inspected it for mold before taking a small bite off the corner. "There was this one night where I was completely alone on the deck. The water was calm and quiet and I'd been leaning over the rail when a mother whale surfaced with her calf right there beside the boat. They swam along the side of us for a while, making these beautiful noises each time they'd come up for air. The whole thing felt almost… spiritual. Like I'd just experienced something truly majestic. And that little moment I shared with them gave me this overwhelming sense I was on the right path."

His eyes seemed to drink me in—exploring all of me despite never moving from my own. "Do you still feel you are on the right path?"

I hid a smile. "Do I feel like the path that took me to a whole other century to alter the future and become completely enchanted by a strange man for the first time in my life is the right one?" I shrugged. "Meh."

He chuckled. "You never had any suitors after I prevented your marriage to Owen?"

"Not really. There was this guy I dated for about six months after college, Greg, but…" I lowered my gaze, not wanting to admit he'd been my only real sexual experience in life and using the term *'dating'* was a stretch on the word. "It wasn't serious."

"You blush," he noted, catching my chin in his grip and tilting my face up so he could inspect it. "This Greg… you shared his bed?"

I hadn't realized I'd blushed, but I certainly did after he asked the question. "I did."

"Tell me where you met him," he joked, his thumb moving over my lower lip, "and I shall appear in another of your memories."

I giggled. "Jealous?"

"Selfish."

Before I could think of a witty response, he covered my mouth with his and there was no restraint in it this time. This kiss was passion and possession and fire. His lips moved with fervor over mine, parting my lips as the fingers of one hand embedded in my hair, prompting a noise to escape my throat and vibrate between us.

This was the kiss I'd been expecting from him the first time; raw and full of desire. He was a flame, and I, his accelerant… or perhaps it was the other way around because I felt incandescent beneath his mouth, glowing brighter with each sweep of his tongue against mine.

I wanted this… all of it… for as long as I could possibly hold on to it.

'I'm looking for my wife,' he'd said in the memory, and, foolish or not, I couldn't wait to be her.

I'd been prepared to climb over the counter and tell him as much when the screech of the galley door opening forced the kiss to come to an abrupt end.

Both of us were out of breath and likely looking quite guilty as we spun toward the sound.

Bruce stood frozen in the doorway with a crate of milk in his arms, his pudgy cheeks turning as red as mine felt. "Should I come back later?"

"No!" I hopped off the stool and patted the counter. "Please, put that down. I thought you had kitchen staff to help you with things like this?"

"I do," he admitted, placing the milk on the surface with a grunt. "But I gave them the morning off. You two seemed like you needed a minute." He grinned as he examined my hair. "And I believe I was right."

"It's nearly noon," Juan observed, straightening uncomfortably. "I'll need to relieve Gabriel. Shall I escort you back to your cabin, Cecelia?"

I smiled up at him as he attempted to appear unbothered by the interruption—or rather, what had come before it. I wasn't quite sure which since he refused to look at me. "I think I'd like to stay down here for a while and help Bruce since we've scared off his staff. Will you *escort* me to dinner later?"

"Aye." He bowed his head, then, as if he couldn't do so fast enough, hurried out of the room.

I turned back to Bruce and pulled my lips in to hide my laugh. "I'm not sure which one of us frightened him away."

Bruce chuckled as he reached up to secure a pin that had come loose in my hair. "It couldn't possibly have been you, dear."

I stared back at the door he'd practically sprinted through, my heart still racing with the feel of him lingering on my lips. "You think there might be something in the air that makes us all lose our minds in this century?"

"Maybe," Bruce said, following my gaze, "or it could be a lack of distractions that might otherwise have prevented us from seeing what's right in front of our eyes."

Humming with a sigh, I spun back toward the counter. "You and Anna never…?"

He shook his head, blushing even further as he began to unload the milk bottles from the crate. "You ever just love someone without needing anything more from them?"

I pulled a few bottles out to place them on the counter. "You mean like a really strong friendship?"

He turned the bottle in his hand as if he might be reading an invisible label. "More than that… like family. She was my family in every way… my mother, sister, wife, and the best friend I ever had… I didn't need anything more to love her."

"You must miss her a lot."

Smiling, he placed the crate on the floor and pulled a roll of fabric from a cabinet built into the island counter. "I do, but I have more hope today than I did yesterday. If Juan showed up in your memories, that can only mean she'll live again. I'll see her soon… Pretty sure she's gonna love *you*, by the way."

"I hope so." I grinned. "Cause I think you might be my favorite and you'll never be rid of me."

He looked back toward the galley door. "I doubt I'm your favorite, but I'll take runner-up and consider it an honor."

I pulled out the stool and sat down. "You don't think I'm insane for letting this go on with him? With everything…" I let that trail off.

"Life is insane, Cece." He unrolled the cloth on the counter to cut a square. "Look at us. Changing history and making new memories… What's the point of any of it if we don't enjoy a bit of the insanity here and there?"

I sighed, smoothing my hands over the counter. "What kind of insanity can I help you with now? What's the milk for?"

He smiled. "We're making cheese."

Chapter Twenty-Two

Alaina

"You can't make decisions for both of us," I said as Jack stood behind me, tightening the stays I'd avoided wearing all day in preparation of attending dinner. "We've been over this. You and I have to talk about these things together. Especially something so big as this."

Tying the ribbon, he leaned in, sliding his nose along the nape of my neck. "You're mad at me? *In my last days*?"

I spun around and shoved him hard enough to wipe the smirk off his face. "This isn't a joke, Jack. I'm serious. That whole '*if I have to die so you can live*' crap isn't good enough. I don't want to live fifty more years without you. I won't. Especially not when we have a way to prevent it."

"Or a guarantee it'll happen," he snapped right back. "What if Juan Jr. went to Cece as a means to ensure I'm led to the very death he's claiming I'll avoid? If he was such a good guy and he had the ability all along to bring us a warning, why not come to any one of us with a message to leave Tahiti with Captain Cook instead of staying behind to be captured by his father?"

I hugged my arms around my shoulders, considering it. "Maybe it's too late for that. Think about it. Cece only remembered Juan Jr. *after* we gave him a location in her past to show up at. And for me and Chris, nothing after the crash changed even though the new memories should've altered our behavior… What if that's how it works? What if you can only change things here *after* you can remember what happened there?"

"She has a point, you know," Terrence said from the doorway, startling us both. "For a mysterious man to just show up and kiss Cece—even if she was blackout drunk—that's not something she's likely to forget… She can count on one hand the number of guys she's kissed in her entire life. She'd have recognized exactly who he was to her the moment she got on this ship. It struck me as odd she hadn't remembered sooner… I think you're right."

"Even if that's the case," Jack huffed, "it doesn't change the fact that I don't trust him; doesn't make me think my children are any safer in that jungle than on this ship."

"Can I make a suggestion?" Terrence asked.

"By all means," I said, blowing out as I plopped down on the bed beside the babies.

"I think Jim was onto something about the ancestry charts." He strolled casually into the room with his hands behind his back. "If we can change memories, we should also be able to change the dates printed on those charts…"

He spun to face Jack. "So, why don't *you* get off the ship in Panama while she waits with the babies on board? Then you're not putting them in danger."

I sat forward in the bed. "But what if it's not instant? What if the chart will only change once the moment he would've died passes?"

Terrence pursed his lips in thought. "If someone on this ship wants you dead, then we should assume they might've done it pretty shortly after you were separated from half your group. There's time to keep this ship anchored for a few weeks if need be. I'd be happy to stay on board and keep an eye on things." He tapped the Glock strapped against his rib. "And if, during that time, the date on the chart changes, then you know Juan is telling the truth and someone can return to retrieve your family. If it doesn't change before we have to leave, you get back on board and we start picking off the crew one by one until it does."

I raised an eyebrow at Jack. "It's not a terrible idea."

He shook his head. "And leave you and the babies here with whoever intended to kill me? I don't like that any better."

"We have automatic rifles," Terrence reminded him. "Kyle, Jacob, Michael, and I can make sure we are the only ones on board with access to them… We'll remain armed and on guard while you're away, and we won't let your family out of our sight. We also have time before we get there to do some reconnaissance. As a detective, I can sneak around the shadows on this ship and see if I can't sniff out any possible threats."

Jack squeezed the bridge of his nose. "I don't know… Say we don't find anything… Every time I have been apart from her something terrible has happened."

"We will live," I said. "That chart says so… And so long as the dates beneath *our* names remain unchanged, you'll know we're safe."

"We'd be putting a whole lot of faith in the idea that we can alter what's printed on that paper," he argued. "What if it doesn't work like that? And what if I get off this ship and it sails off with you still on it?"

Terrence frowned. "There's only two people who can captain this ship. Take Gabriel with you."

"Take Gabriel where?" Cece asked, limping into the room.

"What's wrong?" I jumped up from the bed. "Is the tetanus flaring up again?"

"I'm fine," she groaned, waving me off when I attempted to support her. "I just have a little cramp in my leg… Which is a perfectly normal thing for someone who has been in bed for as long as I have." She looked past me to Terrence as she eased herself down into a chair. "Who's taking Gabriel with them? And where are they taking him?"

Jack ran a hand down his face in surrender. "I'm *considering* taking Gabriel with me *if* I get off the ship in Panama to test this warning. The rest of you will wait on board. If the death date on the chart doesn't change, I'm getting right back on the ship and we're going to that storm the way we intended."

Cece leaned forward to massage her calf. "He said *all*, not some. You really think the paper will change?"

Jack shook his head. "No, but it's worth a shot."

I sniffed the air around Cece as I leaned against her chair. "Why do you smell funny?"

She straightened, horror washing over her features. "I was making cheese with Bruce." She glanced toward the open doorway and back, pulling her sleeve to her nose to get a whiff. "Juan's supposed to escort me to dinner any minute! Is it really bad?"

I chuckled. "Well, it's not the worst thing I've smelled, but it's not exactly pleasant. Why on earth were you making cheese anyway? You've been in bed for two weeks dying of tetanus. You should be taking it easy and giving your body time to heal."

Disregarding the latter half of my statement, she stood from the chair with a grunt to limp to the entry table where she'd left her purse. "Maybe my perfume will cover it up. Do you think I've got time to wash—"

"Hey y'all," Jim poked his head through the doorway beside her, "dinner's ready and I'm 'bout starved to death... By the looks of things, this one is too." He winked at Cece. "If we don't fatten ye' up soon darlin', you're liable to fall straight through your ass and hang yourself. Ooh Lordt, what's that smell?"

"It's me," Cece pouted, fishing out a little champagne colored bottle and spritzing it over her hair, neck, and wrists in a panic. "Is that better?"

Jim choked, fanning both hands to direct the aroma away from his face. "Christ darlin', we don't *all* need to smell pretty. Ye' done burnt the hairs right out my dang nose. Ain't none of us gonna' be able to smell nothin' but flowers for the next two weeks." He snickered. "I suppose that's better than spoilt milk. Come on then. Junior's out here waitin' for yuns."

Jack and I plucked up the babies, and we all made our way through the cloud of her daisy fragrance to the hallway where Juan Jr. was leaning against the wall.

I watched as he silently offered Cece his arm and she took it, staring up at him while he kept his eyes forward.

There was a stiffness in his spine and, although it wasn't outside his character to be reserved, the rigidity seemed particularly in response to Cece. I noticed her noticing it too and she frowned, her own shoulders tightening as we came out of the stairwell into the corridor.

"Ay, Goose," Jim whispered behind me, falling into step with Terrence. "How long you been workin' on our case?"

"Goose?" Terrence scoffed.

"Don't try to fight it," Jack tittered. "Once he's decided on a nickname for you, it's permanent… whether you like it or not."

Terrence smirked. "I've been investigating it for about two years now. Why?"

Jim lowered his voice. "Ye' ever met my ex?"

"June? A few times."

"Ye' seen my son then?"

Terrence softened. "Yeah, I met him once. Great kid."

Jim took a deep breath. "Did he seem smart to ye? Happy?"

"Oh, he's smart, alright," Terrence assured him. "He spoke like an adult—in more ways than one. After he'd finished cussing me out, he expressed himself eloquently, answered with intelligence; he was cautious about the way he responded to questions about his momma, even though she had nothing to hide. He's a good boy. Seems happy."

"His momma," Jim continued. "She seem like she's good to him? She ain't beatin' on him or nothin?"

"No," Terrence laughed. "She's unpleasant, but that boy is her whole world and you can tell she does everything she can to make sure he doesn't want for anything."

Jim sighed. "Before ye' left… do ye' know if she got that money I left for her?"

"I believe so. She quit her two jobs and put their house up for sale about a month before we left. My partner thought it was suspicious."

"Good." Jim cleared his throat. "Ye' don't happen to have no pictures of 'em on your phone, do ye? Photos of Beau or the house he grew up in?"

"I do," Terrence said as we all filed into the dining room to greet the rest of our group. "But my phone's been dead for weeks."

"We got a solar panel," Jim informed him. "It's got enough juice to power up a phone. I wanna' see him… See what kind of life he's livin'. Maybe after dinner?"

Throughout the meal, we went over our idea of using the report as a means to verify Jack's death date would change if he got off the ship. We discussed all the possible risks and ultimately agreed it was worth a shot—well, most of us agreed. Cece remained adamant that we shouldn't ignore the *'all'* part of his statement while the rest of us crafted a haphazard plan.

Chris, Maria, Jack, Jim, Lilly, and Juan would go to Panama. While the bulk of the group would move inland in search of Bud and Izzy, Jack would wait at a small inn in Panama City with Gabriel and a shipman named Tomás.

I would make a handwritten copy of the chart to keep on board with the rest of us. If Jack's death year changed, those of us on board would join him at the inn.

If it didn't change, or if the dates beneath any of our names were made sooner as a result, Jack would return.

Once we had our result, Tomás would then go ahead of us, since he was the fastest rider, to inform the others of our plans.

It was not likely we would run into another ship anchored on the Pacific side of the isthmus. If, by some miracle, we did, we would offer no small amount of gold to be taken to the coordinates of the small island and left there with a cutter. If we didn't, we would need to cross over to the Atlantic side and pray we found a merchant willing to sail us back around Cape Horn.

As dinner wrapped up and we all sat pondering our own roles in the plan, I noticed again the thickness in the air between Cece and Juan. It wasn't just her resistance to our plan. Something had happened between them. Neither of them had said a word to each other during dinner, and although she stole several glances across the table at him, I hadn't seen him return even one.

"I don't feel well," she announced, pushing her chair back from the table to stand. "I think I'm gonna' go lay down now."

Juan rose with her. "I'll walk you back."

"No need," she said with her chin held high. "I can walk myself. Thank you for dinner, Bruce. It was wonderful. Goodnight."

I frowned at Juan as he watched her hurry off, then turned to Jack. "Will you—"

"Go," he insisted, shifting Zachary to one leg and reaching to take Cecelia from me. "I've got them."

Handing her off, I excused myself, jogging once I'd exited the dining room to catch Cece at the top of the stairwell. "Wait up, turd!"

She groaned, but she waited and let me wrap an arm around her for support as we made our way down the stairs.

"You gonna' tell me what's going on?" I asked.

She huffed. "Your guess is as good as mine. We had this amazing conversation this morning that ended with a kiss and he's been acting strange ever since. He won't even look at me. Whatever. I'm too old to feel insecure about it and there's too much going on right now to spend even one more second worrying about it."

"Is that why you're skulking off?" I teased. "So you can not worry about it the rest of the night?"

"I'm not *skulking*," she said, resting her head against my shoulder as we moved toward our room. "I just didn't want to sit there and watch him avoid me anymore. And I really *don't* feel good. My legs are cramping and I need to lie down."

"Hey!" Lilly called from behind us, her footsteps filling the corridor as she caught up and looped an arm through Cece's opposite one. "You alright?"

"I'm fine," she said, forcing a smile. "My legs are just sore."

"Mmm hmm," Lilly hummed sarcastically. "My legs get sore too when the guy I like is being weird. You want me to kill him?"

Cece snickered as we entered our room. "No, it's alright. I'll figure out what his deal is tomorrow… Tonight I just want to lay in bed and not think about what an idiot I am."

"I'm sure you're not an idiot," Lilly snorted. "Men are ridiculous creatures. They blame us for being complicated when they're the ones that have a million different moods. Come on, we'll all take the big bed and Jack can go snuggle with Jim if he gets lonely."

I chuckled at that. "Wouldn't be the first time the two of them cuddled, would it?"

Lilly laughed at the memory and it felt good to hear the sound after weeks without it.

Cece raised a brow. "What exactly did you all *do* on that island? Do I even want to know?"

I grinned, turning her so I could begin to loosen her stays. "Nothing like that, *pervert*. Jim and Jack both got far too drunk one night and passed out together."

Lilly sighed as she reached for the pins in Cece's hair. "I miss being there… When we only had to worry about rescue coming for us and we weren't trying to change history. It was so much simpler."

Cece twisted her lips to one side. "What if we can't change history in the way we think?"

Lilly pulled the final pin for a cascade of blond hair to fall down Cece's shoulders. "What do you mean?"

"Well," she took a deep breath as I tugged the stays away from her body. "We remember the changes, but we didn't go back to live them, right? And things here haven't changed because of it… Only our memories…"

"Right," I said, untying her skirts. "And?"

"Well, I keep thinking about this other life of mine. Where did that other version of me go? What happened to her consciousness? It couldn't have just vanished."

I frowned as Lilly began untying my own stays.

Cece pursed her lips. "Is there some reality still playing out in some other universe where the woman I used to be and the child I used to have still exist? What if we're not altering our lives in the way we think but creating alternate realities instead—ones we might not necessarily get to witness first-hand? Let's say we change history and Anna comes back to life… Is there some other reality where she remains dead? And which one will we end up in? If we were to kill the Albrecht ancestor right now, does Juan just vanish before our eyes? Or do we all stand there looking at each other with new memories of a reality we're no longer a part of?"

Lilly pulled the stays off my ribs. "You lost me."

Cece laughed. "Think about it. We didn't exist in the 1700s, but now we do. Every breath we take here alters something—however big or small—about the world we knew; about our childhoods and the lives we lived before we got here… Our childhood happened; the memories we have are real… But they can't be at the same time. In theory, our past *is* an alternate reality because now that we're here, we are changing small bits of the world before any of us can ever be born to live in it."

"Alright Einstein," I joked, leading her to the bed. "You're either going way over my head with this or I'm just entirely too exhausted to comprehend any of it."

I reached for Lilly's stays but she waved me off. "I'm gonna go back up later." She sat down on the bed beside Cece, intrigued. "Like we're creating different dimensions? You think that's possible?"

Cece shrugged. "Maybe… Who knows though. A month ago, I would've told you time travel was impossible."

Lilly slid further into the bed as I joined them, laying down on her back to contemplate the theory. "Well, now that my brain hurts and I'm terrified of running into myself in some other dimension… can we talk about something we might actually be able to figure out? Lainey? You wanna fill us in on the Chris situation you've been keeping a secret?"

"It's not a secret. You've been preoccupied." I sighed as Cece pulled me to lay down beside her, both my sisters snuggled up with me at last. "And there's not much to tell. The new memories are making it hard for him to go on living like we'd been and he doesn't want to feel that way. He'll be fine. He just needs time."

"And Maria?" Lilly asked, the familiar trill of excitement at the opportunity to gossip lighting her voice. "Where does she fit into all this?"

"Don't know," I admitted. "She's been pretty quiet about the whole thing. Honestly, I've barely seen her lately. I know he cut things off with her, but I don't know if it's temporary or if he made things permanent. I hope it's not permanent."

Lilly let out a dramatic breath through her nose and poked Cece's rib. "What's your take on Maria?"

"Oh," Cece shrugged. "I don't really have one. I was too convinced she and Chris killed A.J. for the first few months to really have an opportunity to get to know her. Why?"

Lilly braided a piece of her hair. "Just curious if I'm the only one who thinks she's rotten and Chris is better off without her."

"Don't start, Lilly," I cautioned. "She's been nothing but nice to you."

"So?" Lilly balked. "Some of the most rotten people I know have plotted behind my back while being nice to my face. I don't like her."

"You've made that clear several times," I groaned. "We don't need to go over it again now."

"Fine." She tossed her braid to the side. "What's going on with Juan Jr.? What was all that tension about in the dining room?"

"You noticed?" Cece asked, her brows high on her forehead.

Lilly nodded. "Honey, I'm pretty sure all your other dimensions noticed it too."

"I don't know." She stretched her arms over her head and yawned. "He told me about his wife and kids this morning… it was nice… and he kissed me. And he's been weird since then. Maybe I'm a *really* bad kisser."

"Or…" Lilly leaned over Cece and sniffed, "maybe it's this weird smell coming off you. What the hell is that?"

"Ugh," Cece pulled a pillow over her face and growled. "It's cheese."

"For the love of God," Lilly chuckled. "Let me wash your hair for you."

Chapter Twenty-Three

Chris

It felt good to feel the vibration in his sword as it made contact with Juan Jr.'s. He'd come up before sunrise and found Juan happy to take on the lesson, evidently needing to work out his own issues in the process.

Juan made John Edgecumb's swordsmanship look like child's play. Where John was methodical and technical, Juan's technique came naturally; he seemed to dance with the sword, his blade an extension of his arm.

The first hour was spent almost entirely relearning footwork and posture John had gotten wrong before they moved onto advance techniques and fades.

"Where did you learn to fight like this?" Chris asked, blocking Juan's advance and spinning away.

Juan smiled as he circled, entirely in his natural element. "My wife's father was a master swordsman in the Spanish army who learned from his father who studied under the great Gérard Thibault. Thibault's techniques are based on mathematics; on natural proportion and the geometric relationships between us. Every move is a calculation, every step measured according to your build and that of your opponent. I have a diagram he called the mysterious circle. When we train, we draw it on the ground. Tomorrow, I shall show you, and we will change your blade for one that suits your size. This one is too short and far heavier than what you require." He clicked his tongue. "You are facing me."

"Sorry," Chris angled his body so that he offered his profile instead.

"Toes too," Juan reprimanded, frowning at Chris's feet. "And we have to do something about your grip."

"What's wrong with my grip?" Chris asked.

"I'll show you," Juan assured him, swinging his blade before the remark was finished and proving his point when Chris's sword clanked loose on the boards between them.

Juan chuckled. "The English do not know how to hold their swords. This is why they need gunpowder to win a fight."

"Look," he said, turning his own grip so Chris could examine the way he'd wrapped an index finger around the fore quillon. "Hold here," he raised the finger and spun the sword in a fast circle before stilling it just as it was, "and it becomes a part of you instead of metal in your hand. It will move as you will it—just as your arm and your fingers move by your mind's command, as will your sword. Understand?"

"Got it." Picking up his blade, Chris made a mental note of this lesson so he could share it during his afternoon teachings to Jim.

God, it felt good to have his mind filled with something other than self-loathing. For the first time in a long time, he was looking forward to the rest of the day.

"Go again," Juan said, backing up with his blade held out. "Hold it like I showed you."

Chris did, the grip feeling unnatural against his wrist after growing so accustomed to the bad habit. But when Juan swung, Chris was able to block, pivot, and advance with ease.

"You learn fast," Juan said. "You enjoy the feel of the blade in your hands, yes?"

"Yes." Chris smiled. "I don't think anything has ever felt more gratifying."

"But you hesitate during the kill." He motioned for Chris to make the next move. "Swordsmanship is more than just stance and skill. There is mindset that must be learned with it lest you find yourself the most talented of dead swordsmen."

"Of course I hesitate during the kill," Chris admitted as they circled. "It's unnatural. I can see the faces of every single man I killed that night… can still feel their eyes on me."

"Aye," Juan nodded, lowering his sword. "It is not an easy thing to do; to take a life that might've otherwise known greatness… It is in our nature to avoid war, but it is also in our nature to protect our own when war comes for us. There's a balance you have to find if you're to kill another. My wife's grandfather gave me these words to help me find mine: *He who raises his hand against me or the ones I have vowed to protect, has chosen the death I serve him. I have not taken a life he has not offered, and so he goes of his own will—not mine.*"

Juan wiped the sweat from his brow with his forearm. "It is the foundation of war. When you wage it upon another, you do so with the knowledge that only one man shall stand in the end. You did not choose their deaths. They did. You did not kill them. They killed themselves."

"Your wife's grandfather sounds like a wise mentor." Chris raised his blade. "Did you follow that code when you were out hunting Albrechts with your father?"

Juan shook his head, meeting Chris's advance with one of his own. "No. And that is one of the many reasons I'd hoped to erase our time here… To give back lives that were not offered freely."

"You think that's enough to save you in the end?" Chris asked, both of them pushing off to circle each other.

"I hope so," Juan said through a heavy exhale.

"Cece's a good girl, you know," Chris noted, spinning away from a lunge. "Far too good for a man like Owen… Did you prevent their marriage so you could have her for yourself or because you believed she deserved better after what I told you?"

"I *will* prevent their marriage," Juan mended, "for no other reason than that she has asked me to."

Chris grinned. "Oh, you really have no other reason?"

Juan lunged once more, taking out Chris's feet and pointing his sword to his throat when he'd landed on the boards. "What did I tell you about your toes?"

"Juan!" Jack called from across the deck, prompting Juan to remove the blade and offer Chris his hand. "We need to talk about this abstract warning of yours!"

Chris groaned as he took Juan's hand and sprang up onto his feet, not ready to listen to another of Jack's tirades, but not quite done with his lesson.

Juan lifted a brow. "As I've not yet given the abstract warning, Mr. Volmer, I'm not sure I can offer much to the conversation."

"Change it," Jack hissed, his fists clenched tightly at his sides as he came to a halt in front of them. "You have to give more detail. I have to know why it is so important that we *all* get off the ship. I have to know where the threat is."

Juan frowned. "Again, I cannot change what I've not yet done, sir. Forgive me, I do not know what to tell you."

Jack pushed a hand through his hair, his eyes bloodshot from a lack of sleep. He'd obviously been tossing and turning all night worrying about the plan. Chris had too, thus the reason he was on the deck before sunrise. "How can I take my family off this ship based solely on abstract words from *you*? And how can I leave them now that I've heard those words? I have to know what happens here. You can't leave it at that. It's not enough."

Jack extended his hand, offering Juan a piece of paper. "Vipers, pirates, slavers, jaguars, malaria, floods, and yellow fever," he said shakily. "That is what I risk taking my family off this ship… I risk only my own life in keeping them on board."

Juan unfolded the paper and frowned as he read whatever was written on it. "What is this?"

"I was in a car accident in 2006. That's the date and location of the hospital where you can find me. Memorize it, go there, and tell me the rest." He squeezed his eyes closed, evidently waiting for a memory to appear.

Chris frowned between them, intrigued at the idea a memory might be that easy to manipulate. It's what they'd done for Cece, after all…

"Dammit," Jack growled through his teeth, a tear sliding past his closed lashes. "I will not let my family die the way yours did. Go there and tell me what to do!"

Chris stiffened at the mention of Juan's family, and he kept an eye on the sword still in Juan's hand as Jack dropped down to his knees. "Please. Tell me what to do."

Juan stared at the paper, scanning the text over and over again. "I give you my word, if it is within my power, I shall arrive here on this date… Have you a memory of it now?"

Eyes still closed, Jack shook his head. "No."

Chris watched as Jack's devastation sank him. He opened his watering eyes and looked between them. "I can't make another mistake."

Juan cleared his throat. "There are additional precautions we might take in addition to the current strategy."

Jack stood. "Such as?"

"When we come into the bay, we'll leave the ship facing the harbor when we anchor instead of turning it away," he said. "If any man should attempt a getaway with your family on board, they shall be forced to turn without the wind. We would see the ship turning and have plenty of time to make our way back."

Chris remembered the nearly twenty-four hours it took to turn Captain Cook's ship around in Tahiti when they'd come in too close and lost the wind. "That's a good idea. Turning these ships is a lot more work than you think."

Jack nodded. "But what if we need to make a getaway? Wouldn't that immobilize us, too?"

"Yes." Juan sheathed his sword. "But we have the guns and it is far more likely whoever might threaten us would be in need of a getaway long before we would. We will anchor the ship in such a way that Gabriel can use the anchor to club haul the ship into a turn should we need to."

"What's that mean?" Jack frowned.

Juan smiled. "We anchor opposite the wind, inflate the sales to turn it against the anchor and cut the line. A maneuver my father has never attempted."

"But Gabriel has?" Chris asked.

Again, Juan grinned. "On another ship where he served as first mate. He and the captain used the trick to navigate between two reefs. He's quite proud of it."

Jack stared down at his feet. "If it were your family and *I* had come with a message you didn't know you could trust... What would you do?"

Juan sighed. "I would do precisely what you are planning. I have seen yellow fever up close and I would not let my children off the ship either."

At this, Jack nodded and inspected Chris's still drawn sword. "Can I..." He cleared his throat uncomfortably. "Can I join you?"

Chapter Twenty-Four

Cecelia

I'd been prepared to march straight up to Juan and demand an explanation for his odd behavior the moment I woke up. Too anxious to bother with a corset, I'd tied on my skirts and wrapped a shawl over my midsection to hide the missing garment.

He hadn't looked at me; hadn't spoken a single word after that kiss… And he'd practically sprinted out of the galley. Why? He had to know how that would make me feel…

It made me feel used, naïve, and ridiculous.

And that made me angry.

I wasn't some daft teenager who shriveled into the corner when a man toyed with her. I was a grown woman, and grown women demanded answers.

At least, that's what I kept telling myself all the way down the corridor and up the first flight of stairs.

On the inside, there was a daft and shriveling girl screaming at the top of her lungs, terrified to no end that she'd never be kissed by this man again… This man, whose name played like a song set on repeat in her mind; who, in the matter of weeks, had completely derailed every life plan she'd spent thirty-four years carefully constructing… This man who, despite her better judgment, she was already falling for…

It had been weeks, most of which I'd been unconscious for. Falling for a man in any capacity in such a short length of time was absurd. I was being ridiculous.

I was halfway up the second flight of stairs, moving toward a gray and purple morning sky, when the all-too-familiar numbness of a panic attack crept over my palms. Moisture formed in my mouth and stars floated around the edges of my vision, forcing me to cling to the railing.

Stupid, broken brain… I didn't need this now…

I lowered myself onto my butt on the stair, bending over my knees to take a deep breath in through the nose and out through the mouth.

What the hell was wrong with my body? How was it able to put up with poison and nearly dying but managed to fall to pieces when a male simply hurt my feelings?

In through the nose… out through the mouth…

There wasn't even anything to panic about. I barely knew the man to be reacting like this to a lack of eye contact.

In through the nose… out through the mouth…

"Mistress McCreary?" Someone called from above. "Are you quite alright?"

I didn't trust myself to speak, but nodded as I counted through my inhale.

"You don't look it," the man said, his steps growing closer until I felt a hand on my back. "You've gone pale. Shall I retrieve the captain for you?"

"No!" I shouted, spinning around to meet Tomás's dusty brown eyes. "No," I said again in a softer tone.

The last thing I wanted was for Juan to see me in this condition. I'd have to demand answers another time. "Are… are you going down to the galley?" I asked. "For your lessons with Bruce?"

He glanced over his shoulder and back, lowering his voice to a whisper. "Yes… but I cannot leave you in such a state. The captain would have my head if he knew I'd abandoned you like this."

I forced a smile, counting through my exhale. "I just lose my breath sometimes. I'll be fine in a moment. Can I walk down with you?" I focused on my inhale before continuing. "I told Bruce I would check on the pigs."

"Of course, mistress."

"Cece," I corrected.

"Cece," he repeated awkwardly, glancing over his shoulder once more. "Are you sure I can't have someone else escort you… someone who may know what to do about—"

"I'm fine," I breathed. "It's almost over. What's that noise up there?" I motioned in the direction of the deck where I could hear a loud clanging sound.

"Oh." Tomás smiled. "The captain is sparring with Mr. Grace and Mr. Volmer. I thought it a good opportunity to slip away for my lessons."

Feeling the pulse in my ears slow its pace, I straightened. I took one last deep breath to clear out the remnants of yellow fuzz from my eyes and tried not to imagine a shirtless Juan swinging a sword somewhere overhead. "I think it's passed now… Help me stand up?"

He did so, and after he'd assisted me down the first flight of stairs, he stoically offered me his arm, a move that seemed to have been practiced but never quite put to use.

"You're very sweet," I said, taking his offered arm and letting him lead us down the second flight. "How long have you been working on this ship?"

"Five years," he said, as if that was no time at all for a man so young—he couldn't have been older than twenty. "Never thought I'd see half of what I've seen here when I took the position."

I smiled. "What have you seen?"

"I saw God take three people up into his light, and then I saw them return unharmed on a white ship with you and the colored man… Saw you give a man with no arm a new one. Are you angels?"

I chuckled. "No, honey."

He eyed me dubiously. "An angel wouldn't say it was an angel… Would it?"

I patted his arm and winked. "You can never be sure, can you?"

I was glad he didn't ask for clarification. I'd been curious about what the crew thought they'd experienced when a modern-day yacht pulled up alongside them. Telling any version of the truth wouldn't do anything to help our cause.

"Tomás, do you know if anyone on board wants to hurt us?"

"No, mis—Cece. No one would ever wish harm upon you. Not after we all saw you come back on that heavenly ship."

"What about the ones that were not on that ship?" I pried. "Mr. Volmer, for instance… does anyone wish to harm him?"

He frowned and shook his head. "Not that I am aware. You think someone intends to hurt him?"

"Not sure," I said as we continued down the last flight of stairs. "Would you do me a favor and ask around? See if anyone might harbor any ill will toward him or any of the others?"

"I'd be happy to."

I set my feet before we could move into the galley. "Tomás, why are you so afraid of the captain? Has he hurt you?"

His eyes widened in horror. "On the contrary, madam, I owe my very life to this captain. It is not fear, it is honor."

"Oh yeah?" I was intrigued by this admission. Where I'd been digging for some kind of flaw in Juan's character to numb the ache of his rejection, I'd instead found more appeal. "Why do you owe him your life?"

"That is for him to tell," he said valiantly. "I will only say that he gave me food and shelter at a time when I had neither, and gave me work on this ship so I would never find myself without them again."

I'd made a quick stop in the galley to interrupt Bruce and Jim's morning gossip. Stealing a cup of coffee while there, I'd promptly gone to the hull with Jim to begin my work with the pigs.

"Ye wanna' see the most beautiful thing in the world?" Jim asked, propped against the wooden fencing that surrounded the pigpen and inhaling his secret morning cigarette.

"Sure." I leaned over, inhaling a bit of his smoke. I might've been the only person in the world that enjoyed the smell of someone else's cigarette. While I'd never been a smoker myself, there was something nostalgic about the scent to me, having grown up with a mother who once enjoyed the habit. It reminded me of long car rides to our grandfather's house, the way she daintily held it between her fingers atop the steering wheel as she gave us clues during a game of I-spy.

Jim pulled a phone out of his back pocket, his thumbs working the passcode until the screen lit up the dim space. Balancing the cigarette between his lips, he swiped through a few photos, then turned the phone in my direction.

The picture he presented was of a young blond haired boy with dark bushy brows. He wore a blue and white baseball uniform with a bat slung over his shoulder, his cap smashing his hair against his too large ears.

I looked from the photo to the man holding the phone and saw the resemblance in the gray eyes, thick brows, and sharp cheekbones. "He's yours…"

He nodded proudly. "Beau Lee Jackson. Ain't he the most beautiful thing ye' ever seen in your whole life?"

"He's perfect," I said, admiring the affection in Jim's eyes as he turned the phone back around and drank in the image, cigarette all but forgotten in the hand rested on the fence.

"I spent the whole night starin' at this picture… I always wondered what he looked like. Never thought in a million years somethin' so perfect could come from me. I's supposed to give this phone back to Goose this mornin' but I cain't let it go."

I beamed at him. "I'm sure Terrence won't mind if you hang on to it a little longer. It's not like he can use it for anything out here. He might, however, mind if you continue to call him Goose."

He pulled the phone against his chest and closed his eyes. "I'll call that man whatever name he wants me to. He give me the best gift I could ever ask for. I hope I get to see my boy in person at least once before I die…"

"You will," I assured him, kneeling down to examine a curious sow that had come close.

Her eyes weren't sunken, nor was there any discharge around them indicative of sickness… Her ears were pink and surprisingly clean with no signs of parasites or swelling. I scratched the top of her head and giggled as she pressed into my touch.

"They don't seem sick, do they?" Jim asked, crouching down beside me to take one final puff from his cigarette before stubbing it out against his boot.

I touched her nose, and finding it cool, I went on to smooth my hand over her back and belly.

"No," I said, pursing my lips. "She's got no signs of infection, parasites, or nutritional deficiency. Her temperament is curious, as it should be, and the pen looks good—nice and clean… I don't see any reason for concern, but to be safe, I'd like to examine them all."

"Ye' gonna' be alright for a few minutes while I go refill my coffee? Need at least two cups before I start shovelin' shit."

I grinned. "Take your time. This is what I'm made to do."

"Careful with that male over there." He pointed at a large black pig on the opposite end of the pen. "He's ornery as shit. Bit me twice now just for lookin' at him."

"I've been bit on more than a few occasions," I said, "I'll be alright."

I watched him head toward the galley before spinning back around to climb into the pen. Hoisting one sore leg over the fence, I noticed movement in the shadows where the fresh straw was kept… *human* movement.

"Hello?" I called out, reaching into my pocket to ensure the taser was still there. I felt my heart ease when I touched its handle. "Somebody in here?"

"Sí," Maria said defeatedly, climbing down from the bales she'd been resting on, her face pale and sullen. "It's only me."

"Maria?" I hopped back over the fence. "What on earth are you doing down here? Did you actually sleep here?"

She shrugged, picking straw from her hair. "It's not so bad."

I could see she was struggling to keep herself together, her lip quivering slightly and her eyes starting to water. The sight broke my heart.

Unable to prevent myself from doing so, I wound my arms around her. "Oh sweetie! There are plenty of places for you to sleep other than here and Chris's bed. Why didn't you come to the big cabin? What's going on?"

She buried her face against my hair. "I don't want to say."

I held her tighter as she came undone, shaking with the tears she'd been fighting to keep inside. "It's alright. Please don't cry. You can talk to me."

"No I can't," she sobbed. "I can't talk to anybody. Every time I open my stupid mouth, I make things worse. I am better off with the pigs."

"You are not." I combed her hair, pulling bits of straw from it as I did. "You've done nothing wrong."

"No?" She pulled away, wiping both eyes to no avail. "I fell in love with a man I knew loved his wife… I have known all along he would choose her over me and still I clung to him. When we went back to our time, I could've stayed. I knew exactly what would happen if I followed him and I did it anyway. Even though I knew the new memories were making things worse; even though I knew he would leave me because of them; even though I knew I would be out here alone with people who hate me, I followed him…because I am a stupid, stupid woman."

"You're not stupid, Maria, and no one hates you."

She laughed. "*Maria is rotten and Kreese deserves better.* I may be a stupid woman, but I am not deaf. I came to the big cabin and I prefer the pigs."

I crossed my arms. "Who cares what Lilly thinks? She's barely an adult and she is very obviously used to having something to gossip about. I'm sure she didn't mean it. Besides, A.J. adores you, and I'm here now. You're not alone, honey. Not at all."

She sniffled. "You don't even know me."

"There's plenty of time to change that." I motioned to the pen behind me. "You afraid of pigs?"

She glanced past me and shook her head.

"Wanna help me check them for signs of sickness?" I asked. "I'll tell you what to do and while we work, you can tell me about your life, and I'll tell you about mine. We'll be friends by the end of it."

She wiped her nose with her sleeve and nodded, fresh tears spilling from her eyes. "Thank you."

"But you have to stop crying," I said, reaching out to squeeze her hand. "I'm one of those ridiculous people who cries when I see other people crying and I'm about to fall to pieces just looking at you. Trust me when I say, you do not want to deal with me crying on top of everything else you're going through. I have a tendency to ugly cry."

She laughed at that, groaning as she moved her hands over her face. "I am so tired of crying. I can't stop."

I straddled the fence, inviting her to join me. "So let's talk about something that won't make you cry. You were born in Cuba?"

"Sí."

I was pleasantly surprised when she didn't hesitate or complain, but climbed over the fence with me to be instantly surrounded by curious piglets.

"I lived there until I was seven," she continued, sniffling, "and then my father took me to live in Barcelona with his uncle."

I swooned. "I always wanted to see Barcelona. Particularly Montserrat—the monastery there and the stairway to heaven sculpture… did you ever visit the mountain?"

She smiled. "Oh yes. My father went to school and worked several jobs, but Sundays were ours, and he always had an adventure planned for me. We went to Montserrat often. We visited the monastery and all the churches, statues, and caves."

She knelt down to pet one of the piglets. "My father was this brilliant man. I don't know how he walked around with so much knowledge in his brain. He always knew all the history of every place we visited, explaining the background for every statue or painting or carving; who made it, why they made it, when they made it… I know that mountain better than most places in my mind. Could paint nearly every inch of it from memory if I could paint."

She frowned at me as I pulled up the piglet's ear. "What do you want me to do?"

I showed her on the young pig what to look for and how to inspect the eyes, nose, ears, skin, and overall demeanor for signs of sickness, and got a sense of pride as she moved to a larger sow to try it herself.

"So, you and Juan Jr…" She poked, running a finger over the sow's snout. "You are a couple?"

"Honestly," I sighed, "I have no idea what we are. He acts one way one minute and completely different the next."

"He's *Colombian*, mi amiga," she said, as if that was all the explanation I needed.

"And?" I ran a hand over my hog's back, thankful to find the skin soft and healthy.

She chuckled. "Colombians are created different, honey… like all the world is born with a certain rhythm inside them, and then there's Colombians… way out there on a completely different wave length. You kissed him, no?"

I blushed. "Yes."

"Well then you know. Colombian men are…" she grinned, "well, they are something else. They can move their mouths and bodies in a way that will make noises you didn't know you had in you come out of your mouth. You take one to your bed and you would kill to stay in that bed for an eternity… He will say and do things to you that no man will ever be able to top. But…"

She inspected her sow's ear. "They are not good at… well, everything else when it comes to a relationship. It's almost like they don't know what to do with a woman if they're not making love to her."

I snorted, moving to another more skittish pig. "You sound like you know from experience?"

She sat back on her haunches and tilted her head back to let out a long, low hum. "His name was Luis. God, I never had a man touch me the way he did… But if he was not touching me, he was nowhere to be found. Our entire short-lived relationship was spent in my bedroom."

I did a little dance with my pig, attempting to earn her trust. "I dated a guy like that after college… if you'd call late night booty calls dating. We didn't exist outside my apartment. I'm ashamed to admit he's the only man I ever slept with."

"You've only slept with *one* man?" She gasped. "I would think men would be lining up for you!"

"Not really," I chortled. "I'm very awkward when it comes to men… Never knew what to do with myself when one came anywhere near me. Maybe I'm on a different wave length, too."

She laughed out loud, scaring off the piglet she'd been reaching for. "Mi amiga, you need to run—*not walk*—to that handsome Colombian upstairs, if only to get yourself some experience! One man… my God. Of course you are confused about Juan Jr. You wouldn't know how to identify love if it walked up and smacked you in the face."

"Don't go near that one," I cautioned as she moved toward the black hog. "He bites. I'll save him for last."

She wisely changed course to kneel down in front of a much friendlier spotted female. "One man..." she repeated under her breath, shaking her head in disbelief. "...in your whole life."

"If I'd known you were going to make it into such a big deal," I said, "I wouldn't have said anything."

She raised her brows. "I'm sorry. You see what I mean with my mouth? I cannot help it. Stupid words just fall out of it. We'll change the subject now."

As we examined each pig, conversation flowed freely, and we talked about just about everything... from fond childhood memories to broken hearts to choosing the lives we'd ended up in before our arrival in this time.

I actually liked the woman, despite her tendency to almost always say the wrong thing.

I saw a bit of myself in her. Where I was awkward with men, she was awkward with women, and just as I'd once hoped to find love despite it, she desperately craved female companionship the same way.

Craving female companionship was also a feeling I'd experienced before. I'd once been a part of a sorority and knew all-too-well what it was like to be an outsider among women who'd already formed bonds with each other. Coming into that house to always be just outside conversations was awful; and to overhear someone in the group you wanted to be a part of call you rotten—or in my case, *boring*—I knew how much it hurt. Luckily, I'd had Jasmine to cling to. Maria had no one but Chris... and he'd let her go.

"Maria," I said, attempting for the fifth time to coax the black hog into letting me touch him. "I can't imagine how hard this all has been for you.... But, I want you to know, if you need a friend to talk to or just hold on to... like... ever... you can hold on to me. It doesn't matter where I am or who I'm with. You can always drag me away or ask me to pull you in and I'll never think less of you for it."

"Gracias," Maria said, rising off her knees to brush the straw from her skirts. "You will regret that when I drive you crazy by taking you up on your offer."

"Will not," I assured her. "I mean it. Anytime."

"Thank you for this. I needed it more than you know. You have no idea what it means to feel like I have an ally here. Especially right now…" She glanced past me and grinned. "I'll eh… go wash off for breakfast to give you two some privacy."

Following her gaze, I whirled around on one knee to find Juan standing in the doorway. My heart leapt up into my throat. "You don't have to go," I said in a panic. "Really."

She patted my head as she strolled past me. "Yes, *mi amiga*, I *really* do. I'll see you at breakfast."

She climbed back over the fence, muttering something in Spanish I couldn't quite make out to Juan before she disappeared beyond the door.

I stood, dusting off my skirts before I met his eyes. "Do you need something?"

He tilted his head to one side. "I have upset you."

"Not at all," I assured him. "I'm perfectly fine."

"I've had blades cut less than those words," he noted, moving across the room. He was stripped down to only his white shirt and black breeches, the damp fabric clinging to his chest after his time spent sparring to reveal the black ink beneath. "I've upset you, and I've come to explain myself."

I crossed my arms over my chest, praying he couldn't see the pulse pounding in my neck as he grew closer. "Well, go ahead. I've got a cranky hog to examine before breakfast."

He balanced his forearms on the fence, the dimple appearing in his cheek to accompany his smile. "Even covered in mud, you are so very beautiful."

I rolled my eyes. "Calling me beautiful isn't an explanation."

He nodded, drawing a breath. "I overstepped in the galley. It was a moment of weakness driven by some sort of wild desire. I lost control of myself when I had no right to launch myself upon you in such a way. I wasn't thinking. Please forgive me."

"You think I'm upset you kissed me?"

He frowned. "Aren't you?"

I sighed, running a hand hard over my face. "Juan, I haven't let anyone kiss me like that in a very long time—"

"Joseph," he corrected.

"What?"

He raised his brow. "You have only ever called me Joseph when we are alone, not Juan."

"Joseph," I mended, "if I hadn't wanted it to happen, it wouldn't have happened. I am upset because you then went on to give me the silent treatment over dinner and avoided all eye contact with me. Do you have any idea how awful that made me feel?"

"I believed you the one avoiding me," he said. "I was anxious to see you again after leaving the galley. You would spend hours on the top deck before you got sick, and I was certain you would come to speak with me again before dinner. As the day passed without any sign of you, I became convinced my actions in the galley had offended you. I reflected on my behavior again and again and realized I had taken advantage of your affections when you'd given me no invitation to kiss you just then. How could I look at you when I knew I would see disappointment in your face? When I was certain you would put an end to our courtship at any moment?"

I shook my head, breathing out a laugh at the thought of such a powerful man being reduced to such normal insecurities. "So you overthink everything you do, too?"

"Only when it comes to you," he said softly, his shoulders easing. "I am made a complete fool the moment you are near me. I barely know my own name in your presence, let alone what is the right or wrong thing to do. You should know, it is never my intention to offend you or hurt you in any way, and I never wish to do so again. How can I make this up to you?"

I hid a smile. "You can help me with this hog. I need to check his ears but he won't let me get close. He's a bit of a biter." I presented the red welts on my forearm as proof.

"Aye," he hopped over the fence with ease, "he's my father's hog. I don't believe there is a man on board who hasn't been bitten by the petulant little bastard." He took my arm and ran a finger delicately over the red marks. "Has he hurt you?"

"No," I breathed, enraptured once again by the feel of his touch. "It's a fear based bite—just a warning nip. Must've had a bad handler at one time."

Juan shook his head. "He was born cranky."

I glanced at the big charcoal monster in the corner. "If you can just keep him distracted… It'll only take a second."

He nodded, letting go of my arm to move ahead of me.

"Hello Charlie," he cooed softly, crouching and extending his palm for Charlie to sniff. "You're looking very handsome today."

I snuck around the side of him as Juan continued to speak in a soothing tone.

He moved his hand closer, daring to run his knuckles along the side of the beast's snout. "There's a good boy…"

I very gently raised one ear and peeked inside. No parasites or welts… He was a healthy pig… well, healthy enough. He threw a bite at Juan and I stumbled backward, deciding my examination was finished.

Juan chuckled, wiggling his fingers at the hog as proof he'd escaped unharmed. "Missed me you little bastard." He turned to me. "Were you able to see whatever it is you needed to?"

I grinned and nodded. "He's got a clean bill of health as far as I'm concerned. Thank you."

He extended his hand to me. "Come then, let's get you out of this filthy place."

I took it and let him lead me back to the fence, unable to stop smiling when he then lifted me over the rail.

"Joseph," I said as he climbed over, "the young sailor, Tomás… He mentioned he owed you his life. Why?"

He reached out to pull a piece of straw from my hair, a brush of his skin skating over my cheek that sent a shiver down my spine. "That was a long time ago. When Philip was still a babe."

"And?" I probed.

He glanced at his feet as if debating whether or not to say more. Decided, he nodded and drew in a heavy breath. "I had been out for a ride with Tonauac—Elizabeth's grandfather—one afternoon when I heard screaming. It was a terrible, awful sort of scream; one I knew, even at so young an age as seventeen, was the sound of a woman dying."

He ran his thumbnail over his teeth, pacing a little at the telling. "It was my instinct to ride toward it; to draw my sword with the intention to stop whatever was causing her evident torment. I thought it a bear or a beast of some sort. I hadn't considered it might be a man."

He forced a smile that was meant only to reassure himself. "When I rode out, I found three natives on horses—couldn't say what tribe, nor could Tonauac. They weren't familiar to our territory. At the center of their circling horses lay a bloodied man and woman, recently dead, and a young boy stood over their bodies, holding up a small dagger in defiance." The upward curve in his lips raised naturally at the image of the boy, but quickly fell away.

"Even at a distance, I knew they intended to kill that child; could see it in the way they bared their teeth at him. Thinking of the boy of my own that would one day grow to be his size, I did not hesitate. I rode out with sword and dagger, Tonauac at my side, and I killed a man for the first time—three men."

He shook his head. "And it was on that day I recognized the same darkness in me that I'd seen in my father. I went with good intention: to save that child... but the moment my blade struck bone, I became someone else... Someone excited to feel it strike again."

"Anyway," he sighed, straightening his shoulders as the rest came easier, "I couldn't very well leave the poor boy standing there with no one to care for him, so... I took him home to my estate where he found a mother in our cook who'd lost a son of her own several years prior. It was a good match and she raised him well, put him to work in the stables where he grew to be one of the best hands we'd ever seen. He approached me a few years ago and insisted I bring him with me when I sailed out again so he could live a life worthy of the one I'd given him."

I didn't have the words for the warmth that had suddenly taken physical residence in my throat. For him to do such a thing for a complete stranger… it was awe inspiring. I wanted him that much more.

"I've never met your father, but *you're* a good man," I managed. "Maybe the best I've ever met, I think."

I took both his hands in mine as he moved to object. "I mean that. Unless I tell you otherwise, you can safely assume you *always* have an invitation to kiss me… in whatever way you'd like."

The corner of his lip curled upward. "I was not too familiar?"

I shook my head, some part of my soul tingling as he gently squeezed my fingers. "No, I enjoyed it… very much."

"Why did you stay away then?"

I bit my lower lip. "I was… making cheese and I completely lost track of time."

He stared at me incredulously and I at him until we both burst into laughter, each of us realizing we'd been just as ridiculous in our self-conscious paranoia as the other.

I wasn't sure which one of us initiated it, but somewhere midlaugh, I found myself pressed against the fence with his mouth once again over mine.

I inhaled the sweet almond and musky scent of him, letting it override the stench of swine and excite my senses.

Nothing felt like him.

Nothing had ever felt like him.

My whole life was like some mustard blend of desaturated colors—each memory bland and dull and unspectacular in comparison. But wrapped up in him, it was like a spectrum of vibrant blues, reds, oranges, and greens burst into life around me. I could live forever in that kind of color… Could survive on nothing but the hues he brought into my once two-toned existence.

It was my turn to be overly familiar. Twisting my fingers into his shirt, I pulled him closer and wound both arms around his neck, basking in the feel of his body against mine—the taste of his lips over mine. And Maria was right. Noises I'd never heard escaped my throat.

He was warm and his clothes were damp from sparring, but I didn't care, and my fingers found a place in his hair, down his shoulders, over his chest, and back up to re-explore them all over again. I couldn't touch enough of him… couldn't have enough of him.

When our hips began to move on their own against each other, he pulled away to press his forehead against mine, breathing heavily. "I could kiss you a thousand times and never tire of it."

I hummed happily. "A thousand's going to take some time. You're only at three so far."

He smiled, running his fingertips down the sides of my neck. "Oh, I intend to commit a great deal of time to doing only that."

"Is that so?" I teased. "I'm a very busy woman. You'll have to squeeze in more than one at a time if you plan to fit into my schedule."

"I certainly shall," he whispered, "when I no longer am required to stop myself at only the one."

I closed my eyes, moving my nose against the side of his. "What if I said you didn't need to stop?"

"Not yet, *mi alma*." He laid a gentle kiss on my lips. "I intend to share far more with you than my bed. And I won't start things off by defiling you at the side of a pigpen."

I blushed, glancing down at our filthy, straw-covered bodies. "I should probably go clean this off. I wouldn't want to spoil breakfast by stinking up the dining room… *again*."

He held me in place, pressing his lips against my forehead. "May I see you again this afternoon?" His kiss moved to my temple, brow, cheek, and lips. "And this evening? And tonight? And tomorrow morning? And every second you might spare me when your eyes are open?"

I laughed. "Yes, yes, and a thousand more times, yes."

PART II

Just a Blip...

Chapter Twenty-Five

Alaina

With so much planning to do before our arrival in Panama, and with all the argument the plan seemed to spark amongst us, the days began to bleed together.

Cece and I didn't like the plan; neither of us was particularly confident about the idea of being left behind, even if we would be heavily guarded. Juan Jr. had specifically said *'you all get off the ship.'* He'd even made her repeat the words back just to be sure she'd heard him, emphasizing the word *all*. And the closer we got to our destination, the more vocal we became about our objections.

Others began to switch sides in the debate, particularly after Cece repeatedly brought up the rest of our death dates in the report being set in the past and not *'unknown.'* If there was any way for us to make it back through time, those dates shouldn't be there at all.

Maria, Kyle, and Bruce agreed with her, and it became a daily occurrence for us to argue in circles that led nowhere.

Jack and Juan would not budge on their stances that the babies and Cece were better off staying on the ship until they could make sense of the warning.

Cece, whether we all agreed in the end or not, had no intention of remaining on the ship; partly because of Juan Jr.'s warning, and partly because of Juan Jr., himself.

If the man was awake, she had an excuse to be next to him. It was only in the mornings and right before bed that I ever saw her outside his shadow. And I knew, even if we tied her to a mast, she would find some way to make it to Panama to be at his side.

Much as I opposed their relationship, there was no denying they were cute together. She softened him, and he brought her out of her shell. They were both far too timid to display any sort of public affection, but there were small touches and smiles... a certain lightness in the air around them that told me there was something much bigger than infatuation blooming between them.

I wanted to look at them and be happy; to see what everyone else saw in their relationship, but all I saw was Maddy. What kind of sister would I be if I didn't try to save her daughter?

With the babies down for their midday nap and Magna watching over them, I'd been standing on the deck watching the two of them flirt at the helm when the barrelman in the crow's nest cried out, "There's something on the water!"

There was a mad dash for the bow made by every man and woman within earshot of the call. Lilly, who'd lived the past several weeks in that very spot, pressed the spyglass to her eye as I made my way through the crowd to her side.

"It's the yacht!" she screamed, her voice raising several octaves as she bounced from toe to toe. "And there's... there's someone on it!"

"Who?!" I asked, squinting to see the little dot in the distance.

She kept the telescope pressed firmly to her eye, frowning. "I can't tell, but there's movement! Oh, please, please, let it be grandpa and Izzy... Please!"

A hand slid into mine on the opposite side of me, and I turned to see Cece there, staring wide-eyed at the ocean ahead. "What if Bud and Izzy *are* on it?" she whispered close. "We would have no reason to go to Panama... Would we?"

I shook my head.

"We have to," she continued, meeting my eyes. "You and Jack are a part of history because you have children that go on to ancestor generations more. The rest of us don't. We'd be easily forgotten if we died on this ship with him. What if that's what Juan meant by stressing the word: *all*? A.J., we *have* to get off this ship in Panama. Not just for Jack, but for the sake of everyone else on board."

I swallowed, staring back out at the yacht as we grew close enough to make out the multiple decks in the stern. It hadn't occurred to me that anyone beyond Jack was at risk of dying, but she was right. Their names in this century might've easily been forgotten should they die on the ship.

"It's a man," Lilly said, leaning over the rail with the spyglass still held against her eye. "On the sky deck. He's bleeding... Holding up some kind of fabric over his head... It's... I think it's Phil."

"Lemmee see," Jim said, taking the telescope from her and looking out for himself. "Shit. You're right. He's tore up pretty good from the 'mount of blood on him. Christ, I think he's been shot in the gut. That ugly summbitch don't die easy, does he?"

Behind us, Juan was shouting orders, maneuvering the ship in preparation of slowing to a stop at the side of the yacht.

"My dad?" Kyle asked, squinting out at the yacht where we could start to see the blond wood coloring of the outer decks. "He's alive though, right? Can I see?"

"He's in a bad way," Jim assured him, handing off the spyglass, "but he's alive."

Kyle held the lens to his eye and drew breath through his teeth. "When we get there, I'm getting off with whoever boards."

"We don't know who else is on that boat," Jim huffed, shielding his eyes from the sun to try to get a better glimpse. "We'll need to be armed and ready... I ain't gonna' stop ye, but you'll stay your scrawny ass behind me 'till we're sure it's safe."

Lilly trembled. "You don't think... Izzy and grandpa..." She trailed off but the rest of the words didn't need to be said.

"No," I said softly. "They're fine. He wouldn't hurt them."

"We don't know that." Her lip quivered.

"We will soon enough," Jack said over my head. "Jim, let's get a sloop ready. Kyle, you and Michael go down to the armory and get a few automatic rifles. If Juan Josef's still on there, I intend to end this once and for all."

"You think they ran out of fuel?" Chris asked, resting both palms against the railing to tap his fingers anxiously against it. "Or do you think they're waiting for us?"

"Not sure," Jack said. "But I have no intention of letting any of them talk long enough to find out why they'd be waiting if they are. Come on. You know that boat better than I do if they're hiding."

Gradually, the crowd around us dissipated to prepare for boarding, leaving only me, Lilly, and Cece standing on the bow watching the yacht get closer.

Lilly slid her hand into mine as well, and we all held our breath and each other, unsure what our lives might look like after we reached whatever was out there waiting.

As our ship slid slowly along the side of the yacht and ropes attached to hook anchors flew overhead to link the the two vessels, I could hardly keep myself upright.

Cece, Maria, Lilly, and I all stood portside staring down at the yacht two stories below. The sky deck was covered in blood and Phil was slumped against the edge of the hot tub. His midsection was stained red, the sleeve of his shirt torn off and held over his head as a means to signal us.

We'd sent Terrence, Jacob, and Michael down to guard the rooms and ensure Fetia and her father were safely locked in with Magna and the babies while Jack, Jim, Chris, Kyle, and Juan were lowered down on a sloop.

None of us made a sound, not even the shipmen who watched at the sides of us.

Kyle immediately rushed to his father. "Dad!" he sobbed, showing a hint of his youth. He dropped to his knees and held his palm over the wound in Phil's stomach. "What can I do?"

With a trembling hand, Phil reached out to move the hair away from Kyle's face.

"Is my father on board?" Juan Jr. cut in, interrupting whatever Phil had opened his mouth to say. "Are you alone?"

What happened next seemed to go in slow motion.

Phil, with a hand still rested against Kyle's cheek, pushed Kyle to the side, drawing a revolver from his side with the other to point at Juan Jr.'s chest.

Beside me, Cece cried out—a high pitched and panicked scream—before launching herself onto the same ropes that had lowered the sloop.

The distraction caused Juan Jr. to turn in her direction, the bullet Phil simultaneously fired catching him in the shoulder.

I was already on the ropes when Cece hit the deck and limped to where Juan Jr. had fallen as the other men rushed to disarm Phil.

Letting the rope burn my palms for fear he might shoot her too, I slid down to the deck's surface and hurried to place myself between the skirmish and my sister.

"It's a trap!" Phil called out, letting Jack take the gun from him. "Why is he still alive?! Someone was helping Juan Josef the entire time! Who do you think unbolted that bed?! It was him! He's leading you right into his father's trap, you idiots! "

Chris stood with his rifle aimed down the stairwell. "Leading us to what? Is anyone else on this boat?"

"No," Phil said, keeping his eyes narrowed on Juan Jr. where he'd sat up with both his and Cece's palms pressed tightly against the wound in his shoulder.

"What trap?" Juan Jr. asked, wincing. "Where is my father?"

Phil's breathing rattled in his chest. "On his way to Panama on another ship. He promised their crew all the gold they could carry if they waited with him there for his son to *deliver his wife and daughter.* "

A cold chill ran up the nape of my neck.

Juan Jr. shook his head at the accusation that swept over Cece's features. "I have no intention of delivering anyone to him. I swear it. I pursue for the sake of saving Izzy and Bud… and with the intent to kill him once they are back in our care."

Phil coughed, pressing his hands hard into his gut. "You're all fucked if you believe that. Kill him now and go back to wait for the storm. You'll never see home otherwise." He made eye contact with Kyle who knelt once again before him. "They want the baby and Alaina and they'll murder anyone else that stands in the way. Shoot him now, my boy, and go back, or he will see to it that you, your wife, and your unborn child will die before you can ever make it to the storm."

Cece's face distorted and she removed her hands from Juan's shoulder, sitting back on her heels to gape at him. "You unbolted the bed? You told us to get off the ship… to get off and walk straight into the very place he'll be waiting for us." Her eyes watered, but she held up her chin and blinked them away. "How can I trust you?"

His expression was sullen as he searched her eyes, like he was entirely devastated by his own answer. "You cannot."

Faster than any of us could've been prepared for, he pulled a dagger from his thigh, and as I readied to launch myself upon him, he placed it in Cece's hands.

"I did not unbolt the bed, nor have I agreed to deliver you to my father. But I cannot know what happens between now and the time I arrive in your past to shape the meaning behind my warning. I do not trust myself, and you should not trust me either." He presented his throat to her. "The ship and the men are yours if you want them."

She shook her head and placed herself between his body and Jack, who, as their conversation played out, had taken it upon himself to point his rifle in Juan Jr.'s direction. "You might not trust you, but *I* do."

She glared at Phil. "How do we know we can take his word over Juan's? Why are you shot? Where are Bud and Izzy? What happened here?"

Phil certainly *didn't* die easily. Missing several fingers and with a massive scar across his cheek, he sat now struggling to breathe with a hole in his gut. He'd been through hell. It was hard to imagine the same man once pinning me to the ground.

"I was to drive the boat," he said. "They didn't give me much choice." He motioned to the revolver in Jack's left hand. "Had their own weapons hidden in the walls."

He took a concentrated breath, grimacing as he exhaled. "We didn't know Bud and Izzy were in the galley when we boarded. Dario was ordered to search the yacht while Juan Josef hauled me up to the pilothouse. Bud heard us come on board, though. He hid Izzy down behind one of the vents in the crew's quarters before returning to the galley for Dario to find him."

Another ragged breath…

"With Bud and the keys, there was no fancy hot wiring required, and we drove right off. Bud and I used Izzy's language. I, to tell him I was on his side, and he, to tell me Izzy was hidden below… We couldn't fight them. We had no weapons of our own and no way to take care of Izzy if we attempted to fight and lost. All we could do was keep her concealed and pray you all would catch up before they found her."

"Did ye?" Jim asked, looking toward the stairwell. "Keep her concealed?"

Phil nodded. "Bud and I took turns going down to feed her and make sure she was alright. She's here." He chuckled, raising his hands from the wound on his stomach to present a blood-soaked band-aid stuck onto his shirt. "When no one came down for her last night, she came up. She tried to help."

And then it was Lilly who launched herself onto the ropes, impressively walking her hands and legs down it in a way that prevented the burns that were presently tormenting my palms. "Where?" she panted. "Where is she?"

"In the crew's galley, off to the side, there's a work area. She's hidden behind the vent. I saw the ship coming, didn't know who was in control. Told her to hide and wait for someone to come get her."

As Lilly and Jim both sprang for the steps, Phil's next words stopped them both in their tracks. "Your grandpa's been shot, too."

Lilly slowly turned around while Jim went ahead down the stairs. "What do you mean, *shot*?"

"We didn't know where we were heading," he said through a wince, "but we knew we were almost out of fuel and must've been getting close to our destination since Juan Josef didn't seem concerned. Bud was worried about Izzy. He crept down and put a hole in the fuel tank to stall us out here until you could catch up."

He shook his head and laughed. "Should've known, with my luck, we wouldn't be stalled for long. It wasn't twenty-four hours later when that slave ship pulled up alongside us. Twenty-four hours…"

With a rattling breath, he continued. "Juan Josef had no intention of taking us with him, but we couldn't let him leave with that binder. We knew what he meant to do with it if you went back through the storm. Bud and I agreed to rush him for it. He shot us both. Bud didn't blink at the wound in his chest, but took the binder and launched it into the ocean. He told him the only way he was ever going to get any of the information on those pages was by taking him with them… So they did. Left me that revolver with one bullet in it should I get tired of waiting to die."

"When did this happen?" Juan Jr. asked. "How far ahead of us are they?"

"It happened about this time yesterday… don't know how fast that slave ship moves, but I know it's got a full crew."

"We are within a day of reaching the isthmus," Juan said, looking past Cece's shoulder to Lilly then me then Jack. "But we have Izzy. Bud is an old man capable of taking care of himself. You could return to the storm."

Jack shook his head and locked eyes with Lilly. "We're not leaving him. We're not leaving anyone."

And the world stood still—the conversation placed on pause—as Jim emerged with Izzy's little figure wrapped tightly around his torso.

"Christ," Jim grinned over her tiny body as Lilly flung her arms around them both, "what the hell yuns been feedin' her? Cain't hardly hold her up no more."

Lilly sobbed, collapsing with her arms wound tightly around Izzy the moment Jim handed her off. She laid a dozen kisses on her cheeks, smoothed her hands over her hair, and might've squeezed a little bit of life out of the poor girl.

I waited patiently for Lilly to let go—which meant I waited a good long while—and then knelt to give her my own too-long and too-tight hug. She giggled as I shook her from side to side, then shouted, "Yag!" as she caught sight of him.

He chuckled, swinging his rifle to his back and crouching down so she could immediately run into his outstretched arms.

"Welp," Jim said casually, placing both hands on his hips, "we killin' Junior or not?"

Cece hadn't moved from her place in front of him, and at the suggested threat, she extended both arms out as if they might shield him further. "We are not."

"Alright then," he leaned back against the rail with a wink, "if we ain't killin' nobody, I reckon we orta' get whatever we need off this yacht and sink it before we really turn history sideways. These two's gonna' need stitchin'," he motioned to Juan Jr. and Phil. "And we gonna' need to figure out what direction we're fixin' to go. No sense in us standin' around yackin' when we got shit to do. We got our girl, and I ain't lookin' to spend no more time with the rest of yuns than I have to. I promised her I'd have a Got damn picnic before all this and that's exactly what I plan to spend my night doin.'"

Chapter Twenty-Six

Cecelia

While the others scoured the yacht for anything valuable, Lilly, A.J., and I took Phil, Juan, and Izzy back to the ship.

With Terrence's help, we got Phil set up in the infirmary, and I removed the bullet lodged in the fatty tissue in his gut.

Lucky for him, it didn't appear to have hit any major organs. Unlucky for me, I had to play doctor to a man who'd attempted to rape my sister and was very nearly successful in that attempt.

When she'd come on deck, she'd straightened her shoulders and might've, to the untrained eye, appeared perfectly unaffected by him. But I knew my sister inside and out, and I saw a piece of her reliving their encounter every time she looked upon his face. I saw her look away, saw her fingers twitch, saw all the subtle movements of a woman fighting to prove to both the world and herself she remained unscarred.

I saw her scars and I hated him for them; hated myself for using my hands to heal him when they would better be used to return a scar or two on his fat, clammy skin.

This was why I'd chosen to be a veterinarian instead of a physician. As a physician, I would've had to save the lives of even the most vile human beings… and some… well, some just didn't deserve it.

I kept my eyes focused on my task as I steadily stitched him; drowning out the *who* beneath the stitch and letting my mind only know the process. Squeezing the needle driver, sliding it through the skin, pushing the lower skin up with the forceps to allow the curved needle to return through, then pulling the needle back with the forceps to do it again… and again…

'Deep breath in through the nose, out through the mouth…'

I didn't want to be stitching this waste of a man, especially when Juan was up on the deck with a bullet still lodged in his shoulder. So very unlike the man laying before me, he'd declined my offer to treat him first, insisting Phil's wound was much more life-threatening than his.

I'd spent nearly every waking hour of the last two weeks alongside him, flirting, talking, and stealing little moments tucked away in shadows with our mouths pressed together. I missed him the second I was apart from him, and couldn't wait to get back to his side.

"You're the sister?" Phil asked through his teeth, making it much more difficult to ignore who I was stitching.

I supposed *the sister* was good enough as far as he was concerned. I certainly had no desire to hear my name fall from his wretched mouth. "Mm hmm," I hummed stiffly, pulling the thread and looping it back through.

"You a doctor?"

"Mm hmm," was my only response.

"She's a vet," Kyle informed him.

I saw Phil's shoulders stiffen out of the corner of my eye, but wisely, he didn't address me again.

"How's the baby? Fetia must be getting big now?"

Kyle spoke sweetly to the man, but I could tell it didn't come easy for him. "She is. The baby's kicking a lot lately. She thinks it's a girl, but I hope it's a boy."

"You decide where you're gonna' raise him yet?" He flinched as I pushed the needle through again, perhaps a little harder than I might have with any other human on my table. "Your mother would spoil him rotten, you know."

"I know," Kyle said, loosing a breath, "but we're waiting to see what happens before we make that decision. I want to raise him with Zachary and Cecelia... wherever they end up."

I bit the inside of my cheek as I kept my mind focused on the stitch. Curious as I was about that statement and whether that meant A.J. was considering staying in this time, I would not lower myself to converse with this man.

'Deep breath in through the nose, out through the mouth...'

Almost done...

And then I could sprint to the top deck...

Where Juan was increasingly suspected by the people around him as a threat...

Where someone could, at any moment, put an end to the only thing that had ever been magical about my life...

Where I might very well return to find my magic lying lifeless on the wood boards, eyes permanently frozen in time to render a part of me forever frozen with them.

Almost done...

'Deep breath in through the nose, out through the mouth...'

"Will they lock me back up, you think?" Phil asked.

"No," Kyle assured him. "You'll stay in here and rest. I'll keep an eye on you."

I felt Phil's eyes move to my face but refused to look away from the last few stitches. "I would never touch your sister again," he said, "or anyone for that matter... It was a mistake. One I'd give anything to undo. It's not who I am."

Again I pushed the needle through his skin, A.J.'s twitching fingers playing behind my eyes.

"I will never not be sorry for that mistake... not ever."

One more stitch...

Just one last loop...

His stare slid over my arms like an ice cube, and it took physical effort not to shudder. I hooked the needle in one final time, knotted it, and cut it loose.

Pushing my glasses up to their rightful position on my nose, I turned to Kyle. "Can you wash this up and bandage it?"

Kyle offered a knowing and grateful smile. "Yes. Thank you."

That was all the goodbye I needed to drop the surgical bag and first aid kit from the yacht into my purse, spin on my heel, and race out the door.

I didn't care about the still healing cut on my foot burning beneath the bandage as I began to jog down the corridor. I didn't care that my muscles ached at the motion or that my lungs, after so long without exercise, protested. I ran, taking the stairs two at a time until I was once again on the top deck.

And my mind and heart settled just to see him. My burning lungs expelled the air I'd held trapped inside them with the image of him alive and well. Hip rested against the railing on the quarterdeck, he hugged his shoulder as he chatted casually with Gabriel. His face was a little paler than normal, but my God, he was beautiful.

I'd doubted him for all of ten seconds on the yacht and it was the worst ten seconds of my life... I thought, at the time, it would've been illogical not to suspect him when all signs pointed to him being the guilty party. Letting myself believe him capable of anything so foul and unlike the man I'd come to know, however, felt far more illogical than I'd ever been in my life.

Mid-sentence, he caught sight of me and froze, his lip curling up into that easy smile that set my pulse to a more suitable rhythm. I watched him excuse himself from Gabriel, then rise and stride toward me with his palm still firmly curled over his shoulder.

And right there, with the sun's rays surrounding him as it set behind his back, I knew, without any reservation whatsoever, I loved him. My entire body was both calmed and excited by it; both shaking and completely still when he took the hand I offered and let me lead him below deck.

I loved him.

"Gabriel has volunteered to sail tonight," he said as we turned down the second set of stairs. "I will need to be on deck early for when we arrive..."

At the bottom of the steps, I smiled ahead of me that there was no quiver in my muscles, no hesitancy in my step… I was not nervous or self-conscious or afraid… I was in love for the first time in my life, and I was anxious to tell him.

I pushed the door open to his room and motioned for him to sit in the chair beside the bed while I lit the lanterns by the door, on the makeshift vanity, and on the bedside tables.

He sat, just as silent as I was, but with that knowing smile on his lips, watching me move across the room.

Blowing out the match, I placed my purse on the bed and stood over him, pulling his fingers away from the wound to get a peek. "This is going to hurt," I said softly. "Do you want a drink first?"

He nodded. "There's a bottle of very good scotch in the bottom drawer of my desk. Will you have some with me?"

I bit my lower lip. "You'd have a drunken veterinarian dig a bullet out of you?"

He flashed his teeth in a wide smile. "Maybe just for me then. Have a drink with me after? If I live through it?"

"Deal," I whispered, placing a kiss on his brow before moving to the desk to retrieve it. "I've never had *very good scotch.*"

"Then you've never truly lived, *mi paloma.*" His voice was light and playful. "There are few things better than a very good glass of scotch."

I fumbled around in the drawer, reaching past additional stacks of journals until I felt the bottle hidden behind them. "You know," I teased, returning with both the scotch and the two glasses it had been hidden with, "for a man who speaks so few words, you seem to have an awful lot to say. What would I find if I thumbed through these journals that cover nearly every inch of your room?"

With one hand still plastered to his wound, he held the bottle with the other and pulled the cork with his teeth, proceeding to pour a small bit of the amber liquid into each glass. Even from where I stood, I could smell the slight caramel aroma as he placed the bottle and cork on the table. He plucked up his glass and inhaled it, humming before he took a sip and closed his eyes. "You are welcome to thumb through them any time you wish… They are my attempts to describe the places I've been, the people I've met, and the things I have seen. Ramblings really. I'm afraid you'll find it all quite dull."

"Really?" I beamed, testing his offer by lifting the cover on one resting atop the table beside my glass. He made no move to stop me, but kept his eyes on me as he took another sip, the dimple visible in his cheek. Curious, I let the journal fall open to a page that had been marked with ribbon. "You'd really let me read your most intimate thoughts?"

The candlelight danced over his smile. "I've nothing to hide from you, Cecelia."

I moved my fingers over the exquisite cursive on the page. "Have you written about *me* in any of your journals?"

He raised a brow, holding the glass near his lips. "I have."

I pushed the journal closed. "Perhaps then you can read me something about myself while I stitch you up?"

He tipped the glass up to finish off the scotch. "You wish to see me tortured *and* embarrassed then?"

"A little," I admitted, giggling. "Like I said before, I like it when you show me your softer side. It makes me feel like I'm privy to some great secret no one else knows about."

He chuckled. "Then you don't want this journal. Top drawer, bedside table behind you, that's the one you want."

I heard him pour himself another drink as I pulled the worn leather journal from the bedside drawer. "There's something about me in this one?"

"Aye, Cecelia," he took a sip, "there's a great many things about you in that one."

I hugged it to my chest, tucking my lips in to stop the ridiculous grin that would've otherwise taken up my entire face. "And you'll read one of them to me?"

He chuckled, placing his glass on the table. "Are you giving me the choice to say no to you?"

I held the journal tighter against my bosom, the ridiculous grin appearing anyway. "No."

"Well then," he straightened in his chair and took a deep breath, motioning to the journal with an outstretched palm, "let's get this business over with."

Handing it to him, I moved my fingers over the collar of his shirt, sliding them down to unbutton the top two buttons with surprisingly steady hands. "Can you lift your arms? If not, I can cut this off you."

With candlelight dancing over his pupils, he held my gaze, his lips turned upward as he lifted his arms.

And there was something so very significant in the act of pulling his shirt up and over his head, in watching his hair fall away from its ribbon as the fabric pulled it loose, and in the way he held my gaze as he slowly lowered his arms back down...

I could've done it over again a million more times and never gotten tired of the way he looked as I did so.

"Even covered in blood," I said softly, mimicking his own words to me, "you are so very beautiful."

"Such pretty words from a woman who intends to dissect me."

I'd never wanted to touch anyone more... to press my lips against every inch of that glorious tattooed skin beckoning me in the soft lantern light... to watch him in that same orange light as he pressed his lips against mine...

I turned away lest I act upon the desires welling inside me and risk the bullet remaining lodged in his arm forever. I fished the first-aid kit and surgical bag from my purse, opening both on the bed.

"It is your turn for pretty words, Joseph," I quipped as I opened several small alcohol packets and disinfected the two sets of forceps I'd need to dig out the bullet.

"Are you sure you wouldn't prefer to read them yourself?" he asked as I turned toward him, his eyes widening at the tools in my hands. "Perhaps when you are alone in your room and I have long since passed out from the pain you intend to inflict upon me?"

"Nu uh." I grinned. "Besides, if you're preoccupied with embarrassment, you might not realize you're in pain." I held the forceps out, clicking them once for good measure. "Are you ready?"

Nodding with a sigh, he laid the journal over his thigh and flipped through the pages, tensing only a little as I moved an alcohol pad over the wound.

I pulled the lantern closer and could see the bullet. It was lodged deep, but it had gone in clean. If I could keep my hands steady, it might come out quick.

"Deep breath," I said to him, preparing both forceps in each hand. "It'll be out before you know it, and the hard part will be over." I pointed to the page with the pincer. "Read me the first line there."

He inhaled deeply and I positioned the first forceps against the edges of the bullet hole to keep it open, allowing the second to slide in and grip each side of the bullet.

"She sleeps," he read through his teeth, "as she has slept every day since I held her for the first time... My—"

His head fell forward and he groaned as I pulled the bullet out and pressed gauze against the wound.

"Well don't stop there, Shakespeare," I teased softly, holding the bullet against the lantern to make sure it was intact and no part of it could remain inside him.

He shakily continued. "My arms, which had once..." He coughed. "Are you quite sure you wish to hear this? I hadn't realized just how embarrassing this would be. I am no poet. I could read something else... *anything* else..."

"I most certainly wish to hear this one," I laughed, "if only to watch you continue to squirm. It's very adorable."

He grumbled something about being called *'adorable'* under his breath as I dropped the bullet with a clang onto the table and turned to prepare the stitching.

Letting out a defeated exhale, he continued as I threaded the needle. "My arms, which had once been sufficient in my body's requirement of them, seem flawed and inadequate without her weight upon them... Now that they have known the feel of her, it is as if they are not quite whole... not quite my own. Some part of me now severed and asleep as she sleeps… I fear, if she does not wake, I shall never be whole again, my arms shall forever feel empty and deficient, and the world shall forever be too heavy without her in it."

I hadn't breathed… nor had I moved. I stood with needle and thread, unable to move my mind away from his words for fear I could miss one.

He'd written those words while I slept… He'd felt that deeply after spending only a few days together…

As had I…

He looked up from the journal, glancing at the stitching in my frozen fingers. "Do you wish me to stop?"

"No," I breathed. "No, please don't stop."

His lip twitched with amusement. "I'm afraid I might have to if I run out of blood."

"Right," I blinked, moving back to the wound in his shoulder. "Sorry. Please… Go on…"

He waited until I'd pushed the needle through to keep reading and I fell into a trance, working the stitch pattern in and out in perfect rhythm with his words.

"She sleeps, as she has slept every day since I pressed my lips against her brow. As I wait for her eyes to open, the scent of her lingers upon my upper lip. She smells of happiness. As if God had looked upon her smiling face and gifted her an aroma to suit the joy her smile had given him. To inhale her fragrance on my skin is my greatest comfort, but I loathe to exhale and diminish its bouquet. I feel her scent fading more each day and I fear I might never know happiness again lest she wakes."

He turned the page. "She sleeps, as she has slept every day since the last day I knew myself complete. Mere days spent at the side of her and I recognized the man I'd at last grown into. As if she'd scrubbed away the old to make me anew… to mold a man worthy of standing at the side of her. Wake up, Cecelia. I have only just discovered you. Please wake up, or I shall forever be half a man without you."

Blushing, he closed the journal, drumming his fingers once over the leather as I knotted the final stitch and cut it.

After applying the bandage, I wiped my hands on a damp towel, then tilted his face up so I could finally meet his eyes. "And are you embarrassed now?"

"Very much so," he admitted, raking his teeth over his lower lip. "I'm afraid my cheeks might catch fire any moment."

As the words *'I love you'* sat on the edge of my tongue in response, the little voice of reason appeared in the back of my mind, urging me to swallow that sentence lest I regret it.

1999, my mind reminded me. That's where he'd go when all this was over. I wouldn't know who he was until 2020, or possibly 2021 depending on when we found Bennet.

Saying those words now would be cruel; indulging him in any way when he was destined to return to a time I wouldn't was only setting him up to have a life of loneliness. I didn't want that for him, even if he decided to come back here and shorten that time. It was too much—too selfish to have him wait based solely on a few weeks spent together. I wanted him to be happy; I wanted him to live his life.

The words he'd written and the way he was looking at me... The kisses we'd shared and the stories we'd both told each other... If he wasn't in love with me already, he was very close to it. And as much as I would've loved to have had him forever, I couldn't condemn him to so many years spent alone as a result of my own desires.

'I'm looking for my wife,' he'd said in my memory...

Maybe I wasn't her after all...

Or maybe some other version of me hadn't been considerate enough of his time to stop it from happening.

How many times had I already lived this moment with this man? And how many times had I ruined his life?

Clearing my throat, I let go of his chin and took a step back. "We'll be in Panama tomorrow," I said, staring down at my feet. "You should rest. It's going to be a long day."

He took my hand and stopped me before I could turn away to collect the first-aid supplies. "Should I not have read it? Have I embarrassed you?"

I swallowed the lump in my throat. "No… it's not that. I just… you really do need to get some sleep before we get there."

His grip tightened around my fingers. "You promised to have a drink with me. Stay."

"I can't," I said softly. "It's not right."

He stood from his chair to tower over me, his expression painted over with concern as he brushed the hair back from my face. "What's not right?"

"What we're doing—what *I'm* doing."

His lip twitched. "What is it, *mi alma*, you think you are doing that I have not directly sought from you to do?"

I laid a hand on his chest, memorizing the lines in his tattoos as my fingers moved over it. "Twenty years, Joseph. It's too much. Whatever this is between us—while it has been earth-shattering— it needs to end now. If we let it go any further, you could not be convinced to live those twenty years fully, and I won't condemn you to a life spent alone because of only a few weeks spent with me."

He shook his head a fraction of an inch. "Cecelia, it is too late for that."

Standing taller, I raised my chin and blinked the threatening tears from my eyes. "You barely know me."

He breathed out a laugh and slid his arm around me. "I knew you before I met you and I loved you then. I love you now, and I cannot imagine how I will love you when I know you after a month, or a year, or a decade."

My heart sank nearly to my toes. No man had ever uttered those words to me, and to hear it from this man's lips, under any other circumstance, would've absolutely made my life. Under these circumstances, it nearly broke me in two.

He pressed his lips to my brow, his words brushing over my eyelid. "*You* are what I want; now and twenty years from now. I will wait for you whether you end this courtship or not because I have seen what life could be with you and I intend to have it. Stay."

"I can't," I insisted. "Over the course of twenty years, you could have a whole life with someone; a family and a chance at real happiness. I can't be the reason you turn something better away."

"Something better?" he scoffed. "I already have all the happiness life has to offer right here in my arms. I waited this long for you to come into my life. I can wait again."

I shook my head, sliding my hands over his chest. "You say that now because I'm here, but five years from now? Ten? Fifteen and twenty if you stay? You'll start to resent me for it, and I won't be that to you."

He pulled back and frowned. "*If I stay?*"

I pulled my lips in to prevent them from saying anything else.

"Cecelia, did I say more to you in your memory than what you've told me?"

Slowly, I nodded. "Yes but—"

"And a part of that had something to do with me coming back to this time?" He let go of me to sit down on the edge of the bed. "I cannot come back here to meddle in the past even further. I need you to tell me everything I said to you."

My stomach dropped. I'd refrained from giving him all the details of my memory of that night, terrified he'd only say the words because I'd told him to. I wanted to be his wife, but I didn't want a proposal only because I'd given instruction.

I couldn't hide from him, though. Now that I'd let it slip, I could see in his eyes I couldn't keep those details to myself.

Surrendering, I sat down beside him and told him the whole thing, start to finish. I told him every single word I could remember him saying, including the part where he said he'd come back to wait and how he wouldn't be an old man when his wife was returned to him.

"Why did you not tell me this before?" he asked when I'd finished, his fingers toying with the fabric of my skirts between us.

I shrugged. "I don't know. I suppose I was afraid to influence you in some way by giving away too much."

"You were afraid I would marry you simply because I had eluded to you being my wife in your memory?"

Abashedly, I nodded.

"And you did not wish to be married to me?"

I stared down at my hands in my lap. "The right answer and the honest answer to that question are very different from each other."

He slid his hand into mine. "So give me both."

"The right answer," I started, tracing a scar on his knuckle, "is no, I do not wish to be married to you. That's the only answer I *should* give you, and if I were the kind of woman I want to be, I would get up right now and walk away before I could make things worse."

He squeezed my hand gently. "And yet you haven't."

"I can't," I admitted softly. "Because the honest answer is that I barely knew you when that memory came to me and I have never wanted anything more. I really want to do what's right, but I've never felt like this about anyone. One part of me is screaming to have you and the other is arguing all the reasons I will hurt you if I do. How can I take twenty years from you after you've given me my life? And how can I give you up when my life feels like it has all been leading me to you? I can't very well ask you not to change history when I know what it means to you… nor can I ask you to wait for so long when we've barely spent a few weeks together. I don't know what to do."

Raising a knee onto the bed, he turned to face me, taking both my hands into his. "You asked me to give you the life of your choosing because you wanted to be in control of your own destiny. Correct?"

"Yes…"

He smiled. "Then let my destiny be mine to control as well. Stay, Cecelia."

I glanced around the lantern-lit room then back to him. "But…"

"Do you love me?" he asked simply.

I hadn't been prepared for that question and I might've fallen off the bed had he not been holding my hands. "That… What… You don't just ask someone who hasn't said the words yet if they love you."

The dimple appeared in his cheek as his smile widened. "I was not aware there were rules, *mi alma*. And since I have already broken them… It is a simple question."

"Maybe for you…"

He shook his head. "You could've ended this on that boat; could've taken my life and control of the ship, but you did not. You chose to trust me when I don't even trust myself. And I have to know, is it because you love me?"

My head was nodding on its own long before I answered, "Yes. Very much."

I drew in a breath as he slid his palm around the nape of my neck and pulled my lips within an inch of his. "Then stay," he whispered before he pressed his lips to mine.

His lips were soft, his kiss gentle, giving space for me to answer him, and I did. "Okay."

With my fingers embedded in his velvet hair, I tasted his mouth, tasted that *very good scotch* and all the words he'd spoken once he'd drank it. I traced every line and angle in his face as his magic sprang to life between our lips, a simple white handkerchief pulled away to reveal a flame. And that flame engulfed us as his arm curled round my waist, burning hotter as his fingers spread against my back and drifted up over the corset to the thinner fabric between my shoulder blades.

He moved past my lips and over my jaw to my neck. His lips and tongue gliding over my skin like music through my ears, awakening my soul like a growing crescendo to call every hair on my body to attention. His arm tightened around me as I tilted back, and he explored the length of my neck, each taste growing more enthusiastic until the feel of him there was a glorious mesh of warmth and wetness; a chill with every breath, instantly heated by the lips that replaced it.

Every breath was wonderfully vocalized as I held him to me, feeling him taste, not just my skin, but *me*... The logical woman, the shriveling girl, the romantic little spirit locked away too long...

And he took them with lips, teeth, tongue, and fire, and I felt so very light and free for the exposure.

"If I asked for your hand now," he breathed against my skin, "you would not say yes. But will you wear a ring if I give one? So you might say yes at a time of your choosing?"

"I already wear your ring," I said, guiding his hand to the chain round my neck. "I haven't taken it off." I sighed audibly as his palm followed it down my collar to pull the band from where it had been tucked inside my bosom.

"I've another I'd like you to wear on your finger," he whispered as he pulled away to look at me. "My moth—*Gloria's* ring. Not the one my father gave her, but one she wore long before she met him. One she never took off. Will you wear it?"

I laid my hand over the ruby ring in his. "Does that mean you want this one back?"

"No." His expression hardened. "I gave this to you for a reason and you're to keep it on—especially if we should..." He trailed off.

"This ring," he said instead, "many men know it and know it belongs to me... If we should be separated, those same men might see it upon you and know you, too, belong to me."

I brushed the hair from his face and smiled. "I *belong* to you, do I?"

"Aye." His lips curled upward. "From the moment I laid eyes on you, you belonged to me... just as I belong to you. Will you wear my ring?"

I nodded shyly.

Reaching out to the table, he placed the glass of scotch in my hands. "One moment, *mi alma,*" he beamed, turning round to climb over the bed and rummage through the opposite bedside table.

I admired the view of his bottom and broad back as I took a small sip and held it in my mouth, the smooth, almost buttery taste serving as a surprisingly welcome interlude. A symphony of flavor erupted as I moved it toward my throat, oak and spice and warmth sitting on my tongue as I swallowed and felt its heat stoke the flames still burning in my core. It tasted like him... and he was right. There were very few things I'd consider better.

He returned to sit on the edge of the bed beside me, the movement of the lantern light seeming to bring the serpent in his tattoo to life.

"Give me your hand," he said softly, and I sat forward, extending my left hand for him to take in his.

He slid a ring on my ring finger and my heart warmed at the feel of the metal against my skin, like it belonged there and I had been missing it... Like he belonged there all along and I'd been missing him.

"She wore this always." He smoothed his palm over my fingers as he admired it among them. "And she gave it to me as she lay dying in my arms. Said she wanted me to have it. I don't know why it meant so much to her that I have it; who gave it to her or when, but I know she would've been as happy as I am to see it on your finger." He smiled. "I know it is soon. And I know what we might endure when we interrupt this timeline we are on... but I want no one else but you for as long as I live."

I held my hand up to appreciate the silver Claddagh ring that would live permanently on my finger. Two hands holding a heart beneath a crown... I'd seen my own mother wear one similar and it brought tears to my eyes to be so close to him, to her, to Alaina and baby Cecelia and all the descendants that came after...

I spread my fingers wide and stared at the lantern light dancing over the silver band. "Do we really have to change everything? Can't we just... skip it? Take this ship to some remote island and sink it instead?"

He took the scotch from my other hand and placed it on the bedside table. "Had I not killed so many men in this time, I would go wherever you wanted... But I cannot forget what I have done; how I have changed the future with my own darkness. I can never be the husband I wish to be for you while carrying the weight of their deaths on my shoulders. If I do not change it, I'm afraid I shall become no better than my father."

I sighed. "What if I don't come through time in the changed memories? What if I forget you the same way I have forgotten Owen?"

He flashed his teeth in a wide smile, gently removing my glasses to place them on the table as well. "Then I shall enjoy courting you a second time."

I stared at the ring on my finger then back up to him. "You're sure this is what you want?"

"Aye," he leaned in, "this is all I ever want."

And this time, when his lips landed upon mine, they were not gentle or submissive. With his ring on my finger, he was emboldened to take what belonged to him—and I belonged *entirely* to him. No kiss had ever been right before him, nor would any that wasn't him for as long as I lived.

He made a sound deep in his throat as his arms tightened around me and the two of us collapsed onto the bed in a tangle of tongues and exploring arms.

His palm was part way up my calf when a light rap on the door halted everything. "Cece?" Alaina called from the other side. "Are you in there?"

I wanted to grab hold of Juan and bury my face in his chest; hide under the blankets and shut out the world for as long as I could… I didn't want to answer her call. I wanted to stay right where I was; wanted to experience what would come with my agreement to stay.

"Cece," she said again, "the men are back and there's something I need you to see. It's important."

I met Juan's eyes, pleading with him to find some way to make the world go away.

He forced a smile and shook his head, pulling me up to sit beside him. "She is here," he announced. "Come in."

Chapter Twenty-Seven

Alaina

Jack, Jim, and Chris had searched the yacht, returning with food, bedding, mosquito nets, solar panels, a few books, and, most importantly, Bud's laptop, which Juan Josef had overlooked as something valuable.

Lilly and I had opened it and we'd both been surprised to find 7% remaining on its battery. She'd unlocked it with Bertie's birthday and we'd been able to find folders upon folders with what we could only assume was every bit of research Bud and Chris had done during their time in the future. There were folders labeled Gloria, Juan Francisco, Time Travel, Ocean Portals, Genealogy, Dahlia, Strange Artwork, and one which I'd immediately opened entitled, *'Jack.'*

I hadn't seen the handwritten Master's Log where Jack's name was listed with the cause of death, *'died at sea'* before that moment.

I'd snapped the laptop closed instantly and rushed to Juan Jr.'s door with Lilly at my heels.

Hugging the computer to my chest and ignoring Lilly's questions, I pushed the door open when Juan instructed me to come in.

Cece sat on the edge of his bed beside him, both of their heads turned toward me.

I'd never seen Juan without a shirt and I was momentarily taken aback by the black ink crawling over his chest and bicep. He seemed darker—more sinister with the snake climbing down his arm, and I couldn't help thinking it didn't suit my beautiful sister.

It didn't fail to escape my notice that her hair and skirts were ruffled and both of them were breathing a little heavily.

This turned my stomach. The truth was, I didn't trust him; couldn't trust his warning when it was leading Jack to the very place his father would be waiting… While I'd once thought the two of them endearing in the way they interacted with one another, I now only saw my sister as a helpless mouse in the grips of a fox. He was his father's son… and trusting him would be a mistake.

"What is it?" Cece asked, her eyes landing upon the laptop in my arms.

I pointed to the desk beside me and the quill and ink that sat upon it. "I need you to write something."

"Ohhh," Lilly drawled where she was leaning against the doorframe and staring at Juan's tattoo. "You think that was her handwriting?"

I turned toward her. "I know it is."

"What's my handwriting?" Cece asked, standing.

Again, I motioned to the desk. "I'll show you in a second. Take this quill and write Jack's name on that paper."

She pursed her lips, but moved to the desk and did as instructed.

I peered over her shoulder, and, just as I had suspected, the sharp angled cursive was an exact match.

I'd recognized the slashing loop in the 'J' almost immediately as her writing, and seeing it now made my heart beat even faster.

I placed the computer next to the paper and opened it, typing Bertie's birthday in to reveal the photo I'd left open. "You wrote this," I said, pointing to Jack's name, "but you didn't write the name above it or the one below…"

She frowned at the screen and I noticed a Claddagh ring on her left ring finger when she moved it over the trackpad to zoom in. "That's definitely my handwriting… But I don't know any men on board with these names. Juan, come tell me if you recognize any of them or the writing. Maybe it's a clue?"

I bit the inside of my cheek when he crossed the room to stand behind her, his non-bandaged arm sliding around her small waist as he looked over her shoulder at the screen. "The writing is mine." He pointed to the names written above Jack's. "Manuel Valdés and Alejandro Suría were both men we buried on the beach… I logged all their deaths the moment we returned to the ship, but this name," he pointed to the one beneath Jack's. "I do not know any man by the name of Simón Bacallar."

"You have this log?" I asked. "Can I see it?"

"Aye," he said, still staring at the screen with a bit of amazement. "It is here."

He pulled out the center drawer to his desk with a clunk and placed a leather-bound book on its surface, opening to a page marked with ribbon where I found the identical passage halfway down the page. Jack and Simón had not yet been added to the list of dead men.

The list was hefty though, and I couldn't help but stare at the nearly forty names that spanned both open pages in the same elegant handwriting. Swallowing, I ran my finger over the page. "These men… they all died on the beach that day?"

He nodded. "But they will live again when we are finished. Won't they?"

I read each name and my heart grew heavy with the weight of what we'd done. They would live again. They had to.

As I read them, an image of Mr. Gil came to mind; an image of him holding the rope Jack dangled from as I beat Kyle, and I searched the list again for an entry with his name.

I'd assumed, since I'd never seen him after the poison, he was buried on the beach with the others, but his name was not among them. Where was Mr. Gil?

Cece moved out of Juan's grip and closer to the screen, squinting to see without her glasses. "I have an idea…"

Quickly, she dipped the quill and held it over Alejandro Suría's name in the log, letting a single drop of ink fall over it. She put the quill back and pointed to the screen. "Look."

The image on the laptop changed to reflect the droplet of ink now covering the 'o' in his name.

"If this can change," she said, pressing her thumb into the spattered ink to create a thumbprint both on the page and on the screen, "that means our fate is not concrete—it's not married to what's on screen. If this little drop can change the image, one little action—like getting off this ship—can erase Jack's name from it as well… just like we'd hoped."

"So what if we wrote someone else's name there?" I asked.

Cece shook her head. "No. This photo is cropped to show only these four slots… If I wrote something else, we'd have no way of knowing for certain getting off the ship works. We don't know that the printed papers can change the way this does. We do know that if another name appears while he is gone, Juan's warning was true and we can all get off the ship with him."

She straightened and bit her lower lip. "Terrence has his phone… He's been charging it with the solar panel and, with no service out here, the battery lasts for several days. What if he took a picture of the screen and sent the phone along with Jack as backup? We can use the solar panel to keep the battery on this charged; check it every hour or so… What do you think?"

"Or…" I said, glancing at Lilly, "we could turn the ship around now and head to the storm. We have Izzy and if the effects of Cecelia going through are somehow immediate, your grandpa would be safe."

"And if they're not immediate?" Lilly asked. "You'd leave him with Juan Josef and a bullet in his chest? Leave him here with no one for the next twenty years? Let Juan Josef live on to pursue our ancestors or come through time to attempt to kidnap Cecelia?"

I shook my head and glared up at Juan Jr. "No, but I don't trust this. He's leading us straight to him!"

"Where I intend to kill him," he said, "and take you home so you will never have to fear him again."

Cece leaned back into him, smiling proudly. "And after he takes us home, he's going to Virginia to kill the Albrecht so Anna can go home too."

I took a deep breath and crossed my arms over my chest, still thinking about Mr. Gil and what role he surely had in all this. "How can you, of all people, trust him so easily? We barely know him and that warning to get off the ship is precisely what his father is anticipating… with a whole new crew waiting to outnumber us!"

She raised her chin. "How can you, *of all people*, doubt him? How many times has he stepped in on your behalf? He stopped the hanging, you told me that. He took you off the ship when the crew was poisoned… And he saved you from those men the night I arrived when his brother ordered them to kill you. He could've let the Nikora kill Jack or any one of us when they came on board, but he didn't… Instead, he fought them off and kept us all alive." She took his hand and curled his arm back around her waist. "When you take Cecelia through time, you will take from him the only family he has left, and even with the knowledge of it, he has saved all of our lives. Have you really become so callous you cannot see the good in people?"

"Callous?" I spat, taken aback by her defensive posture. "Cece, I want to go home. That is all I have ever wanted since this whole mess started. He took us captive just as much as his father did. I cannot help it if I find it difficult to see the good in my captor."

She tilted her head to one side. "Has it never occurred to you that, after being stranded here for more than twenty years, all *they* ever wanted was to go home too? You were the first real opportunity he and his family had to get there. Why wouldn't he take you captive if you would not go willingly? I would."

"So I'm the bad guy in this?" I asked, my spine stiffening.

"No one's the bad guy, A.J., and no one's the good guy either. The lines on both sides are blurred by the desperation to go home."

I blew out. "And what would you have us do? If it were your choice?"

She combed her fingers over Juan's where they rested on her midsection. "I'd compromise, A.J., so that everyone can finally get on with their lives. I would go to Panama to get Bud; make sure Jack got off the ship—because Juan has proven himself an ally over and over and his warning should not go ignored. I wouldn't let Juan kill his father, but I'd speak to Juan Josef instead like the human being he is. Reason with him and try to understand what it is he wants to accomplish in all this. I'd let them pursue the Albrecht to make up for the mistakes you've all made here; give back the lives you've *all* taken. Then, I would send you home to spend the next several years with family and friends."

She raised her brows. "And then, hard as it may be to ask of you, I'd ask you and Jack to come back and raise your family in this time so you aren't erasing the generations of people that should've descended from you—once it's safe to do so with Zachary, of course. Then you wouldn't be stealing his family any more than his father has attempted to steal yours. It's a steep compromise, I know, but it's one that wouldn't add to the list of lives already lost because of our presence here. With time moving differently on this side of the storm, you'd have plenty of years to spend with family before you came back."

I frowned. "And what about you? You're my family. You'd expect me to leave you behind again?"

She laughed. "I would be wherever you are, dummy."

"So would I," Lilly added.

"Ay!" Jim called from down the hall. "Yuns come on, all of yas. Izzy's got us a picnic dinner set up in the floor in here and I'll be damned if I let any one of yas break her little heart by missin' it. She's been locked up in a vent for weeks and we're givin' her whatever she wants tonight. She's got her lil' teddy bears set up and everything."

Lilly leaned out the door and burst into laughter. "Where in the world did you get that hat?!"

"Oh, they's one for all of yuns. Apparently our Izzy's a bit of a snoop. She knows where to find all kinds of hidden treasure on this ship. Took me down to the hull and pointed at a chest full of 'em. Made me fish out a fancy hat for everybody."

"You look ridiculous!" Lilly chortled.

"Wait till' ye' see Hoss in his fancy bonnet! Come on! Bring Junior and lightnin' bug with ye.' We're havin' sandwiches and what's left of the ice cream!"

It was a refreshing break to laugh out loud, even if it was just momentary.

Entering our room, I found Jim modeling an enormous floppy picture hat that folded downward in the back and sported two fluffy white ostrich feathers in the front. Seated on a blanket on the floor behind him, Jack wore a wide brimmed straw Bergère hat, a blue ribbon draped around it and tied at his chin.

Izzy stood in front of Kyle, testing out a deep crowned black hat on his head, the big baby blue satin bow shimmering in the lantern light. Fetia, seated on the blanket beside him in a high-billed white and yellow bonnet, roared with laughter.

Magna winked up at me from beneath her burgundy brim, a plume of cream colored ostrich feathers sprouting from its dark ribbon.

I sat down beside Jack, watching as Izzy moved back to her pile and plucked up another straw Bergère, this one with a satin pink trim.

She waited patiently for Cece and Juan Jr., who thankfully had put on a shirt and looked far less sinister, to sit cross-legged beside Fetia. Giggling out loud, Izzy positioned the hat on Cece's head, and of course, she looked like she'd been born to wear it.

"So," Jim said, sitting down beside Lilly to tip his hat back and look at Juan Jr. with one eye closed, "what we gonna' do now? If your daddy's got a new crew with him, that changes things, don't it? We don't exactly got the numbers no more, and we cain't run into a busy port with automatic rifles."

Juan shook his head. "He wants the child… We could go to shore with two bundles; give the appearance we've taken Alaina and the children with us and…"

He paused and grinned at Izzy as she handed him a silk feathered riding cap, not familiar enough with him to stand close enough to place it on his head. "For me?"

She nodded a little shyly.

He chuckled, and turned it over, frowning at the inside. "Wait… What's that?"

Curious, Izzy leaned over the hat. He pointed to the inside, then tipped it over as if something might pour out of it. Waiting for her to look up at him, he spoke when he was sure she could read his lips. "Did you put something in my hat?"

She giggled and shook her head.

Twisting his lips to the side, he looked into the hat again. He reached inside and closed his eyes. "Are you sure?"

Izzy attempted to see inside as he tilted it toward himself.

"Ah! I've got it," he said, and pulled out one of Izzy's small stuffed teddy bears none of us had noticed him take.

She snagged the teddy bear and leaned over the hat to inspect it for any more of her toys.

I hid a smile as she took the cap from him and shook it for anything further to fall out.

"No more there," he said when she'd looked up at him, "but here…"

He reached over her shoulder and produced a gold coin between his fingers. While she hopped with excitement, he let it dance over his knuckles from finger to finger, waved his other hand over it, and when he presented his palms to her, it was gone.

Izzy gasped.

Juan pointed to the hat in her hands. "Check inside now."

She reached inside and pulled out the coin, spinning to stare wide-eyed at Jack as she presented it to him.

"Where'd you learn to do that?" Cece asked, laughing as Izzy pocketed the gold coin.

He folded his hands in his lap. "When I was a boy, perhaps around seven, I was fascinated by a magician who had performed at my birthday party. It was all I could talk about for weeks. My father came home one day with a book of magic tricks. It came through time with us and, with nothing much else to do, I spent many a night studying it and practicing."

When Izzy gave him back the hat, he placed it hilariously on his head and waited until she'd moved on to Maria before he focused his attention back on Jim. "If my father thinks Alaina and the babies are with us, he will have no reason to pursue the ship. He would wait for us somewhere on the trail—likely Hector's…"

Pursing his lips, he tapped the bill of his hat. "With the rain, it would not be uncustomary for us to travel in hats and cloaks… If you and your wife still intend to accompany me, we could give the illusion that you are Mr. and Mrs. Volmer… place the mock children in your arms… put her necklace on your wife's neck."

"And how would ye' get Hoss to that inn?"

Juan considered it. "Whenever this ship has approached land, my father always insisted the men wear uniform. Jack, Gabriel, Tomás, and myself would be dressed in livery. We will give Gabriel's name at the inn and you both shall keep your heads down. The plan to use the duchess's identity as a means to justify our travels will go unchanged."

"Whatcha' think Hoss?" Jim asked, scratching the scruff along his jaw, the feathers in his hat jostling with the movement.

Jack took a deep breath. "Seems like it'd be a hell of a lot easier to anchor further out and wait for his approach."

Cece moved her hand over her face as she shook her head. "Easier for some… deadly for others… And, if he has a crew with him, he could easily overtake us, babies and all." She smiled sweetly at Izzy as she handed her a teacup and saucer. "Thank you."

"He could overtake you, babies and all," Jack said, "even easier once half of us get off the ship."

Cece smirked, pretending to drink her invisible tea. "The same way the Nikora did? They outnumbered us at least ten to one and we fought them off with the same weapons we have on board now. Terrence, Kyle, Bruce, Jacob, Michael and I have us covered."

I glanced around the room. "Where is Terrence, anyway? I haven't seen him all day."

Cece shrugged. "Creeping around in the shadows spying like the detective he is, I would imagine. He hasn't found any signs that anyone on board wants Jack dead, but he'll keep looking all the way up until he gets off the ship."

"We need to get his phone on the solar charger with the laptop," I said. "If we're doing this."

"I'll go find him after dinner," she said.

Bruce appeared with a wide tray of steaming meat, cheese, bread, and ice cream, a fluffy white bonnet tied around his head. He chuckled deep in his chest at the sight of us. "Look at you. You all get the fancy feathered hats while I'm stuck looking like an old amish woman! Thanks a lot, Izzy!"

Izzy grabbed a stuffed bunny and waited for Bruce to place the tray in the center of our little picnic area before she handed it to Juan Jr. and signed for him to *'do it again for Bruce.'*

"Ay," Jim said, locking eyes with Bruce as he sat down with some effort. "Izzy's stayin' with yuns on the ship when we go. I'm lookin' at you to take care of her."

Bruce nodded. "She'll never leave my sight. I promise." He looked at Juan. "She says she wants you to *'do it again.'*" He turned back to Jim while Juan plucked up a cloth napkin. "So we're moving ahead with the plan then?"

"Well, we're definitely goin' to find Bud one way or another." Jim said. "Up to Hoss what he does while we do it."

We all waited and watched as Juan covered the small bunny with the napkin, waving his hands over it once, twice, then lifting the cloth to reveal an empty space on the floor where the stuffed animal had once been.

Izzy squealed with excitement and clapped her hands, then held them over her lips as Juan raised on his knee, removed Jim's massive hat, and pulled the pink bunny from inside it.

"Now how in the Sam Hill did ye' do that?" Jim balked.

Juan handed his hat back to him and winked at Izzy. "Magic."

"Well?" Bruce asked, looking at Jack for confirmation. "Are you going or staying?"

Jack blew out a long heavy breath, inspecting Juan for a long moment as he returned to his seat. "I'm going."

Chapter Twenty-Eight

Cecelia

Stomach miserably full after eating one too many pork sandwiches and entirely too much chocolate chunk ice cream, I excused myself from the picnic. Explaining I needed to find Terrence, I headed down to the lower deck where the women had made a small empty storage room into a sort of private bathroom for ourselves.

None of us could get used to using a chamber pot in the presence of men so Maria set up the space with its own pot we each emptied after use along with a pitcher, basin, soap, and mirror.

Stomach relieved and pot emptied out the small hatch window that had once catered to a cannon, I stood at the mirror, considering what might come next as I washed my lower body, the claddagh ring on my finger drawing my eye.

I thought of Owen, now a blurry face at a party, and some little girl with my face and A.J.'s curls calling me mom... Was I making the right choice?

I thought of mom and uncle Bill and home... tried to imagine Juan among them, conversing casually with my uncle over dinner...

I imagined returning from a day at the clinic to find Juan scribbling notes in a journal on a shared sofa in our home... Nestling up at the side of him on that same sofa in the winter watching Alaina hand out presents to her children... Joking about our time here with Chris and Maria where they'd joined us for the holiday... Could any of us ever fit into that life now that we'd lived this one?

I glanced at the door.

What would happen if I went back to Juan's cabin? What *would've* happened had A.J. not knocked on his door when she did?

'I'm no gentleman, mi paloma,' Juan had said once before, giving the impression he wouldn't require marriage vows to have sex. If A.J. hadn't interrupted us, I was pretty certain that's right where we were headed...

With no kind of protection...

Frowning at my cloudy reflection, I considered my cycle and how likely it was that I could've become pregnant if I'd gotten carried away. Given how long it had been since either of us had been intimate with anyone, we most assuredly would've gotten carried away.

I rolled my eyes at my reflection.

Crazy as I was about Juan, being pregnant wasn't an option—wouldn't be a reason to celebrate. With the changes we were hoping to make to our history, a pregnant person could fall asleep with a child in their belly and wake up in another life with a flat stomach. That would be devastating, and would most certainly put an end to the magic between us.

We would need to be far more careful with each other.

Drying off, I took a deep, resigned breath, and pulled the door open.

I grabbed my lantern and checked the galley and crew's quarters for signs of Terrence before heading down to the hull where I assumed he'd be.

He'd mentioned the night prior he'd seen two men coming up from the hull late one night. When they'd passed him on the stairs, they'd reacted to his presence in a way that made him think they were up to something.

Standing on the stairwell, I spotted light moving around the livestock, and I put out my lantern to creep toward it, deciding I might play detective if necessary.

I leaned against the double doors that led into the hold, watching as Juan circled the room and called out, "Cecelia? Are you in here?"

"I am now," I announced. "What are you doing down here?"

"Looking for you," he said, hanging his lantern on a hook over our heads. "You left in something of a hurry and I wanted to make sure I hadn't overwhelmed you with my proposal after you'd had ample opportunity to think about it."

I bit my lower lip as I moved closer. "Not at all. I thought I'd find Terrence down here and send him up." I smiled. "And then I planned to find you again."

He ran a hand over his hair and let out a breath of relief. "I wanted to assure you that, in asking you to stay, I had no expectations… for something more."

I smiled. "I think *something more* might've happened whether you expected it or not if my sister hadn't knocked on the door just then."

He laughed. "Aye. I think so, too. It wouldn't have been wise given our circumstances… Would it?"

"No, it wouldn't."

He cleared his throat and blushed. "We *are* talking about children, correct?"

Laughing at his insecurity, I placed a hand on his chest. "Yes. To end up pregnant now, with all we're setting out to do, would be devastating for us both. We can't be so careless."

His shoulders eased a bit. "Do you want children, Cecelia?"

"Not at the moment."

"What about in the future?" he asked, his expression much more solemn. "Is that something you would want?"

I slowly shook my head. "I never really had a strong desire to be a mother. It was always kind of an *'if the right person comes along, we'll see'* sort of thing. As I got into my thirties, that optimism has faded and I've gotten used to the idea of being childless. Is it something you want?"

"No," he said, hugging his bandaged shoulder. "After what happened with Philip and Nicolás, I swore I would never sire another child. This does not upset you?"

I shook my head. "No. Cute as you are with Izzy, I'm perfectly happy to have you all to myself."

"Aye?" He closed the gap between us. "I would be enough?"

I smiled, reaching up to rest my palm against his cheek. "Of course you are. I love you, and that will always be enough."

His breath hitched as he pressed a kiss to my forehead and then brushed his lips against mine, turning us ever so slowly as he wrapped both arms around me.

He moved to my ear to whisper, "I would hear you say those words a thousand more times and be brought to my knees by them every time."

I grinned as he nuzzled my ear. "Let's not be one of those couples that says *I love you* all the time. You're only allowed to say it when you absolutely can't hold it in… When there are no other words to express how you feel. Okay?"

"I love you," he said instantly, pulling my lips to his.

"I love you," he said again, forcing me to laugh and squeal as he moved his lips over my jaw and neck while his hands roamed over my ribcage in search of a ticklish location.

"I love you," he repeated through his own laughter, coming back to hover over my lips.

Combing back the hair from my face, his expression turned much more sober. "I love you."

I hummed happily as he wound his arms around me once more. "You are ridiculous."

"I am," he agreed. "Tell no one of it."

Unable to stop grinning, I kissed the edge of his jaw. "Let me come with you tomorrow."

He tucked my head into his shoulder and rocked us gently. "Allow me to handle my father first. I will come back for you, I swear it."

"I'm not going through the storm," I whispered. "You swore you'd never attempt to make me do anything, and I've decided I want to stay. If you're not back when they decide they're going, I'll get off this ship and find you myself. I'm staying with you all the way until you kill George Bennet and we're forced apart. I want every moment I can have with you in this life… Want to make as many memories as I can while I have the chance." I closed my eyes and let my body relax into him. "I want to be held like this for as much of my life as I can."

He pressed a kiss against the crown of my head. "Will you still stay with me tonight? Let me hold you like this a little longer? I'll not make any attempt to engage in anything further."

I smiled against him. "You have a lot of faith in me that I won't make that very attempt once I get you alone."

Smoothing a hand down my spine, he chuckled. "I think I can fight you off, *mi alma*."

"You think?"

He laughed. "I shall certainly enjoy the attempt."

Back in his cabin, I laid tucked into the crook of his arm, our fingers interlaced and rested on his chest, perfectly content and at peace in our stillness.

"Tell me something I don't know about you," I said softly, tangling my legs with his. "Something like the magic…"

His chest rose and fell heavily beneath my cheek. "Have I told you about the man who retaught me English?"

"I didn't know you'd forgotten it."

"Aye," he said, unlacing our fingers to press our palms together. "We all did in a way. My father rarely ever spoke English around us as children. It was Gloria that taught us initially, though she spoke Spanish too when we were around our father. I had just turned seven when we came through time and for the next ten years, we had no need for English. Everyone in California spoke Spanish exclusively. Dario and I forgot most of the language as we grew up, and it was only when we hosted an earl for dinner and neither of us could properly communicate that my father realized something had to be done."

He let his fingers glide lazily down the center of my palm. "So he brought on a tutor for his adult children; a Scot named Alistair Stuart. That man went everywhere we did, and we were all forbidden—my father included—from speaking Spanish to one another inside our home."

"A Scot taught you English?" I grinned. "Is that why you all say *'aye'* instead of yes?"

He laughed, pulling me closer with the arm beneath me. "*Aye.* My father thought it sounded more eloquent and began using it regularly. I suppose Dario and I just picked the word up along the way. Is it odd to you?"

I shook my head. "I like it… very much. Very eloquent. Tell me more about him."

He smiled. "Alistair became like a brother to us. He even sailed with us. He wasn't that much older than we were, and it wasn't long before he, Dario, and I were up to no good—trying to outman each other in whatever way presented itself in the presence of women… It started out as small things… Seeing who could drink the most… Testing our strength against each other or sparring for hours on end to see who tired first. Those tests got considerably more dangerous when Alistair was anywhere near Eleanor, Elizabeth's nursemaid."

His chest shook with a laugh. "He was this beast of a man, a giant with red skin and red hair that only got redder when Eleanor was in sight. And one evening, we were all out for a walk when we came upon a bear down the trail. It was far ahead and not a threat to any of us, but Alistair—fool that he was—had other ideas. He announced to Eleanor he would kill the bear and return with its claw as a gift for her."

I drew a sharp breath. "That's cruel! The bear wasn't bothering anyone!"

He shook his head. "I argued that very same point, but it was too late. Dario had drawn his sword and was already racing him for it. He was just as much the fool as Alistair. I couldn't very well let my brothers run off toward danger and stand there waiting with the women, could I?"

He moved my palm down his chest to his ribs where I knew there was a scar just beneath the fabric. "It was a mother and she had cubs nearby. That bear nearly gutted me, after, of course, *I* retrieved her claw."

I gasped. "You killed the poor thing?"

He laughed. "No. It was a fool's errand. No one could've killed that monster. It ran off when my blade pierced its paw, but not before slashing me open and nearly taking Alistair's leg."

"So she lived?" I asked, resting my chin on his chest so I could see his face.

He scratched the top of my head and grinned. "Aye, Cecelia, the bear was fine. So was Alistair. He was not the brutish fool we all took him for. Eleanor, though she had never once shown any indication she had been impressed by his feats of strength and courage—or that she'd been interested in him at all for that matter —was a mess over his injury. She did nothing but dote on him for weeks; stayed at his bedside morning and night until his leg was healed. I'd given him the bear claw since he'd only sustained the injury by pulling the beast's attention away from me, and in turn, he gave it to Eleanor. They were wed not three weeks later."

I smiled. "Where are they now?"

He ran his finger over the bridge of my nose. "They boarded a ship to Scotland about a year before Nicolás was conceived. They wrote to inform us they'd had a daughter and named her Elizabeth. I think about them often… I wonder if they will remember each other when I am done here or if I will be robbing them of their love or robbing the world of all that might have descended from them… I wonder if I am truly doing the righteous thing or if I am being selfish to want to right my wrongs… And I wonder who will suffer most for the death of George Bennet. What will become of Tomás if I am not there to intervene? Or Alistair and Eleanor? Or any of the men we have employed on this ship over the years? Or you?"

"Me?" I raised up on my elbow to look down at him. "What are you afraid of with me?"

He tugged on a piece of my hair. "I am afraid I am robbing you of the opportunity to be a mother; stealing a much more meaningful life from you. Your sister says you were a natural mother and I will never give you that."

I shook my head. "I might've been a natural at a great many things in various versions of my life. In this one, I am perfectly happy with being a vet that's madly in love with a time traveler. It's *my* destiny to control, remember? You're not robbing me of anything. As for Alistair and Tomás… you've had far more years to think this through than I have. While I would love to use them as a means to beg you not to go through with it and just have you come back through time with me, that wouldn't be fair to you. Would it?"

"I don't know what's fair anymore," he admitted. "I thought I had an idea of it before you came along, but now… What you said to your sister earlier… Would you really return here to ensure my family would live?"

"Of course I would," I said. "I don't want you to lose your family. Besides, I keep trying to picture you there… in the future… I don't think you would be happy in that kind of stillness, and now that I've lived this life, I'm not sure I could be either. You want to be at sea, and I want to save exotic animals. There's no reason we can't do that here. We'll still go there for a while, and since time moves slower on this side of the storm, we'll have plenty of time to spend with the rest of our families while we wait to come home."

He furrowed his brow. "And how is that fair? How would I be any different than Owen if I let you do such a thing? You asked me once to save your life so you could never lose yourself so entirely to another person. How could I let you abandon what you've worked so hard for in that time to live in mine where a woman's accomplishments mean so little?"

"I'm not twenty, Joseph. I'm old enough now to know what I want and it has nothing to do with the rest of the world's opinions of me. I still have my accomplishments. With my knowledge, I can help animals—ones that have already gone extinct in my time even—and I don't need anyone but me and you to be proud of that accomplishment… doesn't matter what time we live in… so long as we're together while I do it."

He rolled to face me, tracing my brow with his fingertip. "Would you be happy here?"

"I *am* happy here." I slid my palm up over his ribs to let it glide along his back muscles. "And just think, we'll have all that untouched gold in California for the taking. We'll grab a couple handfuls and spend our lives doing what we love together. I can't imagine a better future."

"So, does that mean you intend to marry me?"

"*Aye,*" I teased. "I'll marry you."

"Oh, I like that sound on your lips," he all but growled, rolling over me to bring his mouth to mine.

"Aye?" I asked sweetly.

"No," he rasped, "the other bit… Say it again."

I was fairly certain I'd never stop smiling. "I'll marry you…"

My words were clipped by a gasp as his mouth found the spot on my throat that made my entire body liquefy beneath him. "Say it again."

Words were gone from my mind and the only noise I was capable of making slipped out in a single guttural syllable that was both *oh* and *ah* blended into one.

"I like that sound, too," he purred, coaxing several similar noises to escape my lips as he performed his magic against my skin. "Do you intend to sleep in *all* these clothes?"

"All these clothes," I managed between breaths, "are the only thing keeping us from being careless… good thing too, since you insist on doing things like that with your mouth."

He laughed against my skin, that deep throaty sound that always made me feel like I was the most important woman in the world for hearing it.

"What if I wish to touch you?" he whispered heavily, moving mouth, teeth, and tongue down my throat with growing enthusiasm. "What if I need to hear more of these sounds come from you? What if I must learn all the places on your skin that might provoke these beautiful noises?"

Tilting my head to allow him further access, I shuddered at the blissful torment he was delivering. "You're not putting up much of a fight, Joseph."

"I never claimed to be any good at fighting," he uttered, dragging his nose down the center of my bosom to create an ache in my breasts where they were confined beneath my fabric restraints. "Besides, *mi alma*, there are plenty other ways I might see you pleased."

I loved this part of him most; the unabashed, playful side that made me laugh and want at the same time. I loved the way we were becoming together; the familiarness... the permanence of having his ring on my finger.

He and I were no longer two souls dancing carefully around each other in search of signs of a shared desire. We were blended, and there was no hesitance or timidness left between us. We were free to just be... To take and touch as we liked...

I wanted him to touch... to know my body the way I intended to know his; to have a memory of me that would last through the years he'd spend without me. He was right... there were other ways to be intimate that wouldn't lead to an unwanted pregnancy.

Biting my lower lip, I reached beneath me to pull the laces of my stays, anxious to feel whatever pleasure he intended to serve.

And pleasure was something he indeed was proficient in. I hadn't even gotten the stays halfway unlaced when he pulled the fabric of my shift away to take my breast in his mouth.

Floating somewhere above the bed, I was wound into a ball of sensation; tongue and lips and breath against my flesh, spinning me uncontrollably into a euphoric hypnosis.

Nothing had ever felt like him...

Nothing would ever feel like him again...

I wanted more...

Lost in my rapture, my hips moved on their own against him as he reached back to finish loosing the laces, impatient with my halted progress.

My fingers moved to the ties around my waist, anxious to remove the layers of petticoats between us, but that effort was halted when I began to pull the first skirt away and grazed his hardened length where he hovered above me. He let out a soft whimper as if no one had touched him there in a very long time, and the sound of it set my whole body afire.

It was such a vulnerable sound for such a powerful man, and I no longer cared about whatever satisfaction he wanted to give me.

I'd never made a man make a sound in such a way that his pleasure brought me enjoyment beyond any physical touch. His ecstasy was a song in my ears, a beautiful airy note dancing over my skin, and I'd do anything so I could hear it again... and again... and again.

Abandoning my skirts altogether with piqued curiosity, I touched him once more, sliding my fingers up the front of his breeches where his solidness was nearly bursting through the seams.

His mouth stopped its movement and he whimpered again at the touch. That sound against my skin made even my bones turn liquid.

Pleasing him was more exhilarating than anything I'd ever done. Everything inside me heated when I made another pass and that sound came again... and again... and again.

He swore under his breath, raising up on his forearms so he could look down at what I was doing. "You'll have me undone if you keep doing that."

"I want you undone," I breathed, sliding my hand beneath the fabric to feel the warmth of his skin; to run my fingers over the fine hairs that surrounded him.

He trembled over me, his whimper turning into a deep groan that rumbled through his chest when my fingers tightened around him; iron wrapped in silk in my grip.

"You d-don't need to do that," he attempted to argue, his words a struggle as his undoing intensified with the movement of my wrist.

"Oh, I most certainly do," I assured him with a smile, reaching down with the other to pull the ties of his breeches loose. "I don't think I've ever enjoyed anything more than the sound of your delight."

And then his mouth was on mine and those wonderful sounds were made against my lips. Whimpers and throaty groans and the most exquisite hum passed between us.

He was the loveliest instrument I'd ever played.

I began to recognize what gave him more satisfaction; began to know his body the way I'd come to know his mind… I enjoyed the way he moved with me, indulging himself in my touch. I lavished in the little flinches and jerks as he was driven deeper into his euphoria. And I nearly came apart when his breathing grew too erratic to be contained, and he buried himself against my neck once more.

His heaving breath against my skin brought every hair on my body to stand on edge, and I was writhing with my own excitement as he pulsed in my grip and, losing his quivering hold, released to collapse heavily against me.

"Christ," he panted with a laugh as he raised back up on his forearms to look down on me. "You didn't need to do that."

I grinned. "I wanted to. I've never wanted to please a man so much in my life."

He pressed his lips gently to mine. "I've never been more pleased, *mi alma*."

"If that's true," I teased, "then there are a few more things I think I'd like to do with you this evening."

"Mmm." He slowly slid down the bed to hover over my waist, a wicked smile turning up his lips. "Not this evening, Cecelia. We won't have time. I intend to take a while pleasing you in return."

I playfully pursed my lips. "After all that, I won't take much time at all to please."

"Oh aye?" He raked his teeth over his lip. "You might not need much the first time… but if I'm to commit you to memory, I'll not be able to stop at just one."

I squealed when he suddenly dipped his entire upper body beneath my skirts, and I was forced to sit upright when I felt his breath against my inner thigh.

"This man who was not serious," he whispered heavily, his lips grazing the overly tender skin of my thigh, "did he kiss you here?"

"No," I said on a sharp inhale as he tasted the flesh a few inches above my knee, his mouth like fire against me.

"What about here?" he asked, moving inward.

"No…" I managed, my heart racing as he taunted me further, his calloused palm gliding up the inside of my other thigh to warm it as his mouth danced even higher.

"And what about here?"

Without any warning, his tongue made one long slow sweep over me and dragged every bit of air from my lungs. My head fell back and speaking became impossible.

If I'd thought his mouth was magical before, it became absolutely transcendental once he landed it fully upon my center. He did not tease or torment, but feasted—or rather, *devoured*—with tongue and teeth and breath and hands every last bit of me… cementing his touch on my body like a brand, over and over and over again so I would never forget who I belonged to.

Joseph…

Chapter Twenty-Nine

Alaina

I stood on the bow holding Zachary against my shoulder, staring at the endless green hills of Panama turned gray by the rising sun behind them. Wispy white mist lingered around the rolling canopy that was Panama's rainforest, and aside from one little opening indicative of the harbor, the entire continent appeared undisturbed by human activity.

Had Jack and Bud's lives not been hanging in the balance, it would've otherwise been one of the most beautiful landscapes I'd ever seen. As it was, the sight of it made my stomach uneasy.

There was a single ship in the bay far ahead, less than half the size of ours. I imagined it was the slave ship Juan Josef had commandeered, and my heartbeat quickened at the knowledge he could be waiting just there for our arrival.

I wasn't ready for this; wasn't ready to watch Jack move away from me the same way he had when he and Bud had left our island.

I hated the world… How cruel it was to give us so much while constantly threatening to rip it all away. Why couldn't we have stayed on that island forever? Why couldn't Captain Cook have just sailed right past us?

I dreamt endlessly of being there, safe and undisturbed by the world and its problems.

"Trade," Jack whispered, and I spun round to exchange Zachary for Cecelia so he could hold him just as tight as he had her. He bounced him softly with his lips pressed to the top of his head, and I prayed this would not be the last time I'd see the two of them together.

He'd been given a uniform similar to the ones Juan Jr., Gabriel, and Tomás wore and he looked positively majestic in it. A navy blue waistcoat with bright red and gold trim made his already impressive stature that much more intimidating. He wore white breeches and black boots with a sword sheathed at his hip. Brass buttons glistened in the morning sun and I watched this imposing creature rock our son gently with a sense of awe that he was mine.

"Remember our agreement," Cece was saying just behind him, her hands tangled with Juan's where he held them against his uniformed chest. "No matter what happens, you swore you wouldn't leave Panama without me."

"And I meant it." He pulled their hands to his mouth and laid a kiss against her fingers. "The moment it is safe, *mi alma*, I will come for you."

Beyond them, Jim and Lilly were knelt down in their cloaks, speaking their goodbyes through hand signals to Izzy who clung to a little brown teddy bear. Her little hazel eyes welled with tears and her lower lip jutted out as she fell against Jim's shoulder.

I hated goodbyes. We'd all had to say too many of them to each other, and I couldn't wait to go home and never say one again.

Maria approached me first, the roll of mosquito netting tucked under her arm. She looked every bit the duchess she was masquerading as in cream and blue colored skirts, a baby blue flowered Bergère hat on her head, and with shimmering pearls around her neck.

I'd attempted to talk her out of going, but she was unmovable in her determination. Despite everything that had occurred between them, Chris was her world, and I knew she'd rather give him the silent treatment at close distance than risk being apart. I hated that

I was the source of her misery, but I hoped their time away from me would mend both their hearts.

"Come on and give me a hug then," she ordered, spreading her arms wide. "If I do not come back to you, it is because I have run away with some handsome gypsy to live out my days making love like animals in the jungle."

I chuckled, leaning into her embrace with Cecelia squirming between us. "You're so full of it."

She squeezed me playfully. "I know."

"Be careful out there and…" I sighed, "take care of them."

She pulled away and laid a kiss on Cecelia's forehead. "I will. You take care of them. Now…" She stood back and theatrically opened her cream and lace parasol, resting it against her shoulder as she announced loudly, "I am off to find my new Panamanian lover," before moving past me to hug Magna.

Chris rolled his eyes with a smile as he replaced her in front of me, dressed in a similar uniform to Jack. "You couldn't talk her into staying, huh?"

I laughed. "I take it she's still not talking to you?"

He shook his head. "No, and she's going to be sorely disappointed when we get to that trail and she finds out we're sharing a horse."

I smiled and glanced at her where she was saying her goodbyes to Kyle. "I doubt she'll be disappointed. Are there not enough horses for everyone?"

He ran a hand over the back of his neck. "Oh, I'm sure there are, but… I've never ridden before and she has. I'm not saddling up with anyone else."

I pulled my lips in to hide a laugh. "So… Maria's going to be your knight on a white horse?"

"Shut up," he grumbled, chuckling despite himself.

"That's new," I said, pointing to the swirling silver handle on the sword at his hip.

He placed a hand on it. "Juan's been teaching me a new technique." His mood shifted from playful to serious as he glanced down at Cecelia in my arm. "You sure you're okay with all this?"

I shook my head. "Not really, but I'll be alright. So will you."

He didn't make any move to hug me and I saw him struggle with the decision not to as he straightened. "Take… take care, Al."

I nodded. "You too."

And as he moved past me, I said a prayer for him too, that he'd return safely with a healed heart and mind.

"Lainey," Lilly said, winding her arms around me, "we're going to get grandpa and then we're all going home. All of us. Together. We'll be back together before you even know it so let's not make a big dramatic goodbye anyway."

I rested my cheek on her cloaked shoulder, my swelling throat threatening to make a dramatic goodbye in spite of her. "I love you," I managed.

"I love you most," she said, pulling away to coo over Cecelia. "And I love you too, little angel. Auntie Lilly will be right back!"

Jim winked as he curled an arm around Lilly's shoulders. "That's right. Ain't nothin' to be worried about now. Hoss is gonna' be livin' the high life at a fancy motel gettin' hisself some peace and quiet for a minute and then we're all goin' home."

With a grin, Jim discreetly lifted his cloak to reveal an automatic rifle strapped to his chest. "Just in case."

I forced a smile. "Be careful out there."

He flashed his teeth. "Honey, careful's my middle name. I'll see ye' soon."

"Oh! Wait!" I grabbed Lilly's hand. "The necklace."

She clicked her tongue. "You don't need to take that off, honey. I'll be holding a fake baby and that should be all we need. You keep Evelyn with you."

I shook my head and handed Cecelia to Jim. "No. I don't want to take any chances."

I reached back to unclasp it and my throat felt odd without its weight when I extended it to her.

"You sure?" she asked.

I nodded. "I'll get it back. Evelyn can watch over you for a change."

She forced a smile as she hooked it around her neck. "I won't let anything happen to it, I promise."

"And I won't let nothin' happen to Hoss," Jim said, giving Cecelia back to me before turning to pull Lilly's hood up over her hair.

As the group began to load their sloop with clothing, gold, water, and camp essentials, Jack handed Zachary off to Fetia and stood with a long face in front of me.

"If this proves to be another mistake," he said, "forgive me now."

I shook my head. "There is nothing to forgive. We all agreed to this, and everything is going to work out. We're going home. One way or another."

He blew out, his eyes watering. "I have a terrible feeling about all this. I just… I don't know what else to do."

I took his hand in mine and squeezed. "You stay alive and I will too. That's all. You don't come back to this ship, not for any reason, no matter what happens. If you see it turning, you send anyone else, but you stay put. Our babies need you. If that date changes, you stay right where you are and I will come. Our death dates are years away so you'll know we're safe. Promise me you'll stay put."

Taking a very deep breath, he nodded. "I promise."

"No matter what?"

"No matter what," he said softly.

He laid a kiss on my lips, far too brief, and before I knew it, I was standing with my sister watching the sloop row away, surrounded by our new guards. Kyle, Michael, Terrence, Bruce, and Jacob were armed with automatic rifles and vowed not to leave our sides until it was over.

"You okay?" Cece whispered.

"Not yet," I answered. "Not until I know he is."

Chapter Thirty

Chris

There were moments in Chris's life he knew as they occurred he would always remember; riding a bike the first time, graduating high school, marrying Alaina, crashing into the ocean, kissing Maria in Tahiti, being wheeled into the operating room for brain surgery, and… arriving in Panama.

They'd stopped first at the slave ship in the hopes of finding Bud and Juan Josef there. It was one thing to know slavery was happening in this century, but knowing wasn't the same as seeing. Once he stepped off the sloop and onto the deck, he understood he would never be able to unsee that ship; would never again feel quite the same now that he'd witnessed in person the sobering reality that was the slave trade.

Standing on that ship's deck, the hair on the back of his neck stood on end. There were no slaves on board as the little remaining crew were waiting for them to cross over from the Atlantic side, but evidence of what they would endure upon their arrival was enough to turn his stomach.

Where he had a sword strapped to his hip for protection, the crewmen wore whips, clubs, and pistols for dominance. Rusty chains and shackles sat in a tangled pile to one side of the deck.

Everything about the vessel felt haunted and vile, like the wood itself had absorbed years of sadness from its occupants.

There was an iron hatch in the deck boards that made an icy chill creep up his spine. He couldn't bring himself to go near enough to it to get a glimpse of the conditions beneath it, but he knew, strictly by the impression the hatch left upon him that it was where they kept their human cargo.

Jim had snuck an automatic rifle beneath his cloak and he debated snagging it and taking out every remaining crewman on board. Surely, history wouldn't miss them.

Before he could, however, Juan had gotten the information he needed and motioned them back toward the sloop. His father had gone to shore the morning prior.

Hatred in his heart, Chris settled for simply leaving the ship, and it was a relief to step onto the sloop once more.

With each row of the boat away from that awful vessel, he felt his tensed muscles easing more and more.

In contrast to the dark, lifeless energy of the slave ship, the docks of Panama were bright and full of life, and when he placed a foot on the pier, he found himself sobered once more by the sights and sounds around him.

The city climbed up a hill ahead of them, brilliant colonial architecture lining the cobblestone horse path on each side in shades of white, red, green, and yellow. Merchants, locals, and travelers bustled between buildings on foot, horseback, and at least one in a shiny black stagecoach.

With so many horrors written in the history books, this was hardly the image he'd had of an 18th century Panama. It was absolutely stunning and full of life.

While Juan inquired in Spanish with a few men on the dock as to Juan Josef's whereabouts, Chris found himself entirely hypnotized by a group of toucans—*actual* toucans, with bright turquoise-orange beaks and black and yellow bodies—clicking and chirping in a tree over their heads. He was surprised at their sound —more resemblant of crickets than birds, and fell into a trance watching them interact with each other.

"They came on land," Maria translated in a hushed voice, pulling his attention from the birds to their group where Juan Jr. conversed with two old men while Maria listened in and relayed the message. "Juan Josef went to the Ruiz stables yesterday morning… He had several others with him… one looked injured."

Lilly hopped from toe to toe, hugging the little bundle in her arms. "Grandpa."

Juan Jr. bowed and his gratitude needed no translation. He turned toward the city and motioned the rest of them to follow.

Chris plucked up the two heaviest of their canvas bags as the others collected the smaller ones and they made their way down the main street.

Three story buildings stood pristine and tightly clustered together on each side of them, all with wide towering windows and balconies lined with iron balusters. They passed ale houses, shops, cafes, and countless churches before Juan set his bags down in front of a bright red door above which a metal sign simply read *'inn'*.

"Mr. Volmer," he said. "You, Tomás, and Gabriel shall remain here. Come, I will arrange your accommodations before we head to the stables."

While the four of them were inside, Chris turned a circle, staring up at the buildings and brightly colored birds that sang and hopped between rooftops. He could hear the rainforest ahead, even tucked away beyond the city… chirps, howls, and coos of every octave singing far in the distance.

"Ain't what ye' thought it'd be, eh, Beanstalk?" Jim cackled, bouncing his fake baby against his shoulder. "I's expectin' snakes and spiders and murky water… Not a whole dang civilization walkin' round sippin' coffee and pickin' out lace!"

"Oh, I imagine we'll get to the snakes and spiders soon enough," Chris said, still taking in the wealth of the city spread out around him as men and women in fancy attire passed between shops and cafes without a care in the world.

"Grandpa's here somewhere," Lilly said, scanning their surroundings with less wonder and more inquiry. "He's alive… And he's here… We're going home soon."

"Cain't get there soon enough." Jim moaned, fanning his face beneath the cloak. "It ain't even eight o'clock in the mornin' yet and it's already hotter than a goat's ass in a pepper patch. I don't know how these people wear all this crap. Look at that one." He pointed to a woman in a shimmery burgundy dress. "Here I am sweatin' like the devil's nutsack while that one's covered head to toe and ain't got nary a single drop of dew on her head. These people must have different blood in they veins."

Chris chuckled. It was indeed hot. The heat was heavy and damp, and he already felt his shirt clinging to his torso beneath the uniform. "We'll need to bring all the water we can carry. In this heat, we'll be sweating it out almost as fast as we take it in."

Jim nodded, unscrewing the cap from his canteen and taking a long swig before offering it to Lilly to do the same.

With Jim distracted and Juan off with Jack, Chris took the opportunity to lean in to Maria and speak in a low voice. "I need to ask you something."

She raised her chin and looked away.

Laughing to himself, he spoke to the back of her head anyway. "I don't know how to ride a horse. When we get to the stables… can I ride with you?"

She looked up at him from the side of her eye. "Oh, you need me now, Superman?"

"Please?"

She shook her head. "No."

"Come on, Maria," he quietly pleaded, "I don't want to hold us up."

"Then why did you come with?" she snapped. "You knew we would be riding horses, asshole."

This caught Jim's attention, and Chris pulled her down the walkway a few feet. "Because I *need* to help get us home. I can't just sit idle on the ship and let everyone else do the work."

"And now you *need* me to put you on my horse so you don't look like an idiot to your friends?" Her dark brow shot up on her forehead. "The answer is no."

"I know you're hurt," he said, treading lightly, "but we don't have to be uncivil to each other. We're not strangers, you know."

"We're not?" She coiled her fingers into a fist in his shirt and dragged him several more feet away from the others before spinning on her heal to glare up at him. "I understood that *you* needed time. I understood that we rushed into things and *you* needed to work out your bullshit. I really did, and I would've been willing to give you all the time in the world because I thought I understood you, Kreese; because I thought I knew who you were and was not innocent myself in letting us both rush into things."

Her eyes watered but she tightened her jaw and blinked the moisture away. "But the man I knew wouldn't have left me in that bed alone all night after those men attacked the ship. He would've come and held me and made me feel safe, even if it was just for that night; even if he didn't really want to be there. It didn't matter to me that you still loved her and were going to end things with us. *I* needed you then. While you were falling to your knees and telling her how much you loved her, I was trembling in that bed, terrified more men would come and I might have to kill again or be killed. Do you have any idea what I went through? How scared I was? How alone I felt? While you were having your little internal meltdown over who to love, did you ever consider I might be afraid? With no one else to go to for comfort than you?"

She didn't pause to let him answer, but continued with her eyes narrowed. "I went through time forward and backward because *you* needed me. And the single time I needed you, you disappeared. Not just for the night, Kreese… but for days. And not once, *not once* during that whole spiel you gave about still loving me and me waiting for you, did you ask how I was."

Taking a deep breath, she squared her shoulders. "The answer is no, Kreese. You don't get to treat me like a human only when it's convenient for you. We *are* strangers. And you can get your own fucking horse."

On that note, she pushed past him and hurried back to the rest of their group, leaving Chris to watch her walk away with his heart heavy in his throat.

On the edge of the city, they came to the Ruiz stables after a long walk in the heat. Chris had replayed Maria's words over and over during the trip, unable to come up with any excuse for his complete disregard for her well-being that night.

She had every right to be angry on so many levels, and he had no right to ask anything of her, especially for her to wait. He'd been careless with her; his confidence in her devotion to him making him selfish and negligent to her emotional state. There was no amount of apology he could offer to make up for the way he'd treated her since his memories had changed… but he'd give them anyway. Over and over… Just so she'd know.

The stables were housed beyond a seemingly endless brick building with windows on the second story and arched double doors lining the stalls of the main floor. A spindly old man on horseback greeted Juan by name as they came through the gate.

Maria leaned into Jim. "The man's name is Alonso Ruiz. He and his family own the stables… Juan is asking if Juan Josef already came through… Alonso says yes… they took five horses and a mule and headed up the trail yesterday…"

Maria frowned as they continued. "Juan is asking about the man's sons… Asking if *'Lucas'* or his brothers would be willing to keep an eye on the ship while he escorts us through."

She pursed her lips. "Juan says he'll pay no small amount in gold to have one of his sons inform our rider at the inn if the ship makes any move to turn…"

A younger man with dusty blond hair and a quizzical brow came riding from the far side of the building, his hand in the air as he shouted out, "Juan! I did not believe my own ears when I heard *el cazador* was riding toward our home! It has been far too long!"

Two other men rode up behind him, all of them with a resemblance to each other and observing Lilly and Maria a little too closely.

"Adrián," Juan said in greeting, his tone far less jovial than Adrián's had been. "Lucas… Benito," he added as the others caught up, smiling a little more at them than he had the first.

Again, Maria interpreted softly. "Juan is telling them he has been hired to escort the Duchess of Parma across the trail to the Atlantic. He says his father and brother were supposed to ride ahead and check for threats…"

After the men examined her with wide eyes, she watched their continued conversation closely, nodding. "Lucas… the pretty one," she added with a smirk, "he says he'll watch the ship. Juan's explaining where to find Tomás. And now the old man is going on and on… Basically kissing Juan's ass while they discuss payment. Says they'll load the horses and mules for us and they're more than happy to give him anything he needs. Asking if we'd like to come in for tea…"

She chewed her lower lip as Juan spoke. "Juan says no. Told him we're running behind and have to rush if we're to catch our ship in Portobelo."

Adrián smiled at Maria, the man named Benito smiling similarly at the chest of gold she held in her arms. "We would be honored to serve you, Your Grace," Adrián said in English. "Juan and I are old friends. There is no one finer to escort you safely across the trail. We shall ready our best horses for your journey."

He dismounted easily, taking the horse's bridle and returning to Spanish as he led Juan toward the stables.

"He says his other brother, Jacinto, rode ahead with Juan Josef and a group of slavers. Wants to know why I'm so far from Parma…"

She tilted her head to one side and grinned. "And Juan basically says it's none of their business. I think these men are afraid of him."

Chris gazed ahead and noticed the way the four men kept their eyes on Juan and their heads slightly lowered… He'd seen Juan swing a sword and wondered if his own posture wasn't similar during their morning lessons. The man was definitely formidable when he had a sword strapped to his hip.

And Juan's image was proven even more imposing a half hour later when the horses were brought out and he effortlessly swung himself up into the saddle of a gold and black one.

Chris swallowed and his palms began to sweat as Jim hoisted Lilly up onto a spotted brown male, then mounted his own similarly colored one.

He was the only one without experience… And he was about to make an ass of himself.

Maria climbed up into the saddle of a white horse and expertly guided it to a stop beside the remaining black mare reserved for Chris.

She held a knowing grin across her features as he shakily put a hand on the horse's muzzle. "Please don't kill me," he whispered to the beast, petting its nose for a good long minute. "Does she have a name?" he asked Adrián as he moved past him toward the mules.

"That one's Medianoche," he replied over his shoulder. "I wouldn't stand so close to her mouth. She bites."

"Great," Chris groaned, moving to its side to stare up at the walnut saddle over his head. How hard could it be? He'd seen it done in movies a thousand times…

"Oye," Maria said when he took hold of the saddle's horn. "Gather the reins first, but don't pull her." She looked ahead to where the others were distracted supervising Benito and Lucas as they loaded the mules. "Left foot in the stirrup, hold the saddle, and swing the right over. Sit down lightly with your legs loose. Do not squeeze her with your legs or pull those reins."

Grateful beyond measure at her discretion, he smiled, and was pleasantly surprised when the horse remained still while he mounted as instructed. At eye level with Maria, he looked to her for what to do next, unwilling to ask directly since he had no right.

She looked absolutely radiant on her horse. Like she was glowing… And the sight of her ripped his heart in half.

Something inside him shifted—or rather, quaked. With the sun detailing the little splash of freckles across her nose, he was reminded of the way she'd looked when he opened his eyes in Eimeo and found her hovering over him. He felt that... That deep, undying love that had warmed his entire body at the sight of her then. That feeling had been missing since they'd gone through the storm and memories of Alaina had drowned him.

What did it mean that he felt it now? And was he only feeling it because of his guilt or was it legitimate? He wouldn't take any more risks with her. Not after everything he'd already done to hurt her.

She presented her gloved hands where they held her own reins. "Hold it like this. Elbows in and with slack in the reins so you have control but you're not pulling her. You pull her mouth and she'll go backward; pull too hard and she'll buck you off or bite you. If you want to go forward, squeeze gently with your legs. If you want to turn, extend the rein in the direction you want to go—*gently*. You can't have your big man attitude with a horse."

She sighed, softening her tone a little as he nervously adjusted his grip. "Don't worry too much. She'll want to keep pace with the other horses so you won't have to do much. Just keep the reins loose. Come on, ride beside me for a minute."

He'd never been on a horse before, but the minute he squeezed his legs against her and she stepped forward, he was captivated. The act immediately became something he wanted in his life... Even though he'd hardly learned more than making it walk forward, he could already imagine himself riding at full speed through undisturbed wilderness... The freedom of it... He considered Jim's words and added horseback riding to his list of life requirements; horseback riding *with Maria.*

"Turn this way," Maria instructed, turning her horse toward the stables.

Chris gently moved the reins that direction and grinned uncontrollably when the mare obeyed.

"Keep your eyes forward, ahead of the horse," she commanded. "You are her eyes. She can't see the path like you can and you have to watch where you lead her, especially once we get on that trail. Keep her away from anything that might frighten her on the ground… like a snake or a rodent."

He followed her instructions closely, adjusting the reins to the left and right until the horse was moving straight again alongside hers.

She continued the lesson with him, showing him how to stop and speed up, circling the same several yards over and over until he felt confident. By the time the group was loaded and ready to leave, he had grown comfortable enough to lead her into a trot, stopping a little too close to Jim's horse as they joined the group.

"You ain't got a clue what ye' doin', do ye?" Jim grinned, reaching over to run a palm over Medianoche's neck. "I didn't neither first time I got on one. Ye'll figure it out right quick when ye' find yourself danglin' from a stirrup with 'em hooves threatenin' to trample your face."

"That's… helpful," he said. "Thanks, Jim."

"Anytime, Beanstalk," Jim chuckled. "You just keep to the middle and she'll be fine."

So he did.

With Juan in the lead and two mules in tow, they ventured out of the stables. Growing more confident in his saddle, he couldn't contain his smile as the cobblestone path turned to dirt, and the sounds and sights of the rainforest enveloped them.

Above the constant vibrating thrum of crickets and the sweet soft call of singing birds, howler monkeys rumbled their warnings as they swung from the canopy high above… They were but black shadows in the tree tops, following for a time with piqued curiosity.

Maria rode to his right, slightly ahead of him. He remembered the way she'd flinched on their small island at every noise in the trees… Not here though. She rode without fear, her eyes set forward, vibrant in her cream and blue colored petticoats.

"Thank you," he said to her, holding up his reins in illustration when she glanced back at him.

"I did it for me, not you," she answered proudly. "I want to go home and be done with this nightmare."

Chapter Thirty-One

Alaina

With Kyle standing guard outside our room, Jacob and Michael doing the same on deck, and Terrence inside the room with us, I sat down with Cece on the sofa and fired up Bud's laptop. I needed a way to keep my mind occupied so it wasn't dreaming up all the ways he might die.

The familiar opening note played and my heartbeat quickened with excitement as I considered all the research I might find... all the extra content beyond our genealogy we hadn't had a chance to review together. The time travel conspiracies and photos... the paintings and altered history...

"I transferred some of my own research onto it from my phone this morning," Terrence said, perching on the opposite arm of the couch with his rifle. "Flight log, passenger photos, things like that. I thought it might come in handy to have it all in the same place down the line."

"Good idea," Cece said, not looking away from Zachary where she bounced him in her lap.

"Where should we start?" I asked when I'd unlocked the home screen to be overwhelmed with folders of research. I took a quick glance at the unchanged master's log as they all spoke at once, disappointed to see Jack's name still written upon it.

"Who is Juan Francisco de la Bodega?" Cece asked when I closed the image to return to the list of folders.

I hovered over his name. "He's Juan Josef's ancestor. Before Chris and Bud went through, I asked them to pull his genealogy as well in case we needed to change our plans."

She drew in a breath, sitting Zachary down across her legs. "Juan Francisco isn't in Panama, is he?"

"No," I assured her, "he's in Yorktown... safe and sound."

She sighed a breath of relief. "Good."

Magna, who was hovering behind the sofa with a chatty Cecelia in one arm, pointed to a folder called *'Ocean Portals'* on the screen. "That sounds like a good place to start."

Terrence chuckled. "So you want to go down a very dark and deep rabbit hole, eh Magna?"

She chuckled. "Why not? Bud saw enough value in it to save it. Might as well dive in."

Over the next half hour, we indeed found ourselves deep inside a rabbit hole of conspiracy. The *'Vile Vortices,'* as the author called them, were a set of triangular coordinates along the equator, one of which was the Bermuda Triangle. All the locations shared similar bizarre phenomena in that ships, airplanes, and people tended to disappear when they got too close, and they all shared the same linear coordinate either just above or just below the equator.

There was one particular location that stood out to me, Hamakulia in the Hawaiian Islands. In the ocean just northeast of Hawaii—very close to where our airplane met the storm—there was a volcano. Local legends told of strange disappearances of both ships and airplanes throughout history when they got too close. Some locals had even claimed to have witnessed bizarre lightning in the area. The triangle on the map contained the coordinates we'd gone through.

This made me immediately think back to our island and Magna's story of Maui, the demigod. That legend stated when storm clouds would gather over the volcano Haleakalā in Hawaii, the people would hide in fear that Maui might hurl them so far they could never return… Perhaps there was truth to the legend after all.

There were similar spots and stories throughout the world as I explored all the other vortices. There were the Algerian Megaliths in the Sahara Desert where several flights disappeared and navigational tools regularly stopped working. There was Mohenj-Daro in Pakastan where an entire civilization perished at once with no explanation. There was the Dragon's Triangle in Japan and the Bermuda Triangle, both of which had become famous for airplanes and ships disappearing without a trace. There was also a spot near Easter Island, very close to the coordinates we'd come through that was known for similar bizarre events.

I wondered if any one of those locations might open up in March should we find ourselves closer to one of them than our own… And I wondered which ones went backward and which ones went forward. If we somehow found ourselves in Virginia against our will, could we find a way home in the Bermuda Triangle or would we find ourselves even further back in time?

Cece, thinking the same, ran her finger over the map on screen. "Look how these triangles make a perfect line above and below the equator… We went through here," she said, tapping the triangle over Hawaii, "above the equator. But we came out here." She touched the triangle near Easter Island. "Below the equator. What if that's how it works? Say we went to the Bermuda Triangle…" she touched the spot where it sat above the equator line. "Would we then come out further back in time down in the South Atlantic Anomaly near Rio de Janeiro?" She dragged her finger to the corresponding triangle below the equator.

"Maybe," I said, noticing they were the exact same distance apart as the ones we'd traveled through. "It would make sense."

She leaned in, adjusting her glasses down her nose to inspect the screen, the gears in her mind obviously spinning. "Open up the *Strange Artwork* folder. Chris mentioned Bud found bizarre photos and paintings throughout time. I wonder if they all travel the same distance or if some take you further back than others… Maybe those photos are unfortunate people who found themselves too close to one of these vortices during the equinox."

I opened up the folder and found countless 1940s photographs containing people with more modern cameras, one person appearing to be holding a cell phone, and one man wearing definitively modern sunglasses.

"See," Cece grinned, adjusting Zachary in her lap. "I was right. They have to work differently. That camera looks like one of those digital ones we used to carry around in the early 2000s. Same with those sunglasses and that phone… It almost looks like a flip phone. I wonder if all these people were on the same boat or airplane, and I wonder which location they went through to end up sixty years in the past instead of more than two-hundred?"

Terrence squinted at the screen. "How do we know those haven't been photoshopped?"

"This article says the photos were checked for tampering and were confirmed to be legitimate," I said, scanning the words in the article once more.

"And," Cece added, "you can't photoshop a painting. There's those, too. Look!" She took over the trackpad, closing the article to open a painting labeled, *'Mother and son by John Singleton Copley - Philadelphia, 1775.'*

My mouth might've fallen open. The painting was exquisite. A brunette woman with thick brows and pale skin sat in a chair wearing a flowery cream dress, the arms and petticoats heavily ruffled and trimmed with pink lace. The source of the conspiracy however sat in her lap. A young boy, no older than six, was smiling at the artist. He wore a gold waistcoat and vest with matching gold breeches and white stockings. On his feet, though, was what appeared to be black and white tennis shoes, a distinctive white 'swish' symbol on the sides.

This made me return to the woman and, while there was nothing evident about her clothing that would give her away as a time traveler, she did have three piercings in one ear… Something that wasn't a trend in this century.

Cece frowned at the screen. "Does she look familiar to you?"

I shook my head. "Never seen her before."

"She had to be on your plane. That boy would've outgrown those shoes if she'd come before you. There's a possibility she could've come after, but... 1775... and to be in America?"

"Let me see that," Terrence said, moving from his perch on the edge of the sofa to squeeze his large figure between us on the cushions. "Shit, I think... Holy shit. I'm pretty sure that's Charlotte Miller and her little brother, Chase!"

"Who's Charlotte Miller?" Cece and I both asked in unison.

He took the computer from me and placed it in his lap, leaving the painting open to one side as he skimmed through a folder called *'Terrence Phone Files.'*

"Why do you have a folder in there with my name on it?" Cece asked, frowning at the screen as he moved his cursor over various files and folders.

"Not now," he said, landing upon the image he was searching for and opening it—a family photo of the Millers.

The family looked like they'd been pulled from a magazine. They wore fall sweaters, scarves, and boots and posed in front of a dried out cornfield, pumpkins surrounding them as the sun shone brightly at their backs.

A graying mother and father stood proud, a teenage daughter to one side with long brown hair and thick eyebrows. She had a hand on a little boy's shoulder, both of them an exact match to the painting.

"The Millers were on flight 89," he said. "Seated in the back of the plane."

I swallowed. "But Phil told me he saw the back of the plane explode... Lilly saw something similar... There's no way they could've survived that."

"Obviously, there is," Terrence said, putting the images side by side. "You can't tell me this isn't a painting of Charlotte and Chase Miller."

"This painting is titled *woman and son*," Cece noted, pursing her lips. "Which would mean, if it *is* the Millers, the parents didn't make it and this girl is posing as the boy's mother… How old was she when she went through?"

"Seventeen," he said. "Chase was four."

I stared disbelievingly at the screen. "I wonder if there are others with them? How many of us actually survived that crash?"

"We have to find them," Cece said slowly, "She's probably scared and desperate to get back. She won't have the information we do and we can't very well abandon her. Can we?"

"Do you have any idea how hard it will be to find her in the short amount of time we have before we need to head back to the storm?" I asked. "We can't afford to delay with another mission."

Cece shook her head. "I'm not going to the storm. I'm gonna stay until Juan kills George Bennet. I'll have time to look for her."

"What?" I stared disbelievingly at Cece where she sat opposite Terrence.

"Juan asked me to marry him," she said, bouncing Zachary once more in her lap. "I'm staying."

My mouth fell open. "He *what*?"

She trilled her lips at Zachary and smiled, presenting me her left ring finger as evidence. "He asked me to marry him."

"And you said yes?" I couldn't help the shock in my voice. "Cece, you've been here less than a month, and you spent two weeks of that month unconscious. I know you're smitten with him, but—forgive me for being so blunt—have you lost your damn mind?"

She nodded, laughing as Zachary kicked his little legs. "Oh, I've lost it entirely I think! But…" She swooned. "It's freeing to be this crazy about someone. And I've decided, since I'm not dying, I want to stay with him as long as I can before things change, which will give me plenty of time to find Charlotte."

"Don't be irrational!"

She clicked her tongue. "We love each other. It's not an irrational thing in this century for two people in love to get married so soon. Besides," she pointed at the screen, "this poor girl needs us. We can't leave her behind."

"This is about sex, isn't it?" I balked, ignoring her excuse to save Charlotte and focusing solely on the marriage proposal. "He won't sleep with you unless you're married and you've agreed to spend your life with him just so the two of you can have sex, haven't you?!"

She rolled her eyes. "Give me a little credit, A.J. I'm not that desperate and he's not that traditional. It's so much more than that."

My eyebrows might've shot past my hairline. "Please, Cece, elaborate, because I cannot fathom how you—a person who refuses to let me even speak about the family you once had because of your need to be independent—can decide to marry a complete stranger so hastily and leave behind your life for him."

"*That's* what this is about," she drawled. "You don't disapprove of me getting married, you'd just prefer I was married to that little twat, Owen, who made me into a bet. Right?"

"No," I said. "I didn't approve of that marriage either. I thought you were too young and giving up too much. I just… It's too soon, honey. You can't just go off and marry the first guy you fall in love with. You haven't even had your first argument yet. How do you know this is what you want?"

Cece groaned, placing Zachary on his butt in her lap. "I'm not twelve years old, A.J., I'm plenty old enough to know what I want. You don't know the person I do. He doesn't show you the gentle, playful, sweet person he shows me. Do you know we've spent almost every waking hour of the past two weeks together? All we've had is time to talk, and we have talked about *everything*. There's no noise out here to get in the way of us getting to know each other. You, of all people, should know that. He's told me what he wants out of life, what he's lived, what he regrets, and what he loves; told me where he's been and where he wants to go; what he believes in and what he hopes for in death. I've told him the same. And I fell in love with everything about him… his kindness, his heart, his mind… I love him, and I love the way I feel about *me* when I'm with him. I don't need more time to know I'll take that for the rest of my life easily."

I sighed. "Honey, everybody loves those things about a person when they first start dating. You don't really know him yet. Not fully."

"Do any of us ever fully know each other?" she asked, her blond brow raised. "No, we don't. And just like you took a chance agreeing to spend your life getting to know your *two* husbands, I'm ready to spend whatever's left of mine getting to know Juan. I know enough about him to know he's what I want. And I told you, not because I'm looking for your approval, but because I'm happy and I wanted to share that with you. You can't stop me."

"Do you two always bicker this way?" Magna asked, rocking baby Cecelia against her hip as she moved to the edge of the sofa; her intervention perfectly timed as I prepared to defend the *'two husbands'* comment. "Are you never simply happy for each other?"

I frowned up at her. "Of course we are."

"Really?" Magna chuckled. "You could have fooled me, baby. She tells you she is in love with Juan and you tell her she is not because she hasn't spent enough time with him. You tell her you are in love with Jack and she tells you you're not because of too much time spent with Chris... Have you learned nothing about time or love over this past year and a half?"

When both Cece and I just stared at her, she smiled. "When you get to be my age—which seems like the blink of an eye—you realize how silly it is to waste any of it. Love gives you time; makes it stand still; makes every second precious. Time is nothing, you see. Gone like that." She snapped her fingers. "So love as much as you can to still it... Because it's also everything we have."

She leaned against the arm of the sofa and sighed. "Haunui and I married after only a few weeks, too. Sometimes you can recognize the person you're meant to spend your life with right away. Sometimes you need longer. It doesn't make either right or wrong; we're all different. For us, we both just knew, almost the instant we met, what happiness with each other would look like. And our life together was a wonderful eternity, filled with memories that will live on far past our deaths. If you've both found your eternity, don't bicker about time. You're just wasting it.

Now," she flipped her wrist lazily toward the laptop, "enough love talk. Let's see what else is on here while that computer's still got a charge."

We'd spent the next several hours combing through both Bud and Terrence's files.

We'd looked at the various time travel files, spent far too long debating correct and incorrect logos when we landed upon Mandela effects, spent a while admiring photos of Dahlia and her children, found a photo of a young Juan Josef inside a teal-walled cafe, and then moved on to each of our genealogies and the images that came with them.

It had been odd for me to look at images of Gloria. Each one was almost like seeing a photo of myself in a different reality, the resemblance was that strong. I didn't want to rob the world of a person who seemed so full of life, but I also hated the idea of my descendant ending up with a man like Juan Josef; a man who I knew had physically abused her.

Cece would not relent in her insistence that we needed to come back to raise our children in this time once it was safe to do so with Zachary. She'd said that it wouldn't be fair to rob Gloria of a life when she'd done nothing to deserve it. In turn, I'd accused her of being a hypocrite for lecturing me when she was doing the very same thing to Maddy.

That did not bode well. It wasn't long before we'd worked ourselves up into a full-blown, screaming argument. As our fights tended to do, things got personal. I'd accused her of being naïve and immature while she accused me of being selfish and cold. The tension between us escalated to the point that she eventually stormed off to sleep in Juan Jr.'s cabin.

I loved the girl with all my heart, but the two of us had a way of getting under each other's skin.

I sat, still fuming, on the sofa, checking the computer every half hour or so for changes to the master's log as the others settled into sleep.

"Hey," Terrence said softly, approaching with caution. "You alright?"

I huffed. "I'm fine. We've argued like this our whole lives. We'll make up in the morning after we've both had a minute to cool off."

He chuckled, sitting down with a grunt on the sofa beside me. "Me and my brother used to fight the same way… although, I think our fists might've hurt less than some of your words to each other. You two are ruthless."

I ran a hand over my face. "I can't help it. You've known her for a while now. You have to agree she's being irrational with this whole Juan Jr. thing, right? I mean… she barely knows him. *I* barely know him and I've spent months with him. It was one thing to have a little romantic fling, but to stay here indefinitely? What if it takes years to change things?"

"Can I show you something?" he asked, tapping the computer in my lap.

I nodded and leaned in when he opened it up and navigated to the *'Cece'* folder inside the files he'd transferred from his phone. "I told you I'd creep around and spy on the crew for signs of anything suspicious. I didn't find any suspects, but I did find this."

He opened up a photo of Cece and Juan Jr. The sun shone brightly down on them where she held the helm and he held her.

Her head was turned up to gaze at him, his turned down to look upon her, and they both appeared to be laughing.

"I would agree with you," Terrence said gently, "had I not seen them when neither of them knew I was watching."

He closed the photo and opened another, taken later that same evening. Their foreheads were pressed together where they stood at the stern, hands entwined against his chest.

"Your sister," Terrence continued, "she doesn't open her heart to just anybody. She's smart… guarded… This kind of devotion," he pointed at the smile on her face, "she doesn't give this easily. I know you think she's being naïve, but that girl is one of the smartest people I've ever met. If she trusts him, so do I… So should we all."

He closed the photo and moved the cursor over the other files. "I took a few more last night along with a video you can watch on your own time. I wanted you to know their feelings are authentic. And she deserves that. The poor girl has been alone her whole life, and she has absolutely lit up with Juan. Jazz and I have prayed for years she might find something like this. And now she has it and the only person she'd give it up for is you."

"Me?" I balked.

"Yes, you. She loves you enough she'd walk away from him if you didn't approve. Hell, she gave up her practice to spend three years looking for you. You know she's got your name tattooed on her ankle?"

My eyes watered and I shook my head. "No… I just… Maddy was—"

"She cannot feel what you want her to feel for Maddy," he said. "It'd be like me telling you to give up Jack and your children because you have another family in a life you don't know. You'd fight it, right?"

"Yes, but—"

"But nothing," he insisted, handing me the laptop and standing. "You can't push a life on her she doesn't want any more than she can force you to come back and raise your children here. You two can bicker about that as much as you want, but it'll get you nowhere. She wants him." He motioned to the screen. "And she wants your approval before she'll have him. That girl put her whole life on hold to find you. You owe her that."

With a swelling heart, I waited until Terrence returned to the hall to open up the video, and my heart nearly broke in two as I watched them.

They were so mesmerized and delicate as they touched and kissed. He whispered in her ear and she laughed, saying, *'Let's not be one of those couples that says I love you all the time. You're only allowed to say it when you absolutely can't hold it in... When there are no other words to express how you feel. Okay?'*

I couldn't help the smile on my lips as Juan, completely at ease with her, let go of his reservations and said the words four more times, inciting uncontrollable laughter from her.

I quickly played the video again and again. How happy they both—"

"Mrs. Grace," a deep and familiar voice said behind my head, causing the hairs on my arms to stand on end.

Mr. Gil.

"I suggest, madam, if you wish for your children to remain alive, you follow me out into the corridor and disarm your men."

I heard the cocking of a pistol and turned slowly around to find Zachary asleep in the crook of his massive arm, the pistol held casually upward in the hand of the other.

"Why are you doing this?" I asked, trying to remain calm.

"Why do you think?" he responded with a smile. "Surely you would not believe the captain would rely solely on his rather unruly son to deliver you to him? And you could not think he would approach this ship with so many of your men armed and standing guard on the deck? I'll need you to disarm them now so I can signal him. And should you get any ideas to deviate from this order, I'll have no choice but to kill both you and your son. The only life I'm obligated to save is your daughter's. Understand?"

Chapter Thirty-Two

Cecelia

The ship was eerily soundless. Upon waking, I'd initially assumed the quiet was attributed to the more boisterous members of our group having gone to shore, but as I came fully awake, I realized the silence was heavier.

There were no footsteps above of a crew maintaining the ship, no familiar clang of dishes in the dining room overhead of the kitchen staff preparing to serve breakfast, and no cries from Zachary or Cecelia despite the sunlight streaming in to warm my cheeks.

I sat up suddenly in the bed—in *Juan's* bed with his journal clutched to my chest. For a moment, I inhaled the familiar scents of him surrounding me... The sweet almond spice on my skin and hair from his pillow, the hint of dampened dust on the maps and journals that filled the room, and the caramel accent of very good scotch still sitting in my glass on the bedside table.

Had he come back already? Was that why it was so quiet? Had he found and dealt with his father? Was he already unloading our people into sloops and cutters?

I had remained dressed, just in case we would need to make a hasty exit, and without checking my appearance, I slid my feet into my slippers, fixed my glasses on my face, tucked the journal into my pocket, and hurried into my sister's room.

Empty.

My heartbeat quickened with excitement. He must've come back. They had to be on the deck…

But if he'd come back, he'd have come for me first…

I frowned at the open laptop left on the sofa… off the solar charger…

Kneeling, I tapped my thumb on the space bar, relieved to see the screen light up.

Quickly, I opened up the master's log and my heart nearly stopped to find Jack's name no longer upon it.

Closing the log, I hurriedly opened up the genealogy chart and read the dates below each name.

Jack M. Volmer, Birth Unknown - 1825

Jack had a new death year… Juan was telling the truth. We needed to get off the ship. Maybe Alaina had gotten the same idea. Perhaps she'd seen the updated chart and rushed off to be reunited with Jack, forgetting, in her excited state, I was asleep in the room down the hall… Or perhaps, after our heated words, she'd chosen to leave me behind.

I hurried to the side of the bed where Alaina kept her handwritten copy of the chart. Sure enough, the date had changed there as well… which meant Jack would've seen it on his own copy and sent someone to retrieve us.

Trembling with excitement, I tucked the paper into my bosom and headed back out into the corridor. I was halfway to the stairwell when the hair on the nape of my neck rose and forced my feet to freeze in place.

Terrence wouldn't have forgotten me…

Something was wrong.

Remembering the sight of the bed pulled away from the wall and the hole where Juan Josef had escaped, I turned back. If there were indeed tunnels in the walls, I could use them to spy just as he had. And I hoped, as I slid into the room that once served as his prison, I was simply overreacting to a quiet morning and would find them all sitting in silence in the dining room soon enough.

Kneeling at the head of the bed, I spun the still loosened bolts securing it to the wall with ease, proceeding to pull the bed away and slip inside the opening.

It was dark and damp, but the passageway was spacious enough that I could stand and turn a full circle without getting stuck. I pushed any sense of claustrophobia to the far recesses of my brain and instead closed my eyes to envision the ship's layout.

The pathway would need to run along the outer walls of the ship where it could dip beneath windows and not run into doors. I turned to my right, hands out in front of me to feel my way to the exterior wall.

Sure enough, the pathway created a T, and I was able to turn left, ducking beneath where I knew the window was positioned to follow it along each cabin until I reached another turn toward the stairwell.

On my knees, I crawled forward, feeling out and finding, as I suspected I would, a separate set of narrow stairs built into his hidden pathway leading both up and down.

I'd never met Juan's father, but to have had the foresight to build such a system into his ship so long before he ever took a captive made me think he was a man who trusted very few people.

I climbed the stairs up until I'd reached the top deck. The sunlight streamed in through the boards then, creating small lines of dusty light in the space around me. I was at the top of the stairwell, and pressing my face against the boards, I could see out to the deck.

Alaina stood with her back to me, Zachary held against her shoulder. Ahead of her, with Cecelia in his arms, stood the spitting image of an older Juan. It had to be his father.

"Please," Alaina said softly, "I'll do anything you want. Just… please… give her back."

To one side of my sister, Kyle and Terrence stood with their guns at their feet and hands in the air. Around them, men I didn't recognize pointed rifles from every direction.

Fetia, Magna, and Bruce stood similarly on the other side, and Jacob knelt with Michael at each side of Bud, who was looking much paler and older than the last time I'd seen him. I couldn't see his body for Michael's blocking it, but I assumed there was blood there from the gunshot wound Phil had informed us he'd suffered.

"I cannot give her to you," Juan Josef said evenly, rocking Cecelia gently in the crook of his arm. "Just as you and your husband would do anything for your children, I would do anything for mine. I cannot let you take them from me. Now, tell me where my son is!"

The date on the paper had changed... It had changed because Juan Josef would've killed Jack on the spot had he not gotten off the ship.

Somewhere in Panama, Jack would've seen the change for himself. He would be on his way to retrieve her... on his way to changing that death date right back to what it was if he came himself... I needed to do something to stop him. I had to get off the ship; had to warn them all.

A hand slid into mine and I nearly screamed.

I looked down to see little Izzy looking up at me, big crocodile tears in her eyes.

I didn't know the sign language they'd created for her, didn't know how to tell her everything was going to be alright, so I simply squeezed her hand in mine and looked back out at my soon to be father-in-law.

My father-in-law...

With my free hand, I clutched Juan's ring where it hung from my neck.

'Those same men might see it upon you and know that you, too, belong to me.'

I kneeled before Izzy and pointed back the way she'd come, attempting to communicate with only my hands that she should hide and wait for me to return for her.

She shook her head and kept her hand tightly around mine, using her other to attempt to communicate in a language I didn't yet know.

"It's okay," I mouthed silently, remembering she could read lips a little. "I will come right back."

"Get Yag?" she said softly.

I nodded.

"We will get yag. You and me."

She pointed up to a latch in the boards, locked from the inside, then released my hand and moved away to crouch in the shadows of the stairs.

I wondered how she'd gotten inside the passage… Had she followed me or did she get in some other way? Perhaps we should've spent some time asking her about these tunnels. Maybe she knew more than we thought.

Taking a very deep breath, I stood, praying to no one in particular that I wasn't about to make the biggest mistake of my life.

I pulled the latch and stepped out into the stairwell, closing the little door behind me before I called out with a smile, "Father!"

The pulse in my throat was palpable as the eyes and guns of every man on board focused upon me, but I hid my nerves behind a wide smile as I moved toward the man that looked so much like the one I loved.

"You must be my new father-in-law," I said sweetly, presenting the ring around my neck and the one positioned on my finger as I walked toward him with the confidence of someone who didn't believe themself in any danger.

"That is my mother's ring," a man said from somewhere on my left, and I turned to smile just as pleasantly at him. "And that must make you Dario, my new brother-in-law. Joseph has told me so much about you. I have been anxious to meet you in person."

Dario had my sister's eyes… *my* eyes. Slightly more green than hazel, the almond shape was unmistakable. It was easy to smile at him when I saw so much of my own mother and sister in his features.

"You lie," he said, narrowing those very same eyes at me.

I shook my head and laughed. "I know, it's still a little unbelievable even to me… But it's the truth. Joseph and I are to be married today at St. Francis."

"Why are you calling him that?" Dario asked, one dark auburn brow raised as he placed a hand on the hilt of his sword.

"It's what your mother called him, and it's the name he wanted me to call him as well." I turned toward Juan Josef, reminding myself of the changed death date on the paper I could feel against my chest and the need to maintain my composure so I could get off the ship and keep it that way. "He asked me to wait here while he sought you out… He's done what you asked in saving his mother and delivered my sister and her child to you. He expected to greet you on land with the news of our engagement."

Juan Josef held Cecelia closer as I walked casually toward him, eyeing me dubiously. "That is close enough, my dear."

I was very much aware of the rifles targeted on me, but I didn't show my fear as I frowned at him. "You don't believe me?"

He laughed heartily. "My son loved Elizabeth and Elizabeth *alone*. Where is Juan?"

"I told you," I said simply, "he's gone to search for you and to get rid of the others—they believe they are seeking you out; searching for the old man." I felt my sister stiffen at the words, but I would not give myself away to soothe her. Instead, I beamed at him. "And it is true. He loved Elizabeth very much. He's told me all about her and Philip and Nicolás."

I let my gaze slide to Dario's. "He told me about your time as children, how the three of you would go out hunting and fishing with Tonauac, sleeping by a fire out in those woods. Told me all about the time he spent with Elizabeth at the creek bed and the impromptu wedding ceremony Tonauac performed when she ended up pregnant. He has a scar here," I pointed to my abdomen, "from a bear that Alistair promised to kill for Eleanor. And the face of an Aztec god here," I made a circle over my chest, "that winds into a serpent. Three suns and three eagles circle it, given by Tonauac to represent Elizabeth, Philip, and Nicolás surrounding him with their light and strength."

Dario's eyes widened as he looked past me to his father.

I spun back to face my future father-in-law. "I'm telling you the truth. I hadn't meant to fall in love with him, nor he to do the same with me… but we did. I love him with all my heart, and he loves me. Look."

I removed his journal from the pocket of my dress. "You can read it for yourself in his own writing." I opened it to the page he'd read aloud to me and extended it to Dario.

He took it and scanned the text, frowning over the pages as he slowly nodded. "These are Juan's words… His writing…"

"I'm not here to stop you," I said. "I can't let my sister take my niece through time. Without Gloria or Dario or Dahlia, I don't know that my Joseph would be the man he is. And like you, I, too, will do anything to protect him."

"Cece?" A.J. whimpered behind me.

I straightened, raising my chin to keep from giving myself away. If I looked at her, I would definitely show my bluff and I knew Juan Josef was wise enough to see even the subtlest of tells. "He was going to send Gabriel to retrieve me once he found you. Let me go with one of my men to tell him you've arrived so we can have our wedding."

Juan Josef genuinely looked frazzled by my confession. I watched patiently as Dario handed him the journal and he held it out in his free arm to read the words himself.

"I don't care about going back through time," I said as his hardened expression gradually softened with each pass of his eyes across the page. "And I have no intention to interfere with your plans. I just want to be with him; to say my vows and live beside him for however long we have together. Please, let me go to him."

"He is a fool," he whispered, shaking his head at the words on the page. "All that I have done… All this… It has been for him."

I watched him scan the page again, hearing the words he might read in Juan's voice my mind. *'Now that they have known the feel of her, it is as if they are not quite whole… not quite my own. Some part of me now severed and asleep as she sleeps…'*

"You do it for Gloria, too," I said gently, daring to take a step closer. "I know it was your bullet that struck her and I know you would give anything to undo it. He would too. He's a good man—the best man I know. The plan is unchanged, *father*, and all you've done has not been for nothing. We will kill George Bennet in Virginia. We'll remember both versions of our lives just as my sister does hers. You will have Gloria, and he and I will find each other again in the future. Please, let me have him now so we have something to hold onto while we wait."

I saw his throat move; his only tell beneath his returned neutral expression. "You've fooled him."

"What reason would I have to fool him?" I asked. "Or to stand here before you instead of remaining hidden until I could run away? I am not afraid of you because you are the father of the man I love, and you have no reason to be afraid of me. Come and witness our marriage if you'd like. Let me prove it to you."

At this, he laughed loud enough to jar Cecelia and, as her little eyes opened, she began to work into a cry. "You cannot think me foolish enough to step off this ship with you, madam."

"Please," Alaina begged at the sound of Cecelia's sobbing, "give her to me. She needs her mother. I won't try anything, I swear."

Despite my urge to snatch the baby and run with A.J. in tow, I ignored their cries and continued. "Then send me to retrieve him. What harm can it do? If I'm lying, you're rid of me and I will be left at the mercy of your son and the jungles of Panama—just as the others are. If I'm telling the truth, you'll have given your son his happiness, and you will see it for yourself upon our return."

His green eyes remained narrowed as he rocked the now wailing baby in his arms. "Mr Gil!" he called, and an ominous looking giant I'd never seen before appeared at his side. "Does she speak the truth or is she deceiving my son?"

"She tells the truth," the giant answered, a snarled smile pointed in my direction. "The two of them have spent most of these past weeks together despite many protests from both the crew and her own people. I've no reason to suspect her of deception. They spent the night together last night."

I'd never seen Mr. Gil before and I was familiar with every man on board the ship. Had he been with us the whole time? Was Mr. Gil spying on us? And did Juan know about it?

"Dario," Juan Josef said without breaking eye contact with me, "you'll take her to your brother."

"But father—"

"Do not argue. He's no desire to kill *you*. Confirm she is telling the truth and meet me in Virginia. The other slave ship will wait in Portobelo to take you."

"No!" Alaina sobbed behind me. "Please, Cece, please! Do something! We can't leave without them!"

I cleared my throat, reminding myself it would take time for Juan Josef to turn out of the bay. I had time to get a warning message out and send help back if I could get away from Dario. "The little girl, Izzy," I said. "May I take her with me? She's quite fond of Joseph and she's scared. I think it'd be better if she was with us."

He pursed his lips as he considered it. "You make no attempt to talk me out of leaving with the rest?"

I shook my head, standing tall despite every urge to drop to my knees and do that very thing. "I cannot let my sister take Cecelia through time, and I know she will not be able to if they are both with you when that storm comes. I only ask that you not harm them. Everyone here knows what's at stake if they attempt to fight you and I doubt any of them would be foolish enough to do so now. The only one I want to take is Izzy."

"I've no use for a deaf child," he said with a shrug. "Where is she?"

I motioned to the hidden door I'd come through. "Just there. I'll remain in your sight if you let me signal her. She's frightened and I don't think she'll come out for anyone else."

He nodded once and I spun on my heel. Pulling the little door open to serve as cover, I fished the chart from my bosom, wadding it into my fist while I motioned her out of the shadows.

Reluctantly, she crawled out of her hiding space, her pink stuffed bunny clutched to her chest. I mouthed the word "Jack" as reassurance we would be safe.

With her little hand in mine, we strode back, stopping just behind Alaina. "Goodbye, my little nephew," I cooed loudly, tucking the paper into Zachary's dress as I pretended to caress his cheek with my knuckles. "I will see you again soon."

I had time to warn them while they turned the ship… everything would be fine…

With Dario as my escort, I couldn't very well go to the inn to inform Jack, but I had a taser… if worse came to worse.

"Take care of them," I said to Terrence as Izzy and I followed Dario toward a sloop.

Izzy skipped ahead and took Dario's hand in hers, smiling up at him and completely unaware he might be a threat to us.

Stepping inside the sloop, I looked once more at my sister. While A.J.'s facial expression did not change, I saw a knowingness in her eyes when they briefly met mine. She knew I hadn't deceived her, and that was all I could've hoped for. I would hold that look in my heart for as long as it took to get back to her.

Swallowing the lump in my throat, I took my seat beside Izzy. I would see my sister again. So would Jack. We would make this right… We had time…

Maybe…

As the sloop slowly lowered down and Dario's cold eyes met mine, I longed for a glimpse of my own death date.

There were a few men on the dock as we rowed into the bay, and they assisted us out of the sloop.

Dario hadn't spoken a word to me during the entire trip, and I hadn't pushed conversation, too worried I might find myself exposed. Technically, I wasn't lying, but… it felt like I was in some strange way, particularly with the appearance of Mr. Gil.

"Lucas," he said in greeting to the man that had offered me his hand and helped me onto the dock. "I must find my brother straight away."

He spoke in Spanish and I played dumb, frowning between them as if I didn't understand.

"Of course, my friend," the man responded in the same song-like Spanish. "He came through just yesterday. He secured a few horses and mules from my brother and headed up the trail. It was quite a show. Did you know he is escorting the duchess of Parma? Your father rode ahead with Jacinto and a few slavers to secure their path and collect the incoming batch of slaves."

"I am aware," Dario said before waving a hand toward me. "This is the duchess's sister... a woman worth a sizable reward should she be so unfortunate as to find herself taken captive."

This sent a chill up my spine as all three men eyed me like I was a glistening steak and they hadn't eaten in days.

"The duchess," he continued in Spanish, watching me for any signs of understanding, "she travels with a small fortune in gold. No?"

A man next to Lucas exposed rotten teeth as he grinned and nodded. "Yes, sir. A chest full. I saw it myself!"

"What are you on about, Dario?" Lucas asked, smirking mischievously as he crossed his arms over his chest.

"I have received word these women might be imposters. I need to find my brother and see for myself if he is indeed being fooled. I've seen the Duchess of Parma with my own eyes and can confirm the validity of this rumor right away. I cannot ride fast enough to catch him with a woman and child. If she is not an imposter, I will inform the duchess of her sister's capture and come back with a reward for her safe return. If she *is* an imposter, I will return with reward and you may keep this woman as well for your *enjoyment*."

The man with rotten teeth licked his tobacco stained lips. "Both the woman and child?"

I cringed as his dark eyes landed on Izzy.

"No," Dario said sharply. "The child comes with me."

The third man, who hadn't spoken, took hold of my upper arm and began to pull me toward him when Lucas placed a hand between us. "Not so fast, Martín." He frowned down at me. "There is one detail you are overlooking, Dario. The duchess travels under the protection of your brother—*el cazador*—and should she prove not to be the imposter you suspect her of, what is to stop him from killing every one of us?"

"We are old friends," Dario said simply. "He will understand it is only business. Times are hard with rumors of war in the colonies."

Lucas shook his head. "I do not like this. We're talking about royal families here… Forgetting your brother's wrath, we might face execution by the French if they get word their queen's sister is in our possession."

Dario smiled. "You do not have a choice, Lucas. You owe my father a favor and I've come to collect. Take her to your brother's fishing cabin outside town and I will make sure you are rewarded for any burden it might cause you."

I could see Lucas didn't want anything to do with me, but he removed his hand and lowered his shoulders in defeat. "I can't promise she'll be well cared for if Adrián sets his eyes upon her. You know that. Especially with that hair…"

"Adrián needn't set eyes upon her if you head straight for the cabin now," Dario said, winking once at me before he took Izzy's hand and led her away.

"Wait!" I shouted as if I'd only just understood what was happening. "Where are you going?!"

"To find out the truth, my dear. You've nothing to worry about if you've been honest with me." He smiled in a way that resembled my sister too much for the hatred I suddenly felt for him. "Lucas will take good care of you."

He motioned to a white mare tethered to a post off the docks. "She one of yours?" he asked Lucas.

"Yes," Lucas responded in English. "She's quick too."

Without asking permission to do so, Dario untied her reins, and lifted Izzy up into the saddle, saluting Lucas with a nod before hoisting himself up behind her. "With any luck, I shall return before nightfall," he said to me before turning the horse round and pushing her into a full gallop toward the small town ahead.

It was then I realized he was stalling. He knew we'd positioned the ship in such a way that turning it would take time… And that's what this was about. Juan would come for me instead of storming the ship, allowing his father the additional time he'd need to turn around.

"You're a pretty little thing," Lucas pointed out, lifting a strand of my hair. "Let's pray my brother does not decide to go fishing before Dario's return. Come," he directed me toward the second horse, a golden brown stallion with a patch of white painting its nose. "It's a bit of a ride from here to the cabin. We should get going. You're safe."

"I don't understand," I said sweetly. "I thought I was joining my sister and husband here. Why did he leave me?"

I saw him flinch a little, glancing at the other two who had fallen into step alongside us. "You've a husband with you?"

Nodding, I smiled. "Well, soon-to-be my husband. We were supposed to be married today after he secured a means to transport us to Portobelo. I am surprised his *own brother* would abandon me. The church is right there, on the way." I pointed to the spire I knew belonged to St. Francis.

Lucas chuckled. "You, the sister of the *queen of France*, betrothed to *el cazador*? I don't believe it."

"I love him," I assured him, pulling the ring from my breast to present it to the group. "And obviously, he loves me. It doesn't matter who my sisters are. I am free to love who I choose, and I have chosen Juan Josef."

Lucas swore under his breath and met Martín's eyes, returning to Spanish to inform him, "We are dead men if we take her. All of us. That is his ring."

Martín shook his head. "We are dead men if we don't. This is a favor to his father. We cannot let her go after agreeing to it. He would kill us all for deceiving him. She might've stolen it!"

Lucas looked out to where Dario had rode off. "God help us all if she didn't. That man might've cursed us all."

I needed to get to Jack and Juan and Izzy. I didn't have time for this kind of delay; couldn't let this stall Juan in stopping the ship.

So, when Lucas offered me his folded hands to mount the horse, I pulled the taser from my pocket and shot him with it.

The other two men crossed themselves as Lucas fell to the ground and writhed with the electric current being pushed through the little coiled cables connecting us.

"¡Es una bruja!" one of them cried out, mortified as Lucas's eyes rolled back.

When Martín stepped forward, I fired the second charge, and my heartbeat raced as the man with rotten teeth stumbled back several yards to watch his friends convulse.

Dropping the taser, I bolted toward town as fast as my legs could carry me.

Ahead of me, the cobblestone road was framed on each side by buildings. I scanned them for signs of an inn, hoping I could get to Jack before they could catch up.

Far in the distance, a man stood gaping at me… It was Tomás! And just as I opened my mouth to call out for him, something hard and heavy struck me across the face, forcing me onto my back with the air expelled from my lungs.

"Hello lovely," a man said, his figure distorted beyond my broken glasses where he stood over me. "I am Adrián. Pity about your face."

Chapter Thirty-Three

Alaina

"Please," I begged as my daughter screamed in Juan Josef's arm, her face turning as red as the fuzz on top of her head. "Please give her to me."

"As you all can see, after so much time apart, my wife and I have some things we must discuss," Juan Josef announced to the men surrounding us, prompting a wave of male laughter in response. "Inform the rest of her group of my offer, and turn us around while she and I work out our... *differences*... below deck."

He motioned toward the stairwell behind me. "Please, my dear, let us not quarrel in front of the men."

I met Terrence's eyes as I turned, a question hanging in the air between us as to whether or not he should attempt to fight.

I shook my head once, and with Cecelia's wail taking all her lungs' capacity behind me, I hurried down the stairs to the dining room, desperate to comfort her at any cost.

With my back to them, I heard Cecelia draw in breath as I opened the dining room door, and, stepping inside, she let out an ear-piercing scream that I'd never heard from her; a sound full of terror. My breasts spilled out against my stays with the need to end her suffering, and my throat swelled with panic that I might not be able to.

Rocking Zachary against my shoulder, I spun round to glare at the source of her agony. Juan surprisingly seemed just as terror-stricken when her scream stopped and her face turned purple in preparation of another.

"Give her back," I demanded. "You're scaring her."

He nodded, his brows high on his forehead as he quickly placed her against my other shoulder. "I do not want this," he said in a hushed and hurried voice, spinning back to close the door. "Please, sit."

Unable to remain standing as the relief of holding her threatened to buckle my knees, I collapsed into a chair at the edge of the table. Watching Juan through tear-filled eyes, I placed Zachary on my lap while I gently rocked Cecelia against my shoulder, her little breath hitched and accented with moisture as she attempted to recover, hiccups jostling her tiny body every few seconds.

Juan's expression was… haunted, his hands shaky where they were held out in front of him. "Is…" He cleared his throat. "Is it true? What your sister said? We will remember all that has happened here?"

"Yes," I said, running a palm back and forth over Cecelia's heaving back.

He splayed his fingers wide in the air between us as if he might strangle some invisible force lurking there. "You are certain of this?"

"I have experienced it myself," I said through my teeth, my anger catching up all at once with the feel of my daughter's trembling body against me. "Yes, Juan, *you* will remember every single rotten thing you've ever done here."

He paced to the window, one hand curled into a fist behind his back while the other moved over his mouth. I'd never seen him quite so unsettled. Even when he was inflicting torture and switching between Dr. Jekyll and Mr. Hyde, he had always remained somewhat composed. This unraveling and uneasy version of the man I'd grown to hate was unfamiliar.

"I don't want this," he said again with his back to me, gazing out the window with his fist tightening at the base of his spine, "I never wanted any of this, but my son—"

"Oh, don't start that again, Juan," I huffed, rocking back and forth as Cecelia's hiccups worsened and agitated her even further. "You've given me the whole *'my son'* speech before. I don't give a shit about your excuses for why you do the things you do. I need to know what it is you intend to do with me and my family."

Zachary picked up on my frustration and smacked his palms against the edge of the table, shouting angry *'ba!'* sounds across the room in his best show of support.

Juan turned back toward us and ran a hand over his beard, his expression softening as he observed Zachary's face. "Children change everything about the person you thought you were before you had them. You know it too… Alaina, I cannot let you take my children from me; cannot let you take their mother from them."

I rolled my eyes. "So you're taking us hostage *again* because you're this great, caring father who just wants to give your adult children a mother they've already watched you beat and kill? Is that it?"

He slowly made his way toward me with his hands folded behind his back. I could see in his face—in the way his eyes were glazed over—he was deeply disturbed by the revelation he would remember everything.

I swallowed as he grew closer.

Juan Josef had never been a predictable man. Rattled as he was, there was no telling what he might be capable of, and I tightened my hold on both my children as he stopped within inches of us, ready to defend us should he make any sudden move.

His tone was low and shaky. "I'm asking you to travel with me to Virginia as my guest and not my hostage. Give me the opportunity to tell you everything in our pursuit of George Bennet. Help me put things back the way they should've been and save your friend's life… Do this, and I give you my word, I shall never torment you or your family ever again. No matter what life I am returned to."

"You are *asking* me?" I sat back a little in my seat and laughed haughtily. "Like I have a choice?"

"I am *begging* you," he mended. "I do not want to be the man I must become if you say no."

"Right. And what happens after we kill George Bennet? You'll have your family *and* your memories of this place—of the coordinates and dates. You say you would never torment me or my family again, but that's not true, is it? With those memories, what would stop you from seeking me out in the future and making sure I spent my life in this time so they all would live?"

He shook his head. "Allow me time to explain why I have done all that I have. When we arrive in Virginia, the choice will be yours to make and to live with."

I drummed my fingers on the table. "And what about the others? Kyle and Fetia… Jim and Lilly… Chris and Maria… Bud and Terrence… What happens to them?"

His shoulders eased. "As we speak, the slavers are making an offer on deck to escort your remaining crew back to the storm on their ship. Dario will make the same offer to the ones on land when he catches up to them. All accommodations paid by me. I do not wish to be your villain any longer."

My eyes narrowed as I considered what Juan Jr. and Dario might actually be doing in Panama. I thought about Juan Jr.'s warning to my sister… Had he known we would separate? Had he known by that time I would remain on the ship with the babies so his father could take us? Had it been their plan all along? And how far back did that plan go? How much involvement had they had with a twenty year gap between us? Was it really a coincidence that they ran into their own ancestor in this time or had the Perez family somehow found a way to put us on that airplane in the first place?

I closed my eyes and imagined the video of Juan Jr. and my sister in the hull… were the feelings I was so sure were real all a part of some bigger scheme? And what would happen to Cece if they were?

"Is Juan Jr. a part of this?" I asked in a low voice. "Did he help you escape? Is he tricking my sweet little sister so she would do exactly what she's done in defending him; in getting Jack off this ship so you could take it?"

He frowned and shook his head. "It was my assumption your sister was fooling *him* so he would fight on your side."

I breathed out a frustrated laugh, my words spilling out as that frustration overwhelmed me. "On our side? We didn't ask to have a side in this. The only thing we wanted was to go home after being stranded so long on that island. The only thing *Anna* wanted was to get to her son. *You* declared war—not us—when you took us against our will; when you locked us up, tortured us for trying to get away, and killed the best person among us. We just wanted to go home; to live out our lives with the people we love. We would've helped you seek out George Bennet if you'd have simply asked; if you'd just told us it would get us home all the same. There never needed to be a side in this."

"So sail with me and help me fix it."

I shook my head. "You expect me to willingly leave my husband and sister behind? Leave Jack in the hands of your sons and risk them killing him? Take my children away from him for months so he becomes a stranger to them if, by some miracle, he survives? Why would I do that without a fight?"

He knelt at my side and Zachary babbled loudly up at him. "I am entrusting my sons' lives to your people just as you are entrusting your people's lives to my sons. Let their quarrel or their peace be made on their own journey while you and I get our lives back. None will go with us—neither yours or mine—without causing further interruption; without causing more bloodshed and resentment to cloud our judgment. We will never accomplish anything more than war upon each other if we all attempt the journey together… Likely none of us would see the future we are so desperate to be restored to once we'd finished with each other. You and I will end this fight with George Bennet. When it is done, your children will remember this time spent with you and their father instead of with me, just as mine will remember theirs spent with their mother. Whatever happens in between will be irrelevant, some far off dream that never happened; any lives lost will be restored. Let us end this and get on with whatever lives we have left."

Frazzled and desperate as Juan Josef appeared, he was too calculating in his nature not to have some deeper plot in place; some plan to take my daughter in the long run. I needed one of my own.

Slowly, a thought began to form…

I cleared my throat. "You're really letting the rest go home?"

He bowed his head and held a hand over his heart. "Their safe passage is already paid for."

I adjusted Zachary where he was attempting to wiggle free from my lap in pursuit of the brass buttons on Juan's coat. "I want to send a letter to Jack and the others. Let them know we are safe and the fighting is over. You can read it if you'd like—hell, you can watch me write it if it makes you feel better. And I want you to send one to your sons instructing them not to harm any of my people—Jack included."

He nodded. "I'll gather supplies at once and see to it they receive them."

My arms tightened around my babies. "And I want your word that neither you or your men will put your hands on me or my children during this trip; that you will not lock us away in a room or hover behind a wall and watch us. If the fight is over, it is over. Understand?"

"You have my word," he whispered, a hint of shame pulling his features downward. "I'll retrieve the others and writing supplies straight away. I'll not make you regret this."

He straightened and, with a quick bow, left me alone at the table with my mind reeling.

My eyes drifted down the vacant table and I could see them all sitting in their usual seats and sipping coffee. I could hear their voices—their arguments for why we couldn't simply go along with this… Why we needed to get away.

Juan Josef was right. We could not make this journey together without further bloodshed. They would fight; even if I begged them not to… Even if they knew they could die for doing so… Even if the end result would get us home… After all Juan Josef had done to us, they would fight to get away from him…

Looking down at my son where he wiggled in my lap, I noticed a paper peeking out of his collar—my muddled mind having thought it a tag when I'd seen it earlier. Realizing suddenly tags weren't possible in this century, I fished it out.

Every muscle in my body sank into itself when I unfolded it to find the chart and the year *1825* written beneath Jack's name.

I half-laughed, half-cried as I stared down at my own writing. He was alive. He was alive and would remain so for the foreseeable future.

From the moment my eyes opened to find Mr. Gil with my daughter in his arms, I'd been tucking away an image of Jack's dead body in the rainforest somewhere.

I trembled with the knowledge he wasn't dead already. He would see the change on his own chart and send Gabriel for me. Cece had seen the change and that's why she'd begged to get off the ship…

And suddenly I had my plan…

A plan to end this once and for all.

A plan that didn't involve us having to spend the rest of our lives in this God-forsaken century.

While killing George Bennet would save Anna and get us home, home would never be safe as long as Juan Josef lived on with the memories of our time here. My daughter would always be at risk of being swept away.

I couldn't trust Juan Josef's vow to never torment us; couldn't trust Juan Jr.'s promise to kill him either. With twenty years to plot and scheme before any of us remembered what happened, I couldn't place my trust in any of the Perez men.

There was only one way I could be absolutely certain we would get Anna back and be rid of the threat to Cecelia for good.

Juan Francisco de la Bodega. Juan Josef's ancestor.

And Jack, on his *own journey,* would have time to hunt him down after I sent him a message in a way only he could decipher.

I smiled proudly as my scheme took shape.

Never again would I wake up with Juan Josef standing over my children. This fight was indeed over, and I would win it… I would claw him to shreds.

If it destroyed my relationship with Cece, I would take that risk to save my child, and I would spend my life begging for her forgiveness… *if* she even remembered it.

"We're not leaving you," Kyle asserted as he led the others into the dining room and pulled me from my machinations. "I told that other captain we're all going home together."

Terrence and Jacob held Bud upright as they followed behind him. Bud was paler than I'd ever seen him, looking far too frail where his body weight dragged his shoulders down between them. Someone had removed the bullet and stitched him up, but I could see infection on him… a fever lingering on his skin and weighing down his eyes.

"Yes, you are," I insisted, handing Zachary off to Magna when she reached for him. "You and Fetia are having a child and you'll be better off at a hospital than on this ship. Your father and Bud are both in need of a doctor long-term, and the war zone we're headed for isn't safe for any of you. It's time for you all to go home. I can handle this."

"She's right," Terrence said. "You all need to take that offer and go. This isn't a game. I'll stay with her and make sure she's safe." He motioned to Fetia. "You can't take a newborn where we're going."

Kyle stood straighter. "I'm not leaving without you."

I smiled up at him. "Kyle honey, I'm going to fix all this, and it might be that you live safely in the future for a few months until I do, and then you'll be right here beside me again with new memories."

I shifted my attention to Terrence. "And you need to go with them. You have a wife waiting for you and an investigation you need to clear up so we can all live in peace once it's over. Dario is making the same offer to my sister and the others. You need to go and take care of them all."

Terrence frowned down at me. "You want *me* to get on board a slave ship?"

I sighed. "No, I don't. I want you to go home. I'd give my right arm to put you on any other ship, but… this is the option we have. There are no other ships in this bay. It's your choice, and I won't argue if you want to stay, but you know our people can't go back without you."

He glanced toward the window with a furrowed brow. "And what happens to you if we all go?"

I flashed my teeth in a knowing smile. "I'll be fine. None of these last several months will ever have happened once I'm done here." I looked between each of them. "If this works… If we can do it before the storm in September, then we should wake up in Tahiti together with Anna. Go home and wait for me to undo this."

"No," Bruce cut in, limping to the front of the group. "You can list off whatever reasons you need to, but I'm staying with you until it's done."

I shook my head, "Honey, you poisoned the man's entire crew. You need to be the first one off this ship."

"No." He set his shoulders. "I'm not going anywhere."

"We're not scheming or plotting," I assured him. "We're not going to fight him. We're going to Virginia and we're going to kill the ancestor. We'll get Anna back and go home. That's it."

"Fine by me," Bruce huffed, "so long as I'm right here beside you when you do it. I want to be here—want to help get Anna back."

"Alright," I surrendered, patting Cecelia's back where she'd started to doze off against my shoulder. "The rest of you give me a hug and go before I can change my mind."

One by one, Magna, Fetia, Kyle, and Terrence argued reasons they should stay, all resigning eventually to give me their well-wishes and hug me goodbye.

It was Bud's embrace that nearly broke me. Frail and injured as he was, he held me tight. "Be smart," he whispered.

"I will," I promised. "You get better."

He winked as he pulled away. "It won't matter. I'll *be* better when you're done with... *the ancestor*."

I nodded, wiping the tears away from my eyes that came with his understanding. "Okay. This is the last goodbye I ever want to say to you all. Go and be safe. I love you all and... I've got this."

Chapter Thirty-Four

Chris

They'd set up a camp the night before at the side of the road near a creek once it got too dark to navigate the trail. With the jungle canopy overhead, it was hard to see even a foot ahead in the utter blackness of night. Navigation was impossible, even with a lantern as a guiding light.

Unable to go any farther, they'd made a fire and, all of them too exhausted for conversation, had eaten and wandered off to bed.

Sleeping in the rainforest, however, had proved difficult, even tired as he had been.

Their tents were nothing more than fabric draped over a single pole in the center and pinned to the ground around it. With only a few buttons to keep the slithering, crawling creatures that lurked on the rainforest floor outside, every itch on his skin had Chris jumping up to search for a possible threat.

Maria'd ventured into his tent some time in the night after a howler monkey—who she'd been convinced was a jaguar—roared in the distance. She was tucked tightly against his torso where she'd remained glued all night, and he held her despite the rising morning temperature.

He'd missed holding her and would hang on as long as he could before she would inevitably return to giving him the cold shoulder.

Gently pressing his lips to the top of her head, he inhaled her hair. The usual rosy scent had faded and she smelled of the day's exertion; heated skin and soil… and on her, it smelled lovely.

He knew it was selfish to hope she'd take him back one day, but holding her in his arms, he couldn't help hoping.

His marriage was over, and he felt it now more than ever; not in a devastating way, but more as an ending. He didn't want to fight for that life anymore. That life was over and he wanted this one more.

"Ah ha! Gotcha' ye' lil' summbitch!" Chris tightened his arms around her, hoping to drag out the tender moment just a little longer as Jim let the entire camp know he was awake. "Ye' thought ye'd tango with me, did ye? Well, now I'm fixin' to eat ye' ugly ass for breakfast! Ay! Somebody come out here and bring me a knife so I can chop off this summbitch's head!"

Jim's commotion set the howler monkeys overhead into a deep baritone chorus, putting a prompt end to Chris's morning snuggle.

As Maria sleepily rolled away from him, Chris stretched his arms and sat up. "What breed of summbitch?" he called through the canvas.

"Ugly lookin' snake… Tried to bite me while I was on my way to take a piss. Bring your knife out here before I lose my grip on him."

"I've got it," Juan announced groggily before Chris heard the distinct piercing of a blade through muscle.

"Ewww." Lilly scoffed somewhere nearby. "I'm not eating that. What kind of snake is that anyway?"

"Pit viper," Juan yawned, which was enough to make Chris search his blankets for signs of a similar intruder. "If it would have bit you, Mr. Jackson, you would be dead."

"Well, I wasn't gonna just let it slither off and bite someone else. Princess, you stay right there. Imma' take this head and toss it over yonder. Don't none of yuns go out to this side of camp if ye' got to cut rope. It can still bite ye."

Chris chuckled and moved his palm over Maria's arm. "You sleep okay?"

She jerked her arm away and sat up suddenly, remembering she had a grudge to hold. "This doesn't change anything. Oh…" She winced and moved her palm to the center of her stomach.

"You alright?"

"I'm fine," she snapped though a concentrated exhale. "I just… I'm fine."

He grinned, recognizing her torment from their time spent together on the island. "You have to poop. Don't you?"

"No," she hissed, glancing at the tent where the others were still fussing over the snake on the other side. "I'm fine."

"Maria," he held in a laugh, "I didn't see you go down to your little bathroom after our ice cream picnic and you didn't go once on the trail yesterday. Do you want me to go find you a safe place and stand guard while you go? It's not healthy to hold it in."

She straightened. "I told you I don't have to go. I'm fine."

"Alright," he sighed. "But when you decide you can't take it anymore, you let me know."

She rolled her eyes and hurried out of the tent.

Plucking up his sword, he followed, stifling a laugh at Lilly where she queasily covered her mouth while Jim pulled the yellow and brown skin from a large snake.

"Holy shit," Chris laughed. "*That* tried to bite you?"

Lilly nodded wide-eyed. "If that's what's roaming around on the ground, I think I'll sleep on the horse tonight."

"Ye' ever eat snake before?" Jim bounced his eyebrows at Maria, who blanched in response, covering her mouth and shaking her head.

Swallowing whatever had threatened to come up, she straightened. "What eh… what else do we have to eat?"

Jim slid a knife down the center of the body, not moving his eyes away from the task as he informed her, "Snake… snake… and… oh yeah, some more snake."

Maria swallowed again. "I can't eat that."

"You gonna' be pretty hungry then," he teased as he pulled the guts out.

"There's some bread and cheese from the Ruiz stables in the pack," Lilly said, avoiding looking down at the guts herself. "You want some?"

Jim grinned up at Lilly. "You know if ye' eat cheese, you're gonna' have to… *unloose the caboose*… here pretty soon." He winked.

"Shut up," she snarled in return, motioning Maria to join her as she turned toward the mules on the far side of camp.

"That woman ain't shit in almost two days," Jim grumbled when Lilly was far enough away not to overhear. "She's gonna' be a pain in the ass the whole trip… *literally*."

Chris chuckled, rubbing the back of his stiff neck. "Maria hasn't either. You want me to get the fire going?"

"Yeah," Jim's eyes sparkled as he observed the gutted snake body dangling from his hand. "There's some dry wood on the mule. You get us a fire while I go warsh this off. We'll have us a feast this mornin', yes sir."

The sun blazing down on them, they'd stopped a little before noon to refill their canteens and allow the women to finally venture off into the brush to relieve themselves.

Chris and Jim had both had to scour the area for signs of snakes, spiders, and predators before either would officially go.

Waiting for them near the horses, Chris was pouring a bit of water over the back of his neck when he heard the thundering beat of hooves racing toward them—not from down the trail, but from inside the jungle.

Juan already had his sword drawn and was headed toward the sound when Tomás burst through the bushes.

"Captain, there's trouble," he announced breathlessly, pulling his brown horse to a fidgeting halt in the road. "You need to come quick." He glanced past Juan to Jim and Chris as his horse turned a circle. "There's no time for everyone. We need to ride fast and hard to the Ruiz fishing cabin."

"What's happened?" Juan asked, hoisting himself up into his saddle.

"It's Cece…"

And that was all the man needed to say for Juan to kick his horse into a sprint and disappear into the same brush Tomás had come out of.

"Wait here," Tomás instructed, his horse circling once more. "Make camp. We will return for you."

Then he was gone too, and Chris stood dumbfounded, staring at Jim.

"Wait here?" Jim scoffed, glancing back at the tree line they'd darted off into. "And do what?"

"More importantly," Chris said, narrowing his eyes in the same direction. "What was Cece doing off the ship?"

"Ye' think somethin's wrong?"

Chris ran a hand hard over his face. "We rode for a full day almost non-stop. If something's wrong on that ship… we can't get back to it fast enough."

Lilly and Maria came out of the bushes ahead.

"Oye, what's going on?" Maria looked from them to the trail and back into the trees.

"What if Jack was right? What if it *is* a trap? This whole thing?" Chris asked Jim, staring off into the jungle beyond. "What if Juan led us out here knowing he could ride faster back to that ship and take off with his father and the rest? What if the whole warning message… the whole plan… has all been one big set-up?"

"Get ye' gun," Jim said, digging the automatic rifle from the mule before he turned back to Lilly and Maria. "How fast can yuns ride?"

"Faster than you," Lilly teased. "What's going on?"

"Mount up. Now."

Just as they prepared to do that very thing, they heard the sounds of another horse approaching from far down the trail.

Pistol in one hand, sword drawn in the other, Chris moved to the front of the group, Jim standing with his rifle pointed in the same direction.

He lowered it when Dario appeared on a white horse with Izzy in the front of his saddle.

"Iz!" Jim hollered. "What in the hell—"

"Where is my brother?" Dario demanded, paying no mind to Chris's pistol pointed at his head when he pulled the horse to an abrupt stop.

"Give me the girl," Jim said evenly. "She don't need to be caught up in this."

Dario looked down at Izzy where she sat docile in the saddle, petting the horse's mane and unaware she was in any danger. Chris remembered she'd spent quite a bit of time with Dario and his dog on the ship during captivity. She must've assumed he was an ally.

Much to everyone's surprise and relief, Dario lifted her up and over into Jim's outstretched arms.

"I've no quarrel with the child or any of you," he said, straightening. "I must speak to my brother straight away. Where is he?"

Jim handed Izzy off to Lilly and pointed his rifle back up at Dario. "He took off like a bat out of hell lookin' for Cece. What in the Sam Hill's goin' on?"

Dario let out a long breath. "So it is true? He has involved himself with this woman?"

"They're in love," Maria said from her horse where she'd guided it to stand behind Chris.

"Then he is a fool," Dario spat.

"Where is your father?" Maria countered.

Dario lifted an eyebrow. "He is on the ship, readying to turn it round so he can meet my brother and I in Virginia where we will *finish* what we've worked five long years to accomplish."

Chris's heart sank… They were a day's ride away and there was time to turn the ship… Unless Jack could get to it first…

"No," Maria breathed. "No no no! We have to go to the storm!"

"By all means, go," Dario said, waving an arm out behind him. "Your passage is paid for. There's a slave ship waiting in the harbor for their cargo. They've agreed to take you and leave you with a small cutter. I do not intend to hinder your journey home, only see to it that no one hinders mine."

"*Alaina* has to go home," Maria sobbed, forcing Chris's eyes up to the horse where she was falling to pieces.

"This I cannot allow," Dario said. "I am sorry if it displeases you, but you must understand that I would be slitting my own throat if I let her go."

"Please," she all but whispered with a trembling voice. "Please… she has to."

Chris frowned at Maria's breakdown. She'd never expressed any emotional investment whatsoever in the plan, and he couldn't quite grasp why she was so suddenly devastated by its collapse.

"I am sorry," Dario offered. "It is not personal."

"Not personal?" Lilly cut in, holding Izzy tightly in her arms. "You shot my grandpa. Where is he?"

"He is on the ship and his wound has been tended by a surgeon from the slave ship. It was an unfortunate business that no one wished to have a part in." The horse danced to one side and he led it back, tightening his hold on the reins to still it. "You all are free to go to the storm if you wish. My father is making a similar offer to those on board the ship that have no part in our lineage. We do not wish to harm any more of you than we already have. We only want to see our family safe and restored to what it was meant to be. Go home and let your hearts not be troubled by your involvement in this time any longer."

"Cain't do that," Jim said, spitting to one side as he adjusted his aim with the rifle. "We got our own to worry about, and we ain't goin' nowheres without 'em. Ye' gonna' take us to your daddy's ship now."

Dario shook his head. "It is near noon, sir. They will be gone before we can make it back."

Jim sucked on his teeth and held the rifle tighter. "Ye' better hope you're wrong... Otherwise, I'll slit ye' throat for ye. Mount up, y'all. We're goin' home... *All* of us."

Chapter Thirty-Five

Cecelia

I opened my eye, the other being swollen shut with a constant aching pulse, and found myself staring at rotting wooden rafters above my head with a sweet tang in my nostrils.

My stays were gone, as were my skirts, and I laid in a moldy scented bed in only my shift.

It was ungodly hot. Sweat beaded at my brow to drip down into my open eye. I could hear rain pattering on the roof over my head, a teasing relief to my boiling skin just out of reach.

Without my glasses, I squinted to get a read on my location. I was in a house—a very empty and small one, though I had no memory of arriving here. There were men standing around a table not far from me; blurry figures speaking in hushed voices that were sharpened with frustration.

"Adrián, we cannot keep her here," one of the men argued in Spanish. "We might have been able to negotiate when we'd simply taken her for a bounty, but this? If that truly is *his* betrothed, or worse, the French queen's sister, we are all dead men if we do not let her go. Look at her face!"

As my mind came free of its fog, I remembered the men on the docks that Dario handed me over to. Lucas, Martín, and the one with rotten teeth… Remembered the blurry figure of Adrián standing over me in the street. It was then I realized that the smell in my nostrils and the sugar-like taste in the back of my throat was familiar. It was ether, and a panic settled in my chest as I considered what it might have been used for; what they might've done or seen while they removed the bulk of my clothing.

Swallowing, I laid perfectly still. If these men knew I was awake, they might use it again. If they thought I was still unconscious and got close enough, I could fight when they least expected it.

"We are not dead men," Adrián spat. "She is neither royalty nor *el cazador's* beloved. She is a witch, and witches lie."

"What if you're wrong?" a third man asked nervously. "We could let her go. Tell *el cazador* we set her free as soon as we saw his ring. He would not kill us then."

Adrián laughed. "If she were his betrothed, he would kill us, Martín, just for looking at her. And Dario would not sentence us to death. We are friends." I could hear him guzzling what I assumed was some kind of alcohol and the clang of the glass as he slammed it on the table. "He knew she was a witch and gave her to us to be rid of her—likely to protect his brother. Come on, Benny. Let us have some fun with our new toy."

"Benito, no," Martín said through his teeth. "You saw what she did to Lucas and me. Neither of you should go anywhere near her."

"What do you think I have *this* for?" Adrián asked. "She cannot hurt us if she is asleep."

"Where did you even get that?" the other man hissed. "And how do you know it's not going to kill her? If Dario or his brother return for her and she is dead…"

Adrián clicked his tongue. "It's not going to kill her, Lucas. I got it from a man at Hector's. It's a magic little potion. He had a whole ship full of it. Said the rich pay a fortune to serve it at their parties or use it as a sleeping aid. He said if you inhale it through this contraption he had, it makes you deliriously happy, but if you inhale a few drops from a cloth, it makes you sleep like the dead."

"We can't afford to pay a fortune for something like that," Lucas reprimanded. "How did *you* get it?"

"I stole it," Adrián chuckled. "And good thing I did, otherwise that little witch would've had us all shaking in the dirt before we even got here."

"Adrián, stop," Martín warned. "Dario said he would come back with her bounty and would let us have her if she was indeed an imposter. Let's just wait for him."

"Oh, she's an imposter," Adrián chortled, his booted footsteps on the wood floorboards growing closer. "The French queen's sister would not wear *el cazador's* ring. She's likely put poor Juan under her spell just so she could take it from him as additional protection should she be found out. You saw him yesterday. He was certainly more out of sorts than usual."

"All the more reason to keep your hands off her," Lucas added. "If *el cazador* is under some sort of spell… He will kill us all."

"Then go outside, both of you, and stand watch." The mattress dipped heavily as Adrián's knee came down near my hip. "I've not had a woman in far too long and this one is too lovely to miss out on. Benny, bring that bottle in case she wakes before I'm through."

Despite my thickening pulse, I kept my eyes closed and my body limp, focusing on my breathing so I appeared relaxed with sleep. I'd fight him soon enough…

"Witch or not," Adrián breathed over me, his other knee landing beside my opposite hip, "I shall enjoy you."

I was going to hurt him. I would bite and claw and kick just as soon as he was unguarded. I would dig my thumbs into his eyes until I felt them pop, would rip his penis from his body the moment he brought it near… But I couldn't risk making a move too soon; couldn't let him use the ether and have his way.

My stays and skirts had been removed, but I knew I'd remained untouched so far. There was no burn between my legs indicative of him making any attempt prior to this moment… No lingering scent of the putrid stench coming off him on my skin…

Maintaining my even breaths, I held in my disgust as his grimy, calloused palms swept up my thighs to push my shift up… Past my hips… past my stomach… past my breasts to expose the whole of me to him. There was only one man whose eyes belonged on me… and this man's gaze was unwelcome.

I only found peace in the thought that my body would be the last image he'd see before I ripped his eyes from their sockets.

I laid lifeless and listened to the clang of a belt buckle being unclasped… Felt the shifting of his weight on the mattress as he gathered himself between my legs…

My fingers tingled in anticipation.

I would fight to the death before I let this man have me.

"Open your eyes, Benny," he said, his foul breath in my nostrils nearly giving me away. "Look at our witch now."

I assumed *Benny* was the man with rotten teeth, and as his image came alive in my mind, I remembered the eyes, slightly too far apart and nearly crossed, the far off look and slowed speech… Benito didn't have the mental capacity to understand what was happening.

"Have you had a woman before, Benito?" Adrián cooed, moving his filthy paws over both my exposed breasts. "Come on and look at her. She's not going to hurt you now. Look at her."

And just as I had felt the weight of Adrián's stare, I felt Benny's moving over my chest, abdomen and down between my legs as Adrián pushed them apart.

"Watch what I do, sweet brother," Adrián said, his breath sweeping once again over my cheeks as he put a hand down near my head and readied himself. "And then you can have a turn."

Bile rose in my throat as Adrián's salt-sweat lips came down upon mine and he brought the tip of his penis to the exposed skin between my legs.

That was far enough.

I came alive in a blind, mad rage, lodging my thumbs into his eye sockets and using the nails of my fingers against his scalp for leverage. I pushed with all my might into his eyeballs, my yell indiscernible from his scream in my ears.

His fingers coiled around my throat as his other hand attempted to pull my arms away, but I wrapped my legs around his torso and dug in further, feeling his blood drip down my wrists.

Somewhere in the distance there was shouting… sobbing… screaming—or maybe that was us—I didn't look away from my thumbs as I pressed them further into his eye cavities and he clawed at my forearms in an attempt to get loose.

"Benny!" he cried out. "The potion! Give it to her now!"

He didn't belong on me…. His taste and scent lingering on my skin, so opposite to those of the man I loved, was unwelcome. It enraged me, and I squeezed with unrelenting determination, even as his hold on my throat stole the air from my lungs and brought stars to my vision… Even as my legs lost their grip.

"Benny! The potion!"

I'd fight to the death before I gave myself to him.

I blinked his dripping blood from my eyes as I pressed harder, feeling the soft tissue beyond his eyeballs; needing to inflict as much damage as I could before Benny could use the ether… Even as I could feel the life being strangled out of me, I dug my thumbs in deeper.

And suddenly his weight was gone, and I was gasping for air, my hands empty of him as they continued to squeeze nothing.

With blurry vision, I looked up to find him hovering—not standing, not kneeling—*hovering* by his hair… eyes bloodied, and knees bent awkwardly toward me with a blade protruding from his stomach.

My heart beat faster as I squinted to bring the scene above me into focus. Wound tightly in the hair he hung from was a fist… and that fist was held out by Juan, his lips a straight line, his jaw fastened shut, and his eyes black with fury.

Juan…

I sat up to find Lucas, Martín, and Benito all lifeless on the floor around me. I hurriedly pulled my shift down, and, the relief too heavy to contain, I wept uncontrollably.

I wept because I didn't need to hold it in; because I didn't need to put on a strong face and endure; because I didn't need to fight… and because I wouldn't be a victim.

I wept because I knew Juan would come.

I stared up through my tears at the man I loved and my heart doubled, making breathing almost as impossible as it had been with Adrián's fingers coiled around my throat.

I *knew* he would come…

When Dario had handed me off, I'd known.

When Adrián struck me in the street, I'd known.

And when Benito had opened his eyes to look down at my naked body, I'd known he would come…

He slowly pulled the blade back an inch and Adrián gurgled, a thick red dribble sliding from his lips.

"Close your eyes, Cecelia," Juan said softly.

And I did.

Above me, Adrián made an awful choking sound as the blade moved again—a sort of tearing noise accompanying his choke.

"She was not yours to take," Juan hissed through his teeth. "She was not yours to touch…"

I knew the shredding noise I was hearing was that of the blade moving through Adrián's body, and where it should've mortified me, it instead brought gratification… as if it were my own hands holding the blade that tore through him.

'*I shall enjoy you,*' he'd said… and rage made my fingers curl so tightly into my palms I was certain I left indentations.

"Did you think I would not come?" Juan growled. "And do you think I will show you any mercy now after you have taken and touched what belongs to *me*?"

Adrián choked and gurgled in response.

"No, there will be no mercy for you. You will die here with your insides as company. Keep your eyes closed, *mi alma*."

I did, and beyond the blackness of my eyelids, I felt the mattress lighten and heard the thud of Adrián's body hitting the floor, a slow, tortured moan bouncing off the walls around me.

Then I smelled cherries and almonds as a heavy jacket was draped over my shoulders. I wept again when hands my body recognized as welcome slid round my back and beneath my knees to pull me up against him.

"You are safe," he whispered.

They were the first words I'd heard from his lips when I arrived on the ship and I collapsed into him as I felt them all the way to my core.

With my eyes still squeezed shut, I wept harder as he carried me out of that awful house; sobbed as the rain landed on my eyelids and cheeks, cool in contrast to the heavy heat inside the house.

I buried my face in his chest and let the tears overwhelm me as he walked for a short eternity in the downpour before placing me down on a boulder sheltered from the rain.

"Let me see you," he breathed, his damp fingers moving gently over the swelling in my right eye.

I opened my left one and tried to smile.

His eyes had returned to their normal murky green and the rage I'd seen in his face had melted away. He was the Juan I knew once more, and that image made me cry even harder.

He shook his head, raindrops sliding down his brow. "How? How could this happen? My sweet dove, I told you I would come for you once it was safe. How did you end up in this place?"

"Dario," I sniffled. "Didn't he tell you where to find me?"

He frowned. "Tomás came to find me when Adrián struck you. *Dario* gave you to them? How?"

I nodded, unable to stop crying. "Your father's on the ship. He sent me off with Dario to confirm I was engaged to you. He said he would meet us in Virginia. Dario gave me to them to give your father time to turn the ship. He has Izzy, and your father has my sister and her babies and Kyle and Fetia and Terrence and Bud and…and…" Once again the tears overtook, feeling like I was standing at the side of a mountain far too steep to climb.

"Shh." Juan combed back the hair from my face, kneeling in the grass before me. The rain poured around us but he'd sheltered us beneath a big drooping tree so I only felt bits of its drizzle.

"*Mi alma*," he cupped my cheek, "I will get them back, I swear to you. Every single one will be returned to you unharmed. But first, I must know *you* are unharmed."

Again, I sniffled. "I'm not hurt. I fought him. Don't you dare look at me like I'm broken. I'm not."

He clicked his tongue as he examined my swollen eye. "I know that. I saw you fight—I *heard* you fighting before I even came upon the house. Show me where he touched you."

"There's no time," I sobbed. "Jack's death date changed. It changed because your father would've killed him if he'd been with us on the ship. Jack will see it and try to get to the ship to retrieve my sister the minute he sees them turning. We have to stop him. And your brother… he's headed down the trail in search of you. If he gets to the others… if he hurts Izzy… or if your father is able to turn the ship before we can get to him…"

With a subtle nod, he held my gaze and called out, "Tomás!"

Tomás appeared from behind the tree where he'd been waiting, his eyes apologetic as he stole a glance at me before looking down at his feet. "Aye, sir?"

"Ride ahead, fast as you can, and inform Mr. Volmer of my father's repossession of the ship. Send Gabriel to the ship to speak on my behalf before they can turn it around. Tell him to tell my father to remain in the bay. Tell him I shall join him as soon as I'm able *unarmed* and we will work out a plan to benefit us all."

He turned to me. "We cannot catch up to my brother *and* make it to the ship at the same time. My father will not hurt your sister. I cannot be so certain about my brother's intentions if he catches up to the others where I left them waiting."

I swallowed at the thought of Alaina spending any additional time with Juan Josef, but I nodded. Jack had the chart and we could use it to ensure she was alright. We had no similar guarantee regarding the rest of our fates, and that made Dario the bigger threat.

"Tell Jack to await my return at the inn," he continued, facing Tomás once more. "Under no circumstances must he be permitted to attempt to board the ship. My father will kill him on the spot. Do you understand?"

Tomás bowed his head. "Aye, sir."

"Tell him the report is his insurance," I added when Tomás began to turn away. "Tell him his family will be safe so long as their dates remain the same on that chart."

He bowed again, slightly confused, but didn't ask for clarification. Shortly after he disappeared beyond the brush, I heard the hooves of his horse racing away.

"I shall deal with my family," Juan said softly, "but first, I need you to show me where Adrián touched you and how."

"Why?" I asked, still trembling. "It's over now and there's too much we need to do."

He shook his head and combed back the hair from my face. "It's not over for you. Not yet."

"I stopped him," I said, holding my chin high. "He'd have had to kill me before I let him break me."

His smile was tormented. "I saw. I rode as hard as I could to stop it myself. Would that I could've arrived before he laid a hand on you at all." He moved his palm to my swollen eye. "He struck you here? Where else do you feel him?"

"Everywhere." My lip quivered and my nose burned, and I let it all out because I needed to. "I laid still... let him climb over me and touch what he wanted so he'd think I was asleep... I waited while he looked at my body; while he had his brother look..." I grimaced at the feel of their eyes still sitting on my skin. "I waited all the way until he put his mouth on mine and then I tried to gouge out his eyes."

"You *did* gouge out his eyes," he assured me, moving his thumb over my lips. "Look at me, *mi alma*."

Sniffling, I raised my eyes to his.

"You are not mine to touch and take any more than you were his. You are *yours*. You will always be yours, and I shall never presume to have authority over your will, even once we are wed. If you wish to leave now, we will go straight away. But if you cannot bear the feel of him…"

He took my hand and wrapped it gently around his wrist. "Then show me where you feel it, and let it be *my* touch that sits on your skin when we leave here. *My* memory that comes to you when you think of this place. Not his."

My breath hitched, and I squeezed his wrist tightly as he offered me the other.

"I'll not harm you, Cecelia," he whispered, "nor will my touch be anything more than a means to heal. I'll take nothing from you but him. You've my word."

My instinct was to trust him, but I was suddenly afraid of my instincts. Perhaps my sister was right. Maybe I was too inexperienced to understand what love was. Maybe I was blinded by him. I sat holding his wrists as I inspected his face, a sense of panic welling in my throat and threatening to overtake my body that he could ever be anything but genuine. "Did… did you know Mr. Gil was on the ship with us?"

"Mr. Gil?" He frowned. "What do you mean, on the ship *with us*? I presumed the vile man was dead… thought he wandered off on that island poisoned. He was on the ship?"

I nodded. "He knew I spent the night with you… seemed to know everything about these past few weeks." I took a very deep breath to prevent my words from shaking. "I have trusted you entirely from the moment I met you, but… have I been naïve in doing so? Are you using me for something? If you are, you have to tell me. I'll do whatever you'd like, but I can't stand the thought of being deceived by you, of all people."

"No, Cecelia," he said, keeping his hands in my grip but moving his body nearer. "I have never deceived you, nor shall I ever so long as I live."

"What about the passageways throughout the ship? Did you know about them?"

"Aye," he admitted softly. "I knew. It is why I bolted that bed to the wall in such a way. It had to have been Mr. Gil that helped him escape. There was no way he could've gotten those bolts off otherwise. I swear to you, I did not know the man remained alive."

I sniffled. "Why did you never tell my sister or the others about the passageway?"

He blew out. "I was not sure I could trust them—Jack specifically. I did not know if I might need the passageway at some point should I find myself his prisoner as well. Forgive me."

I tightened my grip on his wrists. Any time I had ever asked him for answers, he'd given them openly. He gave them now and, maybe I was naïve for it, but I believed him.

I moved his palms to the edge of my shift where it sat just above my knees, needing to rid myself of Adrián's touch to be done with this place. "Take this away then so we can go."

I trembled as he splayed his fingers wide, but I leaned my forehead against his shoulder and guided his warm hands up beneath the fabric.

Up my thighs… over my stomach… and over both breasts, the touch wasn't sexual, but warm and loving and so very welcome there, as if he were indeed healing everything inside me Adrián had threatened to break.

No, this man hadn't deceived me. I refused to believe he could. He'd come for me… He'd saved me from both Adrián and Owen and had no reason to do that other than love… He'd never done anything to warrant my mistrust and I wouldn't allow myself to doubt him again.

I cried against him, letting go of his hands to wind my arms around him.

"I knew you would come," I managed, clinging to him with a relief transcendent as my heart slowed beneath his touch. "The whole time, I knew I just needed to hold him off a little longer before you could get here. I knew, with all my heart, you would come."

This was what love felt like, safe and free to be vulnerable under his guard; trusting entirely in my asylum in his arms so the weight of the world fell away.

"Of course I came," he breathed, laying a kiss against my head before pulling back to look at me, one palm still fixed against my sternum atop my shift. "I will always come for you. Always. I should have listened when you asked to accompany me. That decision should have been yours to make, not mine. And I give you my word, Cecelia, I will never do anything against your will again, nor will I let any man so long as I live."

I covered his hand with mine. "That decision was ours. I decided to stay behind when I could've launched myself inside your sloop and insisted you take me with you. I'm not mine *or* yours, Joseph. As your soon-to-be wife, I'm ours. So are you."

He met my eyes then. "You still wish to be married to me? You still trust me?"

I nodded. "I do. Very much."

"You'd be better protected out here if it was known you were my wife—particularly from my family." He scanned the space around us before looking back at me. "I've no wish to rush you, but I'll not leave you again. And if we're to approach my father, you'd be safer as my wife. Alistair told me once of a hand-fasting ceremony his brother had with his wife before he'd gone to sea… meant to serve as a temporary wedding… The two of them simply exchanged vows alone together one night. The vows would legally last a year so they could be wed while he was away and then be married in a church when he returned before the year was over. We could say the words, and I'd give you the protection of my name. It wouldn't need to be more until you wanted it to."

I smiled, surprised at how easily my lips made the gesture after all that had just occurred. "My mother is part Scot."

"You would do this with me?" he asked, searching my eyes for any signs of doubt.

I nodded. "I will. But not here. Not with that house still in my view."

"Aye. I should burn it down if I'd the time." He brushed his lips over my brow, his thumb moving ever so tenderly against my breast bone. "As it is, we'll need to go off the trail and ride fast through treacherous terrain to catch my brother before nightfall. I am sorry to make matters worse after what's happened here. Are you up for this?"

"I'm with you," I reminded him, "and I am not broken."

Mounted atop a stunning golden mustang with Juan's solid chest against my back, I sighed. It was, indeed, his touch that sat on my skin as we rode silently through the rain.

I felt him on my thighs, breast, and cheek just as I felt his chest against my back and his arms against my biceps where he held both the reins and me tightly.

The world was a foggy haze of sage green and brown as we sped through it, the scent of ozone heavy in my nose. The rain, though not quite cold, was a blessing on my swollen face, and after an hour, I could even open my right eye a smidge—not that I could see much beyond our horse without my glasses.

When the shower turned into a downpour and the ground below became too soft for our speed, he slowed us to a trot, and placed the reins in my hands. "Can you keep her straight for a moment?"

I smiled, reaching forward to pet her mane. "I'd love to."

I felt him turn in the saddle to rummage through a pack, and had I not been enchanted by the horse, I might've panicked when he then removed his jacket from my shoulders to expose my drenched and transparent shift to the wilderness.

It was quickly replaced by a lighter fabric, a cloak with a hood, and I basked in the feel of his arms around me as he fastened it and pulled the hood over my damp hair.

He made no attempt to take back the reins, but instead tucked his chin against the crook of my hooded neck and held me tighter. "Earlier, you said my father sent Dario to confirm our betrothal... You spoke to him?"

"I did," I said. "I needed to do something to get off the ship; to warn you and Jack he was there. He had everyone else taken captive. So I ran out with my arms open and called him *father*. Told him we were engaged to be married today and you'd gone off in search of him to share the news."

He drew in a breath. "And he believed you?"

"He believed *you*," I said softly. "I gave him your journal and showed him the rings. And he believed Mr. Gil who'd evidently been spying on us in his absence."

He kissed my temple. "You were not afraid of him?"

I shook my head. "It was hard to be afraid of someone who looks so much like you. And I know he's done awful things, but… He was conflicted when I showed him that journal. I really got a sense from him that whatever awfulness he might've done was done solely out of love for you."

At this, a laugh rumbled in his chest. "You would see the good in the devil himself if he stood before you."

"Your father's not the devil, Joseph."

He sighed, moving his thumb over my hip bone. "Give it time, Cecelia, and he'll change your mind. What was your father like? You've never spoken of him."

I shrugged, the little spot in my heart I held for the stranger burning at the mention of him. "I only met him once when I was a girl. He seemed so nice to me then… All smiles and hugs. We had this wonderful day together, me, A.J., him, and my mother. It felt like a real family. But I never saw him again after that, and I couldn't understand how such a nice man could just abandon his daughters like they were nothing to him. Maybe it's the ones that seem the nicest that are the real devils."

"Maybe," he grumbled. "I'm sorry he did that to you."

I tilted my head back against his chest. "I turned out alright, I suppose…. Riding off into the sunset to change history with a dark and handsome stranger. What will you do with Dario when we catch up to him?"

"I will rip his heart right out of his chest, just as he has done mine."

"He's your brother," I reminded him. "And my family doesn't exactly have a history of being honest with yours. You can't really blame him for not trusting me—particularly after what Alaina did with your father…"

"Christ, Cecelia," he balked, "he handed you over to those monsters. Do you never think ill of anyone?"

I held up my chin. "As a matter of a fact, I do. I'm quite pleased Adrián is rotting away in that little house with only his *insides as company*. But what Adrián did is Adrián's fault. Dario is your brother—a man I've heard you speak fondly of on several occasions—and I can't think *ill* of him for simply handing me over to monsters when he thought me one himself."

"I can," he growled. "He knew exactly what Adrián could do and he gave you to them, not because he thought you a monster, but to hurt me."

"Why would Dario want to hurt you?"

He blew out a breath that tickled my brow as he took back the reins with one hand. "That war goes back a long way, *mi alma.* Starting with Elizabeth."

"He was jealous?" I pried, turning my head enough to get a glimpse of his tightened jaw.

He increased our pace as the rain lightened and pulled me against him. "Aye. He wanted her first and was mad with jealousy when it was me she chose. We were boys then, but I think it was a turning point for him. I don't know what might've happened had she chosen him instead… Maybe he would've gone down a different path, maybe not, but…" He paused, his fist tightening around the reins as he debated saying more.

"But?" I echoed.

He shook his head. "But a few years later, my father caught him with a *man* in his bed—one of my father's crew—and their relationship has never been the same since. Dario blames me and Elizabeth for the way he is and for the way my father now looks at him."

My heart suddenly hurt for Dario. I'd seen the disdain in his father when he ordered him to escort me. How difficult it must've been for him to be ashamed of who he was. "It's not Dario's fault or yours or Elizabeth's that he likes men, you know."

Juan cleared his throat uncomfortably. "He doesn't, though. Not exclusively. He's… different, I suppose. Just wants to be close to someone—*anyone,* no matter the sex. He claimed he found it that day my father discovered him… And my father had me throw that man overboard."

"Jesus," I breathed. "Sounds like his heart's already been ripped from his chest."

"It is no excuse for what he did," he said coldly. "He can hurt me as much as he'd like to make up for his pain, but today, he hurt you… and I shall see him pay for it just as I would any other."

At that, he made a noise for the horse and kicked us up into a full sprint, putting a prompt end to the conversation.

Chapter Thirty-Six

Alaina

With the babies babbling softly to each other in the cradle behind me, I sat down with quill and paper to write my letters, Juan Josef scribbling his own beside me.

Gabriel, as I presumed, had come for me, and he waited on deck for the letters we would send back with him.

I dipped my quill and adjusted my fingers around it.

Fifteen years of watching *Fairview Nights* reruns until I could nearly recite each episode verbatim was about to pay off. I had to hope Jack remembered his role as Elias as well as I did…

During season four, Elias's love interest, Maggie, had been taken captive. As her captivity lasted nearly the entire season, the plot made fans who loved the romance aspect of the show infuriated, myself included. I'd nearly given up on the series midway through that season. Luckily, I endured, and it was that season that would help me get a message to Jack.

During one of the final episodes, Maggie was able to convince her captors to allow her to send a goodbye letter to her fiancé, and, knowing they would read it before sending, she coded it to give Elias her location.

She'd used the first letter of every other sentence in the middle paragraphs to send her message. And so would I…

'*Dear Jack,*

Above everything, I want you to know we are safe, safer than all of you. The fight is over and Juan has agreed not to put a hand on any of us so long as we go to Virginia and help him kill George Bennet. It's fine. Once this is done, it's all over for good. We'll be home and free to live our lives in peace.

Don't worry about us and don't let my sister worry either. Make sure she gets to have her adventure. I mean that. Let her make as many memories as she possibly can before this is over. While I watch over us, I want you to watch over her until we're together again.

Since I won't be able to say so for a while, I love you with all my heart. It's funny what separation makes you think of. In your absence, I keep thinking of that kiss in Fairview Nights when Elias finally was reunited with Maggie at the end of season 4. That relief... That love... I think I might dream of having one like it every night until I see you again. That dream will get me through all that I might endure.

Kyle and Fetia are taking Bud, Magna, Terrence, and Phil to the slave ship. It took some convincing, but they're going home, as they should.

I hope Dario can make it to you in time to give Chris, Maria, Lilly, and Jim the same offer. We've been here too long and it's time they all went home too. Lilly and Jim will argue against it, I'm sure, but they need to consider Izzy in all this. She should be tucked away safe in a bed and not out here in this madhouse. Let it be their decision and don't push it. You know how stubborn they can be when their minds are made up.

Juan is being kind. I'm not afraid of him at all. Far from it, actually. I think we might end up as friends by the time all this is over.

I will see you in Virginia or I will see you in a better life. Either way, I will see you soon. You have the genealogy report and so do I. We'll both know we're safe.

All my love,

Mrs. Volmer'

I looked over it again and again. *Kill J.F.* Would he know what that meant? We'd both seen Juan Francisco in the report, and we both had spoken about the option to kill him instead. Would he remember where to find him? Quickly, I added:

'P.S. I've written a letter to Lilly and Jim. I want you to read it first... Want them to hear the same sentiments from both of us as a show of our unity in the need to put an end to this fight. I mean it, Jack. No more fighting. Not with Juan Jr. or Dario or anyone else that might deter us. Let's go to Virginia and end this once and for all.'

Handing his letter to Juan to read, I pulled another sheet of paper and wrote a letter to Lilly, using the same code to spell out *'Yorktown'* for clarity as I sent her my love, Bud's farewell, and advised her to go home.

Lastly, I wrote a letter to Cece. This one held no coded message. If I was going to steal her life from her, I wanted to make sure she at least got the most out of it while she could. If she hated me in the end, so be it, but the least I could do was ensure she'd have memories to hold onto if she didn't forget.

With eyes blurred by tears as I signed the bottom, I looked up to find Juan Josef looking over my shoulder.

"You really believe they love each other?" he asked softly, his eyes on the words I'd just written.

Wiping my eyes, I nodded, feeling that much more guilty as I said and meant, "I do. From the moment she stepped on board, no one could keep them apart. I've never seen two people more drawn to each other."

He placed a hand on my shoulder. "I know this hasn't been easy—it won't be easy to trust me now, but—"

"No interruptions." I sniffled the last of my tears away. "We'll get our lives back. Here." I handed him Cece's letter.

He took it from me and squeezed my shoulder. "I'll go give them to Gabriel now and see your friends off. Would you like to join me?"

Taking every bit of effort not to grimace, I put my hand over his. "No. I've said enough goodbyes for a lifetime. I'm going to take the babies down for a nap. Come down once you're done turning the ship... There's something I think I should show you."

It was early evening when Juan Josef knocked on the doors and let himself in.

Bruce had returned to the galley with Jacob and Michael, preparing dinner under strict supervision from the new chef, and I was alone with my enemy in my bedroom.

Standing from one of the wingback chairs that still smelled like Jack, I motioned to the sofa. "Sit," I instructed, hurrying to the window to retrieve Bud's laptop.

He watched me cautiously, not taking the offered seat as I moved back to sink down onto one side of the sofa. "You intend to kill me with whatever that is?"

My hand hovered over its silver surface and I laughed. "It's a computer, Juan, not a weapon. I have photos on it you might want to see. Look." I flipped it open, punched in Bertie's birthday and opened the gallery containing Terrence's photos. "I wanted to show you what we saw..."

My heart stung as I pulled up the image of Juan Jr. and Cece with their heads pressed together on the deck. How devastatingly happy they both looked in that moment, and how horrible I was to rob her of it and push her toward a life spent at the side of a man like Owen. I would make this up to her... somehow.

Juan sat down hard beside me, his hand over his mouth as he stared wide-eyed at the screen.

"Terrence took photos of them," I whispered, "when they didn't know they were being watched." I zoomed in on their smiling faces; on their hands where they were held together against his chest. "Hard to think either of them could fake that."

I hit the arrow to pull up the photo of her laughing up at him where she held the helm and he stood behind her. "I wanted you to see her," I explained. "The way she lights up everything she touches… The way it reflects on him. Wanted you to know she's… not like me. She's incapable of deceit."

I dared to glance at Juan where he was frozen in place, palm still plastered over his mouth. I knew he loved Juan Jr. in his own weird way, and I showed the photos to him for two reasons. The first was that I needed to defend my sister's name. For whatever reason—perhaps pride—I needed him to know her feelings were pure. These pictures showed that.

The second was that I wanted him to see this gesture as a sign of my willingness to work with him; an olive branch of sorts to set a pleasant tone for the rest of our trip. We would be connected by our love for them, and I hoped that would be enough to survive each other. I was too tired to fight with him over these next several months.

I flipped to the next: the video of their stolen kiss in the hull. I watched as Juan experienced it for the first time; watched his entire posture soften as she rested her palm against his cheek; watched his eyes water as his son laid a kiss on her forehead; and I watched him nearly lose his reserve when their lips pressed gently together.

"I wanted you to know she really does love him," I said softly, my gaze returning to the screen to take in their slow dancing spin and the secret whisper Juan placed in her ear. I nearly lost my own reserve when she giggled and said, *'Let's not be one of those couples that says I love you all the time. You're only allowed to say it when you absolutely can't hold it in… When there are no other words to express how you feel. Okay?'*

I laughed with her when he proceeded to say it four more times between kisses, unabashed in her presence to show his softer side.

Juan drew in a heavy breath when the video stilled, and he straightened his shoulders. "You remember your life before and after it was changed?"

"And they both will remember each other."

"But the time…" He said, still staring at the video where it was frozen on Juan Jr.'s returned laughter. "The years he'll wait…"

"He knows," I said, flipping to the final image: the two of them standing on the bow where she'd raised on her toes to inspect the bandage at his shoulder. I stared at Juan Jr.'s expression; at the undying devotion with which he looked down at her. "They've both had the conversation around what happens after we kill George Bennet and they are both ready for it. Your son has never once been willing to abandon the plan to save Gloria. Even after he found out she wasn't his mother."

Juan nodded, his attention still entirely glued to the screen.

"Who was Juliana Martinez?" I asked. "And why didn't you tell him about her?"

A muscle in his jaw ticked. "Because there was nothing about Juliana Martinez worth telling."

I took a deep breath. "You said you'd explain everything, Juan. I want to know why this man never knew who his real mother was. My little sister is planning to be married to him and I need to know who he is."

"Gloria was the only mother he needed to know." He moved his hands back and forth over his knees, tipping his chin at the image on the screen. "Juliana Martinez was a monster."

"How so?" I asked. "If I'm going to sail with you and be civil, I want to know everything, Juan. That was the deal."

He gazed at the screen for a good long while before his shoulders eased with surrender and he let out a long ragged breath. "Juliana was the woman my father wanted me to marry. Our marriage would've ended a decade long conflict between our families. The Martinez family ran a similar business and my father wanted the war over. Upon his insistence, I tried to make it work.

But I hated her; couldn't stand to be in the same room with her after only a few months. She was demanding and clingy and she hated me just as much as I hated her, though she wouldn't admit it. Nothing could've made that relationship work."

His nostrils flared. "A few short weeks after I turned her away, my father was killed, leaving me to inherit the business. I knew it was her family that did it, but I didn't retaliate… Even though my family wanted me to… I let that be that."

Fingers tightening over his knee caps, his practiced proper English slipped as he ventured back in his memory. "But the Martinez family didn't. I didn't know when I'd turned her away she was pregnant. If I had, I never would've left her. The night he was born, her piece of shit family brought him to lay naked and screaming in the mud at my gate. I found him the next morning nearly eaten alive by mosquitos, wailing at the top of his lungs with a note stapled—*stapled!*—to his chest that read, *'your bastard.'*"

He blew out. "My brother was with me when I found him. He told me to leave him; said there was no way to know for certain he was mine and I should leave him to die." He shook his head. "But I took him in my arms and wiped the mud from his face. And my *son* looked at me. I knew right then he was mine, and I would do anything and everything to keep him safe."

Pursing his lips, he squinted at Juan Jr.'s image on screen. "So I killed Juliana's father and all her uncles, brothers, and cousins for what they'd done to him. I'd have killed her too if they hadn't put her on a boat and sent her to the States after she gave birth."

"I told you once Juan was my whole heart and I meant it." He met my eyes once more. "It was Gloria that truly pulled him out of the mud when she came into his life a few months later, and it will be Gloria that pulls him out once more when we undo this. I sank him in this time and I'd hoped he would forget. He will kill me when it is done, and I will welcome it knowing I did everything I could, in the end, to keep him safe."

I swallowed… Unable to even fathom seeing my own son in such a condition, I couldn't imagine what he might've felt. I didn't want to understand Juan Josef; didn't want to feel sorry for him, but, in an attempt to lighten the mood, I closed the gallery and opened the photo of him smiling in the teal-walled cafe. "You look like him here," I said.

My mission was accomplished, and beneath Juan's salt and pepper beard, his teeth flashed bright white and he laughed heartily. "Do you know what this is?"

I shook my head. "No… what is it?"

He shook his head, his grin widening. "This is the cafe just outside Valle del Cocora where I met her the first time… She was sitting with friends and she just… pulled up her camera and snapped it in my direction."

A knock at the door put an end to the softness in his voice. He placed a hand on the laptop to push it closed.

"Captain?" Mr. Gil called from the hallway. "We've turned South and are ready for you to take over."

He patted my hand before he stood and stretched his back. "Thank you for this. We will continue our conversation later. I must go."

Halfway to the door, he stopped and turned back, his brow furrowed. "Where did you find that photo of me?"

I reconnected the solar charger to the laptop and stood to take it back to the window. "Dahlia sent it to Maria when they went back. She sent lots of photos I'd like to show you."

All the color drained from his face then. "*My* Dahlia?"

I nodded, realizing only then he'd assumed she was dead.

He opened his mouth to say more, but Mr. Gil called again, "Captain? Are you in there, sir?"

Juan closed his mouth, bowed his head, and hurried out of the room.

Chapter Thirty-Seven

Cecelia

It was nearly dark when we saw the others moving toward us on the trail ahead. Chris and Jim held rifles at Dario's back, all of them mounted on horseback and moving in our direction.

Izzy was safely positioned in front of Lilly, both of them covered with mosquito netting the same way Maria was. My heart settled to see Izzy safe.

Catching sight of us, Dario snarled and kicked his horse into a gallop in our direction.

"Take the reins," Juan grumbled in my ear as we approached in just as much of a hurry.

"What, why—"

He shoved the leather into my palms, and the moment we grew close, he leapt from our horse to his brother's, the two men proceeding to roll off and into the brush at the side of the road.

I turned my horse toward them, grabbing the bridle of Dario's mare as she circled confusedly. Directing her to a halt alongside my much more docile mustang, I watched the brawl with some amusement.

I didn't say a word as Juan delivered blow after blow to his brother's face and gut, the two of them twisting in the dirt with the dexterity of brothers who'd grappled a thousand times before; both of them seeming to know the other's next move before he could strike.

"Get off me, pendejo," Dario spat as Juan locked his arm around his throat and pulled him off the ground in a sort of head lock to face me.

"Look at her," Juan growled through his teeth. "Look at her face. You did that to her… You did that knowing who she was to me. Give me one good reason not to break your neck."

"I'll give you three," Dario choked out, jamming his elbow into Juan's rib repeatedly until Juan let go. "Mom, Dahlia, and Lizzie!"

I leaned forward to scratch the twitching ear of my horse as Dario spun round and threw a punch that landed on Juan's jaw.

"You fool!" Dario continued hatefully. "We are *this* close to going back and you decide now's a good time to get involved with a woman?" He landed another jab in Juan's ribs. "You think I would willingly deliver her to you so you could change your mind —change the plan so you could stay here with her instead of saving mom and Elizabeth or seeing little Dahlia again?!"

"Ay lightnin' bug," Jim said at my heel, smoothing his palm over my horse's shoulder while he took hold of her bridle with the other. "Ye' look like ye' seen better days. You doin' alright?"

I smiled as Juan struck back, landing two quick blows to Dario's nose. "Just taking in a bit of a show."

Jim snorted. "Ye' think we should break 'em up?"

"Nah." I shrugged. "Probably best to let them fight it out. They won't kill each other."

"No?" He watched as they returned to the ground to grapple, a blur of swinging fists and kicking legs. "Sure as shit looks like they're tryin' to, don't it?"

"Their swords are sheathed," I said simply, wincing as I swung my leg around to dismount. On any other day, I'd have been too proud to accept help, but on this day, I was grateful for Jim's outstretched arms.

We'd be back on the trail soon enough, and my aching legs needed a break after such a long ride.

"I got a cut of meat you can throw on that eye," he said, tapping his own eye where mine was nearly swollen shut. "We's just on our way to find ye' when Precious rode up."

"I'll be fine." I frowned. "You call Dario Precious?"

"Ooh, and he hates it somethin' awful," he chortled, leading both the horses and myself toward the others up the trail. "He told us what his daddy did takin' back the ship. Told us about Mr. Gil. What's the plan now? You trust these assholes not to screw us over?"

"I trust one of them," I said. "And we sent Tomás ahead. He's supposed to warn Jack to stay put and send Gabriel to the ship to stall Juan Josef until we can get there."

Jim shook his head. "Hoss ain't stayin' put for nobody with his wife and babies on that ship."

"He has to," I assured him. "His death year changed. If he steps foot on that ship, Juan Josef will kill him—would've killed him had he been there with her when he took control of it."

He ran a palm over my horse's muzzle. "That don't matter. He ain't gonna' leave them in danger."

"That's the thing," I said, leaning in. "His date changed. The rest of theirs didn't. We know the chart can be altered now and he'll have it with him to ensure they're all safe."

"Ay mi amiga!" Maria gasped, flinging the netting away from herself and hopping off her horse. "Your face!"

"You should see *his*," I quipped. "I'm alright, really. I've been through worse. No need to fuss."

Maria's eyes drifted downward and I pulled the cloak closed where it threatened to reveal the lack of clothing underneath.

She looped her arm through mine and clicked her tongue. "I brought plenty of clothes with me." She waved at a mule loaded with bags tethered to Lilly's horse. "We'll get you fixed right up."

I took a deep breath. "You don't happen to have anything *white* in those bags… do you?"

She stopped in her tracks and spun to face me. "I might. You going to sneak off and marry that handsome hero of yours while we're out here?"

I glanced over my shoulder where the two brothers spat vulgarities and exchanged exhausted looking punches to each other's bodies. "At some point… after we fix things."

She pressed her fingertip to my swollen eye and shook her head. "Well, you can't be all puffed up like this when you do. We'll put some meat on it."

"Really," I set my feet. "It's fine. We need to head back to the docks as soon as they're done trying to kill each other."

Maria nodded, looking beyond me to the brawl. "I forgot about the fighting," she said, "when I warned you about Colombian men… I forgot how much they love a good fight. They're born to fight and to fu—"

"Here ye' go sugar." Jim placed a slab of raw pork into my hand and winked. "Hold that on your eye for a bit and that swelling will come down."

"You know that doesn't actually work," I informed him. "Might help if it was cold, but…" As I saw the disappointment in both Jim and Maria's expressions, I decided to let this trail off. They needed to help the situation in some way and were helpless to do so for anyone but me right then. I shook my head. "You know what? I'm thinking of cold compresses for fevers… Nevermind. Thank you, Jim." And with some reluctance around the threat of bacteria, I pressed the meat to my face and shut up about it.

"Here," Maria said, ushering me to a mule at the side of the road while Jim ventured back to the horses, "let me see what kind of skirts I brought with me. I think I have an extra shift in here too. A change of clothes helps more than you'd think after…"

She didn't finish the sentence, but I knew, based on the shadow of some dark memory sweeping over her face, she'd likely been through far worse.

I grabbed her hand before she could turn away to rummage through the pack, needing my new friend to know what happened for reasons I couldn't explain. Leaning in, I whispered proudly, "I gouged out his eyes."

She stared blankly at me for a moment, then a wicked grin turned her lips upward and she moved closer. "I stabbed mine in his dick."

Both of us beaming at the other's confession, we stood in silence, our lips gradually turning back downward as we relived our encounters in our minds.

With a deep breath, she wound her arms around me. "Are you alright, mi amiga?"

I nodded against her shoulder. "I will be. Are you?"

"No." She held me tighter before letting go and stepping back to flash her teeth. "But we are women. Eh? So we will wear our pretty smiles while we do whatever it takes to *make* ourselves alright. That's what we do." She glanced back toward the fight where Chris had stepped between the two brothers. "God help those men if they knew what it was really like to live in our skin. I don't think they could survive it."

Juan had dislocated Dario's shoulder, and not trusting his brother to ride on his own in the dark, he'd pulled him up onto his horse.

I rode Dario's white mare, falling into step with Chris just behind them as the sun disappeared to leave the sky a dim purple twilight, the songbirds quieting to allow for the night creatures' orchestra to begin.

Unable to travel any faster than a trot in the dwindling light, I listened to the vibrating hum of katydids blending with the steady metronome of chirping crickets around me, the occasional yip of a Gekko or low moan of a bullfrog mixing in to round out the symphony of clatter. I prayed—unsure who I might be praying to—my sister was unharmed.

"Did she seem... alright?" Chris asked between us, evidently doing the same. "The babies... they're safe?"

I forced a smile—smiling felt so out of place knowing where A.J. was. "Jack has the genealogy chart. His death date changed. As long as hers and the babies' dates remain the same, we'll know they're alright. It's not much, but it's something to cling to."

He ran a hand hard over his face. "Jack should've listened to you when you told us all to get off the ship. This is his fault."

I pursed my lips. "No use in pointing fingers now. I'm sure he'll be beating himself up for it without your help."

"She should be with us," he groaned. "She *wanted* to be with us. He had no right to force her to stay behind. God only knows what kind of torture she'll have to endure with that man if he sails away with her now."

"I don't disagree with you, but A.J. chose to listen to Jack and so did I… So did we all in the end."

Chris huffed. "And look where it's gotten us." His jaw ticked as he examined my bruised face. "Jack did this to both of you. What if Juan Josef already sailed off? What if Gabriel can't stall him? You know Captain Cook said it would take sixty days to sail around Cape Horn? *Sixty days*… with a fucking madman."

"A.J.'s tough," I reminded him, shifting my back in an attempt to ease its stiffness. "Tougher than me and you put together when she wants to be. Mentally *and* physically. She can take just about anything and come out of it with a smile in the end. You remember that time we all went to Cancun and she sprained her ankle jumping off the rocks at Aktun Chen? Refused to acknowledge anything was wrong—even though we all saw the swelling—and proceeded to go out that night in four-inch heels and smile through it? If she can endure four-inch heels, the woman can endure Juan Josef for a few months."

Chris laughed, his shoulders relaxing a little. "She did love those four-inch heels back then." His smile widened. "When she wore them to the office, she'd say they were her power-shoes… said they made it so she wasn't looking up at the men."

"God, she can be brilliant when she wants to be." I tilted my head back in awe of such a simple show of dominance.

"You know, if *I'd* told her to stay on that ship," he said, staring ahead as the horses trotted onward, "she'd have been the first one off just to prove I had no control over her."

"Not in the beginning," I countered. "A.J. would've dove headfirst off a cliff if you asked her to in those early days. She was crazy about you."

He blew out a breath. "I don't know when she stopped being crazy about me, Cece."

I clicked my tongue. "Chris, you'll always be my brother, you know that… No matter what. And because you're my brother, I can tell you now, I have always thought you deserved more than she gave. Don't get me wrong, I love her with all my heart and if you say one cruel word about her, I'll punch you right in your stupid face, but… I saw you two together almost every day of your lives —in the *new* memories you're so suddenly fond of. Sure, she was crazy about you, but not in the way you were crazy about her. Not in the way Maria is crazy about you."

I glanced over my shoulder to where Maria was trailing, deep in conversation with Lilly and Izzy where they rode alongside her, Jim bringing up the rear with both mules tethered to his horse. "A.J. wouldn't have waited for you to get past this," I said softly, tilting my head in Maria's direction. "That one will wait forever if she has to."

He stole a glance at her and smiled with the same deep underlying affection I'd seen him offer my sister. "I'm not so sure about that… Not anymore. I've been so disillusioned with these new memories and thinking I might love Alaina more that I've completely neglected her… I thought I was doing the right thing by putting distance between us, but I hurt her… Abandoned her when she needed me most. She doesn't deserve that."

"Chris, *she* could wear four-inch heels with two broken ankles and dance a jig. She's tough, too. And she knows none of us is perfect. We all make mistakes—especially when it comes to matters of the heart."

He nodded, considering it in silence for a while before he tilted his chin in Juan's direction. "She said you're planning to marry him?"

I bit my lower lip. "Yes. Do you know anything about hand-fasting?"

His brow lifted. "You're going to hand-fast with him?"

For some reason, I wanted to cry. Maybe it was the fact that I was speaking to someone who'd known me longer than a few weeks, but my throat swelled with the admission, as if I were revealing marriage plans to a father. "I know it's... not the most opportune time, and it's fast and... well, unlike anything *I'd* ever do... but... do you think that'd be okay?"

"Are you asking for approval, Cece?"

I blinked a tear from my eye. "I don't have anyone else to ask. Everything's happening so fast. In our time, this would be absolutely insane, but here... now... with him... It all feels so natural. You're my family and your approval would mean the world right now. Tell me I'm not being crazy or naïve. Tell me this is okay?"

He breathed out a laugh. "You do realize I might be the absolute worst person to ask for relationship advice, right?"

I held my breath as I waited for an answer.

"Cece," he shook his head, "sweetie..."

I watched his expression change as he recognized my need for a familiar endorsement, and he bowed his head. "You're a strong-willed woman. Are you sure you're doing it for the right reasons? Will you marry him because you love him and not just to ensure he'll walk into that party and prevent your marriage to Owen?"

"I love him." The tear I'd been battling slid down my cheek anyway. "Which is insane, I know, but despite all logic and reason and circumstance, I love him. And I feel absolutely horrible that I could love anyone while the world is falling apart around us, but I do. Am I being nonsensical?"

He shook his head. "Nothing is guaranteed, Cece. Time is..." he waved an arm out in illustration of where we were, "it's fragile and unpredictable. Time itself is nonsensical. We don't know where we might wake up tomorrow. There will never be an opportune time, so take what bits of happiness you can in this world where nothing is certain."

He paused and examined my eye. "Did he kill whoever did that to you?"

I nodded.

"Well then, he's a far better man than Owen ever was, and I'm happy to give my consent."

I sniffled into a smile. "Thank you."

"You asked me about hand-fasting," he continued, adjusting his grip on his reins as the lead horse slowed. "It's simple. You stand before each other as you would a normal marriage ceremony and you make the same declarations—I, take you to be my wife and all that—then you exchange rings and you're married. Do you have a ring to give?"

I shook my head.

He shifted his reins to one hand to pull a chain from his neck. Dangling from it was a gold band. "Your sister gave me this. I think it's only fitting you should have it now. Perhaps it'll be the start of a new family heirloom. And maybe the end of my… *disillusion*."

I took it from him and held it to my heart as Juan put up a hand, motioning us all to stop.

My spine stiffened as he lowered Dario to his feet and rode ahead into the darkness.

"What now?" Lilly whispered behind me.

I urged my horse forward to stop at the side of Dario where he stood in the road holding his arm. "What's going on?"

"Riders ahead," he mumbled, keeping his eyes forward as rain began to drizzle on us once more.

I followed his gaze, unable to see anything without my glasses, especially in the dark. A chill ran up my spine as I considered the possibilities of who might be approaching. "Maria said there was another Ruiz brother that rode out with your father… Jacinto. What happened to him?"

He continued to stare into the darkness. "My father paid him to take the horses we purchased and ride ahead to Portobelo with the rest of the slavers. It is not him."

"You know your brother killed every one of those men you handed me off to, right? All his brothers?"

"Aye," he said softly, "I presumed as much when I saw what they'd done to your face."

I glared at the side of his head. "Did you know they would force themselves on me?"

He turned to me then, brows lifted. "No. Tell me, what is it you intend to accomplish here? Are you marrying my brother so he will choose you and your family over his own? If that ship remains in the harbor, what is it you plan to do? Will you and your new husband plead with my father to hand over *my* ancestors so they can go back through time? So that I and my sister and mother will cease to have existed in this world?"

"No," I said, but before I could say more, the sounds of approaching hooves spilling out from the darkness forced my attention forward.

Dario drew his sword with his good arm, taking a half step in front of me as the sound grew closer. "Be ready to ride faster than you've ever ridden should my brother not be among whoever approaches."

I swallowed. "Your father's on the ship and Jacinto is on his way to Portobelo. Who else would possibly be a threat to us?"

He held his blade steadily forward. "If someone came upon that fishing cabin... if anyone saw you and my brother leaving it... Alonso Ruiz has the power to bring the whole of Panama down upon us."

"You'll have to tell me to ride if I need to," I said, staring toward the darkness. "I can't see anything without my glasses."

Four men rode suddenly out of the shadows, and it was only once they were upon us that I could make out the faces of Juan, Jack, Gabriel, and Tomás, my rapid pulse easing.

"The ship is gone," Jack said with surprisingly less defeat than I'd have expected for that kind of news. "The fight is over. We're going to Virginia."

He pulled his horse up alongside mine and handed me a letter with my name on it, announcing to the group, "The slave ship remains in the bay and will wait for the next several days for anyone who wants to go back to the storm. There's another waiting in Portobelo that will take us to Virginia. I'm going to get her, but I won't blame any of you if you choose to go home now."

The rain picked up and I tucked the letter safely into my pocket, pulling my cloak back up over my head and shoulders. "I'm not going anywhere."

"Neither am I," Lilly said firmly as Jack handed her a letter of her own.

Jack shook his head, the rain pasting his hair to his temples as it turned into a downpour. "You can sleep on it and make that call before we head out in the morning. The ones who choose to stay won't see home for quite some time."

"We ain't leavin' nobody, Hoss," Jim assured him. "Ain't nothin' to sleep on. Let's go to Virginia."

Juan rode forward, his eyes fixed on me. "We won't make it there tonight… We won't make it much of anywhere in this weather. The trail will flood in this rain. We'll need to set up camp higher up and wait out the storm."

Chapter Thirty-Eight

Alaina

"Let's not be one of those couples that says I love you all the time..."

Cece's words were muffled, as if she were underwater, and I found myself standing in utter darkness, watching my sister dance in a circle with Juan Jr. where a spotlight shined upon only them.

"You're only allowed to say it when you absolutely can't hold it in... When there are no other words to express how you feel. Okay?" Her smile beamed brightly as she spun out and back into his arms.

"I love you," he said, kissing her forehead.

She giggled wildly as his lips moved across her face; as his hands moved over her ribs.

"I love you." He kissed her again, but frowned when he'd finished as something was pulling his lower body away... *I* was pulling him into the blackness... Not the person standing there watching it happen, but another me… A faceless me—my hands and body—tugging him back as my sister attempted to keep her hold on his hands.

His fingers squeezed hers and her eyes filled with tears as his grip began to slip. "I love you," he said again, and the monster I was stapled a paper onto his chest then ripped him away.

She turned to face me—the me that was watching—and I felt exposed; a second spotlight burning bright and hot over my head. Rage and accusation distorted her features as he let out the final, "I love you" and disappeared completely.

I sat up in the bed, my heart beating nearly out of my chest as I blinked the dream away.

Rain beat down against the window beside me, thunder roaring overhead, and I wondered where she might be. Were they out in the storm with only the trees for shelter or had they come back into the city and joined Jack at the inn? Was she with Juan? Was she safe? Had she gotten my letter?

"Let's not be one of those couples that says I love you all the time," her voice came again, unmuffled this time.

I peered out across the pitch black room where a single light shone from the sofa.

Juan Josef laid across it with his back to me, the laptop resting on his stomach as he played the video over again.

"You're only allowed to say it when you absolutely can't hold it in…"

Feeling both babies asleep beside me, my heartbeat eased a little, and I pulled my robe from the edge of the bed, watching as Juan Josef ran his fingers over the image of his son on screen when he professed his love for her.

Tying my robe, I stood and cleared my throat.

Juan sat up suddenly, the light from the laptop going dim as he moved it to the side of his legs. "Did I wake you?"

"What are you doing in here?" I hissed, tiptoeing across the room to stand at the side of the sofa with my arms crossed.

"I told the men from the slave ship you were my wife," he admitted softly as a flash of lightning momentarily lit up the room.

"I needed a new crew and I couldn't very well tell them the truth… They would consider it strange if I slept in a separate cabin."

A rumble of thunder shook the floorboards beneath me and I tilted my chin toward the laptop. "How'd you figure out how to use that?"

He tapped his fingers over the arm of the couch. "I watched what you did. Saw the code you entered and their names on the screen… It took me a moment to figure out what to do from there… I didn't mean for it to wake you." He motioned to a tea set on the side table. "I made some tea. Would you like some?"

I sighed. There was no use fighting him while we were stuck together, and after the nightmare I'd just had, I didn't want to go back to sleep any time soon. "Yes, please."

I sat down beside him on the sofa as he poured me a cup. Yawning, I took it from him and held it near my lips. "You're not sailing the ship?"

He shook his head, taking a sip from his own teacup and waiting for the next roar of thunder to pass before answering. "There's a man named Gines that served as first mate on the slave vessel. He'll captain us through the night."

Letting the tea warm my throat and calm the nerves that had remained on edge from both the dream and finding him in my room, I tapped the touchpad of the laptop. "Did you look through anything else on here?"

He shook his head. "Couldn't if I wanted to. It took me a small eternity just to mimic what I watched you do."

Another strobe of lightning and the slow crawling crackle of thunder put pause to our conversation. I glanced toward the bed for any signs of movement.

"You seemed surprised earlier," I said, returning my attention to him, "when I mentioned Dahlia."

"I presumed she was dead. She was so small when we went through that storm. I did not think she could survive those waves."

His words were methodical, as if he was anxious to move on to the next subject. The lack of affection in his voice at the mention of her threw me off. "You never talk about the twins the way you do Juan. Why?"

He let out a long breath. "You won't understand this until your children are older, but… as a parent, you have a pull to the one that most reminds you of yourself. You love all your children, of course, but that one you are just more drawn to; more concerned about. There's some deep need in you to protect it from becoming anything like you—save it from making the same mistakes you made. The twins had Gloria's love of life in them so I never worried about them the way I worry about him… He has both my and Juliana's darkness in him. I saw it when he was a child." He smirked. "He tried to kill me over Gloria when he was seven. Had this little pocket knife and was intent to stab me with it… He would've done it, too, had I not stopped him. The boy was a ball of rage. I think, maybe somewhere deep down inside, some part of his subconscious remembers that night in the mud. And that's why I worry. He needed more time with Gloria to soften him."

The rain and wind picked up to hiss sharply against the window, rocking the ship in a gentle sway. Since Juan showed no signs of alarm by it, I relaxed against the back of the sofa.

"Will you finish telling me about that day at the cafe outside Valle del Cocora?" I asked, my curiosity about my descendant and her pull to such a sinister man still piqued. "What were you doing there?"

"Oh, I went to the valley often," he said, lowering his teacup to his palm in his lap, "when I needed to clear my head. Taking over the business and then taking out most of the Martinez family at twenty-one wasn't easy… Nor was attempting to raise a newborn when I knew nothing whatsoever about babies. I hired a nanny for him but it was still hard. Feeling overwhelmed, I drove down with the intention of staying only a few hours. Usually, I'd buy a cup of coffee and sit out front to watch the sun set… Figure out my next move… But that day…" He shook his head. "*She* was my next move."

"You knew that just by looking at her?" I asked, taking another sip and closing my eyes to imagine Juan Jr.'s very same reaction to my little sister.

"I did," he assured me, sitting back against the sofa as another streak of lightning lit up the room. "I had turned round from the counter when her group walked in. It was a split second of eye contact… but it was enough. That day, I decided to sit down inside instead, where the view was much better."

I placed the computer on my lap, closing out the video and opening Gloria's folder. I double clicked my favorite photo of her; the one where she stood atop the Empire State Building making a peace sign. "This view?"

With the screen facing us, I could see the delight in his eyes as he drank in the image of my several-times-great-granddaughter. "No," he said affectionately, "she didn't look quite like that on this particular day."

His laughter came easy… Made him seem almost human. "She had on this white tank top and cargo shorts, and she was covered in grass and dirt stains with a silver camera draped from her neck. Her hair was pulled up in this matted bun on top of her head, pieces of green leaves poking out of this one spot toward the front. She was sweaty and dirty and I'd never seen anything so beautiful in my life."

His lips remained upward as he stared at the screen, the storm outside all but forgotten. "She had her knee hugged to her chest, one arm wrapped around it as she drank a Dr. Pepper through a straw. Her group chatted around her and she'd move that straw to one side of her mouth every so often and smile at me."

"You were just sitting there staring at her?" I balked, imagining my terror if I'd been so young in a foreign country and found the same man gawking at me.

"I held a newspaper… But my eyes never left her. I couldn't risk missing her look over."

"And she wasn't scared of you?"

"Far from it," he chuckled. "She was far more dangerous than I was right then anyway. For all I knew, she could've been a DEA agent come to arrest me, and I'd have handed myself over just to have her hands on me—particularly after she pulled the camera up to her eye and snapped my picture."

I leaned in. "So what happened then? Her group just left her there with a creepy stranger?"

He nodded. "They tried to get her to go back to the hotel but she remained in her seat and told them she wanted to *try the pie.* They all laughed and waved at me on their way out."

"And then?" I asked.

He set his teacup down on its saucer. "And then I moved over to her table and asked if I could join her. She motioned to a chair across from her, and the very first thing she said to me was, *'You look like trouble.'*"

Draping an arm over the back of the sofa, he sighed. "So I said, *'I am trouble,'* to which she responded with, *'Good. I like trouble... and pie. You also look like a man that wants to buy me pie.'*"

At this, he laughed deep in his chest. "I asked her what kind of pie she wanted, and she stared me up and down before pointing at the little glass display and saying, *'I want to try them all.'*"

"All?" I said, admiring the carefree woman on screen and the fearlessness she must've had to make such a bold opening request. "How many were there?"

He grinned. "Twenty. And we sat at that table from evening until sometime around two in the morning trying every single one. She told me about college and her time spent traveling in the summers in between semesters... Told me how she wanted this extraordinary life spent snapping photos all over the world; said she didn't ever want to live the same day twice. I told her everything about my life; about the drugs, about my son, about my father... Didn't care if she could ruin me. I wanted her to know what I was; what she was getting into. I didn't want any secrets between us. And when the baker brought us the final slice, she stood from her seat and sat down in my lap, her legs on each side of mine, and she asked me, *'What does the rest of my life look like if I take you to my hotel?'*"

He raised a brow and smirked. "So I told her, *'I'll give you the whole fucking world if that's what you want.'* And that was the end of it. She pressed her mouth to mine and neither of us came up for air for days. I dropped all the cash I had in my pocket on the table and carried her out, her lips leaving mine only long enough to tell my driver where to take us. We spent three days and three nights in her hotel room, and I married her a few weeks later."

"Weeks?" I echoed. "Sounds like you and your son are very much alike."

Remembering that Juan Josef had beaten Gloria on at least one occasion, I prayed they weren't alike in *every* way. "What went wrong? If you loved her so much... Why'd you beat her?"

He leaned forward and rested his elbows on his knees, apparently unable to look at her photo on the screen for this part of the story. "I beat her three times. The first was when I caught her with Richard. I had been so convinced we had a perfect marriage and she could do no wrong, I hadn't seen it coming and I lost my mind with devastation. I didn't know he was DEA then; hadn't realized he was using her to get to me. That man fooled her and I'll never not regret beating her for it."

He ran his hands over his hair. "The second was when she told me she was leaving me for him. I knew her well enough by then to know she had a restless heart. I'd promised to give her the world and came up short. She needed adventure and, too afraid my enemies might use her against me, I'd locked her away instead. So, I told her she could go. I even agreed to let her take the twins, but I said there was no way in hell she'd take my Juan... She knew that boy was my world, and they left with him anyway. Took me nearly a week to get him back. I almost killed her over it, and that time I wasn't sorry."

His legs bounced anxiously. "The third was when she came home two months later with the twins. She found out Richard was an agent and he'd been hiding it from her... When she figured out he'd been using her to get information about me it broke her heart. I watched as she cried for him... Held her until her tears dried... And when she told me she'd given him everything; told him about our marriage and about my business; named names and gave locations away… well, that broke mine… and I beat her for ruining the extraordinary life I was working so hard to give her. I beat him too… for hurting the woman I loved so fiercely. And when we fled to Hawaii, I promised her I'd never hurt her again. She promised she'd do the same… But Richard Albrecht showed up and never gave us the chance to fix things."

"Juan said it was your bullet that struck her?" I asked gently, unsure how he'd react.

He nodded, lightning filling the room once again. "He had his gun pointed at me and I had mine pointed at him. We both fired on each other. She threw herself in front of him… This woman I loved so fiercely… threw herself in front of a bullet to save the life of a man that used her instead of the man that would've given her anything."

He pulled the collar of his shirt to one side and turned toward me, revealing in the screen's light an old scar from a bullet that must've just missed his heart.

"Jesus," I said under my breath. "Why are you so intent on changing things to save her?" I asked. "Aren't you afraid she'll do it all again some other way; find another Richard Albrecht?"

He put his collar back and reached for his teacup. "I'm not doing it for me. I'm doing it for Juan. The way she loved him… the way she absolutely brought him to life and forced him out of his shell… He needed that; he needed *more* of that. If I were a less selfish man, I'd have let her keep him when she left. She loved Juan more than she loved any of us. I deserved what she did to me. He didn't deserve what I did to him. Without her, I'm afraid I have turned him into me—worse than me. If your sister is the kind of woman she appears to be, she needs him to know more of his mother lest he destroy her spirit the same way I destroyed Gloria's; the same way Juan destroyed Elizabeth's."

Swallowing, I tilted my head to the side. "Elizabeth? She wasn't happy?"

He shook his head. "Juan is a difficult man. Soft words and kisses come easy for him in the beginning… But once that fades…

Where Gloria would've taught him kindness and patience, I made him cold. Elizabeth was desperate to hold on to those soft words and kisses. And in the end, it killed her."

"Did he beat her?" I asked, feeling suddenly terrified of their likeness to one another.

"No," he said softly. "He did worse. He avoided her."

Chapter Thirty-Nine

Cecelia

The rain and wind snapped and hissed against the canvas tent surrounding us as I watched the warm orange glow of a lantern bring life to our efforts to setup a dry place to sleep.

We'd found high ground that was sheltered by a few towering willow-like trees and erected our tents in a hurry, all of us drenched by the time we were done.

The tent smelled like damp fabric and sweat, but it was warm and dry, and I was grateful for the break from the weather.

"You'll sleep there," Juan growled to Dario where he was still holding his arm near the tent's flap. "If anything should threaten to get inside, it'll need to get past you first. You're not to leave my sight. Do you understand?"

Dario didn't argue, his face pale as he extended one leg in front of him with a wince.

A ghost of a pain shot up my own shoulder as I watched him attempt and fail to remove his waterlogged jacket. "Your arm's not broken," I said through chattering teeth, my own clothing soaked through to chill my skin. "Your shoulder's out of socket. I can fix it for you if you'd like."

"You don't need to do that, *mi alma*," Juan said softly, peeling his jacket off his shoulders. "He deserves every second of his suffering."

"He won't be able to sleep like that," I argued, "and we have a long journey ahead. The longer we go without fixing it, the worse it'll get and we can't afford the hold up. And you've ripped your stitches." I ran a shivering hand over the red stain running from Juan's shoulder to his elbow. "I packed a first-aid kit for you with your things just in case. I'll need to restitch you if you don't want to bleed out in your sleep. Go grab the kit while I fix his arm."

Juan looked between me and his brother, worry painting over his features.

"He's not going to kill me like that," I huffed, waving toward Dario's lifeless arm, my exhaustion from the day's events clipping my words more than I would've liked. "And a lot of good you'd be if he tried… it's a wonder you're still upright at all with all the blood you've lost already. Grab the kit. I'll be fine."

"So fearless," Juan said with a smile, leaning in to press a kiss against my temple before he crawled toward the tent's opening, purposely kicking Dario in his bad arm as he moved past him.

Still shivering, I raised up on my knees and motioned to the blankets beneath me. "Lay down here and give me your wrist."

He glanced down at the twisted arm he held to his body. "Why would you do this for me?"

"Because it is the right thing to do," I said, removing my cloak. "And because my arm hurts just looking at you."

He did as instructed, crawling toward me and laying down on his back. In the lantern light, he offered a grimace as he took in the bruising on my face up close. "Adrián did that?"

I nodded, thunder cracking the sky overhead.

"And he is dead now?"

I nodded, placing one slippered foot on his chest as I extended his arm. "They're *all* dead now. This will only hurt for a second."

I pulled his arm away from his body until I heard the familiar *'clunk'* of his shoulder falling back into its socket. He let out a long audible sigh and hugged it to his body as he sat up.

"We'll need to put it in a sling," I said. "You have a blade on you?"

"There's a dagger strapped to my thigh," he nodded toward his bent leg as he massaged his shoulder. "What happened to your glasses?"

I pulled the knife from the sheath on his leg and cut a length of fabric from my bottom skirt. "I imagine they're broken in the road where Adrián struck me." I touched my swollen eye. "Lucky for me, I suppose. The damage would've been a lot worse."

"You remind me of her, you know," he whispered.

"Of who?" I asked, not looking up from the fabric as I pulled it loose. The cut was far from perfect with my incessant shivering, but it would work.

"My mother," he said. "Our father would beat her close to death, and she would mend the cuts on his knuckles afterward." He leaned in. "She was too kind to love such a cold man. As are you."

I assisted him out of his jacket and wrapped the fabric around his torso. "Juan is not his father."

"No," Dario breathed. "He is worse."

All too aware of his eyes on me as I did so, I eased his arm into the sling. "What makes you think that?"

He glanced over his shoulder for signs of Juan's return before turning back to me. "He doesn't know how to love. He knows how to kill. Since he was a boy that is all he has known how to do. He'll show love by killing anyone around you that so much as makes you frown. Doesn't matter who it is… Me, my father, your sister… Anyone that hurts you is as good as dead."

I placed my palm against his icy cheek and smiled. "You hurt me *and* made me frown, but you're still alive, aren't you? None of us knows how to love until we do. Just as he will teach me, I will teach him. And this is the only time I will ever let you speak to me about him in such a way. Whatever resentment you might harbor for him is for you to work out with him, not me. I will always take his side, even when he is wrong. Understand?"

He closed his eyes, seemingly soaking up the feel of my hand on his cheek, like he hadn't been touched in years. "I did not—"

Juan reappeared, climbing back into the tent with the first aid kit to put an end to the conversation. Handing the kit to me, he narrowed his eyes at Dario's repaired arm as he pulled off his shirt. "You didn't deserve her aid."

Dario blew out a breath, motioning to Juan's bleeding shoulder. "Neither do you."

"Would you have me break your other arm?" Juan spat back. "Keep your filthy eyes off her. She is not Lizzie and I'll not have you look upon her in such a way, especially after what you've done to her. It's a wonder I haven't killed you for it already."

Ignoring their banter, I focused solely on threading the needle, too tired to make any attempt to create peace. When my shivering hands missed the eye, I caught a glimpse of my fingernails—of the dark grime still caked beneath them—and I froze.

Adrián's skin and blood…

My lips went numb and a thousand tiny pin pricks coated my face, arms, palms, and feet forcing the needle to fall from my fingers.

I stared at my nails and could still feel Adrián beneath them… Could feel the soft damp flesh as I dug my thumbs into his eyes; the coarse skin of his scalp opening up as I embedded my fingernails into it and squeezed.

And I couldn't breathe…

I'd never had a panic attack hit me so quickly.

"Cecelia?" Juan said softly, gripping my shoulder. "Cecelia? What is it?"

I tried to find some far off place to ground me, tried to focus only on my breathing, but the air wouldn't come, nor would the image of Adrián's face leave me.

"What's wrong with her?" Dario asked.

"Panic," Juan said, his voice muffled beneath the pounding in my ears as he moved to the front of me to lay his hand over my cheek. "You are safe, *mi paloma*. Look at me and take a breath. You are safe and I will wash this off you, all of it. Breathe."

He pulled me against his chest, something which, done by anyone else, would've made matters worse, but… the smell of his skin… the warm amaretto fragrance in my nostrils opened my airway just enough to find a path to my lungs and I inhaled raggedly, a sob escaping along with it.

"You're safe," he said again, combing his fingers through my hair as the other hand worked to pull pins and loosen the laces of my stays.

Where I normally needed space and air and distraction, I now needed him, and I clung to him tightly as I exhaled a too-shallow breath, my chest burning with my racing heartbeat.

Bile threatened to rise in the back of my throat as I squeezed my eyes closed and focused only on Juan's smell; Juan's feel; Juan's voice…

"I'm here, *mi alma*. It's alright."

I felt the stays loosen against my ribs and my lungs filled on the next inhale without their confines. I was crying uncontrollably —as the panic attacks often made me do—and I buried my embarrassment along with my face against his bare chest.

'Open your eyes, Benny. Look at our witch now.'

Hyperventilating, I squeezed Juan tighter, my fingers pressing hard against his damp skin. I couldn't let this break me. I'd promised myself it wouldn't…

'Watch what I do, sweet brother, and then you can have a turn.'

"Shhh, I'm here, Cecelia," Juan soothed as a bellow fell uncontrollably from my lips. Rocking me gently, he laid a kiss on the top of my head. "It's all over. I've got you."

I knew it was over, but, in my exhausted state, my mind wouldn't release me from it… it clung to an image of Adrián inches from my face, both my thumbs sank deep into his eyes… His blood seeping down the sides of my wrists… The world falling apart as I tried desperately to kill him…

I felt Juan tip my face up to him, pulling us apart only enough to inspect me. "Open your eyes, Cecelia. Look at me."

I did, my vision rounded and distorted with my tears, but I saw him; saw those murky green eyes where they worriedly examined each of mine. "Do you trust me?" he asked.

I nodded, my labored breath drying my throat beyond vocalization. I desperately tried to focus only on him... On the look of him, the smell... the voice... only him... not Adrián... only him...

"Take a deep breath," he said softly, "and know I will never let anyone hurt you again."

I took a deep breath in through the nose and out through the mouth, focusing on a single section of black stubble that sprouted along the edge of Juan's jaw.

Only him...

He smiled. "Do it again and know you never have to panic because I will always be with you... I will always protect you."

In through the nose... out through the mouth. My arms loosened their death grip on him as I stared at a small pink blemish beneath the stubble where the growth agitated his skin.

"Do it again," he instructed, "and know I will take this burden from you. Whatever memory lingers, let it be mine from now on to live with. You are safe. And you will be safe for as long as I live."

I breathed again and again, my hands remaining on his chest as a means of knowing where I was and preventing my mind from venturing back into that awful house.

"You are the woman who laughs at death," he said softly, the dark stubble moving with his mouth, "and this will not break you."

The pins on my skin and fuzz in my eyes very slowly disintegrated, and, all of a sudden aware of myself as the rain pattering on the canvas overhead brought me back, I wiped the tears from my eyes and straightened.

Mortified, I looked at Dario and back to Juan. "I'm sorry. It just... came out of nowhere. I didn't even feel it coming. I..." I blinked. "I need to stitch you up. I'm sorry." Moving my hands hurriedly over the blanket beneath me, I searched for the discarded needle and thread only for Juan to grip both wrists and pull them into his lap.

"Stop," he said softly. "Let me fix this."

"I need to stitch you," I argued pointlessly, watching as he pushed his thumbnail beneath mine, forcing the muck beneath it out. The feeling of empty space between nail and skin was as liberating as the loosening of my stays; as if the dried blood had been confining my entire body, clamping down on me to make every breath difficult. This sensation amplified as he did the same to each finger... And I breathed deep when the final bits of Adrián's flesh and blood were forced away from me for good.

When he'd finished, he reached behind him for his rain drenched shirt and scrubbed my hands and arms with it until there wasn't a trace of blood or dirt on my skin.

"Better?" he whispered, still holding both my hands in his.

"Yes," I answered hoarsely. "I'm sorry."

He frowned. "For what, *mi paloma*?"

I sighed. "My stupid brain. I have no control over it when this happens... It just... seizes up like that. Sometimes over the smallest, stupid things. I suppose you had to witness it at some point. Thank you for talking me through it. And... well... now that you see me, I wouldn't blame you if you ran for the hills."

He laughed softly. "I see you, Cecelia, and I am not going anywhere."

I shook my head. "This happens a lot, you know. Sometimes I can feel it coming and stop it early, but it's always gonna' be there."

"And I will always be here to talk you through it." He pulled my fingers to his lips and kissed my knuckles.

"If you don't bleed to death first," I attempted to joke, pulling my much steadier hands away and plucking up the needle and thread. "Turn to the side. Let me fix your stitches before you pass out. I'm alright now."

The dimple appearing in his cheek, he folded his knees up in front of him and turned to face Dario, who I'd nearly forgotten remained in the tent.

"What..." Dario cleared his throat. "What was that you washed from her?"

"Blood," Juan said pointedly. "Before I was able to get to her, she took Adrián's eyes."

"Took his eyes?" Dario echoed, gaping at me.

I nodded, raising up on my knees to pull the now red-stained bandage from Juan's shoulder. "I didn't like the feel of his eyes on me."

Dario continued to stare with his mouth open.

"Don't really care for the feel of *your* eyes on me either," I added, moving an alcohol pad over the opened section of Juan's wound.

Juan chuckled deep in his throat. "If that does not frighten you, little brother, you are a bigger fool than I imagined."

"You are the fool, *brother*," Dario grumbled, focusing his attention on Juan instead of me as I pushed the needle through his shoulder. "How can this do anything but deter what we have worked so hard to accomplish? How can you be so careless as to involve yourself with a woman when we are so close to our goal?"

Juan didn't so much as flinch as the needle moved in and out of his skin. "The plan remains unchanged."

"And what about her sister?" Dario spat, forcing my fingers still. "Will you let them go through time and erase us all from existence?"

"No," I answered for him. "You, your mother, and your sister are my family too—not just by marriage. I'm your aunt in a way. You'll have seen your genealogy chart and therefore you'll know as much."

I hooked the needle in and out again. "You'll also have seen Zachary's rapidly approaching death year. My sister has to go back for his sake. She has to try to save her son. I intend to beg for your lives; to plead with her to return here with her children after it is safe to do so with her son, and to raise them into adults in this time so you all can live."

"You've no reason to save us or my mother." He tilted his chin to Juan. "He'll still live."

"Why would I want Gloria erased from existence when she is the sole reason *he* knows any love at all? I've heard enough about who she was to know she was brilliant—a light to you all in a life spent in the shadow of your father. What kind of person would I be to take that light from him? To rob him of his family? It would be cruel."

"Your sister would do it," he offered.

I forced a smile, pulling the needle out. "I am not my sister. You did not take *me* captive and maybe that is why I'm able to understand why you all have done the things you've done. Just as Alaina and Jack fight for their family, you fight for yours. Like it or not, we're *all* family now, and I aim to end the fight."

I looped the stitching into a knot and cut it, sitting back to prepare a bandage.

"You mean that?" Juan asked, his expression conflicted when he turned toward me. "Even after what he's done to you?"

"Of course I do," I said, raising back on my knees to position the bandage over the stitching. "We'll find a way to make it work for everyone. Assuming my sister doesn't have some insane plan of her own..." I pulled Alaina's letter out of my pocket in illustration and scooted back into the corner. "You two try not to kill each other for a second while I see what she's got to say."

I unfolded the paper, and the moment I saw her looping feminine cursive against the lantern light, my eyes filled with tears.

'Dear Butthead,

First, because I know your brain, I have to assure you that we are in no danger so don't worry about me. Juan Josef is seated beside me as I write this and we are drinking tea. There is no fight anymore and therefore he is not my enemy. My trip will be easy. You are likely in more dangerous circumstances than I am, traipsing through the rainforest like the badass you are. I'm not worried about you, so don't you dare worry about me.

You are the smartest person I know, and after everything you've been through, you don't need me to tell you how fragile life is. You also don't need me to remind you of the risks that come with what we're setting out to do.

Live your life. Live it as fast and as much as you can while you have it. Make as many memories as your giant brain can hold before it's too late.

If you love him, wrap your arms around him for as long as you can. Marry him if that's what you want, and don't let our distance stop you. I'm safe, I promise.

I love you and you have my approval.

Enjoy your adventure.

I will see you at home.

All my love,

Skittle-tits.'

I held the back of my hand to my lips and cried and laughed and sobbed as I read the letter over and over again.

I imagined her in the dining room on the ship, scribbling with the quill and cursing as she dripped the globs of ink that were splattered throughout the paper. I pictured Juan Josef there with her, the two of them sipping tea and being civil... being human...

I love you and you have my approval.

Enjoy your adventure.

I tucked the paper back into my pocket and blinked my tears away. The additional exhaustion that came with my relief was almost overwhelming, so I pulled a light blanket up over me, removed my skirts, and laid down.

"You alright?" Juan asked, twisting to smooth a hand over my hip.

I smiled. "I am. She's safe... Drinking tea with your father."

Dario nodded and pulled a letter from his breast pocket. "Father sent one for you... Basically says not to kill anyone... which I'm sure you are quite incapable of."

Rolling his eyes, Juan unfolded his own letter, scanning the text before tucking it into his boot. "That'll be enough for today." Again he moved his palm over my hip. "I'll say goodnight then."

I frowned. "Where are you going?"

He motioned to the open space beside Dario.

I shook my head. "We're engaged. I don't see any reason why it would be considered inappropriate for you to lay beside me now. It's not like we're alone or you haven't had your arms around me on several occasions already. Thanks to Mr. Gil, your brother knows we've already spent the night together. Come lay with me."

Dario hid a smile as he laid down near the buttoned flap. "Formidable little thing."

"Do not speak of her as if you did not just witness the torment you delivered her," Juan growled, putting out the lantern before he ultimately resigned to slide in behind me beneath the blanket.

I adjusted my head against his outstretched arm, forming by body to his as he draped the other over me.

He pressed a kiss to my temple, whispering too close for spying ears to hear over the steady percussion of rain against the canvas, "I love you."

Smiling to myself, I turned onto my back in his arms to run a finger over the scratchy stubble on his jaw. "You still want to do the hand-fasting thing? Even now that your father's taken off?"

He chuckled, raising up on his elbow to hover over me. "Yes, Cecelia. I would very much like to do the *hand-fasting thing*."

I twisted my lips to one side. "You're sure it's me you want… forever? With my broken brain? We haven't even had an argument yet. How can you know I'm worth it?"

"You're worth it, *mi alma*," he said softly, moving his thumb over my hairline. "But if you'd like me to argue with you, I am certain I could dream up some type of disagreement to ease your mind."

"It's not *my* mind I'm worried about," I insisted. "You're this extraordinary man who's trying to save the world and I'm just a boring woman that hyperventilates if I think too much about overusing a word in a conversation. What is it about me that makes me worthy of any of your time?"

"Boring?" He breathed out a laugh as his fingers moved over my brow. "Cecelia, have you met you? There is nothing boring about you. I would say it is I that is the unworthy one, but that can't be true if you have decided it is me you want. You are a woman who would give herself to no one she deemed unworthy. Christ, you altered time itself to see to the destiny of your choosing. And how lucky am I to be considered worthy by a woman who faces death with a smile; a woman that would launch herself into the very pits of hell to save those she loves from danger? You are the extraordinary one. You'll never need a man to protect you, but I'll try anyway, because that is all I can offer, and because *you* are my light in the shadows—not Gloria. I love you for everything you are and for everything you make me want to be. I don't need to argue with you or spend months making up my mind. I have known, almost since the moment you arrived on the ship, that you are worth all I have to give."

I laughed. "Will you always talk to me like that?"

"Not always, *mi paloma*," he said, moving his nose over mine. "Life with me is not always going to be easy. There will be times when you'll want to gouge *my* eyes out, I'm certain; things I'll say in the heat of the moment that I'll not mean; moments where I shut you out because I am flawed or you'll do the same to me; days we might be so angry with one anther we cannot stand to be in each other's presence. I've no intention of worshiping you just as I have no expectation you'll worship me. We'll live our lives together with the knowledge that every day won't be perfect, but we'll love each other as if they were. I am prepared for that life with you… I *want* that life with you. If, that is, *you* still wish to do the *hand-fasting thing*?"

"I do." I said, grinning in the darkness. "The very moment I'm not a cyclops anymore. I won't have you spend twenty years remembering your bride with one eye."

Laughing out loud, he pressed his lips to mine. "Aye, my cyclops, we can do it whenever you'd like."

Chapter Forty

Alaina

It was strange how quickly I readapted to sitting at the breakfast table to one side of Juan Josef. I'd sat in that very seat so many times as his captive… Now, as his guest, I still felt the chains of captivity lingering around my wrists; all the control weighted heavily at the head of the table where he sat. I would only feel free once I was rid of him once and for all. And I would be rid of him soon enough.

I pushed the eggs around my plate, unable to stop myself from glancing at the chair opposite me where Anna had been seated when he slit her throat.

We'd dined in this room on countless occasions without that memory haunting me. Now that he was back in that chair, it was hard not to replay the events of that horrible day over and over.

"You are thinking of your friend," he said, motioning to the seat I'd been staring at.

"How could I not?" I spat. "She didn't deserve to die like she did. She was a great woman."

He dropped his bread onto his plate. "I hadn't thought any of you would remember what I'd done once I killed the Albrecht.

Everything I have done these past years was a game… One I was certain no one would ever know I'd played once it was through."

"You never thought it could be permanent?" I asked, meeting his dark eyes. "Killing her? You never regretted it?"

He shook his head. "It was a move, Alaina, nothing more. Killing her was placing your king in check when I had no other option left. I was certain you'd poisoned me and my sons and I needed to make that move if I was to see them live again. It was the only thing I *could* do with my back against the wall. I knew she would live again. So did you if you finished the game for me."

I thought about the way he'd just sat there as her throat bled out all over the table… the way he'd asked me if *'this was what I wanted.'* Try as he might to appear human, I knew what he really was. I pushed my plate away from me, disgusted. "You enjoyed the game. You loved killing her; the fear it implanted in me… You liked toying with us… torturing us."

"I did," he admitted. "I'll not lie to you now. Twenty years spent in this time will do all sorts of things to your mind. I wanted to hurt someone. I couldn't very well hurt anyone in this century outside the Albrechts for fear they might be connected to my lineage… So I tormented you and your people… and I was certain you would have no memory of it when it was over."

He pursed his lips and stared down at his plate. "Your sister said your memories changed… Do you think your friend will remember her death?"

"Her name is Anna," I clarified. "And I hope not."

He rotated his teacup on its saucer, looking a bit anxious as he glanced at the chair Anna had once been seated in. "You have been kinder to me when we are not in this room. Perhaps we should spend the duration of our trip dining in a place with less hurtful memories in its walls. The journey around Cape Horn will take some time and I'd prefer not to have you scowl at me in such a way these coming months."

"No," I said, feeling a bit more brazen. "We will take breakfast, lunch, and dinner right here. You deserve far worse than whatever scowl I give you. Just as I've had to live with the memory of what you've done, you will too."

He breathed out a laugh as he raised his teacup. "You know, Gloria very rarely got angry with anyone. Those first several years, she was almost always smiling. Oh, but once she met Richard, she would look at me and speak to me the very same way you do. With that same deep underlying hatred you have for me now. I knew you were deceiving me before when you told me of Jack's supposed affair. I knew you planned to hurt me, just as I know you're planning some way to hurt me now. You even lie the same way she did."

I calmly took a sip of my tea. "I won't lie to you now either, Juan. I *want* to hurt you for everything you've done to us; for what you did to Anna. In my mind, there are at least a thousand ways I have dreamt of doing it." I glanced at the cradle where both babies were making noises at each other. "But I'm not stupid. I know they would pay for that mistake."

He smiled at my children before returning his gaze to me. "Since we are being honest with each other, I feel I should inform you that one of the slavers was sent ahead prior to my boarding with another letter. When he reaches the docks in Portobelo, he'll board the very first ship headed for the colonies to personally ensure my letter arrives in the hands of its recipient before your people can."

I swallowed. "Who's it for?"

He flashed his teeth in a wicked grin. "Juan Francisco de la Bodega." He paused for a moment, searching my face for a reaction I would not give. 'I had to assume," he continued, plucking up his cup once more, "since you saw it so important to look into my lineage, you had some secondary plan in place that involved him. He'll not be in Yorktown for long."

I remained calm at this revelation, forcing my mind on any other thought to avoid the devastation of him, once again, being two steps ahead of me. I could melt down later, but not here. Not now. I would not give him the satisfaction of knowing he'd found me out yet again.

For whatever reason, my thoughts drifted to Charlotte and Chase Miller where I hadn't allowed myself to think about them at length before. Were they living a similar nightmare or had they been picked up and taken in by much more pleasant people? Surely, they'd been picked up relatively quickly to not only have made it to Philadelphia, but, based on the painting, to be living in a somewhat luxurious setting.

I stared down at the amber liquid in my cup.

But how did she come to that luxurious setting? She was only seventeen. She'd have been eighteen or nineteen when that portrait was painted… Had some vile man—possibly someone worse than Juan Josef—taken her as a wife? Did she think that was her only option for survival in this time?

It didn't feel right to just leave her. And if my plans were thwarted…

I tapped my wedding ring against the side of my cup and glanced at Juan where he'd dug back in to his breakfast.

"There are more of us stuck here, you know."

He raised one dark brow and swallowed his bite of sausage. "More? From the future?"

I placed my cup back down on its saucer and nodded. "A young boy and girl, Charlotte and Chase Miller. None of us thought anyone from the back of the plane survived the crash, but then Bud found an old painting that proved otherwise. We won't have time to find her now, but you could."

"Me?"

I nodded. "When we kill George Bennet, you and your sons will show up in a life with these memories twenty years before the rest of us will; twenty years before the Miller family can ever get on that plane. I have all their files on the computer where Terrence was investigating the crash. I have their home address, the date they bought their tickets, the time they checked in to the airport… You could find some way to interfere, couldn't you?"

His lip twitched with amusement. "You are concerned for a complete stranger?"

I took a deep breath. "Charlotte doesn't know the way back and she's just a kid. It would eat away at me to know we left her. She has to be feeling the same pull we are to go home; the same level of desperation that's caused both you and I to nearly kill each other to get there. It'd be nothing for you to delay their trip in some way. Hire one of your cartel goons to kidnap her father for a day or two to prevent the Miller family from ever getting on the plane."

He tilted his head to one side. "You're asking *me* for a favor?"

"I am," I said, raising my chin. "You want to get rid of this deep underlying hatred? You want me to stop scowling at you? Agree to do this for me and maybe I'll see you as less of a monster."

Mere days after I'd given Juan Jr. the location and date of the sorority party, Cece's memory changed. If I gave Juan Josef Charlotte's location now, would her painting disappear before my eyes? Would the Miller family's names disappear from Terrence's passenger log? It was worth a shot...

Juan Josef removed his napkin from his lap, dabbing the corners of his mouth before he placed it on the table. "I do not mind the scowling so much, Alaina... However, I might be persuaded to *consider* interfering if you might consider returning to raise your children in this time. Mr. Gil says your sister has asked the same of you and offered even to come back with you should you agree."

I narrowed my eyes. "Mr *Gil*... He's been on board the whole time? Watching us?"

Juan grinned mischievously. "Aye. You did not see that coming, did you?"

"And it was him that put the knife in my bed the night of our wedding?"

At this, he chuckled. "Like I said before, my dear, I did very much enjoy playing the game with you... I thought it more fun when you were given clues as to my next move."

I shuddered as I remembered standing naked in the mirror with the feeling I was being watched. "Did your son know he was with us the whole time?"

"Juan?" He shook his head. "No. Mr. Gil was watching him too. See, I have known for years my boy planned to kill me, and I needed someone to warn me should he decide to follow through with those plans before we could get to George Bennet. This is why I could not wait for him to return to the ship. He would have killed me the moment he boarded and I intend to set history right before he does."

He poured another cup of tea for each of us. "I could agree to interfere with your Miller family, but I very much doubt I shall live long enough to make good on that promise. Juan will see to it that I am dead within days of that life being restored."

"You don't know that," I said. "My sister softens him. She's already told me she plans to talk him out of killing you. It's much harder to get away with murder in the 2000s than it is here. If he has plans to be with her, he can't very well risk being in prison when she wakes up to remember him. Can he?"

Leaning back in his seat, he propped one booted foot on the edge of the table while he sipped his tea. "He could if the two of them have plans to return to this century. From what Mr. Gil has told me, your sister is quite adamant about ensuring Gloria lives; willing to give up her life to live beside you in this time. After he kills me, Juan could flee to the coordinates and have a much shorter wait in this century. It's what I would do."

"You don't seem overly concerned with his plan to murder you. Seems so very unlike you when you've taken so many steps to avoid dying."

He shrugged. "What have I to live for once this is done? A wife that will never love me the way I love her; that may well disappear from existence once you take your daughter home? Sons that will remember the pain I caused them here? My own memories of murdering and torturing you and your friends? I'm tired of this life, my dear. I will welcome my death if he intends to deliver it once this is over."

I sighed. "And if he doesn't? Let's say he has a change of heart and decides not to kill you... What then?"

"Then," he said with a smile, "I shall see about kidnapping your Millers… if, by the time we reach Virginia, you have agreed to come back and live in this time."

Chapter Forty-One

Cecelia

The rain pattered softly against the canvas tent as I laid wrapped in Juan's sleeping arms. I loved the feel of his body behind mine and the warmth of his breath against the nape of my neck. I had never slept more peacefully—nor had he, I presumed, since the daylight was already lighting the tent and he hadn't stirred at all.

Comfortable as I was, and as much as I wanted to stay in his arms indefinitely, I'd needed to pee for close to an hour. Unable to hold it much longer, I surrendered to open my non-swollen eye and found Dario sitting up near the tent's flap staring at me.

He didn't look away when my gaze met his and that would've made me unsettled had he not resembled my family so much. As it was, looking at him was like looking at a masculine version of Alaina, and I smiled where I should've frowned.

"Morning," he whispered, glancing at his brother to ensure he remained undisturbed. "How is your eye?"

"Hurts," I said softly, very carefully pulling Juan's arm from me to sit up and drape the blankets back over his shoulders.

I looked down at his sleeping figure, admiring the way his hair had fallen across his brow and the way his lips were turned upward in a smile. I never could've imagined being this crazy about a person; just the sight of him took my breath away. Cyclops or not, I was going to marry this man.

Turning back to Dario, I placed a finger on the tender bruising beneath my eye. "Does it look as bad as it feels?"

"Aye," he said, wincing on my behalf. "It is worse than it was yesterday."

I sighed, reaching for my cloak and slippers. "I figured it would be. Yours isn't much better."

Dario had similar bruising beneath his eye and on his cheek from his fight with Juan, but where I was swollen and ridiculous looking, his bruising seemed only to enhance his good looks. I was slightly annoyed he didn't look like the monster I did.

"Where are you going in those shoes?" he asked, frowning at the fabric slippers.

"I need to… relieve myself."

He clicked his tongue as I prepared to slide my foot into the first. "You can't walk around out there in those things. Not with vipers everywhere. Here." He toed off his boots and pushed them toward me. "We should arrive at Hector's by nightfall where we can procure some suitable footwear for the rest of your trip. You can wear mine when you're walking around in the brush."

This was his apology. I could see it in his eyes. He felt guilty for what he'd done and needed me to accept this small olive branch he was holding out. Awful as what he'd put me through had been, he was Juan's little brother, and I needed to find a way to let go of his role in my nightmare.

That's all it was, after all. Just a nightmare. It hadn't touched me; hadn't affected me once I woke. It felt as far away as any other bad dream.

I took the boots and was grateful for them. If I'd had a chance to thoroughly prepare for a trek through the rainforest, I definitely would have put on boots before leaving the ship. Pit vipers could launch themselves off the ground and strike above the knee if they felt threatened. My little fabric slippers couldn't even protect me from a mosquito.

I slid my feet into the very warm leather, chuckling at the size and feeling like a child as I attempted to maneuver in them. "Thank you," I said as I crawled past him and out of the tent. Catching sight of Jim and Lilly, I halted in place on my knees in the dirt, letting the light morning drizzle dampen my hair as I fell into a daze watching their interaction.

There were a handful of occasions in my life where I'd witnessed two people sharing an intimate moment. It was always an uncomfortable feeling to be caught watching. But as I crawled outside, I was unable to look away where they stood just outside their tent, their lips locked in a kiss.

I'd arrived just after their wedding, but in my mind, I'd never imagined them as a romantic couple. They were always so argumentative with one another; always teasing or bickering. This was something far sweeter than I'd thought them capable of.

I couldn't help but stare at the way his fingers curled tightly into the fabric of the skirts near her hip as the moment grew a bit more heated. I couldn't look away when her own swept over the nape of his neck and she let out an audible sigh against his lips.

Was I imposing on a goodbye? I remembered the slave ship waiting in the bay to take any of us who wanted to go back to the storm. Was Lilly leaving?

Feeling like an intruder, I waited until their lips separated to grunt as I stood awkwardly in Dario's boots. "Oh!" I said with a smile, spreading my arms for balance. "Good morning."

"Mornin'," Jim responded, seemingly unbothered by the interruption as he pulled Lilly against him and rocked her in my direction. "Christ, darlin', ye' look like ten miles of bad road. That hurtin' ye' at all?"

I waved it off when Lilly turned to grimace at my eye. "I'm fine. It'll heal. Looks worse than it is."

I carefully took a step toward the brush in the oversized boots.

"Where ye' off to?"

I pointed to the bushes ahead and smiled. "I have to pee."

"I do too," Lilly said, untangling herself from Jim's arms. "I'll come with you."

"Yuns need me to check for snakes first?" Jim asked with a grin. "Wouldn't mind havin' me another snake breakfast this mornin.'"

"We'll be fine," I said, snagging a branch from a tree at the side of the trail. "I'm not afraid of snakes."

Lilly wrapped her arm in mine and assisted me through the mud, the boots threatening to remain behind with each step.

"I didn't mean to interrupt you," I whispered as we made our way around the bushes. I moved the long stick around the area to ensure there was nothing sleeping on the ground that might be inclined to bite.

"It's fine," Lilly said, watching the leaves for signs of a snake as I dragged the branch over them. "You weren't interrupting anything."

"So that wasn't a goodbye I just cut short?" I asked, letting her go to squat down and finally relieve the pressure in my bladder.

"No," she said, bunching her skirts to do the same. "I won't leave Lainey. Neither will Jimmy. We probably shouldn't be making out in the open where anyone can see us. It's just, with everything that's happened, we don't get many chances to have a normal moment as husband and wife, you know? We take what we can get. Sorry if I made you feel weird."

She groaned as she relieved herself, unabashed to do so and continue our conversation like it wasn't awkward enough to be peeing beside each other. "I have some makeup if you want it for your eye. It looks horrible."

I laughed. "I suppose a little makeup won't hurt. Thank you…" Staring ahead to avoid making eye contact while I urinated with a practical stranger, I caught sight of something far too dark blue to be found in nature. It was near where the cliff dropped off about a hundred yards in the distance.

"What is that?" I asked, realizing the answer for myself as I pointed at the gold and blue cloak I'd seen Maria wearing the day before. "Maria!"

Standing, I hoisted my shift and cloak up around my knees and ran toward her.

Lilly kept pace beside me; an easy feat since I was hindered by oversized footwear. "What the hell is she doing?"

My heartbeat quickened as I watched her spread her arms. She was going to jump…

"No no no," I breathed, running as fast as I could in Dario's ridiculous boots. I knew she'd been upset, but I hadn't realized it was bad enough for her to want to end her life.

"Maria!" I panted when I was close enough to be heard over the rain pattering on the canopy above us. "Maria! Please! Wait!"

She turned around when we came within a few feet of her, her eyes full of tears. Placing one hand out to instruct us to stop, she shook her head. "I cannot do this anymore, mi amiga. I am sorry."

"Just wait," I said calmly, inching closer so I might be able to grab her if she launched herself backward. "He's not worth this."

She raised her chin. "This isn't about *him*. This is about me. I will wake up someplace else when you are done here just like Anna will. I *need* to do this."

"Tell me why," I insisted, stepping just a little closer. "Why do you need to do this?"

Her eyes darted between the two of us before she laid both hands over her stomach, her expression softening as she looked down at her midsection. "Because if I don't do this, waking up someplace else is going to kill me for good."

I followed her gaze and noticed the very subtle swell in her abdomen against her shift beneath the cloak. She was pregnant, and I couldn't help the horror I felt for her at the realization.

Lilly gasped as she saw it too. "Oh… Maria, no…"

"Yes," she said, tears streaming down both cheeks when she looked back up at us. "It was an accident. A stupid stupid night when we both had too much to drink. What am I supposed to do if I don't jump? Eh? Just… keep going? Watch my belly get bigger and bigger? Hold a child in my arms that will disappear when we kill the Albrecht? I cannot do that! And I cannot do that to Kreese either!"

"How far along are you?" Lilly asked, her eyes glued to Maria's stomach.

"What do you care?" Maria spat. "It doesn't matter how far along I am. If Alaina does not go through that storm… if we have to wait until December to get to the Albrecht, I will hold a child in my arms that will be taken from me. If I jump now, I'll never know what it feels like to give birth to it; to hold it in my arms and fall in love with it; or to watch it grow to be nearly six months old before it's taken from me. If I jump, I'll wake somewhere else, and Kreese and I both would be able to live a normal life without feeling the loss of our child every day for all of eternity. He already has to live with the loss of his first. I cannot give him another to mourn."

"Why didn't you say anything?" I asked.

Her lip quivered. "I know you didn't think so, but I really thought everything would change the minute Alaina went through the storm. And when it did, this," she motioned to her belly, "would go away on its own. I thought no one would ever know it had been there but me. But now she's not going… and *I* have to make this go away."

My heart ached for her that she'd been willing to carry that burden alone—that she'd carried it alone for so long already—but it ached more that she might end her life in such a way.

"What if the pregnancy would've happened anyway?" I asked. "What if there's a chance it could be unaffected by the changes? How did it happen? When?"

She sniffled. "In Albuquerque a few months ago… I've already thought about all that. If Anna lives, she would've gone to Albuquerque, not us. It wouldn't happen the same."

I shook my head. "Alaina shouldn't have ended up on an airplane to Bora Bora with the changes we made to her past, but she did anyway. There's a chance this pregnancy might happen some other way. And none of us knows if what we do here will even bring Anna back to life. You might die for good. Come on, Maria, we'll figure this out some other way. Don't do this. Please."

She took a shaking breath. "I have to. If I don't, I will become worse than Juan Josef ever was. If I hold a child of my own in my arms, I will stop at nothing to prevent you from taking it from me.

I felt it move for the first time yesterday, and just that was enough to make me consider the most wicked things. I will not become the villain here. Let me jump."

"No," Lilly said, setting her feet. "This trip is the first time you and I have spent any real time together and we're finally becoming friends. You can't just kill yourself now, Maria. That would kill all of us... Even if you come back, we'll always have the memory of watching you jump off this cliff. I can't watch you do this."

"Then don't watch," she said. "Go back to camp and I'll do it alone."

"No!" Lilly insisted. "I'm not leaving you. Just... stay a while. Let's see how far we can get, okay? Maybe we'll find George Bennet sooner... You were willing to wait for the storm, right? Give us a few months to search for him. You can still kill yourself if we don't find him. Please? Nobody but us needs to know if you don't want them to. You said this happened a few months ago? How far along are you?"

Maria sniffled. "A little more than three months I think. I didn't realize until we'd already come through time otherwise I would've done something about it there... I thought I lost it after the Nikora came because I started to bleed, but it's still there."

"Three months," Lilly repeated. "Give me two more. Your belly won't be too big and we can keep it covered with these skirts and stays. No one else will know. Help us find George Bennet. If, after two months, we can't find him and you still want to kill yourself, I'll help you do it."

Maria glanced over her shoulder at the massive fall below her and swallowed. "You swear?"

Lilly smiled and extended her hand out toward her. "I swear. Now, please, *please* come down from there and let us hug you. This is all too much for one person to hold in for so long."

Maria looked behind her one more time, taking a very deep breath before she surrendered to take Lilly's hand.

Lilly, continuing on with her surprising level of tenderness that morning, pulled Maria tightly into her embrace, whispering as she rocked her and pet her hair, "I'm so sorry. You poor thing. I've been so awful to you. I'm so so sorry you carried this alone. I've got you now. It's gonna be alright."

Maria clung to her, burying her face against her shoulder as she let out the sob she'd been holding in.

"I've got you too," I said, moving my hand back and forth over her back. "I'm not a doctor, but… if worse comes to worse, there are things I can do to help… so you won't have to kill yourself to make it go away."

Maria turned her head in Lilly's arms, sniffling. "Like an abortion?"

I nodded. "There are certain herbs and plants you could eat. I don't think we'll find any here, but they will be available in Virginia. I can try to find it in the wild, but we'd have better luck searching for it at a brothel. If that's really what you wanted."

"Ay!" Jim hollered from the bushes where we'd been. "What in the Sam Hill are yuns doin' all the way out there?!"

"We'll be right there!" Lilly shouted back. "You stay over there and mind your business!"

"Mind my business?" he scoffed loudly, his words bouncing off the rocks of the cliffs behind us. "Woman, you *are* my Got damn business! You bring your little scrawny ass back over here where I can see ye' right now!"

Lilly held Maria tighter, turning her head to holler back, "Obviously, you can see me just fine from there, smart ass, otherwise you wouldn't be standing there yelling at me! We'll be there in a minute!"

She focused her attention on me, combing her fingers through Maria's dark hair. "Would that be dangerous to her?"

I shrugged. "No more dangerous than jumping off a cliff. The safest thing would be to put her on that slave ship so she could have a real doctor do it."

"Woman!" Jim continued. "You got to the count of three before I march in there and get ye'!"

Maria straightened, running both hands over her tear swollen eyes. "Kreese will not go back without Alaina. I don't want him to know about this and I can't very well ask him to get on that ship with no excuse as to why. What… eh… what kind of herb?"

"Queen Anne's lace," I said. "It's a weed and when the seeds are crushed and mixed with water, it can be both a contraceptive and an abortive. If we can get our hands on some, that's probably our best option. Unfortunately, the plant looks a lot like poison hemlock which is why I'd prefer to find it in a brothel than in the wild. I wouldn't trust myself to know the difference between the two. There are other more risky plants and fruits we can look for, but in Virginia, Queen Anne should be readily available."

"One!" Jim shouted.

Lilly rolled her eyes. "I swear to God, I might just let him storm out here so I can push him off a cliff!"

Maria's eyes danced between the two of us. "You won't say anything to anyone?"

"We won't," I assured her.

"Not even to Jim?" she asked, raising her brow at Lilly.

"Especially not Jim," Lilly said, smirking. "That man's a bigger gossip than I am."

Maria let out the breath she was holding. "Okay then. Two months… not a day more. I can barely take it as it is… you don't think that'll be too late to take the herb?"

"Two!" Jim yelled in the distance.

I pursed my lips. "It won't be easy at any point, but if you're certain that's what you want, I'd recommend you take it sooner than later if we can find it."

"Okay." She pulled her cloak tight and smoothed down her hair. "Do I look like a mess then?"

I chuckled, pointing at my eye. "Nobody's going to be looking at you thinking you're the messy one if you walk out of those bushes beside me."

She frowned as she inspected my eye. "Ay, it's so much worse today."

"I know," I said, looping my arm through hers. "I'll live."

Lilly looped hers through the other and we turned toward camp as Jim yelled out, "Three Got Dammit!"

"We're coming, Jimmy," Lilly snarled.

Maria laid her head against my shoulder as we all strolled back. "Oye, what the hell are you wearing on your feet?"

I laughed and kicked out a leg, flexing my foot to the left and right to model for her. "Dario's boots. You don't think they look good on me?"

Lilly chuckled. "Oh, they're gorgeous darling. Positively *gorgeous.*"

"You going to marry your Colombian in those boots today?" Maria asked.

Lilly bent forward to look past her at me. "You're getting *married* to him?"

I raised a shoulder. "We're gonna exchange vows in a hand-fasting thing at some point... once my eye looks a little more normal."

"You know," she drawled, "I can put some makeup on that eye and have you looking normal in no time."

"We'll see," I said, grinning at Jim where he stood fuming with his arms crossed as we made our way back into camp.

"Ye' scared the shit out of me wanderin' off like that. What the hell was yuns doin' out there?"

Lilly smiled sweetly. "We were trying to surprise you, dummy. Cece very nearly caught you a snake for breakfast. We would've had it too if you hadn't started yelling like a crazy person and scared it off."

"You lie," he said as I broke off to wrap my arms around Juan's waist. "There ain't no way in hell your little prissy ass was out there huntin' a snake."

"Good morning," Juan said, the dimple appearing in his cheek before he pressed his lips to my forehead. "Did you sleep well?"

"I did," I said resting my chin against the center of his chest to smile up at him. "Still a cyclops, though, *obviously.*"

He chuckled, tucking a strand of hair behind my ear. "An adorable one... Especially in those boots!"

I laughed. "Your brother gave them to me. I think it was his way of apologizing."

He made a noise in his throat to express his lingering displeasure with his brother. "We'll purchase you some that fit tonight. Hector has several businesses in town but he keeps additional stock at his primary place of business hidden away in the woods."

I looked over my shoulder at Maria where she and Lilly were rummaging through the pack on the mule. "What kind of businesses?"

"He's a clothing store, an ale house, and… well, a few less reputable places I dare not mention."

"A brothel?" I asked, my excitement uncontainable.

"Aye," he chuckled, "something like that. Why?"

I moved my fingers over his ribs. "You think he might have any sort of… contraceptive?"

I watched his throat move as he glanced around us for any spying ears. "I could ask… is this something you want for eh… yourself?"

I bit my lower lip. "Yes, Juan. For *us*. And for the other women. Wouldn't be fair to expect them to remain abstinent while we hogged it all, would it?"

His cheeks reddened. "If it is something you desire, I will enquire upon our arrival."

"Good." I beamed at him. "And, assuming you haven't changed your mind since last night, I was thinking we could say those vows later… when we stop again."

"Oh, is that what you were thinking?" He cupped my face in both hands and grinned. "I would be delighted—"

"What the hell happened to your face?" Jack growled, barreling across camp toward us as he caught sight of my black eye for the first time in the daylight.

I glanced at Tomás. "No one told you?"

"Told me what?" he snarled, narrowing his eyes at Juan. "Who did that to you?"

"Easy Jack," I said, positioning myself between them, one eye on the tent where Dario was climbing out with his sword drawn. "The man who did this is dead. Juan killed him. I'm not hurt, and that's all you need to know. There's no need to get all defensive. Everything's fine."

But, as I stood there watching his chest heave, I realized everything wasn't fine. This was the Jack I knew; reactionary and quick-tempered. He'd found out just hours before joining us that his wife and children were once again Juan Josef's captives, and yet… he'd been far too calm about it. It was too far out of his character to be so collected and therefore, I had to assume he was up to something.

"Can I talk to you in private?" I asked, motioning to the far side of camp.

Nodding, he led the way, stopping once we were out of earshot to spin back around. "What happened?" he whispered. "How'd you get that black eye? And how'd you manage to get off the ship?"

"We'll get into that in a second," I said in the same hushed tone. "First, why the hell are you so calm about all this?"

"I'm calm because I have to be." He crossed his arms over his chest. "Because panicking would do no good to any of you… and because I'm going to undo it all and get my family back unharmed. I know what I have to do and that makes me calm."

I shook my head. "What are you planning? What was in your letter?"

He presented his palms. "Nothing, Cece. She wrote you a letter similar to mine. You know, just like I do, they're as safe as we can hope for. So long as their dates don't change on the chart, we can know they're alright. There's nothing we can do now but go to Virginia and search for George Bennet."

He took a deep breath. "I saw the date change on my chart. I very nearly took off for that ship, but I got your message in time. This isn't easy, knowing my family is with him, but I know she's alright so long as their dates don't change."

I nodded. "Juan was telling the truth. You would've died if you'd stayed on board with her. I was so scared you'd go running off to that ship before I could warn you."

He laid a hand on my shoulder. "She made me promise I'd stay put, so I did. Now she's made me promise I'd take care of you, so… What happened to your eye?"

"A man named Adrián," I said, a chill running up my spine. "A *dead* man named Adrián." Taking a seat on a fallen log, I ran through the events of the day before, explaining how I'd gotten off the ship and how I'd ended up with my thumbs dug into Adrián's eyes.

He glanced at my left hand, sitting down on the tree beside me. "Are you really going to marry him?"

I spread my fingers wide as I looked down at the little silver Claddagh ring on my finger. "You think it's too soon?"

He chuckled. "No Cece, I don't. I loved your sister within hours and would've married her on the spot on that island if I'd have thought she'd agree to it then."

I laughed a little. "You know, I think this is the first time you and I have ever spoken without her. You're my brother-in-law and I don't know anything about you other than what she's told me."

"We've got a very long trip ahead of us," he laid his hand over mine and squeezed gently, "and since I've promised to take care of you, I imagine you'll know me plenty before it's over."

I twisted my lips to one side. "You really are too calm. It makes me nervous. You swear you're not planning something? If you are, you have to tell me. The last time you all planned—"

"I'm not planning anything, Cece." He squeezed my hand again before reaching into the pocket of his shirt and pulling out a piece of paper. "My wife is strong and she can handle Juan Josef. I've seen her do it before. I'm calm because she wants me to be calm. You can read the letter for yourself."

He stood and wandered back into camp while I sat reading her words over and over.

Folding the letter back up, I sat watching as Jack, Chris, and Juan disassembled camp.

What Jack didn't know was that I had watched every episode of *Fairview Nights* alongside my sister. I knew season four well.

Chapter Forty-Two

Alaina

I stood at the side of the ship looking out at the South American coastline far in the distance, both babies dozing against my chest in the sling.

Closing my eyes, I tilted my face up and let the sun tint my eyelids in its warm orange glow. With it, a memory—one of the new ones—washed over me. I let it come; welcomed it now that neither man was on board and I didn't need to feel guilty about whatever emotion might be tethered to it.

About six months after Evelyn died, Cece booked a trip to Cancun for the three of us. She'd planned out every single day for us; filling our days with hikes and adventures and our nights with good food and good music. She said it was to be the turning point for our lives; a getaway from all the reminders of our loss at home.

Chris and I had never been big planners. Our vacations were generally impulse buys and we'd take each day as it came, more often than not, choosing to lounge on a beach and exert as little energy as possible. When we'd arrived at our hotel and Cece gave us our full itineraries, both of us were a little less than enthused to have so many activities planned on our behalves.

It had been one of the best weeks of our lives, though, and I wasn't sure if I ever properly thanked Cece for it.

We snorkeled and hiked, spent an entire day visiting Mayan ruins, and explored all kinds of local cuisine. We swam with whale sharks and kayaked and danced at the Coco Bongo.

The devastation of losing our child became a faint whisper beneath all the exciting sounds Mexico had to offer.

Having the time of my life, I'd sprained my ankle like an idiot three-quarters of the way into the trip and made it worse by going out that night instead of staying off it.

To me, the risk had been well worth the reward. I wore a tight black dress and felt sexy for the first time in over a year. Chris and I made out like teenagers in the middle of a bumping and crowded dance floor. It was there, under the strobing blue and white lights, that we found each other again where we'd both been lost in sadness after Evelyn.

Everything about him was new. It was as if I hadn't seen him in six months. I'd stared at him in awe as the lights moved over his face, surprised by how handsome he was... Like I'd somehow forgotten what he looked like in my grief... forgotten the way he looked at me.

I remembered the complete weightlessness of letting go of all the thoughts that had been bombarding me to simply let myself be kissed by my husband.

I'd fallen in love with him all over again on that dance floor.

We'd barely made it back to our room when that little black dress was pushed up to my neck and we had our way with each other right up against the door... then again on the bed, much more gently.

The following morning, however, my ankle had turned purple and was so swollen, I could hardly stand to so much as slide it an inch across the bed.

"You mean we're going to have to call off the *zip lining* trip?" Chris had teased. "Not the *zip lining* trip!"

Both of us were far too exhausted to keep up with Cece's agenda, and my swollen ankle might've been the best thing to happen as far as the two of us were concerned that morning.

Instead of zip lining, we decided upon a day of leisure, and, unable to put weight on my ankle, he'd lifted me into his arms to carry me down to the beach.

I remembered pressing my cheek against his chest, inhaling the coconut scent of sunscreen in the hairs there, and feeling like the luckiest woman in the world.

I remembered thinking how very much I loved him and how lucky I was to have found a husband so good and so patient.

My depression hadn't been easy, but he'd never so much as complained even once.

He didn't complain even then as he carried me down the hall, into the elevator, and through the lobby, even though I knew he was hungover and sore from the night before.

"You guys," Cece said when she caught up to us before we could reach the sand. "I found the most perfect thing for both of you."

I groaned and buried my face in his chest. "Cece, can't we just lay around all day and sip margaritas?"

"Yes!" She was hopping from toe to toe with excitement. "But first, we're all going to do a temazcal ritual. It's this ancient Mayan cleansing ceremony where you get rid of all your bad energy. It's kind of like a sauna but with other stuff going on. You can stay off your ankle and then, afterwards, we can go lay around on the beach and be super relaxed without all our bad juju. It's only like an hour and I kind of already paid for it."

And so we'd found ourselves, fifteen minutes later, crammed inside a tiny dark stone hut with damp towels over our eyes and a sense of ridiculousness hovering in the air around us.

Beside me, I could feel Chris's laughter as the Shaman woman performing the ritual spoke words none of us could understand while she poured water over the rocks to create steam.

Within seconds, the space grew so hot, I thought I might faint.

"Why did I let you talk me into this again?" I groaned to Cece in the darkness.

"Shh," the Shaman reprimanded, moving around the tiny dark space with ease and adding even more hissing steam.

Chris's fingers found mine where they were rested on my knee, and I smiled to myself. I didn't need to see him to know how silly he found the whole situation… I could feel it radiating through his fingers.

Given the increasing temperature, I wasn't entirely sure I could keep breathing if I continued to laugh at him, so I swatted his hand away, attempting to clear my mind since it was supposed to be a healing ritual.

But all I could think of was him. I spent the entire time seeing his face lit up with blue and white strobe effect while he kissed me. I thought of the single spot on his shoulder marked with a freckle that I'd pressed my lips against so many times while we'd made love the night before. I thought of the way he'd looked at me; the way he'd *always* looked at me… as if I was a gift to him.

In the darkness, I saw that look over and over throughout various memories of our lives. If I was to heal during whatever ritual the Shaman was doing, I prayed I could be healed for him; a better wife for the husband he'd always been to me.

After a short eternity on the edge of fainting, I smelled mint and I could hear Chris chuckling—not his normal playful laugh, but one he used whenever he was uncomfortable.

My focus—whatever little there was of it—was entirely broken by that sound, and I once again found my lips turned upward, unable to take the ceremony seriously.

It was the Shaman, I learned quickly when she moved away from him to me. She scrubbed my body with a burlap material filled with minty herbs, and I too began to giggle uncomfortably.

It was an odd feeling to be scrubbed in the heat in such a way. While it was awkward at first, it slowly became more and more medicinal. The mint and the sensation against my skin blended with the dark dampness to give me this strange sense of openness… Like my pores were all open and all the bits of darkness inside me were seeping out of them to leave me a little lighter…

Perhaps Cece had been on to something.

With more concentrated effort, I relaxed my muscles and tried once more to clear my mind.

There, with minty steam pushing my consciousness over the edge, I found an image of him that shook me.

We'd been in the NICU with Evelyn. I stood on one side of the incubator while he stood on the other. He had one hand inside the little hole and Evelyn's tiny fingers were wrapped around his thumb. She was smaller than his hand, and seeing something so little struggle for life was hard. What I hadn't considered was how hard it had been on him—how much he actually loved her.

Inside that little hut, I could feel his pain and love as he felt that tiny squeeze around his thumb and prayed out loud for an end to her suffering.

I'd never prayed for an end. Every second I spent in that hospital, I'd prayed she would make it through.

But she had been suffering, and when she finally was set free of it, I couldn't understand how he could be so calm about the whole thing. Why wasn't he as devastated as I was? Why wasn't he sobbing the way I'd been? How on earth was he able to live on after what we'd both witnessed?

In that misty darkness, though, I felt his calm come over me. Our daughter wasn't suffering anymore. She was free. And that knowledge was freeing.

I wasn't sure if it had been seconds or hours that passed, but suddenly the Shaman was massaging my porous skin with aloe; an incredibly cool relief that brought my consciousness back to the hut; brought that image of him and our daughter back with it.

She then beat steadily on a drum as the aloe settled in and told us to let all of our emotions, bad energy, heaviness, and fears out with the steam once the doorway was uncovered.

And I did.

The light came streaming in and I felt transcendental, like all the world had melted off me and I was made new... Made to see the beautiful husband grinning beside me.

Evelyn's death was only devastating for me. It had been a relief for her... and for him... I would not make the end of her suffering my tragedy any longer.

When Chris carried me out of that little hut, I closed my eyes and let the sun beat down on my eyelids, finally letting go of every bit of lingering sadness so I could be the wife he deserved.

I opened my eyes and found myself back on the ship once more... a bit of that enlightenment remaining with me.

Yes, my plans to kill Juan Francisco had fallen apart, but... that was life. Nothing ever went as expected. Maybe my broken plans were the equivalent of my sprained ankle, and we'd all find ourselves better off because of them.

I took a deep breath and ran my palm over Zachary's head. He'd never fully dozed off and was looking up at me with those same clear blue eyes as his father.

"Don't you judge me little man," I whispered. "I'm allowed to miss him a little. It doesn't mean I love your father any less."

I rocked him gently, still buzzing with the emotions from the memory. I missed Chris; missed the way we'd loved each other that week. It made me sad we hadn't been that way on the original timeline... It made me wonder if I'd have done things differently.

I looked back down at Zachary where he was watching me with half his fist crammed in his mouth. "Nobody's that wonderful all the time. The man always had the right answer. I swear to God, I never saw him falter except the once. Ten years I was married to him, and I don't know if he was really that perfect or if he was just trying to be perfect for me."

I chuckled. "With your daddy, I know every little thing he's feeling just by looking at him. Although, so could everyone else who's ever spent ten minutes with him. He's got about four basic emotions he carries on his face at any given time... Hungry, happy, cranky, and... something you're too young to understand."

I stared out over the water at the horizon. "The other one though… I couldn't tell you if he was happy or sad or hungry or anything but perfect. He was always just whatever I needed him to be. And you'd think after ten years of being married to a person, you'd know how to read a person better than that, right?"

Scrunching his nose with a gummy half smile, Zachary's face turned shades of red as he let out a rather loud and long fart in response.

I laughed. "Tell me how you really feel, why don't you? Was that a fart or is there more?"

As if he understood me, he curled his fingers up beneath his nose and his little face turned pink again.

I sighed, turning toward the stairwell. "I *just* changed you. Are you doing it on purpose?"

"Hey," Bruce said as we nearly collided at the top step. He plugged his nose. "What are you feeding this kid?"

I laughed. "Just milk, although…" I motioned him to follow me down the stairs and he did. "I think they're just about ready to start some soft foods. Both of them are mouthing their hands and toys which I read is a sign they're ready to eat."

"Already?" He ran a hand over his face. "My God, it feels like just yesterday you were pregnant."

"I know."

"We're hugging the coast," he said, "and there's all kinds of fruit we could be grabbing up if we could stop for a day or two. We didn't get to restock in Panama, and this area is amazing for fruit supplies. We could gather guava, banana… ooh and babaco— which the babies would love. You think we could talk Juan Josef into stopping? The crew will need fruits and vegetables if he doesn't want us all to get scurvy before we can even make it to Virginia."

I smiled, turning down the second stairwell. "I highly doubt, given our history, he'd let either one of us off this ship to pick *fruit*… But I'll ask him."

He raised an eyebrow. "Jacob says he spent the night in your room. Did he… try anything?"

I shook my head. "No. He's being civil. Or at least as civil as Juan Josef is capable of being. He slept on the sofa."

We turned into the cabin and Bruce closed the door behind him before following me to the bed. "How are you holding up with everything?"

"I suppose I'm holding up alright." I pulled each baby from the sling and laid them on the blanket. "Don't really have a choice, do we?"

He trilled his lips at Zachary. "It's the right thing, you know… Pursuing George Bennet. It wouldn't be fair to Anna if we'd have gone through time and risked twenty years going by without her. We don't know if she'll remember all this—if she'll remember dying. Can you imagine what it might be like to spend twenty years dead and then wake up with knowledge of it? It's already been too long. I know the circumstances aren't ideal, but I really think it's the right way."

I watched as Zachary blew spit bubbles back at him. "What if she *does* remember death? You think she'd despise us for pulling her out of some kind of heaven?"

He shook his head, taking a seat beside the babies while I unpinned Zachary's poopy diaper. "Wonderful as heaven might be, she'd want to be with Liam more than she'd want to be there. He's all she ever talked about when we'd go up to that summit."

He watched as I struggled to keep both babies still while I reached beneath the bed for fresh linens. "I can help with this stuff, you know. Changing them or holding them or… whatever you need. You're not alone here."

I pursed my lips as I inspected him. Bruce and I had had moments of closeness on the island, but we'd since grown apart. It had never occurred to me to ask him for help. Of course he would willingly give it, and I was grateful he'd chosen to stay behind. "You think you'll settle down and start a family when all this is done?"

He shrugged. "It wouldn't be fair to plan out my future when we're not sure if Anna will get to have one. Once I know she's safe, I'll figure out what my life will look like. Besides," he grinned down at Cecelia, "I've got all kinds of family out here."

I smiled at that, holding my breath as I cleaned Zachary's bottom. My son was good at two things so far: blowing spit bubbles and pooping all the way up his back. I hoped introducing more foods into his diet would help with the latter.

"Why did you never make a move on Anna?" I asked. "You obviously love her. We all saw it. She wouldn't have turned you away, ya know."

He let out the breath of a laugh, taking Zachary's wailing fists before he could land one in the mess I was attempting to clean. "Yes, she would've. She was a nice enough woman that she might've indulged me for a bit; might've went along with it on that island if only to escape her own sense of loneliness, but she'd have eventually turned me away. I'm not the type of man she's looking for. I've always known that."

"Oh yeah?" I huffed. "Did you ever flat out ask her that or did you just assume?"

He raised a brow. "Honey, you saw what Dario looks like. That's the kind of man she wants. Not me. I didn't need to ask."

I rolled my eyes, removing the rest of Zachary's soiled clothing. "For someone who cares so much about the girl, you don't give her much credit. She was not the type of woman that cared about looks. She married a good looking guy and he beat her. A kind heart is what mattered to her, and you have it. She *wanted* you to make a move on that summit, but you never did."

"She told you that?"

I nodded. "Twice. Can you grab me the soap and pitcher?"

He hurried to retrieve both and blew out a breath on his return. "It was lonely on that island. It wasn't my heart she was after. And it doesn't matter now. All that matters is getting her back and trying to stay in one piece while we do it."

"You're right," I said, dampening a wash cloth. "You think Bud and the others are safe on that slave ship? You think they'll make it home?"

His lips turned upward. "You don't actually think they'll go to the storm, do you?"

I tilted my head to one side and frowned. "Why wouldn't I? That's the plan, isn't it?"

He chuckled, making a face at Zachary to keep him from throwing a fit about being washed. "Oh honey, you really are lost in your own world if you believe that. Bud won't leave Lilly, and Kyle would never leave you. Magna wouldn't desert these babies without knowing for certain they'd make it home safely. And, had you been watching closer, you'd know Terrence wouldn't willingly board a slave ship without some ulterior motive to take it over. That ship is severely short handed with the bulk of its crew working this one and it wouldn't be hard to take over command. You're looking toward the coast when you should be watching the waters behind us. I have no doubt we'll run into that ship again before this is over."

At that, a memory suddenly washed over me. Before Cece had gotten sick, she'd found a passage in one of the history books on a ship that had burst into flames near our destination.

"Bruce, do you happen to know the name of the slave ship?"

He nodded. "It was painted across the stern. *'Sofia Martina.'* Why?"

"Over by the chairs, there's a notebook of Cece's. Can you grab it? She was writing down all the places we should avoid and one of them was a ship that caught fire near our destination. I'd feel a whole lot better about sending them to that slave ship if I knew the name of the one that burnt."

"The ship you're thinking of is the São Salvador. She said it burst into flames off the coast of Charleston."

"Oh," I said, instantly relieved. "She told you that?"

His cheeks raised with his smile. "Your sister spent a lot of mornings down in the galley while Juan was sleeping. She shared a lot of her research with me and Jim."

I slid a fresh diaper under Zachary's bottom, my shoulders slumping. "I was hard on her the night before she left. Even worse to her after she left."

"She's not the type to hold a grudge," he assured me.

I pinned the diaper and pulled Zachary up against my hip to rock him. "I know, but I am. She had this beautiful little girl in her other life… Smart and funny and maybe I selfishly wanted to see that little girl again. I couldn't let it go; couldn't approve of her relationship with Juan, even after I saw how happy he made her—*even now*. I keep thinking about my niece and it breaks my heart that Cece might never know her."

He shook his head. "Cece has this theory about time. She called it a spirograph pattern. She thinks every little change here is creating a new loop that's still playing out somewhere. And that made sense to me. Maybe there's a loop out there where Cece does know her daughter. Maybe there's another one where Anna lives. Maybe there's one we've dodged where Jack dies. All these looping dimensions could be out there still moving. If you think about it like that, there's really nothing to be sad over. We're just hopping around dimensions, not really changing them. In this one, she loves Juan, but in another one, I'm sure she's raising a little genius right this instant."

I laughed, turning Cecelia over onto her stomach in the hopes she might poop before I left the room to launder their diapers. "It's a very pretty way to put it. Cece always has a pretty way of looking at things."

"You said you were worse to her after she left. How?"

I observed him for a minute, and not trusting Juan Josef not to have a spy in the walls, I drew an invisible J.F. on the mattress beside Cecelia.

"Oh." The way he said it felt like a knife through my heart, like he was disappointed I could've even considered it.

"It wouldn't have worked," I said, backpedaling. "Juan's always been two steps ahead of me and saw that plan coming even before I did. He won't be where we all thought he'd be. Hopefully, she'll never know what I almost did to her."

Bruce pursed his lips, looking down at his hands in his lap. "Alaina, when you panic, you make really bad decisions. You know that?"

"I know," I whispered.

He stood, massaging the back of his neck. "I'll go see what kind of food I can mash up for these babies. You want anything while I'm down there?"

"Bruce, I'm sorry."

He smiled. "I'm not mad at you. Not even a little. I understand you more than you think. I'm telling you to ask for help. You always try to take on too much. Maybe talk to your friends next time so we can let you know what's a good or a bad idea. And for the love of God, let me help you with these two. I'll get some water boiling for their laundry while I'm down in the galley. What else can I do? You want some coffee? You look exhausted."

My eyes burned. "Thank you. I'm so glad you're here."

He reached out to touch my cheek. "I wouldn't leave you alone with that man if my life depended on it, sweetheart."

Chapter Forty-Three

Cecelia

We moved slowly down the trail, an ever present thunderstorm drizzling down on us throughout the duration of the day.

Hot as it was, none of us minded the storm. While the soft ground slowed our pace, the rain kept us cool and prevented the mosquitoes from attacking us. During the brief breaks in the downpour, we were all stifling under the mosquito netting we had to cover ourselves with.

We were hoping to reach Hector's before nightfall, which, at our sluggish pace, meant we wouldn't be stopping.

I was anxious for a night spent out of the rain; excited to sleep in a dry, warm bed.

Hector's was a hideaway of sorts tucked into the jungle where men like Juan Josef often did secret dealings outside city limits. Juan and Dario knew the owner and were confident he would be happy to offer us a few of the rooms he rented upstairs.

Juan held the reins with one hand as the other moved back and forth over my waist in rhythm with the horse's steps.

My eyes remained on Jack's back where he rode in the lead alongside Dario.

I was livid; utterly disappointed with him, my sister, and, most of all myself.

My whole life, I'd considered A.J. my best friend. Yes, she'd always had a tendency to consider her own feelings over others, but I'd always been able to steer her right when she was wrong. We were the kinds of sisters that never held anything back—even the things that were hard to say and hear. We told each other everything, unafraid of whatever screaming match might ensue because of it. We'd always forgive each other quickly and move past it as better people.

This, however, was unforgivable.

She knew what Juan meant to me, but still she'd plotted to kill his ancestor anyway to serve herself.

What an idiot I was for giving her so much of my life.

When she lost Evelyn, I moved home and leased an apartment within walking distance of her house.

Where I would've remained at Ohio State to finish out my Ph.D., I instead decided to transfer to a local school and take night classes so I could be close to her during such a hard time.

She never noticed what I gave up... Never thanked me for it.

When her airplane went missing, I dropped everything. I sold my practice, moved into her house, and dedicated every minute of my life to finding her. I even went through time itself so I could bring her back.

Still, she'd never said thank you...

And now, after I'd completely uprooted my life for her, I finally had something of my own... Something that made me happier than I'd ever been... And she was willing to take that away from me.

I glared at Jack's back. I would not let them take this from me. I could sacrifice a lot for my sister, but I wouldn't sacrifice this.

The easiest way to stop them would be to expose them. Mad as I was, though, I wasn't like her—could never be like her. She might've been willing to steal my happiness, but I wasn't willing to take hers. Telling Juan would put Jack in danger. I'd need to stop them some other way.

I moved my hand over Juan's damp forearm against my midsection. "Since we won't be stopping, can we say our vows now? Is there some rule about where and how you say them?"

"Never done it before," he admitted, opening his palm for my fingers to slide into his, "but I don't imagine the location matters. I *would* prefer it, however, if I could see your face when we say them."

I tilted in his grip to smile up at him. "There. You can see me now. Say the words."

His lips turned up in a laugh. "You really wish to be wed on horseback? In the rain?"

"To you?" I said. "Absolutely. Do I just say '*I marry you*' out loud and slide the ring on your finger?"

His brows shot up high on his forehead. "You've a ring for me?"

Biting my lower lip, I nodded. "Of course I do. How else will other women know you belong to me?"

He laughed loudly then, his fingers tightening around mine. "This is why I love you, Cecelia. You never cease to surprise me."

"Well then we love each other for the same reasons. Can we say the words now? I don't want to wait any longer."

He playfully narrowed his eyes at me. "So impatient. You wouldn't prefer to wait until we arrive at Hector's?"

I scoffed. "*Me*? Married in a *tavern*? No. I prefer horseback in the rain."

He held me in place, the amusement slowly fading from his expression. "Cecelia, what is this about? What is your hurry all of a sudden?"

I frowned back up at him. "I need to have a reason to want to marry you as soon as possible? Have *you* changed your mind?"

"No," he said, pulling the reins and slowing us just enough to allow the others to pass by us. "But there's more to it than just your desire to be with me. You've got a look about you I've not seen before. I've been honest with you from the start. I expect the same from you. Tell me what this is about."

I sighed. I couldn't lie to him, but telling him the whole truth would make me no better than my sister.

"I don't trust them." I stole a glance ahead. "Jack's too calm about all this and it makes me nervous that he might do something stupid. You offered to marry me sooner than we'd planned as protection from your family. I'm offering to do the same for you. I want to marry you before we get to Hector's so my ring on your finger might make someone think twice about any retaliation they might be planning… So they'll see you, not as Juan Josef's son, but as my husband."

He smiled and shook his head. "You really think our marriage would prevent whatever brainless plans at retaliation Mr. Volmer might dream up? And do you really have so little faith in me that I cannot see what he has in mind? Do you believe me incapable of stopping him?"

"I don't want it to come to that; don't want it to be us versus them for the rest of our lives. I want him to see us for what we are together, see you as his family by marriage, and give up on his *brainless plans* of his own accord."

He raked his teeth over his lower lip, looking ahead at the group before those dark green eyes once again met mine. "Does the name Juan Francisco mean something to you?"

Slowly, I nodded.

His lip twitched. "And who is he?"

Of course they'd already figured out my sister's plans. It's what he and his father had done from the start. I should've known; should've had more faith in him that he'd see through their schemes. My heart and mind eased that I wouldn't need to keep secrets from him after all. "He's your father's ancestor—*your* ancestor. He's in Yorktown, very close to where we are headed."

"And is he the subject of whatever brainless plans you are afraid Jack might be forming?"

Again, I nodded. "I didn't want to tell you and start a war. I'd hoped we could change his mind." I furrowed my brow. "You never saw that binder… how do you know about Juan Francisco?"

He smiled sweetly. "Take the reins, *mi alma*."

I did, watching him reach into his boot in my peripherals. "My father wrote with implicit instructions to, one, try not to kill anyone, and two," he placed the letter in my hands, "to make sure, should we ever cross paths with Juan Francisco, to do everything in my power to see that he is protected. He's already sent correspondence ahead that would send Juan away from Yorktown."

I scanned the sharp cursive, past the parts where Juan Josef spoke about his peace deal with my sister to read, *'With that said, your brother and sister are not the only ones with an ancestor here. There is a man in Yorktown named Juan Francisco de la Bodega. He is my ancestor. If it were I in their place, I would be hunting him while you believed I was hunting George Bennet. They will never believe this war I've started will end with Bennet. For as long as I live, they will believe their daughter is in danger. As safe measure, I sent a letter along with a slaver before your arrival that would send Juan Francisco far away from Yorktown. If you wish to remain alive, you must do whatever you can to protect him should he not receive my message in time. You are smart, my dear boy, and I should never doubt your heart, but, as your father, I will always have a need to protect it. I cannot say with certainty this woman is deceiving you, but I will advise that you ask if she knows of the name. You will know if she is true by her answer.'*

Pulling the horse to a halt, he nuzzled my cheek and wound both arms around me. "I have never doubted you, Cecelia, but I was so very afraid to ask you that question and prove myself the fool."

I laughed, folding the paper back up and placing it in his hand. "Why do you think it took me so long to ask you about those passageways? I was afraid of the same thing. Will you do anything about this now? Will you fight Jack?"

"No, *mi paloma*," he said softly. "Not unless I must. We will do things your way for now. But I'll not say my part on a horse." He rose in the saddle, swinging a leg over and dismounting. "If you wish to do this now," he extended both hands out, "I'll see your face while we do it."

I blinked the rain from my eyes and looked ahead where the others were growing farther away. "Shouldn't we stay with the group?"

He kept his arms outstretched. "We will catch them. The rain is picking up and they'll slow. If you wish to wait, however—"

"No," I said, leaning over into his arms to let him help me off the horse. I grinned as he held me in place against his dampened chest, the rain flattening his dark hair against his temples to make him that much more beautiful.

"You're certain you wish to do this?" he asked.

I nodded, sliding my arms around his neck. "On one condition. You said hand-fasting lasts one year and then we have to have a ceremony otherwise we're no longer married. We will have the ceremony on the other side of time. My vows will still be good when I wake up with my memories. Yours will expire during the years you'll spend waiting. Promise me you will live a *full* life while you wait; that you won't turn down any opportunities at happiness. I expect you to become my husband again when I remember you, but I won't have a shell of the man you are now. Swear to me you'll live your life. I won't do this if you insist on spending that time in misery."

He lowered me to my feet. "I will live, *mi alma*. I swear it."

I pulled Chris's ring from my pocket, opening my palm to present it to him. "This will disappear when we change things." I held my left hand up beside it, admiring the silver Claddagh ring. "So will this…"

He nodded. "We will get them back when we are wed again."

The rain and wind picked up just as he'd predicted, soaking both of us even through the cloaks we both wore.

"How… eh… how does it work?" I asked awkwardly, looking around us. "Should we be kneeling or standing?"

"I suppose we should kneel… that seems right." He looked down at the damp ground beneath our feet and frowned. "…or stand. Which… whichever you prefer."

"Okay," I said a little breathlessly, taking the lead and lowering down to one knee. "Are you ready?"

"Christ," he laughed as he did the same, balancing his forearm on his bent leg, "I haven't shaken like this since I was a boy."

I saw the tremble in his hands as he lowered the other leg so he was balanced on his shins.

"Are you scared?" I asked, feeling the cool dampness soak my skirts where my knees rested in them.

"No, *mi alma*, I'm not scared," he said with shivering breath. "I am happy, and I think I might just be overwhelmed by it."

"Oh." I smiled like an idiot because I was shaking just as fiercely with the same overpowering sense of emotion. "Should… should I go first then?"

"Please," he exhaled in a nervous laugh.

"Okay," I took a deep breath, "Umm… give me your hands."

He obliged and I squeezed his quivering palms in mine as I tried to remember any piece of a traditional wedding vow. "I, Cecelia—"

I frowned. "I think I'm supposed to put the ring on your finger first."

He laughed that deep throaty roar of his which settled my nerves enough to slide Chris's ring partway onto his finger where it became too tight to pass the knuckle.

"I'll have it widened before morning," he said, putting an end to the panic attack that might've ensued as a result.

Straightening, I took another deep breath, and as I met his eyes, now sparkling against the gray of the storm, the words came easy. "I, Cecelia Ruth McCreary, take you, Juan Josef Perez Hernandez to be my husband. I give you my whole heart and promise to never offer it to any other. From this day till my last day, I will love you."

The dimple appeared in his cheek. "Ruth?"

"My grandmother's name," I whispered. "I… didn't know the actual words so…"

"Those were perfect… Ruth."

I shook his hands. "Stop stalling and get on with it before they realize we're gone and come back for us! I'd like to kiss you at some point."

He took my left hand in his. Touching the ring already on my finger, he recited his vows purposefully slower than he would've otherwise. "I, Juan Josef Perez Hernandez, take thee, Cecelia *Ruth* McCreary to be my wife, to have and to hold from this day forward, till death us do part."

The two of us knelt in silence then, each staring starry-eyed at the other, grinning like the fools we might've been.

"You, eh…" He blushed. "I think that's it. You can kiss me now… if… eh… if you want to."

And I did.

I kissed him with a fervor that had been building inside me for thirty-four years. Every fairy tale I'd ever read and dreamt of, every romantic movie I'd ever watched and envied, every jealous dinner spent with Chris and Alaina—all of it spilled out of me in a moment no amount of my imagination could've anticipated.

I was his wife…

And some part of me felt it; felt the change of title—the permanence of this moment… Like I'd been waiting my whole life for the rain to pick up.

I sat back on my heels, heedless of the stains to my skirts, and held his face in my hands.

"What?" he asked, neither of us able to fully stop smiling.

I shook my head. "Just want to look at you for a minute… Memorize you in this exact spot… I think this will be my new favorite memory, and I don't want to mess it up in my head."

He chuckled, sliding his thumb over my cheek. "Aye. *Podría mirar a mi bella esposa durante días.*"

I leaned into his touch. "And *I* could look at my *beautiful husband* just as long."

His entire face lit up then. "You speak Spanish?"

"Sí." I grinned.

"Why didn't you tell me before?"

I slid my finger along the bridge of his nose. "Couldn't give away *all* my surprises at once."

"You are too perfect to be married in the mud," he said, wincing as he looked down at my white skirts against the damp ground. "I'll give you better, I swear."

"I happen to like the mud," I assured him, sinking a hand down into it as proof and smearing a glob of its darkness over his cheek.

His eyes narrowed playfully as he dragged a finger along the stain and inspected it. "In some cultures this is considered an act of war, you know."

"Is it?" I teased, scooping up another handful and raising an eyebrow. "What's the matter? Don't like to get dirty?"

He bit his lower lip, fire burning in his eyes as he lowered both hands into the mud on each side of our tangled knees. "I have no desire to arrive at Hector's with you covered in sludge, *mi alma*. But if you do that again—"

Hiding a smile, I laid my clay soaked palm on his other cheek. "You'll what?"

I screamed with delight as he raised over me and took my face in his hands, the cool damp grime wetting my cheeks as he covered my mouth with his. With his silt covered fingers sliding into my hair and his other arm snaking round my back, I hummed against his lips. I didn't care if every inch of me was caked with soil before this moment was over.

"Ay!" Jim called, forcing us to freeze in place. "What the hell are yuns doin? Everybody's stopped up here waitin' for yas."

I laughed out loud. "We're coming!"

"Hey," Juan whispered, taking my hands before I could stand. "What I said yesterday... I meant that. I will never do anything against your will. And after what happened at that house, I've no assumptions about what comes next. I am perfectly content to simply call you my wife. Nothing else needs to happen until you are ready."

I smiled. "And I meant what *I* said yesterday. I'm not broken, Joseph, and I *look forward* to what comes next."

Chapter Forty-Four

Cecelia

Tucked away on a separate path that was nearly hidden from the trail, the tavern was a large brick structure with a wrap around wooden porch. Warm orange light glowed from its two stories of windows, an upbeat piano drifting from the ones on the first floor where they were pushed open. The only thing differentiating it from a colonial house was a sign over the door that simply said, "Hector's."

As we rode up, a stable hand greeted Juan and Dario by name, taking the horses off for the night.

Under the cover of the porch, Juan turned to our group and spoke in a hushed voice. "Before we go in… You two," he addressed Chris and Maria, "you will remain quiet. We will use the duchess's story but we'll leave it to Hector's imagination as to which duchess we escort and who among you might be royalty. Understand?"

Chris nodded and offered his hand to Maria. She stood closer to him but didn't take it.

"Let me and my brother do the talking inside," Juan continued. "Got it?"

The group collectively nodded their heads, and on that note, Juan took a deep breath, wrapped my arm in his, and we headed inside.

The atmosphere was like looking at an old painting. Several men in black breast coats and white stockings lounged casually around a wooden table with their drinks while an older woman played a joyful tune on a harpsichord in the corner. Lush wood paneling lined the space, decorated with rich oil portraits of what I assumed were brilliant men, the entire room alight with lanterns hung in evenly distributed sconces throughout.

It was only when the faces of several men wearing powdered wigs turned in our direction that I became aware of my mud covered skirts and bruised face.

"Juan Josef!" the oldest of the men called, placing his glass of amber colored liquor on the table and adjusting his wig before he hurried over to join us.

"I was not expecting you this night!" He tried not to be obvious as he examined our muddied clothing and bruised faces. "This is a most pleasant surprise!"

"Hector," Juan bowed, "this is my wife, Cecelia, and some of her family. We've just wed this afternoon and I was hoping you might have a few rooms to shelter us from the storm."

Hector's eyes widened and he quickly took my hand and pressed it to his withered lips. "Pleased to meet you, madam!" He turned toward the rest of our rain-drenched crew. "And your family! I am honored to be of service. How many rooms might you be in need of?"

"We've no wish to put out any of your guests," Juan said, glancing at the table of men as they gradually fell back into conversation. "How many rooms have you available?"

Hector leaned in, tilting his head to the table behind him. "Frenchmen, all of them." He snarled as if the word tasted foul in his mouth. "I can offer you four and put a few of them in the stables once they've drank themselves stupid."

Dario bowed his head, his eyes dancing to a younger man with green eyes who sat at the table mulling over a paper. "You are too gracious, Hector." He turned toward Jack. "You take the fourth room. Gabriel, Tomás, and I can sleep in the stables as well."

"Carlota!" Hector called, putting an abrupt end to the happy music as the old pudgy woman turned in her bench. "Ready four rooms for our new guests," he grinned at my muddied dress, "and tell Pedro to take the water we'd been preparing for Mr. Moreau and his guests to the tubs in their quarters instead." He spun back to us. "Hang your garments outside the door and Carlota will have your attire ready by morning."

"Gracias, Hector." Juan bowed. "You really are too kind. We're in need of some additional supplies if you have them. My wife requires a pair of riding boots, we'll be in need of some more water, and there is one other thing I might ask of you… in private."

Hector, apparently a man who enjoyed a good bit of drama in his old age, all but hopped with excitement. "Of course, my friend. Come, all of you, I shall pour us a glass from my private stock to celebrate this most happy day while Carlota readies your sleeping arrangements!"

Juan took my hand and we followed Hector through a white door to a private study lined with books, a bar cart, and several leather sofas positioned in a circle.

"How is your father?" Hector asked, making his way to the bar cart and wiggling his fingers over the selection.

Juan stood tall with a palm rested on the small of my back. "My father is well. He remains on the ship."

"I've never understood why that man won't give his ship a proper name," Hector complained. "It's bad luck to have a ship with no name. I have told him this many times."

It was odd to hear someone talk about Juan Josef in such a normal and affectionate tone. I'd only ever heard the name spoken with disdain. It was refreshing to feel like the man my sister would be stuck with was human after all.

We all waited patiently as Hector proceeded to pour out glasses of scotch for everyone and distributed them with steady hands, raising his own in my direction. "¡Salud!"

I raised my glass and we all responded, "¡Salud!"

I took a sip, reminded of the very good scotch I'd shared with Juan the night he'd asked me to marry him. I wasn't sure I would ever sip it and not taste a memory of him.

"Now," Hector said, exhaling in a hiss as his scotch made its way down his throat. "If you leave your slippers near your door, I'll have Carlota replace them with a proper set of boots. What else can I do for you?"

"Well," Juan motioned for the others to sit and they all made their way to various sofas before he leaned in. "We're to be at sea for some time, and…" he glanced shyly at me. "We do not wish to have a child until we know we shall be settled on land."

Hector held up a hand. "Say no more, dear friend, I understand completely. Especially after what happened with…" He peered at me and let this trail off. Lowering his voice to a whisper, he said, "I've a new batch of elixir made with Queen Anne's Lace in the store room… but…"

Favoring one leg in a slight limp, he crossed the room to one of the bookshelves. With a wink in my direction, he pulled out a drawer masqueraded as a stack of books. Small glass bottles clanked against each other as he pilfered through its contents.

"Ah!" He pulled out a little blue vile and crossed back to place it in my palm. "Here you are, my dear. Drink this now and you'll not conceive tonight." He turned back to Juan. "As I said before, I've more in the store room if you'd like to take some along with you?"

"Yes please," I blurted.

Hector hid a smile and nudged Juan with his shoulder. "¡Que suerte!"

Lucky indeed… I was anxious to share it with Maria. She held her chin high where she sat quietly, but I knew the pregnancy was weighing heavily on her mind.

Dario, who'd been the only one not to take a spot on the sofas, straightened, motioning toward the door with his glass. "Was that Pierre Beaumarchais I saw out there?"

"Indeed," Hector said, spinning round to face him. "There's war coming in the colonies, as I'm sure you've all heard by now. I'm host to all sorts of rebel supporters these days."

Dario frowned at the door. "*Pierre Beaumarchais* is a rebel supporter?"

"Oh yes," Hector said, eyes alight with mischief. "He's personally invested a small fortune in the rebel cause. I wonder if the poor man has any money left at all!"

There was something in Dario's feet that gave him away. He was anxious to join the other men; or, more specifically, to join *Pierre,* who I presumed was the young man with green eyes.

As he made an excuse to leave the room with Tomás and Gabriel in order to inquire about the rebel status, I uncorked my elixir and drank it, wincing at the licorice-bark flavor. Juan placed his palm against the small of my back; a small gesture of support, and one I was grateful for as Hector's eyes swept over me with the smallest hint of judgment.

"What brings you to Panama?" Hector asked, waving a hand in invitation to one of the empty sofas, "aside, of course, from marrying this lovely young woman?"

"We're escorting a duchess across the isthmus," Juan said, making no move to take the offered seat.

"A duchess?!" Hector sank into a chair across from Jim and Lilly, eyes wide over the rim of his glass as he looked at each member of our group with suspicion. "Who?!"

Juan smiled. "One who is paying a great deal of money to keep both her identity and the trip itself secret. We are old friends, Hector, but you are the last soul I'd reveal her secrets to. The whole of Spain would know before I even left Panama."

Hector chuckled and sipped his scotch, explaining to Izzy, "I've little else to do with my time, dear, but converse since I became old, decrepit, and left to rot in this place." He raised his brows. "And I suppose the last thing any of you young ones wish to do is converse with an old man after being stuck out in that storm!" With a grunt, he stood. "My apologies. Come, I'll show you to your rooms. I'm certain your baths will be drawn by now."

Juan pulled a small leather purse from his breast pocket and laid it with a heavy *'clank'* on the bar cart. "For your troubles and the supplies. We'll be off before sunrise."

Hector shooed us toward the main room, falling into step at our backs after he'd collected the bottle of scotch. "I'll have the supplies loaded on your horse tonight. And I'll see to it that your clothing is ready before I retire. Come."

He led us upstairs, and after showing the others to their quarters by opening each door for them, he led Juan and I last to a large room not unlike the cabin on the ship. A velvet curtained fourposter bed sat against one wall with a bay window just beyond it overlooking the jungle. A copper tub sat steaming beneath the window, fogging the center panel of glass, toiletries set out for us on the windowsill. Built into the wall opposite the bed was a large stone fireplace with a white mantle. I doubted it ever got used with the heat, but it was decorated with fresh white Peristeria orchids that gave the room a sweet honeyed scent.

Near the door was a set of wingback chairs and a coffee table, a tea set placed between them. Elegant rugs made the room cozy, and candlelight from sconces surrounding us lit the room in a warm orange glow.

It was the perfect place for our wedding night.

Hector placed the bottle of scotch on the tea tray. "If you need anything at all, do not hesitate to ask." He winked once more at me. "Buenas noches, young ones."

And then he was gone.

And Juan's eyes darkened with desire as they scanned the length of me.

We'd already been intimate, but it had been touch and taste without really seeing each other. My heart leapt into my throat as he closed the gap between us and I imagined how it would feel to have his eyes on me; to watch him move over me...

"You," he breathed against my lips, "are absolutely covered in mud, *mi alma*."

I laughed. "So are you. Poor Hector was trying so hard not to stare at the sludge on your cheeks."

"Oh, aye," he said softly. "He was far too preoccupied examining the clay caked in your hair."

I reached up and felt, for the first time, the dried mud which had wound large sections of my hair into dreadlocks. "You really got in there with it, didn't you?"

His fingers slid down my arms. "I warned you I would. Shall we have a bath, Mrs. Perez?"

I draped my arms around his neck. "Mmm. Only if we make it a fast one, *Mr. Perez.*"

He pressed his forehead against mine and smiled. "Oh no, my lovely wife, nothing will be made *fast* this evening."

As proof, he kissed me, slow and deep, his hands exploring my spine as he backed me up toward the tub with his body pressed against mine.

I sighed heavily when he turned me to face the window, watching our blurry reflections in between the flashes of lightning.

"That night you came to me on the deck," he said, moving his nose along the length of my neck, "you asked me if I knew you... I wanted to tell you then that I did; wanted to tell you I'd recognized you the moment I saw you as the woman I would one day marry. I've never wanted anyone more than I wanted you. It confounded me that I'd never so much as heard your voice and could know with such certainty I'd found my mate."

I hummed with my content, leaning back against him. "I felt the same... It wasn't just you that was familiar... It was the way I felt about you... Like I'd been waiting my whole life to find you. I was so nervous to approach you that night. I was sure I'd lost my mind and I was terrified you'd think the same and turn me away."

He tugged the laces on my stays. "I tried to turn you away. But you had me overcome when you informed me you had no intention to *maul* me."

I chuckled, reaching back to curl my fingers in his hair. "I'm so glad I decided to maul you after all."

"Cecelia, I—"

Someone cleared their throat loudly and both of us spun around in a hurry.

Dario stood between the wingback chairs with a box in his hands, staring down at his feet. "My apologies," he coughed out. "I've something for you." He held out the box.

"It couldn't wait?" Juan growled, moving toward him.

"It's not for *you*," he snapped, defensively pulling the package back to the side of him. "It's for her."

"For me?" I smiled, joining Juan in front of him. "What is it?"

He presented the black velvet box once more in my direction. "All the spectacles Hector had in his inventory. I'd... well, I'd hoped at least one might suit your vision. Consider it a wedding present."

My throat warmed at the gesture and I took a step forward to receive it. "Thank you. That's very sweet of you, Dario."

He bowed his head and spun back toward the door.

"Wait!" I called, clutching the box of glasses to my chest. "The man downstairs, Pierre. You know him?"

His spine stiffened as he slowly turned back to face us. "A little. Why?"

I could feel Juan's curiosity behind me as I took a step closer. "He's a rebel supporter, right? He's spent time in the colonies?"

"Aye." He frowned. "This concerns you? The rebels?"

I shook my head. "I'm looking for an artist named John Singleton Copley. He lives in the colonies. Could you ask Pierre if he or any of his friends know where I might find him?"

"Is this Copley fellow a relative to one of us?" he asked, his auburn brow raised.

"No," I assured him. "He painted a portrait of two people we believe were also on that airplane. If there's time, I'd like to try to find them, give them the knowledge we have about the way back."

Slowly, Dario nodded and turned back around. "I'll enquire. Goodnight to you both." He paused when he reached the doorway, grinning at his brother. "I'd advise you lock the door if you've no wish of being interrupted again, brother."

Juan stared at the doorway, a troubled expression pulling his features downward.

I raised on my toes and pressed a kiss to his cheek. "He's your little brother and you can't stay mad at him forever. He's trying to make things right. Go make peace with him. It's obviously bothering you and I can't have you bothered on our wedding night. I'll be here when you're done." I glanced at the still steaming tub. "Nice and clean…"

He pursed his lips, not looking away from the door. "This, I *will* make fast."

I'd washed my hair twice and scrubbed my skin until it hurt. Feeling clean for the first time in over a month, I stepped out of the tub and wrapped the dressing gown loosely around my body.

With no signs of Juan's return, I dabbed a small bit of Lilly's foundation on my eye to cover the bruising, relieved the swelling had gone down so it appeared almost normal beneath the makeup. I then sat on the bed with the box of glasses in my lap, trying each circular pair on until I found a close match.

I scooted to the edge of the bed, focusing on the two wingback chairs near the door. Placing the glasses on, the two seemingly plain chairs transformed and I could make out the gold damask pattern of the fabric I hadn't noticed even at close range.

I giggled with excitement, taking in the fine details of the room with eyes that could actually appreciate it. I noticed the little violet splash of color inside the Peristeria orchids on the mantle, saw the matching orchid pattern in the hand tied rug beneath my feet, and admired the gold pattern overhead in the crown molding.

Hector certainly had expensive taste.

The prescription wasn't as strong as my normal and the bridge was made wide so the glasses sat halfway down nose, but I didn't mind… It was a wonderful thing to have my eyesight back.

Perhaps the most glorious sight of all, however, was that of Juan when he reentered the room. His hair was wet, falling over his face in wavy dark ringlets, and he'd changed out of his uniform into a long hunter green and gold dressing gown.

My cheeks burned with the size of my smile as I watched him lock the door and stroll casually toward the bed.

"Fancy digs," I teased. "I told you to go make peace with your brother, not *bathe* with the man."

He chuckled, propping one arm against the bedpost to look down at me, his eyes ablaze with lantern light. "I made what peace could be made and decided to wash downstairs. I could not share a tub with you, *mi alma*, and expect either one of us to get clean."

My eyes moved to the gold band glistening on his finger. "You resized it?"

He nodded. "Hector had the tools."

Biting his lower lip, he inspected the nearly sheer material I was wrapped in. "Fancy robe."

"Isn't it?" I raised my arm, showing off the translucent cream fabric and lace sleeves. "Carlota left it by the tub."

He extended a hand to me. "I would very much like to admire you standing in it."

There was command in his tone that set my core on fire. I wanted to bend to his will; to give whatever he demanded; to be entirely his to dictate for the rest of the evening as he would be mine.

I took his hand and stood at the foot of the bed, shaking with excitement.

When he stepped backward, I lowered my arms, allowing him the full presentation.

My breath trembled as his eyes moved slowly downward. I knew what he could see through the fabric and his evident desire to have it excited me. Just having his eyes on me was enough to create a fire between my legs.

Unabashed in front of him, I pulled the tie keeping the robe together and let it fall open. I watched his throat move; watched his tongue subtly wet his lips as I shrugged the soft fabric off my shoulders and let it pool on the floor around my ankles.

No man's gaze had ever been so welcome on my skin.

"Now you," I said with the same hint of command he'd had with me.

The dimple appeared in his cheek as he moved his fingers to the buttons of his robe, his eyes never deviating from my body. Just as I had, he let the fabric fall to the floor, exposing a loose collared shirt that sat just above his knees.

He took a deep breath and pulled it up over his head, tossing it lazily to the side to watch my reaction to him.

I let my eyes take their time moving down him, that much more grateful for the glasses as I drank in the deep cut lines of his chest and abdomen, the tattoo that painted his right side, the scars that lined his left, and the small bits of dark hair that crept down his naval to the imposing length of his arousal.

I'd felt him before, but seeing him… I was breathless.

I returned my gaze to his and smiled. "You're stunning."

He slowly shook his head. "God help me, Cecelia. Looking at you now… I don't know if I can leave you. Not for all the righteousness in the world. I am torn between taking you in my arms and running out of this room here and now to destroy every person in this world that might threaten to part us."

I extended my hands out in front of me, beckoning him to come closer.

He obliged, taking a single step so my palms landed on his chest, then another so my hands could glide up around his neck, then one more so I felt his entirety pressed against me.

He was trembling, his breath shaky against my forehead where he removed my new glasses to gaze upon my face.

I swept my fingers down his jaw and let my thumb trace his lower lip. "You're mine now, Joseph," I whispered. "And I won't let anyone part us if we don't want them to."

I held his face between my palms, smiling as I took in every line and angle of his face.

Moments like this, when he was so young, might not last much longer. I just wanted to stare… and he let me, his expression softening as he did the same.

This was an image I'd hold onto forever… My young husband in my hands… A husband I would show how to love; that would teach me to love in return.

His fingertips brushed softly down my shoulders and arms, circling back to float up my spine, turning my insides to ice and fire all at once. Tremors swept from my toes to the very top of my head and back as he circled again.

I did the same, moving the tips of my fingers over his chest, along his ribs, and around his waist, enjoying the soft feel of his bottom and the shiver that ran through him in response.

And there was only one word that came to mind: home.

Home for me had always been wherever my family was. It was never a house or a town or some piece of furniture that gave the word meaning. It was the people. And staring up into my husband's eyes, I found the only family I needed… He was home in a way no person or place had ever been home to me before. Nothing would ever be more mine than him.

When he laid his lips on my brow, I felt my very soul escape on my exhale, drifting up somewhere over our heads to watch him move his kisses gently across my face.

He kissed the corner of my mouth, the edge of my jaw, and the place just beneath it that made my hair stand on end. His lips were delicate and featherlight as they made a trail along my collarbone to my shoulder and back, a thousand words seeping into my skin with each tender kiss.

Much as the feel of him threatened to pull my eyelids closed, I fought to keep them open, needing to watch him as he moved lower. My body prickled and chilled as he pressed his nose against my stomach and dragged it up to my sternum, every one of his exhales pulling me deeper into a trance.

I rested my palms on his shoulders and let him explore, his fingers splayed wide against my sides to gently move my body on his way back down so he could run his nose and lips over my breast.

My eyes did close then and I made fists in his damp hair as he took each one gently.

Then his mouth was on mine, no longer patient or delicate, but hungry and urgent. He made a thick sound in his throat, pulling my body against his.

That sound blended with the feel of his arousal against me awakened something just as untamed inside me. I was not the timid girl I'd been when I stepped on the deck. I was his wife, and he was my husband.

I moved my mouth down his throat, anxious to have him as unleashed as I felt.

He let out another similar groan, this one deeper than the last, as I dragged my lips and tongue over his neck with the same haste, his hands seeming like they were everywhere all at once… In my hair, on my arms, breasts, thighs, and spine…

The backs of my legs met the edge of the bed and he folded himself over me when I collapsed onto it.

He took my mouth once more as I backed up onto the mattress beneath him, our lips bruising each other's unapologetically with the desire for more.

Every breath of mine was audible, and every breath of his against my skin dragged me further and further away from reality.

My body seized as he ran his thumb slowly over my center, shifting from ice to fire and back as I reached for him and guided him to me.

And with his fingers in my hair, he pulled me back to press his forehead against mine, our breath blending between us to become one collective inhale as he pushed inside. There was a second of pain—a welcome tear as my body was transformed to fit him exclusively—and then, on our exhale, I was entirely home.

Far far away from the rest of the world, I clung to him and he to me as our hips developed a slow, gentle rhythm of their own.

This was home…

This sweet almond sent and caramel scotch kisses…

This pulse inside me and breath against my cheek…

This warm skin against mine…

Maybe none of us knew how to love… I certainly hadn't until this moment with his eyes on mine as he moved inside me. And if this wasn't love, I couldn't wait to be proved wrong.

We were whatever our bodies wanted us to be; gentle at times, desperate at others; hands and mouths and hips exploring and taking as they pleased.

Wave after wave rose to release and recapture me, pushing me up and up and up its swell then breaking over me to nearly drown me before catching me once more in its tide.

This was the happiest moment of my life, and unable to stop the swell of emotion, I let my tears fall as I rolled over onto him and gave the last of myself over.

My skin tightened as I felt him quake with restraint, his arm around my waist tensing as he fought to both remain in his delirium and be freed from it at the same time.

He sat up, guiding my hips with his own as he pulled my lips to his, our bodies a shuddering vise around each other. The hum of his release shook my insides, and I tightened my arms around him until there was nothing left of him either.

Home.

This feel of his surrender inside me…

This absolute vulnerability of his muscles turning slack beneath my arms and inside my body…

This sound of his heaving breath in my hair and his whisper against my ear.

"I love you," he said, and I knew no other place would ever be my home again.

"I love you," I said in return, and I realized that I, too, would destroy anyone that threatened to take this from me.

Chapter Forty-Five

Chris

His head was pounding when he groggily made his way to the stables that morning.

While he'd started to grow accustomed to Maria's ongoing silent treatment, she'd been particularly cold to him when they'd settled into their room the night before. Unwilling to dance around her mood after such a long journey, he'd decided to give her space and joined the men downstairs for several more glasses of Scotch than he'd intended.

The instant the men had heard his voice, they'd taken him for a colonial, and, upon the arrival of Dario, assumed he was an ally, discussing the rebellion openly.

Pierre Beaumarchais, he learned, was a devout supporter of the rebels and was there in secret to purchase arms from the Spanish that would then be shipped out of Portobelo to the north. Finished with his business in Panama, Pierre volunteered to accompany their group across the isthmus.

The night had rounded out with a game of cards and it was late before Chris wandered up to bed.

He was certain he hadn't slept more than an hour before Juan Jr. had knocked on the door to inform them they were preparing the horses. Maria hadn't been in the bed beside him when he woke.

Since it seemed to habitually rain in Panama, he was unsurprised to find himself walking in a downpour toward the stables in search of her.

Each drop on his face seemed to pull his befuddled mind that much closer to consciousness. He found himself much more aware by the time he reached the group. Maria was there, huddled in hushed conversation with Lilly and Cece. There was redness and swelling around Maria's eyes. Had she been crying? Had she slept at all?

He watched her for a long moment, frowning as Lilly pulled her into a tight hug and Cece massaged her back.

Pierre, clad in layers of white ruffles beneath a gold framed turquoise jacket, appeared at his side. "Bonjour mon ami! Did you sleep well?"

Chris laughed at the question, examining Pierre's bright green eyes and wondering if the man was human. He'd still been awake when Chris had ventured off to bed and yet he appeared as refreshed as if he'd slept for days. He'd ditched the powdered wig and Chris was surprised to find a light chestnut head of hair pulled back at the nape of his neck. He'd imagined his hair darker based on his nearly black eyebrows.

Yawning, Chris shook his head. "I don't think I slept at all."

Pierre leaned in and nudged his elbow, his eyes landing on Maria. "Nor she from the looks of it! Is she yours?"

The question seemed to linger in the air between them. Maria did not belong to him, but he wouldn't have Pierre drooling over her either. "Yes," he said stiffly, feeling guilty for possession he had no right to claim over her. "If you'll excuse me."

He had no idea what he was doing, but his legs moved him forward until he found himself in the middle of Maria's little support circle.

She looked up at him, and the redness of her eyes was that much more pronounced up close. Every one of his heartstrings was pulled tight at the sight of her. "Can we have a minute before we go?"

He wasn't entirely certain who the question was directed at, but Lilly and Cece stepped away to busy themselves with loading their horses, leaving Chris and Maria some room to talk.

"Will you ride with me today?" he asked. "Just for a while?"

Her lips were a tight line across her face. "Why?"

He ran a hand over his hair. "Because I miss talking to you."

"Oh?" Her dark brow raised as she peered past him. "A new man is joining us and suddenly you *miss* talking to me?"

Blowing out a heavy breath, he shook his head. "I have missed talking to you from the moment you started this silent treatment. This isn't working. Neither one of us is sleeping for thinking about the other. Can we just… try something else?"

She scoffed, crossing her arms over her chest. "I sleep just fine, Superman. If you are losing sleep thinking about me, that's your problem."

He gently touched the darkening skin beneath her eye. "Your eyes are redder than mine, Maria, and I can't stand that I'm the one causing it."

She swatted his hand away. "My life does not singularly revolve around you, estúpido. You are very full of yourself, you know that? I can have tears that are not caused by you."

"Then ride with me and tell me what's causing them. Tell me why Lilly hugs you like she's trying to keep you together. Tell me why you seemed so devastated that Alaina's not going through the storm. Or spend the whole day telling me you hate me over and over. Just talk to me, for God's sake. I can't stand the silent treatment anymore."

He watched her chest move with a deep inhale. "Fine," she ground out, "I will ride with you because I am too tired to stay upright in a saddle by myself. Cece!" She pushed past him. "You want to ride my horse today?"

Cece glanced between the two of them and smiled. "Sure. I'd be happy to."

"You're not riding with me?" Juan asked, snaking his arm around Cece with a casualness that hadn't been there the day before.

"No, handsome," she said with a laugh, spinning in his grip to drape her arms over his shoulders. "Maria's exhausted and I kind of love the idea of a horse to myself today. It's hot already and I don't want to be all sweaty later. I'll ride beside you though, might even decide to race you at some point."

"Oh, aye?" He chuckled. "I do believe I'd win."

She grinned and adjusted the frames of her glasses. "We'll see about that."

What Chris hadn't taken into consideration when he'd asked Maria to ride with him was the view. She sat in the saddle in front of him, positioned in such a way that whenever he looked down, her cleavage—and the raindrops beading upon it—was put on full display.

This was a woman he'd been attracted to from the start; that he was still very much attracted to and wanted back. The view made his position behind her... a little awkward.

She knew it too. While she hadn't decided to converse with him yet, there was a slight upward curve in her lips that told him she was pleased with his discomfort.

Chris sighed. "Are you going to tell me why you were up all night? Why your eyes look like you've been crying?"

"No," she said, laying her head back against his chest. "I'm riding with you so I can get some sleep, not so we can pretend to be best friends. I'm tired."

Chuckling, he moved the reins into one hand and attempted to slide the other around her waist, but she gripped his wrist firmly with both hands before he was able to.

"What the hell do you think you are doing?" she hissed.

"You said you were going to sleep." He frowned down at her, seeing little else but the swell of her cleavage and returning his eyes to the trail. "I don't want you to fall off."

"I'm not going to fall off." She tossed his hand away from her. "Keep your hands to yourself."

He leaned to her ear, winding his arm around her anyway. "You are the single most infuriating woman I have ever met in my entire life. You know that?"

"Says a man," she grunted, attempting to pry his arm from her, "who cannot take his head out of whatever woman's ass occupies his thoughts on any given day!"

He tightened his grip. "It is not always a woman's *ass* that occupies my thoughts. You knew that well when you decided to put on *this* little outfit."

She gasped, yanking a small patch of hair from his arm in an attempt to get him to remove it. "¡Pervertido! Let go."

He laughed, tucking his chin into the crook of her neck. "Why on earth would I let go when it is the single reason you are talking to me this morning?"

She growled. "Let go or I will squeeze this horse and make her bolt so you'll be forced to let go."

"You do that and you'd better be ready to take the reins because I'm not moving my arm. It's comfortable there."

"Ooh, I hate you." She shrugged her shoulder so he would sit up straight. "¡Vete a la puñeta! I knew I shouldn't ride with your annoying ass."

"But you did," he said. "You knew I would annoy you, but you rode with me anyway. Why?"

She let out a long exhale. "Because I am too tired to ride alone and I thought—*stupidly*—I might get some rest. But now I've got your stupid arm squeezing the life out of me and your annoying little pinga pressed up against my ass and there is no way I will ever get any sleep!"

He laughed loudly then. "God, I miss arguing with you."

She adjusted her spine against him. "Is *that* what you miss doing with me, Superman?"

"I miss doing everything with you, Maria."

He saw her lips form a smile for a moment before they were dragged back down into their scowl. "And I am the infuriating one? *'I love you, Maria.'* Oh wait… *'I can't do this to you, Maria.'* Oh… no, wait… *'I miss doing everything with you, Maria.'* Jesus, how many personalities did they put in your brain during surgery? Can we take you back and exchange you for the broken one? At least you knew what you wanted when your head was damaged."

He leaned in again, inhaling her damp hair. "I want you, *asshole*. I just want to do it the right way."

"The *right way*?" she spat. "It's way too late for the *right way*. What? You think we're just gonna' forget everything we already did wrong? Go on a first date and maybe I give you a kiss on the cheek if it goes well? Are you crazy? We've already done it wrong. What the hell are you talking about, *the right way*?! There is no right way. There is only together with our bullshit or not together with the same amount of bullshit and no one to hold on to."

"What if I—"

She sat up suddenly. "Pull over. Stop the horse."

"What? Why?"

She pasted her palm over her mouth and motioned to the side of the trail, grunting anxiously.

He pulled the reins and Maria practically leapt off the horse and onto the trail, muddying her hands and skirts as she fell on all fours and vomited.

"Jesus," he breathed, carefully dismounting. "Are you alright?"

"Ugh," she groaned, sitting back on her heels and tilting her head back to sniffle. "I'm fine. It's some kind of stomach bug. I've been up sick all night."

He pulled his canteen from the side of the horse and extended it to her. "That's why you were up all night?"

"Uh huh," she tilted the canteen to her lips, swishing the water around her mouth before spitting it out.

He laid his palm over her forehead.

In traditional Maria fashion, she swatted it away. "Oye, I don't have a fever. I'm just sick to my stomach."

He sighed. "You should've told me you were sick. We could've stayed at Hector's an extra night and had Pierre ride out with us tomorrow. We would've caught up to the others in Portobelo."

Another wave of sickness forced her back on all fours and she retched again. Her misery made him wince on her behalf.

He glanced at the trail behind them. They weren't that far. He could still take her back.

Waiting until she'd rinsed her mouth and stood up, he wound an arm around her back. "I'm taking you back to Hector's. You can't ride a horse all day like this. You need to be in bed."

She shook her head. "I'm fine."

"No you're not. You're sick. I'm taking you back."

She shoved him away with much more strength than a sick person should've been able to muster. "If I need to throw up again, I'll tell you and you can pull over. I don't want to go back to Hector's. I want to go home."

He placed himself in her way, narrowing his eyes at her. She didn't look sick. Quite the opposite, actually. She looked radiant, even soaked as she was with rain and mud. It was early morning… Her breasts were definitely bigger… And Lilly had never hugged Maria before…

Feeling his own bit of nausea creep up his throat, he swallowed, his palms going numb at his sides. "Maria, are you sick or… pregnant?"

Her lower lip flattened for a moment as if she might cry but she pulled it in and blinked. "I'm sick." The words came out in a whisper that gave her away.

"Fuuuuck," he breathed, suddenly unable to stand still. He paced on shaking legs. "Oh no, oh fuck… How did this happen? When did this happen? Why didn't you tell me? Oh fuck."

"It's alright. I'm gonna' deal with it. You can stop saying *fuck* over and over like it's gonna' help in some way. You sound stupid."

Taken aback, he stopped his pace and frowned at her. "What do you mean, *deal with it*?"

"Cece gave me some medicine that'll make it go away. Just… don't worry about it."

Suddenly his clothes were too tight, his collar suffocating him. "Don't worry about it? Of course I'm worried about it. When did this happen?"

"Albuquerque," she said. "You need me to tell you *how* it happened too?"

"Albuquerque?!" He definitely couldn't breathe. "So all this time… that night with the Nikora… And… all my bullshit… You knew?"

She nodded. "Sí. I realized almost as soon as we went through time that I hadn't had a period in two months. I should've realized sooner but with everything going on… It doesn't matter. What's done is done and I'll make it go away soon."

He stumbled over various combinations of words, the result a stuttering *'wuh uh uh'* sound until he landed upon, "Why would you want to make it go away?"

She narrowed her eyes at him. "I don't *want* to make it go away. I have to. When we kill George Bennet, it's going to go away on its own, isn't it? Without Bud in the future, you and I will not end up drunk in Albuquerque that night. I can't risk giving birth to a child that will disappear from my arms. I don't have a choice."

His arms fell slack at his sides. "Were you even going to tell me before you did this?"

She shook her head. "No."

"Why?"

"Because you have already lost one. I wanted to save you from losing a second. I thought, if I stopped speaking to you, there'd be no way it could slip out and you'd never know it had happened."

And now he really couldn't breathe. It felt like all the air had been punched out of his lungs. He tugged on the collar of his shirt. "Ah fuck." He bent over, clutching his thighs as he attempted not to hyperventilate, the rain soaking through the shirt on his back and making him feel like he was drowning. "I should've seen it on you sooner. You've been carrying our child alone while I'm running around acting like some lovesick fucking teenager… Like you're not the most important person in the world right now. Jesus, I'm sorry."

"Stop it," she snapped, jerking his chin so he could look at her. "Don't make this about you. You're not allowed to call it *our child*. It won't exist soon. This is just a blip."

"It's not a blip," he said breathlessly, combing back the wet hair that was pasted to her face. "You know that."

"Don't you dare do that either." Her lip quivered as she smacked his hand away. "This is not a reason for you to touch me. This is nothing."

"Then why are you up crying all night over *nothing*?" He straightened and reached for her, but she took a step back. "Maria, we both did this and you never should've felt like it was only yours to deal with. Let me help."

"Help?" She did cry then, like he'd never seen any woman cry before. Her entire face transformed with it. "What the hell are you going to do to help? You gonna reach in there and take it? Make me forget it was ever there? You gonna go back in time and pull out faster? How you gonna help me?"

He took a step forward and wound both arms tightly around her. It was a relief when she didn't fight and sank into him to let the tears fall. He felt guilty that he was comforted by the feel of her there, even if she was falling apart.

"I'm so sorry," he said over and over.

"My whole life has been one awful thing after the next," she sobbed against him. "And that probably sounds like I'm feeling sorry for myself, but it's true. You know, when I was a kid, I used to pray every night for God to save me; to come take me away from that horrible house of my uncle's. But every single night, that monster would come to my room anyway, and I'd wonder what the hell I did wrong that God would keep ignoring me; that God would let him do that to a *child*… Every night. For years. Then one day God gave me you… and I thought my prayers had been answered because what my uncle did suddenly didn't hurt anymore. So I begged him to let me have you. I begged God for a married man and this is my punishment."

He held her tighter, his own tears sliding down his cheeks. "You haven't done anything wrong, Maria."

"Yes I have!" She cried harder, her fingers curling into fists in his shirt. "I always do. My mind just thinks wrong. The other day I felt it move for the first time. It was this little flutter like bubbles in my belly and it took me a minute to realize what it was… And do you know what my reaction was? I thought… Anna is not worth this to me. What a terrible thing to think! To want her to stay dead —a woman who was kinder than all of us—for a child that isn't even a child yet! What is wrong with me?"

He kissed the top of her head. "Nothing is wrong with you."

"Then why do things like this keep happening? Why does everyone around me get to be happy and not me? Why can't I be normal?"

"You two alright?" Jack called out, and Chris looked up to find him on his horse waiting several yards ahead.

"We're fine," Chris assured him, waving him off with one arm as he held Maria tighter with the other. "You guys go ahead. We'll catch up. We just need a minute."

"We're all stopped not far from here." He offered an apologetic smile. "We'll wait for you."

Chris nodded. "Thanks."

Jack turned the horse back and rode off.

He peeled Maria from him to look down at her face, her tear-swollen expression nearly ripping him in two.

"You said Cece gave you medicine. You haven't taken it?"

She shook her head, every muscle in her body sunken with defeat. "Not yet. I was going to wait until we get on the ship."

"I don't want you to take it."

"I have to." Her eyes welled once more. "It's small right now and I can pass it. The longer I wait, the harder it will be without a doctor."

He peered out to the trail they'd come from. "You can't take that medicine. The bleeding could kill you too. I could take you back… We could go get on that slave ship with the others and head for the storm. You'd have doctors in the future that could help you.

Or…" He turned back to look up the trail ahead. "We could save George Bennet's life and keep it."

She frowned up at him. "But—"

"Anna's not worth it to me, either." He held her upper arms firmly. "I know I've had a messed up way of showing it, but I love you so goddamn much it hurts. Giving those memories any merit was a mistake; a mistake I will never allow myself to make again. Tell me what you want and I'll give it to you. Do you want to get rid of this baby?"

Again, her lower lip trembled and she shook her head. "It's not even a baby yet. It doesn't even have eyes or ears or anything to love… But… I love it more than I have ever loved anything in my whole life and I don't want to get rid of it. How can I choose this thing with no eyes or ears over Anna? It's cruel."

He moved his grip up and down her arms. "Anna chose her fate when she poisoned those men. She knew she was risking her life and she did it anyway. It has never been our obligation to fix her mistake. We were only doing it because we felt it was the right thing to do… But you… our baby… neither of you has done anything to warrant dying over what she did that day. Saving her is no longer the right thing to do here. We don't owe her a life. We don't owe her the life of our child."

Her eyes were so big just then, hope and devastation wrestling behind them, he couldn't help but sink down to his knees.

"And what will that make us?" she asked. "Will we take everyone who intends to go through the storm or kill George Bennet onto *our* ship and lock them away? Do we become the evil ones now?"

"I don't care what that makes us." He slid his palm over her midsection, his heartbeat quickening when he felt the smallest swell in her lower stomach; so small he might've imagined it. "We're family. I should've been there for you from the start and there isn't enough apologizing I could ever do to express the depths with which I am sorry. I'm here now, whether you'll have me or not, and I'll do whatever it takes to make sure you never have another awful thing to pray over again."

She rested both hands on his shoulders as he moved his fingers over her stomach. "We can't do this."

"We can," he said softly, sliding his arms around her and pressing his brow against her abdomen.

She sniffled. "No, *mi amor*. It was a mistake that we even created it. We should go back to that slave ship and go home right now. I can take the medicine once we get there and you can take me to a hospital to miscarry. If you want a baby when all this is done, we'll do it the right way."

He held her tighter. "There is no right way, Maria. Remember? Please, let's not make the decision yet. Let's talk about it."

She let out a long breath, sliding her fingers into his hair. "We will only try to talk ourselves out of doing the right thing."

He shook his head. "We would've gone to Albuquerque for Jim either way. Wouldn't we? To search for June? We don't know for certain this wouldn't have happened."

"Yes, we do," she said softly. "*Anna* would've gone to Albuquerque. Not us. She was going to California for Liam. It wouldn't make sense for us to travel so far when she would be closer. If, by some miracle, this pregnancy happens some other way, then you and I will show up in a life where our baby lives when all this is over. If it doesn't happen and we don't give this up now, you and I will be ruined forever. Do you understand?"

He understood, but for the life of him, he couldn't bear the thought of willingly giving up a child.

"That ship isn't going anywhere yet," he whispered. "It's waiting to receive slaves from the other side of the isthmus. We haven't passed any slave traders yet so we have time before we need to make that decision. Give me until then before we turn back?"

"Why? So you can talk me out of this?"

"No." His eyes watered. "So I can talk myself into it."

PART III

The choices we make

Chapter Forty-Six

Alaina

I'd opened the flood gates when I allowed myself the memory of Cancun. All night and morning, my mind proceeded to drag me through one memory after the next of what might appear to be, for anyone not inside it, a very happy marriage.

What I realized, however, the further and further I explored my altered memories, was that the two of us were doomed from the start. It wasn't just my reaction to Evelyn that caused our downward spiral. It was us; the way we interacted with each other; the people we were pretending to be. We'd rushed into our marriage when we were both too young to know what we needed from each other.

I wouldn't ever contest that we had love for each other—we did—but our love didn't go much deeper than the surface; didn't venture away from pretending to be perfect—and that made any feelings of self-worth difficult to come by.

We didn't share our sadness or anger or fears or deepest desires with one another. We hid behind the good stuff; the easy stuff. We laughed when we should've been crying, smiled when our insides might've been screaming.

Maybe Chris thought that *was* perfect, but I felt suffocated by all the emotions I couldn't share with him.

I'd wanted to be better to him after Cancun, but better meant more smiles and kisses and laughter where it should've meant being more open and honest.

There was one memory of Thanksgiving that played out very similarly in both versions of my life, and I couldn't help but keep returning to it all night.

I'd been cooking in my kitchen with Cece and mom while the men had been sent to the grocery store for some ingredient one of us had forgotten.

Cece always tended to get sentimental during the holidays, but on this particular holiday, she pressed mom about our father—a subject we'd silently concluded was off limits.

"Mom," she'd said from her seat at the center island, "we're adults now. I need you to tell us what really happened with dad. I need to know why he left. And don't say it's because he's an asshole. That's not good enough for me anymore. I'm twenty-eight years old and not knowing why the man that helped make me walked away is eating away at me."

Mom had been stirring something on the stove, and I remembered the grimace on her face at the question. "He *is* an asshole, Celia. Why on earth would it matter to you now? I raised you alright, didn't I?"

"Of course you did," she assured her. "But it's hard to know I look so much like him and not be curious about him every day of my life. Am I like him in some other way? I don't know because you have consistently refused to talk about him in any way."

"You are *nothing* like him, baby." Mom let out a long breath. "He was a narcissist. And he didn't leave us for any particular reason outside of loving himself more than he was capable of loving anyone else. There was nothing that went wrong to cause it; no explanation I can give you to justify it. He and I never argued and you two were good babies. We had a good home and nice things and he had a great job. As far as I knew, we had a strong marriage and he was happy." She shrugged. "But then he just…

changed his mind. He woke up one day and decided he wanted a different life. There was no reason for it. He just left; walked out and didn't look back."

I'd been standing at the opposite counter peeling potatoes when my heart sank in my chest.

I, too, had it all: a nice house, a good husband, a close family, and a great job... Chris and I didn't argue or beat each other. For the life of me, I hadn't been able to understand why that wasn't enough.

Had I inherited it from my father? Was I a narcissist? Was my father? Did he have a reason for leaving that my mother just couldn't see? What if, like me, he just needed more?

Their conversation continued, but their voices were far in the distance as I stared down at the potato in my hand.

Chris was a wonderful man, but we didn't talk to each other about anything deeper than dinner options or weekend plans. There was no substance. Our life, on paper, was a dream, but living in it had become... methodical. We woke up, went to work, ate dinner, had sex, and went to bed... That was our life. Where was the passion? What was the point? Chris might have been content with it, but I was slowly drowning.

With Chris, I'd felt every bit the narcissist my mother claimed our father was. But, standing on the ship now and thinking about Jack, I wondered if there even was such a thing. Maybe some of us just came off as narcissists when we ended up with the wrong people.

And that made me sad. I'd spent so many years in the new memories putting on that perfect face and feeling like I was the bad guy for wanting more; like I was the same kind of monster we'd always considered my father.

With Jack, I felt whole.... Felt seen and heard for all my good and bad. How completely different we were together from the start. There was nothing surface about us; nothing to guess. Everything we were was laid out for each other, and I didn't need anything more. I knew him as well as I knew myself and I felt good about the person I was becoming as a result.

Chris deserved so much more than what I was capable of giving. He deserved someone who didn't hide themselves from him. I wished I wouldn't have been so afraid to acknowledge the new memories. If I'd done it sooner, I might've been able to give him some of the clarity I found in them now.

"The babies will stay here," Juan announced as he approached, pulling me away from my thoughts, "with Bruce."

"What? Why?" I smoothed my palms over their heads where I'd secured them inside the sling, spinning to face him. "I'm not going to try to run off with them through a jungle if that's what you're thinking."

Juan had agreed to take a group to the shore to hunt and forage. He'd insisted I accompany him but had never mentioned my children not being permitted to go as well.

Juan shook his head and sighed. "Mosquitos, Alaina, to name only one of the thousands of threats they might face. They'll be eaten alive and could develop sicknesses you and I are immune to. Not to mention snakes, spiders, bullet ants, poison frogs…. I could go on for an hour."

I frowned at him. "I'll stay here with them then."

Juan chuckled. "My dear, I'll not leave this ship without you. This was your idea, remember?"

I looked out toward the shore. It suddenly felt so very far away. "I can't just leave these babies here, Juan. I don't trust you not to have some kind of sinister plan to sacrifice us both and send this ship off with my daughter on it."

"Then it appears we are at a standstill. You want fruit? You come with me. If you would prefer to risk a vitamin deficiency in your milk, we'll move ahead instead."

"Why can't we just send the crew?" I asked. "Then you and I don't have to do this whole trust dance."

The corner of his lip curled up in a smirk. "These are slavers, my dear. The foulest sort of men, and dumb to boot. They might be able to return with a curassow or a deer, but they wouldn't know the difference between an apple and a banana even if they came with a label. As I have been close to poisoned once before, I'll not risk a similar outcome by sending this lot to forage. You and I will collect the fruit while they hunt. This is my offer. Take it or leave it."

I hugged both babies against my chest. We needed vitamins. The galley was running low and with the additional crew, we wouldn't be able to spread out what we had for much longer.

"I don't even know what to look for," I argued. "Bruce does. What do you think's gonna happen if you get off this ship without me? You think I'm gonna' somehow take over the helm and play captain?"

He took a step closer and lowered his voice. "Look around you, Alaina. You are the sole female on this ship. Now, look at those men I brought with me. Do you see the way they look at you? Like lions stalking prey. If I had to guess, I would say it's been years since most of them have even laid eyes on a woman with your complexion. I'll not tell you what men like them do to the women they consider cargo. There is a reason I told them you were my wife. I do not sleep in your room for *my* enjoyment."

I swallowed, suddenly aware of the eyes on my back. "So I'm supposed to just leave my children here with them instead?"

He laughed. "These men have no use for a baby. Mr. Gil will assist Bruce in guarding them. The ones that can shoot are coming with us. The ones left behind," he motioned to a man standing on the quarterdeck with a finger buried in his nose, "will not be concerned with your children."

I chewed my lower lip. "What makes you think the men that stay behind won't just take off with the ship while you and I are away?"

He leaned against the railing and crossed his arms casually over his waist. "Men like them are loyal to one thing. Money. And I've promised them a great deal of it once we arrive in Virginia. They'll not leave us. Time is wasting, Alaina. Are we going or not?"

Again, I looked out to the shore a million miles away. "But I don't even know what kind of plants to look for."

He smiled and waved a hand out toward the coastline. "That is Colombia, my dear, and I know every inch of her by heart." He scanned the length of me. "If we're to go, you'll need to change out of these skirts and into trousers, long-sleeves, boots, and gloves. What we want will require a bit of a hike inland. Are you in or are you out? We cannot stand here all day."

I took a long steady breath. "I'm in."

One thing I learned quickly about the Colombian wilderness was that if you were actively looking for creeping crawling things, they could easily be found.

While Juan cut down bunches of bananas and collected purple and green berries I'd never seen before, I knelt on the ground harvesting chanterelles mushrooms, attempting not to look at the giant black and yellow spider lounging in her web ten feet away.

I was grateful for the pants, boots, and gloves he'd given me. Every little brush of a leaf against the fabric had me jumping to swat away an invisible arachnid. I could only imagine what it might be like to have attempted this in skirts.

Somewhere around the hundredth jump, I decided I'd never get anything done if I didn't find some other way to occupy my mind.

The rest of the crew had gone farther inland to hunt, leaving only Juan as a potential distraction. Glancing once more at my eight-legged tormentor—who hadn't moved from the center of her web—I decided Juan was the lesser of the two evils.

"What was Gloria like as a wife?" I asked, pulling fluffy yellow mushrooms from the mud as I looked up at him. "Before Richard, that is… Did you have deep, meaningful conversations or was it all surface-level stuff?"

He kept his back to me, picking bunches of berries from a bush to toss them into a basket at his feet. He snickered at my question. "There was nothing surface-level about Gloria. She was an artist in every sense of the word. Beyond the photography, she was an amazing painter, writer, and dancer. She could pick up an instrument and have it mastered within the week. The woman was far too complex for small talk. She needed to have her mind massaged with deep conversation at all times… Not always an easy thing for a man to come home to after a long day."

He moved to the other side of the bush, kneeling to collect berries hidden deeper inside the branches. "I used to wonder what it'd be like to come home to someone who would simply ask me how my day was instead of being bombarded with questions about my opinion on the energy crisis in America or women's rights or buddhism or whatever she had on her mind that day… Would've been rather dull, I think."

"You talked to her though, right? You didn't brush it off?"

He chuckled. "No one could brush off Gloria when she was knee deep in a thought process. She had a way of thinking about life that made you *want* to philosophize with her. She could make you look at the world in a completely different way." He frowned. "These are all very specific questions. Why do you ask?"

I shrugged, double checking that the spider hadn't disappeared from her web to attempt a sneak attack on me. "I keep thinking about my first marriage. We didn't talk to each other on a deeper level and I got restless. I think the same thing happened to my father. I was just curious if Gloria was the same since she ran off with Richard… Like maybe it's something genetic?"

"Restlessness comes in all forms, my dear." He plucked up his basket and moved to a bush closer to me. "Hers came from a lack of adventure, not a lack of stimulating conversation. When she and I were first wed, I was young and unafraid. I'd barely begun running the business then, and having my wife and child travel the world alongside me wasn't any more dangerous than a walk through the park."

He met my eyes then, his shoulders slumping. "But as I began to experience the threats my father was always thwarting, I realized even a walk in the park could put them in peril. I'd inherited enemies all over the world, and the surest way for those enemies to get to me was through my wife and child. I couldn't live with myself if something happened to them on my account, so

I locked them away and made our home her prison… Of course she would try to escape it." He grinned. "She came from you, after all. Perhaps it is the urge to escape that is genetic."

I forced a smile. "Did you ever think about giving up the business?"

He nodded, keeping his eyes on his task. "Shortly after the twins were born. I knew I couldn't keep them locked up like that forever. I brought my brother in with the intention to have him running it after a few years. I started investing legitimately so I could still give her the life I'd promised her. Unfortunately, that transition is what killed her. Richard Albrecht had been working our family for a few years undercover, and he'd made a best friend out of my brother. When I gave my brother a bigger role, Richard got one too… Guarding my family."

"Jesus." I stood and brushed off my pants. "No wonder you have trust issues."

I pointed to my full basket. "This one's full. Can I take it back to the beach and get another while I check on the ship or do you not trust me to venture off on my own?"

He flicked his wrist to dismiss me. "You are my guest, not my captive."

I huffed and spun on my heel. "Could've fooled me."

I marched through the bush, one arm flailing like a crazy person in defense of invisible spider webs, and deposited my basket on the sand. Relieved to find the ship still anchored where we left it, I gathered three more baskets and turned back.

My heart skipped a beat. Leaning against a tree with his arms crossed in front of him was one of the men we'd brought to shore with us. He was blocking the path back in, and his stare was heavy where he scanned the length of me.

Remembering Juan's warning about the slavers and the way they treated women, I felt his desire sitting heavily in the air between us.

"You are afraid of your husband," he said in a deep Spanish accent, raising one dark brow. "Why?"

Swallowing, I glanced behind him for signs of Juan.

"He cannot hear us, mi rosa," he sang, pushing off the tree and strolling toward me. "Do you need rescuing?"

"No," I said, attempting to move around him only for him to side-step right back in my way.

"No?" There was something sinister about his smile. "Tell me. What is your name, bella?"

I clenched my jaw tightly as I ground out, "*Mrs. Perez* to you. Excuse me."

He put both hands on my shoulders to still me before I could push past him. "Not so fast, Mrs. Perez. I am trying to make you an offer. Wouldn't you like to hear it?"

"You are supposed to be hunting with the others. My husband," I cringed at the word, "has offered you substantial compensation to work for him until we reach the colonies. No part of that agreement included putting your hands on his wife. If you expect to keep those hands, I advise you remove them immediately and get back to what you're being paid to do."

He laughed playfully and held both palms up in surrender. "Why did you take his ship and run from him? Eh? Why is your husband paying so much to make sure we deliver you to the colonies? Did you steal his money too? If so, I have little use for your husband when I'd much rather be *serving* his wife for the same compensation."

"No," I growled, once again attempting to move around him and failing.

"We could have fun together, you and I." His eyes moved down my collared shirt to my breasts. "I would take care of you."

He reached out to graze my cheek with his thumb.

Realizing the situation was not likely to get any better, I did exactly what Jack had taught me and drove my knee hard into his groin.

I stood proud as he collapsed onto his knees. "Get back to work," I muttered, stepping around him to hurry back into the brush.

Juan had been watching. He waited just inside the shadows with a smirk across his lips.

"You send him to test me?" I asked, tossing him one of the empty baskets.

He shook his head. "No."

"And you couldn't have stepped in at some point and told him to piss off?"

He chuckled, peering past me to where the man was still cupping himself and attempting to catch his breath. "I would have if I thought you needed me to. I warned you they were foul. That one is maybe the foulest among them."

I fell into step beside him as we ventured back into the woods. "Who is he?"

"Daniel Bacallar," he snarled. "He and his brother are the worst kinds of men. "Lucky for you, I left Simón on the other ship. Perhaps unlucky for your friends who joined him."

Simón Bacallar.

I remembered that name sitting just beneath Jack's on the master's log. It remained there on the screen, one slot up where Jack's had once been. If Simón stayed on the slave ship, how was it possible his death ended up in our master's log in Juan Jr.'s handwriting?

Was Bruce right?

Were the others planning a takeover of that vessel this very moment?

Chapter Forty-Seven

Cecelia

Much as I'd enjoyed sharing a horse with Juan, I enjoyed riding alongside him more.

He was absolutely majestic in the way he rode, looking like a statue in the saddle with his freshly pressed uniform and glistening sword. I found my eyes drifting toward him every few seconds to soak up his image. His eyes had done the same throughout the day, both of us grinning every time our gaze would meet.

Neither of us had slept at all the night before, and I didn't mind the fatigue weighing down my bones one bit. We'd made love, then laid awake talking in each other's arms before repeating the process several more times.

I could still feel him on me; could taste him on my lips, smell him on my skin... And there was a permanent smile on my face because of it.

The sun was lowering at our backs when we finally decided to stop for the night near a small pond where we could refill our water supply and give the horses a much needed break to graze on its banks. I dismounted with a wince and stretched my back.

While horseback riding had always been a favorite pastime for me, my entire body was sore after so many days of it. We would arrive in Portobelo tomorrow night and I couldn't wait to get there. My muscles needed a break from the saddle.

I was digging through a saddlebag for my canteen when I felt Juan's hands slide up my sides and his lips press against my temple. "You have tormented me all day in this wicked dress, *mi alma*. I cannot wait to get it off you."

I grinned and leaned back into him. "Does that mean we don't have to share a tent with your brother tonight?"

"My brother," he all but growled, catching my ear between his teeth, "can find his own place to sleep."

"Mmm." A wonderful chill swept up my spine. "I don't think he'll have a hard time finding one." I grinned at the way Dario was watching Pierre unload his horse. "You think those two are…?"

His breath was torture in my ear. "I do not care what those two are. My mind is entirely occupied with the most sinful thoughts of you… I cannot wait to rip this bothersome dress off you."

"Oh yeah?" I chuckled. "You'd better go get the tent set up fast. I've had similar thoughts of undressing you all day."

I moved out of his grip as if I might help Lilly and Maria where they were unloading supplies from a mule. Juan took my wrist instead and spun me back, covering my mouth with his.

It's funny how you can long for a kiss even while it's happening. As his tongue slipped past my lips, I longed for more. I wished I could've known what it was like to love him the moment I stepped on the ship; wished I could go back and spend all the nights from that one to this one wrapped up in him. How much time we'd wasted not knowing each other this way.

"Junior!" Jim called. "We got a camp to make, wood to cut, a fire to build, and mouths to feed. You can suck on her face later."

I laughed, slinking shamefully out of Juan's arms. "Sorry Jim."

He cackled with laughter. "Ooh, and don't you look at me like that, boy. I've stepped over bigger men than you lookin' for a fight! Come on!"

Blushing fiercely, I turned toward Lilly, Izzy, and Maria while Juan headed the opposite direction.

Lilly flashed her perfect teeth as I joined them. "I take it you're enjoying married life Mrs. Perez?"

I nodded, shifting my focus to Maria. "How are you? What happened? Did you tell him?"

Maria glanced over my shoulder to be sure everyone was out of earshot. "Sí. I had to. I puked and I tried to play it off like I was sick but he could see it on me."

"It's good you told him," Lilly said. "He needed to carry this with you. Do you feel better? What'd he say?"

She shrugged. "I feel exactly the way I thought I would if I said anything. He told me how much he loved me and how he chooses me and will do anything I want him to do. And that makes me feel like I'm somehow manipulating him with this pregnancy."

Lilly huffed, unpacking the salt pork from our pack. "You didn't make a baby by yourself, Maria. And you don't have to take him back just because he's decided that's what he wants now. He doesn't get to just decide when you are and aren't worth his time. He's kind of an asshole."

Maria turned to help unload dry wood from the mule. "But I *want* him back. Even if he's an asshole. It just feels like I'm doing something wrong if I take him back now."

Lilly shook her head. "You're not doing anything wrong."

Maria looked over her shoulder, frowning. "Now that he knows, we're thinking about going back to the slave ship to go home. It'd be safer to…"

Her words trailed off and we all froze at the sounds of people moving toward us from the trail ahead—a *lot* of people.

Chris, Jim, Jack, and Dario all slowly abandoned what they'd been doing, backing up to stand ahead of us near the trail. Tomás, Gabriel, and Juan moved ahead to get a glimpse at what was coming.

"What is that?" Maria asked, squinting as if doing so might help her see around the curve and through the trees.

"Slavers," Pierre said, strolling casually up behind us. "They've got at least a hundred of them heading for the Sofía Martina. They're taking them to the Orient."

"Asia?" Lilly scoffed. "I didn't know they had slaves there."

"Of course they do," Pierre said, unbothered by the idea. "They have lands just as rich in crops as any that need tending to."

My stomach twisted in knots as I heard the clamor of chains far in the distance. I knew it wasn't my place to put an end to all the atrocities of history, but how could I stand still and watch what I knew I was about to witness?

"It's cruel," I said under my breath, waiting to catch sight of whatever was about to come around the curve.

"Such is life," Pierre said, poking his fancy cane into the ground near his feet.

"Can we do something about it? Free some of them?" I asked, my heartbeat palpable as the chains grew louder. "God, it sounds like so many."

"What would we do?" Pierre scoffed. "Risk our lives to cut one or two loose so they could fall into destitution here in this jungle? They would never make it back to whatever country they were taken from. It's likely most of them were born into slavery and know no other life. Isn't it just as cruel to set them free in a wilderness they are unfamiliar with where they would have no means to survive? Much as I detest the practice, their masters would keep them better cared for than this jungle would."

"It should be their choice," I growled.

"You have a kind soul, mon chéri," he murmured, "but do any of us really have a choice? If I'd had a choice in life, I'd have been a prince or a duke or a man of leisure, spending my days and nights doing as I pleased with whomever I pleased. As it is," he spun his cane up and caught it mid-air, "I am here in the mud with you."

I glared at him. "Are you so heartless you can't see the difference between being born into circumstance and being robbed entirely of every freedom you'd been born with? Forced into whatever circumstance someone else sees fit for you? Do you really have the audacity to compare your position to theirs while you stand there with every ability to interfere as a free man but are prepared to do nothing?"

Our conversation came to an end then as several men on horseback appeared down the trail. One rode forward and backward, shouting marching orders down the line.

Bile caught in my throat as the men and women he shouted at came into view. Their hands were shackled and each of them was connected to another by a chain that ran from one iron collar to the next, to the next...

The men wore tattered breeches, few of them with shirts, their dark skin shimmering with the rain and fading sunlight on the bits of flesh that weren't lined with scars. The women wore dresses that had faded to a pale yellow, the hems of their skirts torn to shreds and stained to the knee with mud. Most of them had no shoes. Some carried babies...

Everything inside me clenched like a fist in the throws of rage.

It was one thing to read about the horrors of slavery. It was another to witness it.

Every single body was scarred; every face dragged downward with fatigue, hunger, and torment. The rags they wore showed signs of blood near the sleeves and on their backs. They were herded like animals to the slaughter—no, animals were treated better even than this. This was... pure evil.

I wanted to vomit. More so, I wanted to grab the automatic rifle behind me on the mule and shoot every one of the horsemen riding alongside and in front of them. To hell with history. This part of it should've never happened in the first place.

A voice of reason reminded me this would not last forever; the future I'd seen would place the descendants of these people in a better world. Who was I to alter the lives of their descendants?

Another voice, however, screamed at the top of its lungs to do something—*anything*. What if I'd been pulled into that storm so I could find myself in this very spot? What if it was my destiny to give these people a better world sooner? What if those spots on the ocean were a means to make history better; to erase the atrocities of human nature?

As they were herded past us, my eyes landed upon an emaciated young boy, and both the arguing voices in my head were silenced.

He wore a shirt that hung too loose, his pants torn above the knee to reveal skin clinging like damp cloth against a skeleton. His eyes were sunken and I could very nearly make out his skull beneath his cheeks. Linked to the chain with an iron collar round his neck, every one of his steps seemed labored and close to his last. He would not make it across this trail.

We might've been in an existence that would be erased, but my lungs still drew breath inside it, and I could never look at myself and feel whole again if I simply let him march toward his death. There was nothing that could stop me from running toward him.

Nothing, that is, save for an arm round my waist to pull me off my feet and spin me away before I could reach him.

"Stop," Jack whispered, holding me against his chest as I fought to get loose. "We can't help them."

"Did you see that kid?" I screamed, all logical thought lost on the image of the boy's skeletal figure. "We have to try!"

"We can't do anything for them. This is not our place; not our time. You can't save them. It's already happened this way."

"No, it hasn't!" I growled, squirming in his grip. "He's not going to make it across this trail! Let me do *something*!"

"We won't save anyone," he breathed. "You and I won't ever even end up in this place once we're finished in Virginia. You know that. You'd be risking your life for nothing."

"Bonsoir Monsieur Bacallar!" Pierre called out behind me. "Quite the heavy shipment you've got with you!"

I kicked my legs in an attempt to get free but Jack only held me tighter, blocking me from seeing what was happening at our backs.

"Señor Beaumarchais!" a man responded, the clop of his horse's hooves halting entirely too near. "Good evening to you!"

I was starting to panic. My lips had gone numb. I closed my eyes and took a deep breath. I couldn't panic now. I had to get to that boy; had to figure out some way to help him. No amount of history classes could've prepared me for what I'd seen when I looked at his sunken face. It was like standing at the side of a swimming pool and watching a baby drown while being told there was nothing I could do to stop it. Of course there was something I could do. I was here, wasn't I?

"Are they all paid for?" Pierre asked casually.

"They will be," the man said, "if we can keep them in one piece during the crossing. We lost a few over the cliffs yesterday. Watch your footing when you go across. The trail is treacherous."

I cringed at the way he spoke so unemotionally about losing human lives, as if they'd been little more to him than names on a paper that had blown away in the wind.

"Would you be willing to spare one or two more?" Pierre asked. "That boy… are his parents among you?"

Realizing what he might be doing, I relaxed a little in Jack's arms as I awaited the man's response.

"This one?" the man scoffed. "He's an orphan. They all are these days. Thinking of buying a little toy for yourself, Pierre?"

"Perhaps," Pierre chuckled. "Does he speak?"

"Spanish. Some English, but not much."

I heard the jingling of coins and my heart nearly tripled. Pierre was going to buy his freedom.

"Have you lost your mind, Señor Beaumarchais? The boy is haggard. This is too much."

"I'll feed him," Pierre said. "And I want the man beside him, too. The big one. And that woman."

The man clicked his tongue. "You've no need for slaves… what do you intend to do with them?"

"Whatever I want," Pierre laughed. "Do we have a deal or not, Monsieur Bacallar?"

"Oh, we certainly have a deal, Pierre. Allow me a moment to prepare their papers." I heard his horse trotting toward the front of the line, chains rattling loudly as word of their purchase moved from one end of the group to the other.

Suddenly Pierre stood before us, a cocky grin plastered across his cheeks as he twirled his cane. "Satisfied, mon chéri?"

"You did that on *my* account?" I asked, wiggling free of Jack's grip. "Why?"

"Boredom?" Pierre grinned. "They are yours now."

"Mine?" I scoffed. "What do you mean, *mine*?"

"You are the one that wished for us to do something, and now I have on your behest. They are yours to set free. See if they go or if they run back to their captors."

"You did this to prove yourself right?" I asked.

He shrugged, eyes on his cane as he twirled it again. "Perhaps. Or perhaps I'm not so heartless after all." He peered behind me. "Pardonnez-moi, mademoiselle. I must collect our new friends."

"What in the Sam Hill is goin' on?" Jim asked, replacing Pierre in front of us.

Jack crossed his arms and gazed down at me. "I believe Cece is going to free three slaves."

Jim blinked, looking past us toward the trail. "Only three?"

"Best we could do for now," I said, moving to the mule to rifle through our supplies. "Do we have extra clothes? I know we have enough food…. Did we bring extra boots?"

"I got some extra boots and britches in there," Jim said, scratching his stubble. "Where we takin' 'em?"

Fishing out a loaf of bread from Hector's, I turned toward the trail where a man and woman stood with the boy, unchained and staring wide-eyed at our group. "Wherever they want to go, we'll help them get there," I said. "I'm not leaving them to get on that ship and be beaten, starved, and God only knows what else. Philadelphia was a free state and we'll be close to it when we arrive in Virginia. Maybe I can get them there…"

Jim shook his head. "Philadelphia wasn't free in this time. It was made free after they forced men of color to fight in the frontlines of the war that's comin. We cain't take 'em to the states with us. They'd end up right back in chains and we ain't no kind of heroes in this if we let that happen."

I stood taller as Pierre approached with the three of them, my mind moving a million miles an hour. "Mademoiselle," he sang, "here you are."

"What's this?" Juan asked, taking a spot at my side and placing his palm against my lower back.

Jim smiled at me. "We gonna' set these three free… Know of somewhere safe we can take 'em?"

I nervously handed the boy the loaf of bread in my hands. "What are your names?"

When none of them responded, I asked again in Spanish, earning little more than shocked looks from both Maria and Dario. The boy held the bread in his hands but made no attempt to eat it.

"We won't hurt you," I said gently in Spanish. "You're free. Tell us where you want to go."

"Free?" the woman asked, pulling the boy against her. "What do you mean?"

Pierre leaned back on his cane, observing the interaction with skepticism.

"We mean, no one will ever hurt you again." I glanced at the scar across the man's eye and cringed. Someone had hit him with a whip across the face. "You are free to go wherever you'd like. We'll make sure you get there."

"Wherever we like?" The woman shook her head. "There is no place to go."

"There are communities," Juan said, placing his hand back over my spine, "made up of escaped slaves from as far back as the 1500s. They've built their own colonies here over the years. They are free men and women. No slaver would dare set foot in their territory. There's a village not far from here. We can feed you for the night, provide some fresh clothing, and take you there in the morning if you'd like? Otherwise, we can sign your papers and help you find another way. The choice is yours."

"Why us?" the woman asked, looking back to the trail as the rest of slaves were pushed ahead. "Why not any one of them?"

I pointed to the boy. "He needed help."

She let out a sound that wasn't quite a laugh. "They all needed help. Every one of them looked like this boy at some point. Do you know what they do to people like us on those rice farms?"

"I'm sorry," I said, unsure what I was apologizing for as I lowered my eyes to my feet. "I… I—"

"Thank you," the man said in English, narrowing his eyes at the woman. He nudged the boy and motioned to the loaf in his hands. "Eat."

The boy immediately tore off a piece of bread and put it in his mouth. It almost looked painful for him to chew.

"Are you thirsty?" I asked. "Come and sit," I waved toward the partially erected camp. "You're safe here."

The man inspected Jack and Juan for a long moment, pulling his attention away only when Lilly appeared with a canteen for each of them.

"We have friends and family who will be hitching a ride on the Sofía Martina," she informed them. "If I know them as well as I think, they'll try to free more of them—if not all."

I thought about Terrence then. He would take one look at the marks on those slaves and fight to the death to see more than just three freed. Kyle, righteous as he was, would try to help him… And from what I'd been told about Bud, he would help too. Part of me was terrified they'd try while the other part of me hoped they would… but what would that mean for Maria? She and Chris would be returning to that ship to go home. Would they make it there or would Terrence's wrath kill them all?

"*Mi alma*," Juan whispered, pressing a kiss against the crown of my head, "are you coming?"

I blinked and realized I'd been staring blankly ahead while everyone had ventured into camp with our new guests.

I looked up at him and saw nothing but admiration in his eyes. "You're not mad about this?"

He smiled and shook his head. "Quite the opposite, Cecelia. I couldn't be more proud. We've enough food and blankets to share, and the colony I spoke of is not far from where we are now. Tomás can escort them in the morning if that's where they wish to go and catch up to us by midday. They'll be happy there. Happy and safe and free. They'll live good lives thanks to you."

I nodded, looking toward camp where Jim and the man were building a fire. Jim, of course, was cracking some kind of joke he found hilarious while the man's expression remained neutral.

"When we come back to live in this century," I said softly, watching the boy accept a chunk of cheese from Maria, "there will never be an instance where I can stand by and let that happen. If we intend to travel, I imagine we'll encounter slaves from time to time. I will *always* need to intervene. Okay?"

Juan leaned into me. "I cannot think of a better way to spend my life."

We'd stayed up far later than we intended for the lack of sleep most of us had gotten the night before.

It took time, but our guests eventually grew comfortable with us after their bellies were full of pork stew, cheese, bread, and wine.

They'd informed us that they'd been slaves as long as they could remember and knew only the names they'd been given. The man went by Miguel, although it hardly suited him, the boy was named Antonio, and the woman—who spoke very little—had always been called 'Dee.'

They'd come from Spain and spent the past several years in Cuba working on a large sugar plantation. The living conditions were dreadful and it had come as a relief when they'd been sold. When they found out they were going to work a rice field, however, that relief turned to terror.

Miguel had been told by another slave during the ship ride about the Cimarrones in Panama. He'd heard they'd often ambush slavers and help their captives go free. He hadn't allowed himself to hope they'd come across such a group, but he'd prayed for it all the same. Upon learning he'd soon be joining one, he'd gradually come to life, even smiling on occasion throughout the meal.

He was excited to start a life here.

Antonio had slowly come out of his shell as well, and it warmed my heart when he and Izzy began to draw pictures in the dirt to communicate.

Dee remained quiet, almost angry she'd been chosen, and I imagined she had something resemblant of survivor's remorse. I might've too had I been in her shoes.

If I was honest, I had mixed emotions about the whole thing. Freeing them had given me a sense of purpose and gratification, but there was guilt that accompanied the small accomplishment.

This wasn't an achievement. It was a basic human requirement. Any person with morals should've stepped up in the same situation. I shouldn't be allowed to feel good about what we'd done when so many more had still been taken to that ship; when we were setting out to undo all this and they'd be taken anyway.

By the time we all ventured off to bed, I'd been so exhausted that my eyes closed before my head had even hit the pillow.

It was early morning when they finally opened again.

My cheek was rested on Juan's chest, one leg draped over both of his. He was lazily moving his fingertips up and down my thigh.

He'd removed my skirts, stays, stockings, and boots in the night—hardly ripping them off since I had no memory of it—and I laid in only my shift against him.

Smiling, I pressed a kiss over the tattoo I'd been sleeping on, and the arm beneath me coiled around my body to pull me closer.

"Good morning," he whispered, his hand flattening against my outer thigh.

I hummed, sliding my palm up his warm chest. "Good morning. Did Tomás leave yet?"

"Aye," he yawned. "I heard them head out a few moments ago. The woman, Dee… She left in the night. Went back to the slavers."

I sighed. "We didn't really free them anyway. They'll end up right back on that ship once we change things."

He scratched the back of my head. "I've been thinking about that…"

Raising up on my elbow, I gazed down at him. "When have you had time to be thinking about that? Do you ever sleep?"

One corner of his lip curled up in a smirk. "When I must. I've been thinking about what I said to you in your memory… about coming back here."

I moved my thumb over the stubble on his jaw, pouting just a little. "So you're not having second thoughts then?"

He combed the hair back from my face. "I would give anything to change course and never miss a moment with you, Cecelia, but who will stop you from marrying Owen if not me? I'd rather put pause to our lives for a few years than to never know you at all."

Swallowing, I nodded. It was easy to forget about Owen without Alaina there to constantly remind me.

He held my cheek against his palm. "If we wake in our restored lives at our current ages, I would have five years to spend with my family before you show up at that party. Tell me, do you really wish to return to this time?"

"I do."

The dimple appeared in his cheek. "Then, after I intervene in your past, I shall return to this century to wait for you. I would have seven years to prepare for our life. I could take my father's route to the gold in California. While I'm there, I'll try to right the injustices of our undoing things; seek out Alistair, Eleanor, and Tomás and try to give them the lives they belong in. I could then attempt to purchase the same ship my father did. It was already outfitted with hidden passageways meant to hide royalty at sea. We could use it should we ever have need to hide slaves. I could acquire land and have homes built for us and your sister… I could come here once more and make sure Dee, Antonio, and Miguel are set free just the same as they were last night. And I'd be forty when you remembered me; young enough that I could…" He swallowed as he let this trail off.

"Young enough that you could what?" I asked, tugging on a piece of his hair.

"Young enough that I could still give you children… if you wanted them."

I smiled. "I told you already, you would be more than enough. I don't need children to be happy, and I know how you feel about having any more."

"How I *felt*," he amended. "Everything I thought I wanted or didn't want has changed with you. All night I imagined the life you and I will spend together… the great things we would do and the places they would take us… and I couldn't help but see a child both mine and yours alongside us; a child that would learn from your goodness and grow up to make the world better."

"Tell you what," I said, stroking his cheek. "We'll wing it."

He raised one dark brow. "*Wing* it?"

"Yeah." I laughed. "We don't need to write out our *entire* future right here and now. We know enough to plan for it, and if we're both open to the idea of children by the time we get there, then we'll wing it… see what happens." I glanced up at the tent where a dim blue hue was lightening the space around us. "We'll get to Portobelo tonight, right? Will we be traveling with the men that took those slaves captive?"

He shook his head. "No, *mi paloma*. After yesterday's events, I realized I could not put you on a slave ship and feel like a man for it. Pierre has a ship transporting supplies to Virginia and he's agreed to provide us rooms on board." He ran his finger down the bridge of my nose. "I daresay he's quite fond of my wife."

I bit my lower lip. "Jealous?"

He nodded, but his expression was playful. "Did I not tell you I would be a jealous husband? I might be tempted to duel the poor man if he cannot keep his eyes off you."

I chuckled. "I doubt I'm his type."

With a spark in his eye, he rolled over me. "You would be any man's type, my little dove. But I don't suppose I can keep all the eyes of the world off you…"

I giggled wildly as his hand roamed up my inner thigh. "What are you doing? The others will be up soon!"

"Then you'd better be quiet," he purred. "I'll not leave here until I'm certain you're rightly disheveled. How else am I to deter all the men in all the world?"

Chapter Forty-Eight

Chris

Chris paced back and forth near the horses while the others loaded up camp, the faces of every slave that had passed by them the day before burned into his mind.

"I can't put you on that ship, Maria. I can't put *me* on that ship and go with the sole intention of reaching the storm. There'd be a fight… there's *going to be* a fight if Terrence has really agreed to go with them—he wouldn't agree to go if that's not what he had in mind. Much as I would love to be a part of that battle, I can't put you and our child in danger; can't risk you being caught in the middle of it. There's a very real possibility we won't make it to the storm at all if we go that way."

Maria smoothed her hand down Medianoche's snout, making small kissing noises as the horse pressed into her touch. "Kreese, I am going to take this medicine and miscarry one way or another. That decision is made. It is *your decision* where I do it. We have antibiotics with us and I have faith in Cece if you don't want to go back."

Hands on his hips, he looked down each end of the trail. There was no easy choice. Both directions would put her life in danger, and neither direction would prevent the loss of their child.

At one end of the trail there was hope for medical staff if they could get to it without all hell breaking loose during the trip. But even should they get to the storm without incident, going through it came with its own risks. They'd gotten lucky when they went to the future before and encountered a barge right away. They might not be so lucky a second time. They could find themselves stranded on the water for far too long, or capsized if they ran into bad weather...

At the other end of the trail, however, they'd be among friends. They had antibiotics and Cece had enough medical knowledge to know what to do if things got rough.

"Kreese," Maria said softly, pressing her forehead against the horse's nose. "I won't die. Not permanently. There is no wrong choice when the end will be the same either way."

He ran his palm over the stubble around his mouth. "Yes, but there's a hell of a lot that could traumatize us both along the way."

"Do you want to know what *I* think we should do?"

He kicked a rock at his feet. "What?"

She grinned. "I say we get on this horse and we ride out with guns blazing and take out as many of those slavers as we can hit before they kill us both. Then, once we're dead, we'd get to skip over all the headaches of having a miscarriage or finding George Bennet. We'd just wake up in our new lives after someone kills him."

He sighed. "Why did I think you'd offer up any kind of *reasonable* advice?"

She chuckled, returning her attention to Medianoche. "Fine, if you don't want to be a badass, I think we should stay with Cece. A lot of women miscarry at three months and never go to a hospital. I know I'll be alright with Cece. I don't know if I can say the same for that slave ship."

"I don't want you to miscarry at all, Maria."

She groaned. "We're back to this? Kreese, this is hard enough as it is. You know I don't want to do it. I've told you, we don't have a choice."

"Hear me out." He took her arms and turned her to face him. "Juan Jr. showed up in Cece's past."

"Yeah, so?"

"So he and Dario will have their memories of this place long before you and I will have made that first trip back to the future. One of them can make sure you and I end up in Albuquerque on that exact same night at that exact same hotel with the exact same amount of alcohol in our systems. We don't have to give it up if we can guarantee it'll happen the same. Right?"

She stared at him for a long moment, slowly shaking her head. "Are you sure they fixed your brain in that hospital? Do you have any idea how crazy you sound? *One*, the last thing Juan Jr. or Dario is going to be concerned with when this is over is our sex life. *Two*, even if they agreed to help and we could trust them to follow through on it, there's no guarantee we'd end up in bed together the same way—you could say just one stupid thing and the whole thing would go to hell. And *three*, for the last time, I am not willing to take the risk of falling in love with a child that could disappear when this is over. Period."

He let out a long ragged sigh. "I'm sorry. You're right. I'm being out of line. I don't mean to make this harder on you. It's hard for me, too."

"I know." She returned to petting the horse. "And I didn't mean to call you crazy. It's not like I hadn't thought of that before. I forget you haven't had the time I have to process this. Trust me, I've thought of just about every possible alternative and there's nothing we can do."

He looked ahead toward the curve in the trail. "How long can we wait before you absolutely have to take the medicine? Is it possible to give us enough time to try to find George Bennet first?"

"You thinking about saving his life again, Superman?"

He shook his head. "No. I'm thinking I'd rather you didn't have to miscarry at all. If we can get to him in the next two months and kill him, it'd be the same as what you'd hoped would happen when Alaina went through the storm."

She turned back to the horse. "If we can't find him, a miscarriage that far along will be more difficult… But… I'm not ready to do this yet, either. I can wait one more month to get to Virginia. Depending on what information we can find on him during our first few days, we can make a decision then."

He let out a long sigh of relief. "Will you ride with me again today?"

She didn't look at him, continuing her long strokes down Medianoche's nose as she considered it. "Tell me this, mi amor. If Alaina came riding down this trail shouting your name, listing all the reasons she was sorry for not choosing you and vowing to never make such a horrible mistake again, would you take her back?"

"No, I wouldn't."

She stilled her palm against the horse's nose, meeting his eyes as she raised her brow. "Then why wouldn't I make that same decision for myself?"

The question felt like a punch in the stomach; one he knew he deserved from her but hadn't been expecting after she slept in his arms all night. He opened his mouth as if he could have any kind of response, but closed it when he realized there was nothing he could say.

She moved away from the horse and stood in front of him. "Look, I knew when we started this it was too soon for you. You were married for ten years and the wife you'd spent a year searching for had chosen another. Of course you needed time, and I didn't give it to you. That was my mistake."

She took a deep breath, her fingers flexing at her sides. "But once *you* realized it was too soon for you, you treated me like some old dog you'd grown tired of playing with—left me out in the cold like I meant nothing to you. You didn't come to me and say *'I need some space'* or *'we need to take a break'* before you disappeared for over a week. You just… walked away. That night the Nikora came was the worst night of my life. I cried and cried until it hurt to keep crying. Then I got scared, not of more Nikora coming, but because I started to bleed, and I thought I was having a miscarriage. I laid in that bed all night, terrified, waiting for you to come make it better. It didn't matter to me who you loved more. You were my best friend and just having you there would've made everything okay. But you never showed up. And that was your mistake."

She held her chin high. "Every bone in my body wants to grab onto you and never let go; to say we both made mistakes and move past them. But how can I do that and have any self respect? How do we do it the right way after we've both done so much wrong?"

He shook his head. "I don't know. I can't change it by saying I'm sorry but I'll keep saying I'm sorry because I am. I never meant to make you feel that way. And there's nothing I wouldn't give to go back and do things differently."

Her lip quivered ever so slightly. "Why did you just disappear like that? Why didn't you come talk to me first?"

His shoulders sank. "The thoughts that were going through my mind when I came face to face with her after getting those memories were torture. I found myself making unfair comparisons and thinking in the most selfish ways. I was so convinced I'd given up too easily on my marriage that I couldn't see that marriage wasn't worth fighting for. Even in our happiest memories, she and I barely knew one another. Yes, I should've come to you and been honest about what I was feeling, but I was a coward; terrified I'd lose you completely if I told you the truth. So, I disappeared at the worst possible moment, and I will never not regret that. I truly believed it would be easier for both you and Alaina if you didn't have to deal with me and my feelings—I didn't even want to deal with me right then. It was a mistake. All of it. I know I have been the worst kind of dick to you and I don't deserve a second chance, but if you gave it, I swear I will never make you feel like anything less than the most important woman in the world… because that's what you are to me.

She let out a long breath as if she'd been holding it the whole time. "If I was not pregnant with your child, would I still be the most important woman in the world to you?"

"Of course," he said. "I should've never put you in a position to feel like anything less. I should've given myself the time to get over her first."

She raised a brow. "And all of a sudden you're over her now? Less than a month later? You're not in love with her anymore?"

"No, I'm not." For the first time since the plane crashed, that was the truth. He felt the freedom of that admission all the way to his toes.

She pursed her lips. "Fine."

"Fine?" He laughed.

She crossed her arms over her chest. "Yes, fine. I'll ride with you today… which might make me the stupidest woman in the history of the world… but… I'm tired of being mad at you."

His heart might've floated right out of his chest. He flung his arms around her and held her as tight as he could. "Thank you."

"¡Ay dios mío! Are you trying to suffocate me?" She pried him off her. "Get the horse ready while I go put on something else so you can't be looking down my top all day. And don't think just because I'm riding with you that everything is back to the way it was between us. It's not."

He'd held Maria against him throughout the trip with an arm around her waist, trying not to think about the baby developing beneath it.

It was hard, though.

For so many years, he and Alaina had tried to conceive, and he'd spent those years looking forward to fatherhood.

He'd had a picture in his mind of the type of father he would be, and after they'd lost Evelyn, he'd had to let go of that image. It had been difficult to accept that he would never have a child of his own, but he'd accepted it.

Now, that image of himself as a father had returned.

He imagined teaching his son to be a man—how to build things, work on a car, and treat a woman. He pictured himself with

Maria showing their child how to ride a horse the first time and telling stories about the glaciers they'd seen as they rode. There was so much he could offer; so much more he wanted to give… Wanted to teach his son to swing a sword in the ways John and Juan had taught him or show him how to shave the way his father had shown him.

He saw himself fishing and camping and hiking through the wilderness where he could now teach a child how to identify what was edible, medicinal, and poison. He imagined learning Spanish alongside their baby and beaming with pride when he watched his growing child converse naturally with Maria.

He *wanted* to be a father.

Thoughts of fatherhood remained with him well into the evening. It was nearly dark when they reached the docks in Portobelo.

The town was unlike the one they'd arrived at. While its harbor had several ships inside it, Portobelo lacked the life and luster of Panama City. Or maybe it didn't and he was just too tired to notice.

They hardly had time to explore it anyway. Pierre led them straight to a sloop where they all were paddled out to a ship significantly smaller than any he'd been on in this time.

There were only two lower decks and a hull, and he was grateful for a cabin, even if it was no bigger than a closet. He imagined the accommodations were significantly better than whatever they might've been offered on the slave ship.

Pierre said his goodbyes on the top deck after introducing them to their new captain, Sebastian Navarro, an older man of few words. Pierre had kissed them each, informing them he wouldn't be joining them in the colonies as he had business to return to in France.

Chris was a little sad to see him go. He was an odd man, but one that reminded him very much of Johann Forster. He imagined they might've been quick friends if he'd chosen to travel with them.

Once he got Maria settled into their tiny cabin, he returned to the top deck where Cece and Juan had remained with Jack and Jim to converse with their new crew.

Running a hand over his hair, he took a deep breath as he looked out at the darkening sky ahead of them. "So what happens now? How do we find this guy?"

Cece grinned. "Captain Navarro is a friend of George Washington. The supplies on this ship are headed for Mount Vernon. We're going to meet Washington in the flesh, if you can believe it! His spies might have an idea where we could find the sixty-third infantry."

Jack, beside her, crossed his arms over his chest. "Assuming the sixty-third infantry is even in the states so early. The war didn't officially start until April. We'll get there in February. Bennet could be anywhere."

Cece leaned into Juan's side. "He'll be there. And Mount Vernon isn't too far from Philadelphia. Juan and I can take a trip there while you search for Bennet. We'll see if we can find Charlotte."

"Charlotte?" Chris asked.

Cece nodded. "After you got off the ship, A.J. and I went through the research you and Bud put together on his laptop. You know that old painting of the woman and the kid wearing Nike's? They're an exact match to two passengers Terrence had on his flight log."

Chris scratched his head. "Won't finding her be pointless after we kill Bennet?"

"No," she said, biting her lower lip to contain her smile. "We'll know where she is. We'll know if she's in trouble. And if she is, Juan can intervene just as he did with me... Prevent her from ever getting on that airplane. If she's not, then when we come back here, Juan and I can give her the coordinates to go home. Just so she has them."

He met Jack's eyes and he saw his disapproval. Subtly, Jack tilted his head toward the bow.

While Jim and Cece conversed about Washington and important historical dates, Chris slipped away to join Jack on the bow.

"I need to get to Yorktown," he said, his eyes remaining on their group on the quarterdeck. "Not Mount Vernon."

Chris crossed his arms. "You're planning to go after Juan's ancestor?"

Jack nodded. "I have to. I cannot live the rest of my life not knowing if that man will creep up behind us and try to take my daughter. You have to help me get there."

He glanced at Juan Jr. where he was engaged in conversation with the captain. "You realize we'd be killing him, too?"

Jack softened as he followed his gaze. "I know. Is there any other way to be rid of his father?"

"Yes," Chris said, lowering his voice. "We kill the sonofabitch once and for all and we stop this whole ridiculous plan to kill Bennet. Once Juan Josef's dead, we all go home and it's over."

Jack pursed his lips. "What about Anna?"

Chris shrugged. "People die and don't come back all the time. I hate to say that, but..." He sighed. "Maria's pregnant. She's talking about forcing a miscarriage, and I don't think I can let her do it. I can't watch her give birth and lose it when we change things either. If we just go home... If we kill the single person who serves to prevent us from getting there... Can't that be enough? Then none of us will lose anything. We ran into Juan Josef *before* your babies were born. You really want to take a risk that something might go differently?"

Jack shook his head. "Juan Jr. and Dario won't go for it."

"They might," Chris said, glancing back at them once more. "Juan Jr. will lose twenty years with Cece if we go ahead with this plan. We've talked about that when we spar in the mornings and I know he's dreading it. I don't think it'd take much to change his mind."

"Wouldn't she end up married to that other guy if he doesn't go back to intervene?"

"Owen was a prick," Chris said, "and she would've left him eventually. She fell in love with Juan once, why wouldn't she do it a second time? Yeah, it might take a year or two if she lost her memories of him, but that'd be better than twenty years, wouldn't it?"

"And what about Dario?"

Chris twisted his lips to one side. "If we can persuade Juan, maybe he can persuade his brother. We could continue to spar with them in the mornings while we head toward Virginia; start planting those seeds. Figure out where their father would come to shore and take him out there. With Juan Josef dead, there's no more roadblock. We could just go home. You and your babies, me and mine. All of this over for good. What do you think?"

Jack rested his hands on his hips, peering out over the water. "If we can't get them on board with it?"

Chris dragged a hand over his face. "Then we go to Yorktown, me and you when Cece takes off to Philadelphia with Juan. I can't let Maria miscarry and I won't risk her giving birth while we look for Bennet. We don't know where Bennet is, but we know exactly where Juan Francisco will be."

Chapter Forty-Nine

Alaina

After my encounter with Daniel Bacallar, I spent my time nearer to Juan Josef. He'd gone from being the most dangerous man in my life to being my single source of security on a ship full of lewd men.

I'd noticed it when we returned from our trip to shore; the way the men gawked at me. I could fight off one if I had to, but two or three could easily overpower me.

Juan was my only protection.

While I would never consider him harmless, I at least knew him well enough to know he'd never force himself on me.

And so, as the weeks passed in forced proximity, I grew increasingly comfortable in his company, even finding myself relieved on occasion to wake up in the night and find him asleep on the sofa.

Conversations got easier between us as the barriers we'd built through our mistrust in one another fell away. I talked about our time on the island, and he told me more about Gloria.

She reminded me so much of Cece in the way she made the world around her prettier; in the way she saw the good in people.

Juan Jr. was so much like his father in the way he'd fallen for my sister, it made me worry they'd end up with a similar outcome.

I sat in one of the wingback chairs considering it.

Juan Jr. had already interfered in her life as a means of protecting her from a man he deemed unworthy. Would he, too, lock her away from the world to keep it from hurting her? Would she grow restless and regret her decisions in life?

Yawning, I stretched my legs out in front of me as Juan took his usual spot on the sofa.

The babies were down for the night and we'd developed a sort of ritual out of sipping tea and making small talk before bed.

"God, I miss showers," he groaned, scratching his beard.

I smiled at that. "What did you miss most about the future when you realized you were stuck here? Aside from people, of course."

He adjusted his back against the cushions, crossing an ankle over his knee. "Music."

"Music?" I laughed. "Not hot showers or telephones or ice-cream?"

He shook his head. "No. I can live without all that. I missed the music. I had records and the gramophone with me, of course, but it wasn't the same. To stand in a crowd and feel a bass drum in your chest, or to watch a man's fingers glide over the frets of a guitar like magic…. That feeling of being swept up in sound with all the people that surrounded you… There's nothing else like it."

I smiled, thinking about my first concert and feeling those very same things. "You missed a lot of good decades for music. The hair bands of the 80s and the grunge of the 90s… I have some of it with me if you'd like to catch up."

"*With* you?" he asked as I stood and moved to the boxes near the bed.

"Yeah," I said, digging out the iPod Chris had loaded up for me along with a set of earbuds. "You can carry just about every record ever made in your pocket now. Unfortunately, you'll be limited to *my* preference in music, but we seem to have similar taste in the old stuff so I think you'll like it."

I took a seat on the sofa beside him, handing him the earbuds as I scrolled through albums for a good place to start.

"What do you want me to do with these?" he asked, staring down at the white ear pieces in his palm.

I chuckled, plucking one up. "This part goes inside your ear. They're headphones."

"*These* are headphones?" He laughed. "All the sound in this little thing?"

I nodded, landing upon Stevie Ray Vaughn's *'Pride and Joy'* and deciding it might be a good way to ease him into the 80s. I doubted starting out with Guns N' Roses would be the best start.

I waited until he'd positioned the earbuds in each ear to press play and I laughed as his face lit up in a smile with the opening notes.

I could hear little bits of the song trickling out, and I sat back to sip my tea, knowing each progression enough to feel everything he might've been as he experienced it for the first time.

His love of music was evident. I saw the hairs on his arms rise with it, watched the way his eyes closed when the vocals came in, and laughed to myself when the foot rested across his knee began to twitch with the beat of the drum.

Juan Josef was a human, after all.

For the next hour, I took him on a journey through time, introducing him to Prince, Van Halen, Mötley Crüe, and Metallica before shifting into Nirvana, Pearl Jam, and Alice in Chains.

I was surprised he leaned toward Eddie Vedder's voice over the others, and when I pulled up his later solo album, he fell in love the same way I had.

Side by side, each of us ending up with an earbud in one ear, we sipped tea and listened to the entire album together. The simple acoustic guitar and sorrowful vocal made us each a little lighter; made us more familiar in our love for music.

"My sister said you fought in the seven years war?" I asked, lowering the volume enough that we could still enjoy it as we conversed.

He smirked. "I wouldn't say I fought, my dear. I funded it as a means to meet powerful people. In my mind, I was convinced someone in power had to know about that storm… So I sought out whatever power I could get my hands on. I was given title in exchange for my contributions to the war effort, but I didn't fight. I dined with other leaders and helped with strategy."

"And no one had any clues about the storm?"

He shook his head. "Not a one of them. So I thought… to hell with it, I'll buy a ship; a big fancy one we could all live on. I thought we'd sail the Pacific until lightning struck us again." He let out the breath of a laugh. "I bought this one, outfitted to transport the king of Spain, himself, and I sailed home with a plan I was sure would work. I knew where we'd ended up—*roughly*—and I would sail back to that same spot and wait."

He raised a brow. "My coordinates were so very close to being right… If I'd have gotten Juan on the ship that day and left, I might've caught that storm. As it was, my dear boy had a wife and child when I arrived. What could I do? I wanted nothing more than his happiness and there it was."

"But you didn't give up," I said, frowning. "Cece said you and Dario went back out."

"We did. A few months later—after the storm had already passed. I was determined to find that lightning; to mark the location and at least know there was a path home should we ever decide to take it." He shook his head. "We found nothing but headaches. A Portuguese captain saw my ship and attempted to overtake us. I had modern weaponry and it was nothing for me to conquer him and overtake his crew. That's where I first met Mr. Gil."

He chuckled. "We did have fun those first few years after that. Developed a bit of a reputation. I didn't mean to become a pirate, but… what else had I to do with my time? We overpowered four slave vessels coming from the isthmus, and we ventured into the

Atlantic to pillage what we could from the British before they went to war with the colonies. We were enjoying ourselves so much, I'd almost forgotten about the way home. When Juan lost his family, however, everything changed. It was no longer fun. We couldn't just go home after that. I had to find a way to undo his suffering. And the only way I knew how was to search for the right Albrecht man—Richard had to have gotten the name from somewhere."

I pulled the earbud from my ear. "But you didn't kill those men. Juan Jr. did. Why?"

A muscle in his jaw ticked. "Do you know what it takes to lead a cartel?"

"No," I said. "What?"

He took a deep breath, tugging the earbud from his ear to sit forward. "The illusion of power and ruthlessness. You have to give your enemies an image of someone to fear. You have to appear to be a monster—become the devil, himself, if you can pull it off. I gave that illusion well when I killed off the entire Martinez family, but I was a twenty-one year old boy who only ever wanted to get lost at a concert when my father left me in charge. I'd never killed a soul… Even with the Martinez cartel, I only gave the order. My hands remained clean. When I came face to face with the first Albrecht—Moses, was his name—I could not pull the trigger. My son, however, could. There's not been a single moment between that day and this where I haven't regretted letting him do it."

"You do realize you are dissolving my own perception of you being this ruthless monster by telling me as much, right?"

He laughed heartily. "I have no desire to frighten you, Alaina. Despite our history, I've enjoyed spending time with you these weeks. If we'd met under any other circumstance, we might've even become friends."

I poured myself another cup of tea and sat back. "You have far too many trust issues for me to have befriended you. I'm insecure enough as it is. What's with the secret passageways? What were they used for before us?"

Folding his hands behind his head, he stretched both legs out in front of him. "King Charles had those put in when he owned it. He liked to travel but didn't like people knowing where he went. There's a secret entrance and private quarters hidden away down on the bottom deck where they'd sneak him in. That's where Mr. Gil's been hiding."

I rolled my eyes. "Of course he was. Did this ship have a name before you bought it?"

"Aye," he said, yawning. "It was called the São Salvador."

My entire body went rigid. This ship was going to burn, and I wasn't sure if I wanted to watch Juan Josef burn with it or save him from it.

Chapter Fifty

Cecelia

I sat in Maria's bed while Izzy braided my hair, smiling at the head of the bed where Lilly was doing the same for Maria.

The past few weeks had gone by quickly, and with little else to do and no other females on board, the four of us spent more and more time below deck with each other. We lounged around in our nightgowns and robes most mornings, and we'd began to develop a bond I was grateful for.

"How are things with you and Juan?" Lilly asked, keeping her eyes on her task.

I smiled, running my thumb over the ring on my finger. "Things are perfect… Sometimes I feel bad about how perfect they are. Like I'm enjoying this life too much while A.J.'s out there somewhere, miserable without Jack." I squeezed Maria's leg. "And while you're in here trying to keep from falling apart."

Maria moved her palms over her stomach. "It's not so bad as you think. She's been moving around in there lately… I know that should make me sad but it doesn't. I kind of like the idea of remembering the way she feels. At least I'll have that, you know?"

"She?" Lilly asked, frowning at me.

Maria looked down at her midsection. "I dream of her."

"Oh, honey," Lilly dropped the braid to rest her chin on Maria's shoulder and curl her arms around her shoulders. "You can't do that to yourself. I told you waiting to take the medicine wasn't a good idea. You're getting attached."

She shook her head. "No, I'm not. I know this is temporary. I think she came now to prepare me; to show me the person I need to become for when she comes again for real."

I smiled at that, moving my palm up and down her calf. "You'll make a wonderful mother someday."

She laughed out loud and sat forward. "Oye, Cece, we all know I would be a *horrible* mother."

"Why would you think that?"

She stood up from the bed, wobbling a little with the ship's movement as she grabbed a biscuit from the tray and leaned against the opposite wall. "Most women have some kind of foundation to build from, you know? I have nothing. I didn't have a mother to set an example of what to do. No aunts or grandmothers or even close girlfriends. I barely know how to be a person, let alone a mother."

Again, she smoothed a palm over her belly as she held the cookie against her lips. "This one never would've had a chance. I would've screwed her up from day one. But now I know that. She came to tell me… So I'm gonna work on it and be better for when she comes back in a few years."

"What happened to your mom?" Lilly asked, curling her legs up beneath her.

"She died when I was too young to remember her."

"I didn't know that." Lilly sat forward. "Mine did as well. When I was two."

Maria let her back slide down the wall, sitting on the floor with her knees against her chest. "Yeah, but you had good, loving people like your grandparents to show you how to be a person."

"You had your father," I said. "You told me how wonderful he was and how much you loved him."

She turned the cookie between her fingers. "I've been thinking about him a lot lately. I don't know if he was as wonderful as I imagine him being. When I think about this baby… I could never imagine leaving her alone all day and night with a man like his uncle. Even if he didn't know what he was right away, he had to have figured it out at some point."

"What he was?" Lilly asked, her eyes sliding to me and back.

Maria smirked. "You didn't think I became this messed up of a person from having a totally normal childhood, did you?"

I swallowed. "His uncle abused you?"

Slowly, she nodded, her attention moving to Izzy. "I was younger than she is now when it started… And I just thought it was normal. I thought it was how all families showed their love. When I became old enough to realize it wasn't, I was too ashamed to tell anyone. I thought *I* had done something wrong. You know? So it kept happening… And then I started lying about my life to make up for it… To my teachers and the kids at school… I told so many lies for so many years it's hard to even know what was real. Was my father a wonderful man? Or did I make it up as a way to escape the fact he gave me to that monster?"

She tossed the cookie back onto the tray. "So that is the foundation I ended up with. Sex and guilt and lies to make up for myself and to hell with anyone who didn't like me for it." Straightening her legs on the floorboards, she smiled down at her stomach. "But she came to tell me I needed to be better than that. I need to become someone who has a little bit more to offer her. Maybe she came to bring me closer to you two… to give me a stronger foundation."

Lilly's eyes welled with tears that immediately streamed down both cheeks. "Oh my God, I had no idea. I would've never been so cold to you if I'd known."

Maria picked at a thread on her robe. "I'm not sorry so don't feel sorry for me. Hard as it was, that life taught me what to look for in order to keep my future babies safe from men like him. It taught me to be strong…. Taught me all the things I didn't want to be again. Just because my childhood was tragic doesn't mean I have to be." She hugged an arm around her stomach. "Especially when I have her to look forward to some day."

"Have you ever talked to anyone about it?" Lilly asked. "Like, professionally?"

She took a deep breath and shook her head. "I went to this support group a few years ago in Miami for survivors of childhood abuse. I had no idea there were so many women with childhoods just like mine. It made me want to cry when I saw all those women in that room. How could there be that many monsters in this world that one little Miami support group would be so crowded? I just sat and listened to their stories. And every one was always the same… the initial confusion about love… the shame and lies to cover it up… the feelings of inadequacy that follow. But it was the stuff that came after they left their experiences that affected me most. Most of them couldn't have a relationship at all. Some became prostitutes or strippers because they needed that sexual validation… They all spoke about trying to kill themselves on multiple occasions. It was hard to be surrounded by so many broken people. It sounds awful, but when I left there that night, I thought… maybe mine wasn't so bad. And messed up as that may be, it was almost therapeutic to know I wasn't the worst off for it."

I clicked my tongue. "I'm sorry. If you ever need to talk about it, we're here. Sometimes just having someone listen is therapeutic."

"I know," she said, massaging her abdomen gently. "I tell her."

"Fucking men," Lilly sniffled, groaning as she wiped both cheeks. "Is there something attached to the penis that gives them this sense of entitlement to take what they want when it pleases them?"

Maria grinned. "Yeah, it's called their brains."

I dabbed my tears with the sleeve of my robe. "Does Chris know about your uncle?"

"Sí. I told him one day when we were stranded on that island." She let out a long, audible sigh. "I think that is when I fell in love with him… The way he held me in his arms afterward. He loved your sister and I knew he was only holding me to comfort me, but I never felt so protected in my life… Never felt so at ease with a man before he showed up."

"He's a good man." I pulled Izzy into my arms, every strand of my hair pulled tightly back into one of at least twenty braids. "Are you two officially back together?"

Maria smiled, crossing her ankles in front of her. "No, mi amiga. I'm not going to make it so easy for him. He abandoned me for another woman. Yes, I understand why, but I cannot be someone he thinks will always forgive him so easily when he treats me like shit. He's got to earn my love… Can't spend *all* his time up there playing with his sword."

Lilly leaned back against the headboard, combing her chestnut hair where it was draped over her shoulder. "It's not just him. All our boys have been up there sparring with Juan and Dario every chance they get. I snuck up last night to get a glimpse of Jimmy doing it. I thought I'd get a good laugh before bed." She swooned. "I wasn't laughing at all. Watching him swing a sword with confidence was the sexiest thing I've ever seen that man do."

Maria cackled. "I don't think I've ever associated the word *'sexy'* with Jim before. Is that why you sent Izzy to sleep in here with us?"

Lilly bit her lower lip and nodded. "I'm going back up to watch them again tonight. Their penises might be attached to their brains, but they sure do look pretty when they fight."

I laughed. "I'll come with you. I wouldn't mind watching Juan spar for a while."

"I'm sure you wouldn't with that body of his," Maria snorted. "I suppose I could use a bit of entertainment and a reason to change out of this gown. I'll come too."

Lilly had been right. Watching the men spar was an aphrodisiac of all sorts. The sun setting at our backs, I was mesmerized by the show they put on for us.

They'd drawn circles on the deck to control their footing, and they paired off inside those circles to battle one another. Juan and

Chris fought in one, Jack and Tomás in another, while Jim and Dario faced off in the one closest to us.

Maria, Lilly, and I sat with Izzy on a pile of sandbags to cheer them on. I felt a bit like a teenager, swooning at the sight of my big handsome man showing off his agility.

The men felt our presence, too, going a little harder than they might've without us there.

Jim and Dario were by far the most entertaining to watch. Jim was sorely outmatched, but he loved to irritate Dario with smack talk, and there were several occasions when I was certain Jim wouldn't make it out alive. They tired out faster than the others with their constant attacks on one another.

Where Jim and Dario would clang swords almost nonstop, Jack and Tomás were methodical with no females to impress, focusing on footwork and posture more than their swing. They were respectful of each other, offering pointers as they moved slowly.

Juan and Chris, however, were the most elegant. Neither even looked down to ensure their feet were on the circle. They danced with each other, their lunges and fades perfectly executed. Every movement was fluid and graceful. It was hypnotic watching them fight.

Maria enjoyed them as much as I did, and I wondered if she'd remain resistant to Chris's advances when they ventured back down to their room.

Holding Izzy tightly in my arms where she'd dozed off in my lap, I fell into a trance as each battle continued, my mind drifting off in thought.

I thought about Alaina and the babies on the other ship. Mad as I may have been at her for plotting the death of Juan's ancestor, I couldn't hold onto that grudge now that the plan was thwarted. I missed her deeply and worried about her safety with Juan Josef. It didn't seem fair that I was so surrounded by the ones she loved most while she was forced to manage him on her own.

I thought about Bruce there beside her, and that eased my heart. Of all the people I'd met during my brief time spent in this century, he was the most treasured. He was kind in every way and deserved everything this world could offer. I missed my mornings with him and hoped Alaina would get as much value out of his company as I had. He was a great friend to have at your side, and I was confident he'd lift her up in times of darkness if she let him.

I smiled at the thought of Anna and what it might be like to see her interact with Bruce; to see him love her in-person. It warmed my heart to consider the day he'd wake beside her. I hoped she loved him with the same intensity he loved her. I couldn't imagine a happier ever after than for him to wake in a life where she'd confessed to shared feelings and offered him her heart.

That intense level of love brought my thoughts to Jack. I wondered what it might be like to feel your wife and daughter were in constant danger of being snatched in the night. He loved them fiercely and I knew the driving force behind his plan to pursue Juan Francisco was desperation to keep them all safe. Would I tell him his plans were already foiled, or would I let him sneak off to Yorktown to discover it for himself?

And then I thought about Juan. I thought about the life he intended to get started for us while he waited; considered what it'd be like to wake up every day beside him with no doom lingering over our heads. I wanted to see him interact with my mother and uncle, and I was anxious to get to a life with him that wouldn't be interrupted ever again.

Or would it?

I thought about time then. My one simple request to control my own destiny had meddled in more than just my own history. I'd altered memories and erased a daughter. How many other lives had I tampered with by jumping onto that boat?

Had I even tampered at all?

If we killed George Bennet, would he remain dead once we landed ourselves on another loop through time? How could he if we'd never run into Juan Josef? Had any of us really changed anything or were we just delaying a predestined outcome?

Would any of us even remember this life?

I didn't remember Owen and Maddy. Was it merely a glitch in the spirograph that Alaina and Chris remembered or was there some special formula that decided what you could or couldn't recall?

What was time?

And what was even real inside it?

"S'at all ye' got, Precious?" Jim cackled, pulling me out of my head and back to their fight where he barely dodged Dario's advance. "Boy, you couldn't knock a hole in the wind with a sackful of hammers!"

Before I could laugh, Jim's legs were swept out from beneath him and he was on his back with Dario's blade pointed at his jugular.

He chuckled and blew Dario a kiss. "Well, look who *finally* showed up to fight. Where ye' been? I's done fightin' you ten minutes ago!"

Dario grinned and offered Jim his hand. "Do you ever stop talking?"

"Ye' wasn't hittin' nothin' when I was quiet. Figured I'd help ye' out some." He grunted miserably as he stood, hunching over to place a hand on his lower back. "Christ almighty, I think my asshole's broke."

Maria nudged Lilly's arm. "That's your idea of sexy?"

Lilly shrugged, smiling at Jim as he hobbled toward us. "Everyone's got their own ideas of what's sexy. He happens to be mine. Right, Jimmy?"

Jim winked. "That's right, Princess. Scooch over and let me sit my sexy ass down for a spell. I'm wore out."

Smiling, I watched as Jim collapsed beside her and she massaged his back.

How unique the two of them were; such polar opposites in both upbringing and personality, and yet so perfect together.

I rocked Izzy gently as I admired the two of them, and a new thought occurred to me as I wondered if they would've come together without intervention.

What if time was a living thing?

What if it watched us?

What if it bent in order to serve itself better?

What if a gap was created solely for Lilly and Jim to meet inside because time saw some future where their descendants accomplished great things?

Or, what if it saw its own destruction at the hands of a descendant from Adrián or Lucas or Benito or any one of the Nikora who had attacked our ship? What if time bent for us to change an outcome it didn't want?

I sighed as Dario knelt to offer Jim his canteen.

What a strange mixture we made.

Jim and Dario couldn't be more opposite either, and yet, over the passing weeks, they'd become bantering best friends.

Dario had a rough life here. More than anyone, he needed to be surrounded by good, loving people that would accept him and support him in ways his father never had. Despite Jim's almost constant teasing, I could see Dario's appreciation for his easy friendship; could see him coming out of his shell a little more each day.

Maybe time simply saw a mix of people that needed one another. I'd only just arrived and already I couldn't imagine my life without them.

I glanced at Juan where he and Chris had wrapped up their fight. Two months ago, my life looked so completely different. What I thought was a meaningful existence now seemed so lacking without these people inside it.

"There's your America," Dario said, standing to point out over the water.

"Where?" Lilly asked, raising up beside him.

"You see that dark line there on the horizon?" Dario asked, turning her a little to follow his finger. "That's what you call Florida."

"Oh my God, I see it!" Her feet danced beneath her. "I can feel it even! Do you guys feel that? Like… we're finally home?"

I glanced to my left where Juan and Chris were walking toward us. Everything in my face smiled when Juan's gaze met mine. Whatever time was, and wherever it might lead us, I *was* finally home after a lifetime of searching for it.

My life had meaning and purpose and good, loving people inside it. Time gave that to me and I would forever feel home now that I had it.

I just needed to help a few others get there as well.

Gloria, Dario, and Dahlia…

Chris and Maria and their baby…

Alaina and Jack and Zachary and Cecelia…

Charlotte and Chase Miller…

I would help them find home too.

Epilogue

Alaina

I laid in bed, lazily combing the bits of fuzz on Cecelia's head while Zachary dozed beside her.

Her eyes were open, and in the mid-afternoon light, I admired the colors developing in them. Where Zachary's eyes were showing signs he'd inherited Jack's blue, Cecelia's were beginning to look like mine... like Gloria's.

Gloria had the same coloring I did, grayish with hints of both blue and green. I knew that because I'd obsessed over her photos in Jack's absence. Day and night, I looked at them; saw the life in her and recognized a mixture of both myself and Cece in the bits of her personality that shone through the photography.

The more I'd learned about her, the harder it became to remain firm in my stance to never return to the past. She was this woman full of life and creativity and kindness. She was a part of me, a part of my daughter, and someone I couldn't help but feel a little bit of pride in having helped create.

Who was I to take such a woman from the world?

Then again, who was I to take my daughter from a future that might be better for her?

I stared down at Cecelia, those questions weighing heavily on my mind.

"Where do I take you, little love?" I whispered, smiling as she gummed her fingers. "You could be anything you want to be in the future, you know... A doctor... lawyer... president even, if you wanted... Here, you'd only be a wife and mother."

Sighing, I caressed her damp little cheeks. "But you'd create some pretty amazing people if we came back here. I know you'd live a long, healthy life because I've seen it on that chart. I don't know if I can say the same if we stay in the future. Who knows if you'd be safe there long-term?"

I raised up on my elbow. "Here, life wouldn't be easy, but it would be simple and guaranteed. I know you'd be married for a long time, and you must end up really loving the man to give him four children. Right?"

I smiled at Zachary where he let out a gentle snore.

"You'll be eight or nine before it's safe to come back with your brother... Definitely old enough to get used to that century. You'd be pissed at me if I brought you back here and you no longer have access to cartoons or ice cream or family and friends."

I chuckled. "Although, your grandma is going to be mad about you both. She'll follow us wherever we go. Oh, can you imagine Sofia McCreary in the 18th century? With no hair dye to cover up her age? She'd either be a nightmare or she'd finally find a man to live up to her insane expectations of male chivalry. Maybe she'd live happily ever after with some handsome Scot in a cottage next door to us."

I kissed her foot where she'd raised it near my face. "How can I possibly make this decision for you? Or for Gloria? Or Jack or Cece or Juan?"

Her little lips curled upward and she made a 'bah' sound.

"One thing's for certain," I said, leaning in. "I have to get you both off this ship before we get anywhere near Charleston. It's going to catch fire there. I haven't told Juan yet. I don't know if I should."

I placed my finger in her grip. "Want to hear something crazy? I picked up one of our history books this morning and did a little searching for Captain Cook. He's going to be sailing around Cape Horn very close to the time we reach it. Maybe, if we can find him, he can give us a ride to Virginia to find your daddy. I'm gonna talk to Bruce first and see what he thinks before I do anything. Mommy makes bad decisions on her own. I can't be trusted, you know."

I sighed and laid on my back beside her. "I'll tell you this much, little love. No matter what we plan or where we go, nothing is going to end up the way we think… It never does."

What's Next:

Book 5: The Stars that Call us Home
The fifth book will wrap up the first part of the series and will release spring/summer 2023. This book will give closure to this series but leave an opening for a continuation down the line.

Adrift Origin & Side Stories
I'm not ready to leave this world or these characters just yet. I have a few plans for side and origin stories. These will be standalone books, and I have outlines ready for Frankie, Dutch, and Zachary (The characters from the journals in book 1), Bertie and Bud, and Jim Jackson.

Charlotte & Chase Miller
Yes, there will be a new series to follow these two. I plan to start this one the minute book 5 is wrapped up.

Acknowledgements

I've never sat down to write an acknowledgement because the list of people I have to thank feels so very lengthy, it'd be impossible not to leave someone out. I will make the attempt now, but know the list, done properly, might take up an entire six-hundred page book itself.

First, I have to thank my husband, Richard, for being so very patient with me as I have transitioned from writing as a hobby to building my career as an author. Thank you for putting up with zombie-like responses, one too many delivered dinners, and a somewhat messy house while I've been glued to my computer morning and night for two years straight. Thank you for helping me brainstorm and come up with this story. And thank you for being the type of husband that inspires so many amazing male characters in this book. I never could've written any of this without you.

Second, I have to thank my mother, Karla, for helping create these stories. She reads every word as I write it in a shared document, encouraging me every step of the way with feedback, fresh perspective, and new ideas—oh, and lots of Jim-isms! Thank you for keeping this moving and giving me the confidence I need every single time I hit "publish."

To my family—yes, I'm grouping y'all together because if I gave you all a paragraph, this acknowledgement would go on forever. To my sister, brothers, nieces, nephews, aunts, uncles, cousins, and my all my beloved in-laws, you are the personality in these characters. I have been blessed with such a diverse family through both blood and through marriage. Watching you all interact has given me the ability to create interactions with these characters who are as unique and opposite as all of you. Thank you for being so delightfully weird and wonderful, and for always having my back.

To my friends—y'all know who you are. Thank you for being the first ones to buy and share and review and recommend and make me feel like this was something I could actually do. I cannot imagine how obnoxious it was to receive those early chapters and graphics and name ideas and then have your social feeds littered with nothing but Trinity Dunn content for weeks at a time. Thank you for surrounding me with positive energy and standing by me with whole-hearted support as I discovered mid-life what I love doing.

Okay, now this part gets tricky because I love every single reader, but I absolutely could not do an acknowledgement without naming a few of my biggest supporters.

Before I do, let me say that I never could've imagined when I sat down to write chapter one having the types of readers that would be so die-hard and amazing. All of you deserve credit here because I could not be here without your readership.

To Katelin, your video reviews of the first book caught me completely by surprise and had me crying at all hours of the night that this complete stranger could love my words so much to share so often. Thank you so much for making this girl feel like she wasn't a fraud after all.

To my Brandi's. Yes, I have two of you! I have no idea what I ever would've done without you. Thank you for sharing, responding to comments before I even see them, for reading early and finding flaws, and for always being a source of inspiration on days I'm feeling demotivated. Sometimes a bad review can hit harder than others, but the moment I see one of you on social media hyping me up, I am alight with encouragement.

To Kayla, Layla, Lindsey, Kristina, and Alysha, I absolutely love your feedback and support both in beta and in social. Your excitement makes me excited! Where I might have taken a month or two off between books, I see your feedback and I am compelled to jump straight into the next installment. Thank you for keeping the fire beneath me burning!

To Paula. Girl, write that book and I will be your number one supporter! Thank you for sharing your real-time emotions and thoughts chapter by chapter. I love being in your head, and I seriously cannot wait to read and share whatever you put together!

To Randi, same! Write that book that's living inside you and share it! Thank you for your words of encouragement. You brought me to tears and have inspired me in so many ways to keep going. I cannot wait to see your first novel published, and I am there for anything you need along the way.

I couldn't possibly write an acknowledgement without thanking my partner-in-crime, Amelia Hugh! You have brought this story to life with your amazing narration. I keep throwing curve-ball accents at you, and you keep on knocking them out of the park. Thank you for being so thorough, for finding errors or plot holes no one else saw, and for really understanding these characters in such a way that you narrate them exactly the way I hear them in my head. I am so glad I found you. No one could've done what you have with these books, and no one else ever will. (You're stuck with me now.)

This has been, and continues to be, an amazing journey. Thank you to everyone who has read, shared, or talked about this story to make this journey possible. I would love to name each of you individually, and at some point, I just might.

I cannot wait to see where we go next!